THEY COULD BE SAVIORS

DIANA COLLEEN

PLH PRESS

Published by PLH Press

Printed in the USA

Publisher's Cataloging-in-Publication Data

Names: Colleen, Diana, 1974- .

Title: They could be saviors / Diana Colleen. Description: Seattle, WA : PLH Press, 2026.| Summary: A group of billionaires is abducted and held captive in a high-tech facility by a well-funded sisterhood of psychedelic therapists seeking to dismantle their egos. The women's goal is to use psychedelic assisted therapy to show the men that they are destroying society and the planet and get them to work together to solve climate change.

Identifiers: ISBN 9798999808516 (pbk.) | ISBN 9798999808509 (ebook)

Subjects: LCSH: Climatic changes – Fiction. | Billionaires – Fiction. | Psychotherapists – Fiction. | Hallucinogenic plants – Therapeutic use – Fiction. | Hallucinogenic drugs – Therapeutic use – Fiction. | Responsibility – Fiction. | Captivity – Fiction. | Moral development – Fiction. | LCGFT: Ecofiction. | BISAC: FICTION / Political. | FICTION / Psychological. | FICTION / Dystopian.

Classification: LCC PR9199.4.C65 T44 2026 | DDC 813 C--dc23

Thank you to...
My mom, who gave me life—and the courage to face it.
Marie, who saved my life when I could not save myself.
Mykle, who made life worth living again.
And the medicine that showed me the way forward.

Want to help cure billionaire-ism and save the planet?
Leave a review—it's powerful!

And sign up for my newsletter for updates, giveaways, and to join the movement for change.

CHAPTER ONE

YOU CAN ONLY SELL YOUR INTEGRITY ONCE, SO YOU BETTER GET A GOOD price for it.

Josh Latham's business school professor had been fond of that line, but Josh found it naïve. Integrity was a commodity, and he'd sold his many times. He didn't care about the diminishing price tag.

Flexing his principles had become as commonplace as flexing his muscles at the gym. Now, straddling the bench press in his private gym with sweat sliding down his back, Josh took a swig of Tupalik Polar Iceberg Water. Bradley James, his head of sustainability, had gifted him a case as a nod to Omnicia's upcoming EcoStar campaign. At $100 a bottle, the water was less about taste and more about perception. It promised to help the melting icecaps, but to Josh it was nothing but bottled PR.

Hiring Bradley had been a deliberate act of pragmatism. Josh knew the man's reputation when he brought him on: slick, shrewd, and utterly indifferent to the environment. It was that indifference which made him perfect for the job. Josh hadn't wanted someone weighed down by conviction or principles.

But Josh didn't dwell on ethical reckonings—especially not his own. Rising sea levels? Not his problem. If he was honest, which was rare, he didn't give a shit about the planet. His sons would live comfortably for the rest of their lives, thanks to his relentless drive that took Omnicia from a thought to the largest corporation on Earth. If his kids were dumb enough to bring their own children into this mess, well, that was on them.

What he *did* care about was the financial boost EcoStar could provide. Omnicia had more than doubled its market cap during the CryoSpora pandemic by playing up concern for essential workers. He saw EcoStar as the next big score—a chance to cash in on the growing demand for sustainability. He'd let the public *think* the campaign was about the planet, as perception was reality, and he was a master at shaping it.

Omnicia wasn't just a company; it was an empire. It transcended industries, borders and even governments. It was the answer to every problem society could be convinced it had. The slogan 'Your world. Your way.' was imprinted on the consciousness of billions; a promise the company could, and would, deliver anything.

His phone buzzed, interrupting his thoughts. He snatched it up, glancing at the screen before answering. "Hey Brad, you ready for this?"

"Damn straight I am. Bring it on!"

Josh loved how enthusiastic Bradley was about the campaign. "Good. Have you touched base with Susan yet?"

"Not this morning, but we spoke last night. I think she got her shit together. Shouldn't have to worry about her."

Josh didn't share his optimism. Susan had been wavering. She wasn't built for the ruthlessness required to thrive at the corporation. Still, she had her purpose.

"We'll see about that. It might be time to move on. Shame, though. She brought a certain... aesthetic to the team."

Bradley's laugh crackled through the line. "Yeah, gonna miss those low-cut blouses. Hey, I know a guy down south who'd be great. He led Texon's rebranding campaign after the big spill in the Gulf. Actually had people believing they cared about climate change. All it took were pictures of the CEO standing next to some solar panels."

Josh's pectoral muscles danced, one, then the other. "Nice. I'd look pretty good in a field of wind turbines. Maybe lose my shirt ... You at the office yet?"

"Just pulled in. You?"

"Finishing up my workout. Should be there in about an hour. If you see Susan, tell her to brea... shit, she's on the other line. Okay, I'll see you soon."

He braced himself. Susan hated talking on the phone.

"Morning, Susan. How are you feeling?" His tone was syrupy and calculated like sweet vermouth.

Her voice cracked. "I can't... I can't do this, Josh."

Pulling the phone away from his ear as Susan sobbed, he pinched the bridge of his nose, summoning patience. "Aww, Susan, I know this is difficult for you. But you're the heart of this campaign. I need you."

"Thank you, Josh." Susan sniffed before continuing. "I don't know how to handle the accusations of greenwashing." Her words tumbled out in a rush. "The whole campaign, it's all just lies."

He bit his lip so he wouldn't snap at her. Lies? The entire corporate world thrived on lies. They were just called narratives, strategies, and branding.

He looked heavenward, as if pleading for divine intervention. "You're overthinking. And anyway, Brad and I will handle the tough questions. You just focus on what you do best, and we'll have your back. It all ultimately falls on me, so I'm the one who has to defend it. Plus, do you think they're going to care after they see the profit projections?"

Silence.

"Susan, you still there?"

"Uh, yeah...Josh?"

"Uh huh?"

"Why can't we actually do some good? Why is it always about money? Don't you have enough?"

His jaw locked, teeth pressing hard enough to ache, while his free hand curled into a fist. Enough? The concept was laughable. Empires weren't built on *enough*.

"There's no such thing, Susan. And if you think saving a few trees is going to make a difference, I have some iceberg water to sell you. You don't stay at the top by doing what's moral. You stay there by doing what works."

"Goodbye, Josh."

The line went dead.

He hurled the glass water bottle across the gym, its impact exploding into sharp echoes in the otherwise silent room. Frustration coursed through him, not from Susan's defection, but at her naivete. She'd known what Omnicia was when she'd signed on.

He left the mess behind as he headed for the shower, knowing his staff would clean up after him.

Hot water slammed against his skin, the heat failing to pierce his growing frustration. Each brisk scrub felt mechanical, as if he could erase his emotions with sheer efficiency. Streams of soap slid down his body, pooling at his feet before swirling down the drain. Once clean, he dried off just enough to throw on his clothes. In front of the mirror, his fingers moved deftly down his shirt as he fastened each button.

The board would be furious about rescheduling the meeting, and now he had to handle the fallout with Susan, too.

She better not go to the fucking press.

Getting to the office was a priority, but arriving disheveled was never an option. He reached for his hair gel. His hand didn't move. His brain fired the command again, but his fingers wouldn't budge.

What the fuck?

His body refused to obey; muscles locked in place as though the thread between thought and motion had been severed. Something was frighteningly wrong. Was he having a stroke? He tried to pick up his phone, but again, nothing moved.

Josh Latham never panicked. Not when investors turned on him or the market crashed; not even when *The New York Post* broke his affair with Lisa. He was the guy who walked into a room of chaos and made it bend to his will.

The pulse in his neck quickened as he stared at the mirror, its surface rippling like a lake disturbed by a thrown stone. The distorted glass made his reflection waver. His features blurred, as if the confident, unshakable image he projected to the world was melting away. Steely eyes, typically composed, flickered with dread the longer his body remained rigid and unmoving.

A moment later, the mirror exploded with a torrent of water, crashing to the floor and surging through the room. The water rose, churning around his legs, creeping up to his shins, and continuing skyward with inexorable force.

This isn't real. The thought pounded through his skull. His chest heaved as water surged over his ribs, uncaring of his denial. There was a thundering in his ears, which he recognized as his own heart, hammering with primal terror, as water reached his neck. His lips submerged as he fought for one last inhale through his nose before the water filled his nostrils.

CHAPTER TWO

"Open your eyes, Josh."

Blackness.

I need to get to the meeting.

He strained to open his eyes, but they were lead weights. A stabbing ache swelled behind his temples, twisting tighter, like a vise clamping down on his skull. This wasn't the familiar pain of a headache or the dull throb a night of excess on his yacht earned him. This was deeper, sharper, foreign. A buzzing itch crawled beneath his skin like an army of ants was marching through his veins. Somewhere distant, the soft murmur of a woman's voice urged him to do what his mind screamed for, but it was like trying to hear through water—distorted and unreachable.

"Open your eyes, Josh." The voice again. More insistent this time. "I know everything feels wrong, like your body isn't yours. That's because your brain is scrambling to make sense of things. It's trying to stitch itself back together in a way that feels familiar."

Where is she?

"For a while, you're going to feel clumsy and heavy. It'll feel like you're trapped in quicksand. You're going to ask your body to do simple things, but they'll seem impossible. Your body will ignore you."

Confusion was too small a word for the storm ripping through Josh's mind, too tame a term for the way his thoughts splintered and re-formed, only to collapse again.

"You'll have to relearn how to do everything, but it shouldn't take long for your brain to adjust," the woman's voice continued. "I've been through this myself. I'll try to help you."

Who are you? Where am I? The questions echoed in his mind, but when he tried to form the words, his mouth refused to cooperate; lips pulled tight, as though bound by unyielding nylon thread.

His throat constricted, a fresh swell of dread rising and crashing against his chest. His heart pounded in his ears, but his body remained paralyzed. A prison of flesh. Desperation. His thoughts raced back to the last moment he remembered—at the gym, talking to Susan.

Shit, the meeting. Bradley would be the only one who showed up. Despite his haze of panic, he had little anxiety about Omnicia. Bradley was competent. Everyone knew he was Josh's heir apparent. The board would follow Brad's lead without hesitation, and Susan would be back at the table before the coffee cooled. The real problem now wasn't the company. It was this. Whatever *this* was.

Oh my God, I've been kidnapped. Fear knotted in his stomach. *Is Lisa okay? Fuck! What about the boys? Are they safe?* His chest constricted. *Fuck, fuck! How did this happen?* His thoughts were scattering in every direction. *FUCK FUCK FUCK!!* He forced himself to slow his breathing. His body responded to the command. *Think goddammit!*

"Josh, you're probably wondering where you are and who I am." The woman's voice again.

"Right, know... want...me... damn it. Where is this... and me and... who you are?" The words sputtered out of Josh's mouth, disjointed fragments of a conversation, each one struggling to find coherence. His tongue was a dead slug in his mouth, unable to move.

Relief flooded his gut the moment he heard his own voice, though it didn't sound normal. Gone was the authoritative tone that cut through a room, replaced by something frail and unfamiliar. Thin and shaky, reminiscent of a nervous teenager. The kind of voice that would falter in the face of a bully, cracking under pressure. The sound grated in his ears, each word sounding weak.

"Who the hell are you and where the fuck am I?" he managed to growl, his voice cutting through the air with more bite than before.

"Good! Well done. That couldn't have been easy. My name is Mel, but I can't explain where you are until you're up and able to move around. It'll be much easier to show you rather than trying to tell you."

Josh heard relief in her voice, which caused him to wonder if he could have been left permanently damaged.

"For now, I need you to know you're safe. No harm will come to you or your family," she continued. "No ransom has been asked for, so you don't need to worry about that, either. I'm sure you have a lot of questions and I'll do my best to answer them, however; there are some that won't be answered for quite some time."

Quite some time. What the hell does that mean? The effort to ask was too draining. His mind was still in pieces. The two sentences he managed earlier had depleted what little energy he had. His eyelids were still glued shut with every attempt to open them, a frustrating failure.

"Josh, I'm going to leave you alone now so you can concentrate on getting your mind and body to work together."

What's her name again? Mel?

"Once you have the energy and coordination to get up, there'll be a few things to look for. There's a switch on the wall that'll allow you to open the blinds for some natural light. You might want to open them a little at a time, as your eyes will be sensitive today."

Simple things like getting up to open blinds seemed impossible. Josh tried to open his eyes again, with no success.

"There's a stocked fridge in the next room with some of your favorite foods and beverages. Things might taste strange for the first bite or two, but once your brain recognizes what you're eating, the flavors will settle in like you expect. Actually, the food here is going to be a lot better than what you're used to."

Her words swam through his mind, disconnected from the reality he was trapped in. Food. Fridge. The details felt absurdly mundane when contrasted with the chaos in his head.

"Your stomach will be angry, but only for a minute or two, so try to relax. Any discomfort will subside quickly. The bathroom has all the essentials. If you need anything else, push the button on your wristband and ask for it. We'll do our best to get it to you."

"We? Who is We?" This time, the words were easier to spit out, so Josh kept them coming. "When will I get answers? Why do I feel like this?" He paused, but didn't wait for a reply. "What have you done to me? Why the fuck am I here?"

"You've every right to be angry and confused. I'll monitor your progress throughout the day, and once you're mobile and totally coherent, I'll come back so we can have a conversation.

"There are no cameras in your apartment. We won't be watching you. Don't worry about your privacy while you're in your own quarters. The band on your left wrist will tell us everything, so I'll get a notification when you're able to meet with me."

No cameras. That should have been reassuring, but the fact that she felt the need to say it meant privacy wasn't a given. If they could choose to grant it, they could just as easily take it away.

"I cannot stress this enough... please take your time today. You may stumble, so hold on to walls and furniture as you make your way around. The wristband will tell me if you injure yourself. As I said before, we're here if you need anything. Just ask. I'll see you soon."

No footsteps. No door closing.

Josh lay there, trapped in a body that refused to work and a mind churning with questions that had nowhere to go.

He started working on his eyes again. Each muscle in his face was alien and stiff.

"Open your eyes, Josh. Open your fucking eyes!" His voice resonated with the unwavering intensity of a seasoned CEO demanding nothing less than absolute obedience.

CHAPTER THREE

Mel reached into the box hidden behind her filing cabinet and found the cool neck of a bottle. Her fingers hesitated, just for a second, before grabbing the merlot. It was easier not to think about the consequences even as her hand trembled, the red liquid swirling into her coffee mug.

Her eyes remained glued to the tiny screen on her desk as a BREAKING NEWS banner flashed across it. She sank into her black leather chair, its worn seams groaning in protest, while every muscle braced for what came next.

She took a deep breath and let her eyes close for only a second. The ache of exhaustion crawled through her body, seeping into her bones, heavy with the weight of what was to come.

The voice of news anchor Walt Meyers pulled her lids back up. She wanted to witness the look on his face as he delivered what she hoped was the beginning of the most consequential news of the century.

"Good evening, ladies and gentlemen. We interrupt regular programming to bring you breaking news. It is confirmed that five of the wealthiest men in the world are missing."

The anchor leaned forward, his brow creased as he tried to absorb the words coming out of his own mouth. "Among them are Americans Josh Latham, CEO and founder of Omnicia, and Matt Aronowitz, head of the social media platform Peepl. They are joined by Australian Joel Berg, retired founder of software giant Aetheria; Briton Mykle Drexel, founder of Mobius, the transportation conglomerate; and German fashion mogul William Becker, founder of the Instant-Mode empire."

Hints of chocolate and berries peppered Mel's mouth as she sipped, letting the liquid rest on her tongue for a moment each time before swallowing. One drink. It didn't have to be anything more than that. The smooth burn that followed didn't register, as she tried to maintain focus on the screen. She continued to wrestle with her eyelids.

"In all five cases, there's no indication of a struggle and, as yet, no ransom demands. We don't have a lot of information at this time, although we do know the families are working closely with Interpol and law enforcement in their respective countries. I'd now like to bring in special agent Randy Stenner of the FBI."

Even the lone potted plant in Mel's cramped office seemed to perk up with anticipation as the TV turned to a split screen. Mel hung on every word, impatient to learn what information the public would receive about the missing oligarchs and what speculation there would be.

"Randy, thank you so much for being with us. What can you tell us about these disappearances? Do you have any theories about whether they've been kidnapped or if they planned this together, and if so, for what purpose? And why the secrecy?" Walt's voice was sharp as his questions hit Randy in rapid-fire succession.

"Thank you for having me, Walt. Unfortunately, due to the nature of the missing individuals, there's very limited information right now. What we know so far is all five men were last known to be in their homes, with staff and family nearby."

Walt's chin dipped in a slow, deliberate nod as he listened.

"There are no signs of break-ins or any kind of struggle," Randy continued, "and of course, all the homes have robust security systems and are heavily guarded. Security tapes haven't provided any clues, but our agents are still combing through terabytes of video and sensor data."

"So what you're saying, then," Walt cut in, "is if there's no appearance of foul play, wouldn't that lead us to believe this could have been planned by the missing men themselves?"

"Well, not so fast, Walt. It's no secret some of these men are friends, but some of them have publicly expressed disdain for each other. They have very different ideas about how they should be spending their money and using their influence." Randy shifted in his seat. "They're all ultra-rich, but they don't have much else in common."

"I think that's a good segue to bring on our next guest. Please welcome to our broadcast, Brooke Berg, daughter of missing billionaire Joel Berg."

The screen split into three as a woman in her mid-forties, with puffy black bags under her eyes, appeared next to Randy. Her hair was pulled back in a loose ponytail and had the sheen of someone who hadn't showered in days.

"Brooke, let me first express how grateful we are you're with us. You and your family must be out of your minds with worry."

"Yes, thank you, Walt. I wish the circumstances were different."

Mel used both hands to bring her mug to her mouth as she listened to the broadcast. Brooke looked more composed than she expected—sitting straight, without a hint of apprehension on her face. Mel admired her for keeping it together in front of the world.

"I want to be sensitive to your situation, what with your father missing, but you have a unique perspective on things. I don't think our viewers know you're on the board of Omnicia and have a close friend on the board of Peepl. This means you have a connection to four of the five missing men, since Mykle is a family friend, if I'm not mistaken."

The anchor's face showed sincerity, but Mel wondered if he was just a good actor.

"As Randy pointed out, there have been disagreements between a few of them," said Walt, "but we've also seen some of them join forces. For example, Omnicia and Instant-Mode brought us the incredibly popular bulletproof clothing line that launched a few years before William retired. I know you're dealing with the disappearance of your dad, but…"

Walt's dramatic pause stretched for a beat too long.

"Could this be a meeting of the minds to bring us something really big?" he finished.

"I can certainly see where you might get that idea from." The corners of Brooke's mouth hinted at an enigmatic smile. "It does seem to be the prevailing theory right now, but the biggest question is still, why the secrecy? Surely they'd at least let their families know, so we wouldn't worry. I know for a fact my father would never keep such an enormous secret from me, and he'd never want resources to be wasted trying to find him. I'm sure the others would feel the same way."

Mel drained her wine. Her entire body protested as she pushed herself from the chair, muscles stiff and aching from hours of tension. She filled her mug again from the half-empty bottle on top of the mini-fridge, pouring slowly, her eyes never leaving the screen. This was the last drink. She told herself that every time.

Walt Meyers was still grilling Joel Berg's daughter. "It's no secret your father has become quite good friends with Mykle Drexel. Do you know if there are friendships between the other men? Do they even know each other? I mean, obviously, Josh and William's companies have worked together, but do you know if any of them are friends?"

"Honestly, Walt, I don't. These men don't like to have their personal lives on display. My father is friends with Mykle, as you mentioned. But other than that, I don't know if the other men have ever met."

Mel could see Brooke was choosing her words carefully. It was impressive, really, the way she navigated the conversation without giving anything away.

"From my time on the board of Omnicia, I know Josh Latham prefers to do things on his own," Brooke said. "The project with Instant-Mode was very calculated. He knew Omnicia had more to gain than Instant-Mode. I just don't see Josh collaborating with anyone, especially not Matt Aronowitz."

Mel filled her mug again. The past few days had been some of the most stressful of her life. The magnitude of what they were doing wrapped around her like a steel trap. She had expected it, but knowing something intellectually was one thing, experiencing it was another.

"So, where does that leave us, then?" Walt leaned back, his voice no longer shrill. "Randy, what do you think? Are we looking at abduction? Should we be expecting ransom demands? And of course, the question on all our minds is how this could have been pulled off? Other wealthy people around the world must be on high alert—what can they do to protect themselves?"

"I clearly don't have the answers to those questions, Walt. Nobody does. I think what we can expect to see is a lot of time, money, and manpower being poured into the investigation. I'm sure each of the missing men's families will cooperate with the agencies involved and will undoubtedly fund their own investigations as well. As for others going missing...I think if I were on a wealthiest person's list, I might not want to be alone in my office for a while."

Mel clicked off the TV, the abrupt silence almost jarring. She eyed her mug. It was empty. Staring at the blank screen, her thoughts were as heavy as her body.

Tomorrow, the real test would begin. And if things went

sideways, she, the men, and her girls would all be living together for the rest of their lives.

CHAPTER FOUR

BEFORE THE MEN ARRIVED, THE DAY HAD ALREADY TESTED MEL.

She had given herself plenty of time to get ready that morning, but it still didn't feel like enough. The founders had planned Josh's extraction for 9:00 AM; 7:00 AM in Seattle where Josh lived. She had reviewed his charts a hundred times and memorized every detail of his medical history. Still, a knot of worry clenched tighter each time she checked her bracelet, the digital clock ticking down like a bomb.

She contemplated doing a centering meditation. Her mastery of the skill, honed over more than fifteen years, allowed her to dissolve into nothingness within minutes. After rehab, the tools she'd learned, like mindfulness, had saved her more times than she could count. Yet, since arriving at the facility two months ago, her thoughts second guessing her abilities had been intrusive and constant. Although she knew meditation would leave her more refreshed and focused, she chose music instead.

Eminem's "Lose Yourself" blasted through her apartment on repeat, the bass rattling the paintings on her walls. The same song had fueled preparation for her TED talk on psychedelic-assisted therapy. She'd thought that talk would change the world. She had aimed to shift the long-standing belief that drugs were all dangerous and convince governments to reopen research, but it hadn't made the difference she'd prayed for. Instead, it led her here. The founders had seen it.

Both men had grown up in the shadow of the Vietnam War and the height of Nixon's campaign against drugs, an era that vilified psychedelics as tools of escapism rather than healing. Despite modern research proving their therapeutic potential, the stigma lingered; an echo of a time when mind-expansion equated to societal collapse. Mel's TED talk, along with Brooke's personal transformative experiences with the drugs, had won the men over.

Checking her bracelet again, Mel's heart stuttered in her chest. One more hour. Bile rose in her throat, leaving her lips puckered and mouth bitter. She swallowed as heat rushed through her and caused a cold sweat on her skin.

Dear God, can we please get this over with?

She needed a distraction. Anything to pull her away from the persistent ticking in her head. Thalia.

Without further thought, she was knocking on her friend's door.

"Hey Mel." Thalia answered the door with her eyebrow raised, a towel wrapped around her head and toothbrush in hand. "What's up?"

"Oh shit, I'm sorry. I didn't mean to bother you. I just..." She hesitated, mouth suddenly dry. "I'll let you know when Josh is here."

"No. No, come on in." Thalia motioned for her to enter. "I'll throw some clothes on. Make yourself at home."

Mel ran her hand along the velvety, multi-colored throw hanging over the back of Thalia's couch on her way to the rocking chair in the corner. The softness of the blanket was a comfort that grounded her. As she walked through the apartment, the warm scent of sage and patchouli wrapped around her, mirroring her friend's calming energy. Thalia's taste in decor differed from Mel's, but she loved the homeyness of the space.

"Tea?" Thalia called as she made her way from the bedroom to the kitchen.

"Yeah, that'd be great. Although I feel like I need a few glasses of wine... or maybe some pot." Her laugh sounded brittle even to her own ears. She sat on the antique rocker, the wood creaking as she shifted, legs bouncing with restless energy. "I need something to quiet my nerves."

"You're not alone there." Thalia plopped the tea bags up and down. "I did a two-hour meditation before my shower, but it didn't help much."

"I couldn't even make myself sit for half an hour. I didn't have faith my mind would shut up."

Thalia handed her a steaming mug, the scent of cinnamon and cloves hanging between them. "I feel like I want to crawl out of my skin."

"Glad I'm not the only one," Mel said as her fingers drummed against the arm of the chair.

Thalia nodded, taking a sip of her tea.

Mel traced the rim of her cup, the steady motion soothing her racing thoughts. "I'm just so restless," she said, her voice barely above a whisper. "It's like there's a constant knot in my stomach."

Thalia eased onto the couch, pulling her knees up. "Restlessness can be its own kind of noise, you know? I used to feel it all the time when I was living under the Principle."

"What did you do about it?"

"I thought I could sit still long enough to make it go away. I wasn't meditating. I was trying to disappear." Thalia paused, the faint tap of her fingers against the ceramic filling the quiet. "Real stillness isn't about shutting it out. It's about letting yourself feel it. Allowing it to pass through you instead of fighting it."

"I don't know if I can be still right now. It feels...too much."

Thalia reached out, resting a hand on Mel's arm. "I know what you mean. It's all so unpredictable, and it's hard not to let that consume us. Please don't think everything falls on you. Just because you're the director doesn't mean you're responsible for *everything*."

Mel found reassurance in Thalia's eyes. "Thank you, hun. I know my girls have my back."

Everyone found it amusing when she referred to them as girls. Monica and Shannon were older than her, and Thalia and Cath were only slightly younger. She tried calling them women, but it didn't sound right.

Thalia squeezed her arm. "Sometimes, it's okay to let yourself feel overwhelmed. It's a natural response to everything that's going on. But remember, we're in this together."

Mel blinked back tears as she thought about the empty wine bottles in her apartment. She masked the thought with a weak smile. "Don't worry, I'm fine."

The corners of Thalia's mouth pulled downward. "I used to say that, too. 'I'm fine.'" She paused and let the silence stretch. "Back then, I had to be. If I weren't, I'd be punished. You'd be surprised how unfine I was most of the time."

"I can't even imagine what you went through on that ranch. It must have been a lot."

"It was." Thalia took another sip of tea. "But pretending you're okay doesn't make you stronger. It just makes you tired. And when you're tired, mistakes happen."

Tired wasn't the right word for what Mel felt after her husband, Lee's, death, when she'd insisted she was fine while drowning in alcohol just to get through each night. She wasn't drinking like that now, but she *was* drinking.

Her bracelet chirped and turned from blue to red. She glanced at her wrist, then bolted from her chair so awkwardly she spilled her tea. Her knees almost buckled from the rush of adrenaline. "I'm sorry, I have to go. He's emerging now!"

"Good luck," Thalia called after her as she sprinted down the hall.

Mel arrived at Josh's apartment as he began to emerge. The sight was both mesmerizing and surreal. It was like watching a Polaroid develop in slow motion, his form gradually becoming solid, the lines of his body sharpening with each second. For a brief moment, she was transported back to her childhood, sitting beside her mom on the couch, laughing at the terrible special effects of old sci-fi shows. Now, the technology that had once been laughable fiction was here, unfolding in front of her eyes.

Josh's body was still except for the rise and fall of his chest. He was naked. She thought she'd be prepared to see them arrive like this, but her muscles constricted. She forced herself to look, though every instinct screamed at her to turn away. It was such an invasion of his privacy, so she dressed him as quickly as possible. Easier said than done.

She was aware of his strict workout regimen, yet wasn't prepared for the muscles that seemed to carve themselves into his skin. The interplay of light and shadow highlighted the contours of his jawline and defined the lines of his abdomen. Despite her best efforts not to, she let her eyes wander below his waist.

"Damn it, Mel, get a fucking grip." Her voice came out in a harsh whisper, a verbal reprimand she needed to hear.

Her hands trembled as she pulled a shirt over his broad shoulders. The fabric slid easily over his skin, but her fingers fumbled with the buttons. Getting his pants on was a battle of tugging and twisting, leaving her breathless and red-faced.

Once clothed, she snapped a red bracelet onto his wrist. It clicked into place, seamlessly affixing itself to his skin like it was fused there. His band synced with the blue one on her wrist, the connection humming softly as his every heartbeat fed into her device. It was a quiet reassurance. She fingered the tiny silver button embedded in her bracelet—a safeguard, one press away from immobilizing him if anything went wrong.

She lifted Josh's arm and examined the contact between his band and skin. No gaps; tailored to deliver precise doses of PLH directly into his bloodstream. The drug was her own design, a compound engineered for one purpose: to suppress impulses toward anger, violence, or escape. To keep the wealth-hoarding dragons compliant.

She hated that word. Compliant. It reminded her of the treatment center years ago, where control had been imposed on her when she couldn't trust herself. She understood the value of control, but here, it felt like a betrayal of her ideals. Compliance was a tool, but it wasn't the kind of healing she believed in.

As she tapped her bracelet, a virtual screen appeared above her wrist, showing Josh's vitals were right on target. The tight coil of anxiety in her gut loosened.

She waited while he tried to gain consciousness, giving him basic information while his brain was scattered. Once satisfied he could manage on his own, she headed toward the gym. She needed a release before the others arrived. Everything so far had gone as planned, yet she couldn't rid herself of the thought that something had to go wrong. It shouldn't be this easy to abduct the wealthiest men in the world.

Mel found Cath in the small, yet well-equipped gym, her body moving in rhythm with the low hum of the rowing machine. Each stroke precise.

For a moment, Mel hesitated, caught between the urge to let Cath finish, and the impulse to check in with the youngest member of the team. But Cath hadn't paused, hadn't looked up, her gaze fixed somewhere beyond the wall.

Mel observed her with quiet concern. Out of all her girls, Cath was the most empathetic. It was why she'd brought her into the project; Cath's ability to read people, to experience their emotions almost as her own, was a gift. But gifts could be heavy burdens, too. Her sensitivity, her openness to others' feelings, left Cath exposed in a way that could endanger her own mental health. The intensity of the project and the countless traumas they'd wade through, would undoubtedly take a toll. Mel feared it would push the sensitive girl too far.

"Cath?" She kept her voice low.

Her friend jerked, releasing the handle and clutching her chest. "Oh my God, you scared me!"

"Sorry. Didn't mean to. Wasn't sure if I should disturb you, but wanted to see how you're feeling and if there's anything you need from me before Matt gets here?"

Cath's lips pressed into something almost resembling a smile. "I appreciate your concern, but no. I'm fine. Thanks."

There was a tightness in her jaw Mel recognized all too well. "If you're sure, then I'll leave you to your workout. Okay if I'm in here with you?"

"Oh yeah, sure, you're good. I was pretty much finished anyway." Cath rose from the rower, breath ragged, sweat streaking her cheeks. She dragged a towel across her face, then turned toward the door.

Mel reached out and clasped her hand, offering a reassuring squeeze. Guilt tugged at her for cutting Cath's workout short; Mel knew she had a tendency to prioritize others' needs above her own and keep her feelings to herself. She prayed Cath would trust her enough to be honest with her, even when things got tough. More than anything, Mel wanted her girls to understand they could come to her without fear of judgment. It would be impossible to survive this without being real with each other. Mel knew she needed to set the example.

After forty minutes on the stair-climber, the alarm on Mel's bracelet chimed, signaling the end of her session. Sweat clung to her skin, breath coming in steady gasps as her muscles burned, the ache sparking memories. She remembered the burn from when she'd hiked up mountains alone to camp overnight—those endless climbs after Lee's suicide, when the silence of the wilderness seemed to be the only place she could breathe.

She'd bring a bottle of wine or a flask of whiskey, convincing herself it was just to take the edge off, to help her sleep. But in truth, she'd been trying to numb the grief lodged in her chest. Mel thought the pain might kill her. Now, the ache served as a reminder of the person she'd fought to rebuild. The person she feared was slipping away.

She wished there was more time to lose herself in the steady pounding of her feet against the machine. It was a meditation of sorts that drowned out her thoughts. But there were things looming over her more important than a few extra minutes of peace. William, Matt…the entire project.

Running a hand through her tangled hair, she grimaced at the sticky strands clinging to her fingers. She needed to shower. Pull herself together. Josh would be awake the next time she saw him, and she couldn't afford to look unprofessional.

Cath was walking from her apartment to the common room when Mel exited the elevator. They walked together in silence. Images of snow-capped mountains and tranquil seascapes lined the walls. Originally meant to induce calm, but now only served as reminders of the stakes of the project.

Cath paused in front of a photo showing the Wadden Sea National Park. "Monica said it doesn't look like this anymore. The last time she visited, most of the beach was gone."

Mel rested her head on Cath's shoulder. "Then we'd better make sure this works so we can save what's left."

Her bracelet chirped as they approached the common room's

door. "The founders are arriving."

The smell of food greeted the women as they stepped into the common room. Spices mingled with the warmth of roasted vegetables while Monica and Thalia chatted by the counter. Shannon was carefully arranging dishes on the table.

"How's Josh?" Monica asked when the two women approached.

"He's waking up," Mel replied. "Faster than I expected."

Monica moved toward the table. "That's great! God, I hope things go as well with William. I'm so nervous."

"He'll be here soon." Mel forced a smile. "Try to relax. Let's have a nice lunch before things really ramp up."

As they settled around the table, Thalia reached for a plate of pakoras. "Wow, Shannon, you went all out. This looks amazing."

Shannon shrugged off the praise, but Mel leaned over and gave her a hug. "Seriously, thank you for this."

The clink of utensils filled the room until Monica spoke. "Can we talk about Josh and Matt?"

"What about them?" Mel asked, although she knew what was coming.

"I just don't see how we're supposed to work with two guys who hate each other."

Thalia smirked. "They're like middle-schoolers. Did you see their latest posts?" She pulled out her device and scrolled. "Matt said, 'It's sad when someone with more money than God has to rip off someone else's ideas.' And Josh? 'Sometimes it takes a genius to polish someone else's turd.'" She laughed. "They're insufferable."

"If this whole thing blows up because of them..." Cath said under her breath.

"It won't." Mel's tone was firm. "It's our jobs to be sure that doesn't happen."

Despite Mel's reassurance, the mood at the table had darkened. As the meal wound down and plates were cleared, Cath's hand trembled on the way to the dishwasher. Mel followed her, sensing something was off.

"What's wrong?" she asked quietly.

Tears spilled over Cath's cheeks as she choked out a response. "What are we doing, Mel? Like really? We're all insane."

Mel held back her own tears as she pulled Cath into a hug. The fragility in Cath's voice broke something inside her. The other women closed in and wrapped their arms around each other. A collective fear settled into their hearts.

"I know..." Mel's voice was almost inaudible. "We all know. It's overwhelming...but we've come this far. We can't lose sight of why we're doing this."

Mel couldn't ignore the contrast from two months ago, when they'd arrived. Each of them had been buzzing with excitement, fueled by the thrill of new tech and a shared mission. But now, that excitement lay far behind, replaced by a crushing sense of reality.

She pulled back, giving the group a final squeeze. "I almost forgot." She tried to infuse her voice with optimism. "There's a new program on our headsets. You can pinpoint any public location in the world and experience it virtually, in real time, as if you were really there. It should help with cabin fever."

Monica smiled. "That sounds amazing. I'm definitely spending time in Paris, people watching."

"Paris sounds lovely." Thalia put her arms around Monica. "Too bad we won't be able to eat the pastries."

Mel's bracelet chirped. She glanced at the glowing display. "Oh shit, here comes Matt." She drained her water glass, wishing it were something stronger. "Cath, I'll keep you posted. Monica, you get ready too."

Mel straightened her shoulders. "Here we go."

CHAPTER FIVE

HAD JOSH IMAGINED THE VOICE TELLING HIM TO OPEN HIS EYES, OR had it been real? And if she was real, where was she?

His eyelids finally receded. The world that greeted him was a hazy, fragmented mess. It looked pixelated, like he had been dropped into some primitive arcade game from the 1980s. Tiny squares blinked in and out, giving him the unnerving notion that reality itself was glitching.

The surrounding darkness wasn't complete, which allowed him to make out the edges of the room. He lay on his back, his body sinking into the soft mattress while silky, cool sheets brushed his skin. Nerves stirred, awakening one by one. Beneath his head, the pillow cradled him with a familiar loft, conjuring the thought of home.

But this wasn't home.

He tried to lift a hand to touch his face, to confirm his body was still there. His breath quickened when his arm refused to cooperate. *Where the hell is my hand?* Thoughts buzzed with frantic energy, but his body remained still.

Fingers tingled beneath the pillow. Slowly, as though his thoughts were dragging his body through molasses, he began to feel his hand. Concentrating, he willed the muscles to obey. His thumb twitched, then his index finger. *Come on*, he thought, forcing himself to focus. His hand crept up and grasped the sheet.

Progress.

Hours later, or maybe it was minutes, he hoisted his torso up. His head pounded. The ache radiated behind his eyes and down his neck. Veins filled with lead made every movement a monumental effort. The room swayed as his vision continued to distort his surroundings. The square edges still refused to smooth out.

He made fists and forced himself to steady, struggling to piece together what was happening. He blinked, and his gaze locked on what looked like a control panel on the wall. The woman, Mel, had mentioned a switch and something about blinds. If he could make it over there, maybe he'd get a better idea of where the hell he was.

Each muscle protested as he tried to move his body off the bed. *Christ, I feel like I weigh 300 pounds.* His pulse thudded in frustration.

The inability to command his own body sent a tremor of fear through him, one he buried beneath a clenched jaw and a low, steady growl while he forced himself to keep moving. If anyone was watching, he'd be damned if they saw him flinch.

A glass of water beckoned from the bedside table. His throat, dry and raw, demanded it. He reached for the glass, but the simple act of lifting it was impossible with only one hand. His arms trembled under the weight. Sweat beaded on his forehead, his palms so slick the glass almost slipped from his grasp.

It took both hands to steady it as he brought the rim to his lips, muscles quivering like he was deadlifting twice his weight. When the water hit his tongue, he winced.

What the hell is this?

A sharp, metallic tang coated his tongue, bitter and unnatural, like licking rusted iron. His throat burned, but he swallowed it down as the pull of his thirst silenced his disgust. The unpleasantness faded. It became so refreshing that he couldn't drink fast enough.

His body responded to the liquid immediately. The cotton left his mouth, and his breathing regulated. Sweat dried on his forehead, and the weight pinning him to the bed lifted. Though a lingering unsteadiness clung to him, his limbs responded when called upon, each one under his command.

He finally had the strength to swing his legs over the side of the bed. The floor wasn't cold or hard. His feet sank in ever so slightly, not like carpet, but more like a gymnastics mat; enough to cushion the impact, yet not so much to cause instability.

The first step was tentative. He had to hold on to the furniture for support, knuckles turning white as his fingers curled around the headboard. He focused all his effort on putting one foot in front of the other. His legs were uncooperative. Every movement, deliberate and awkward, yet he kept moving.

Repeating the process, he forced his feet to shuffle across the room. Each step marginally easier than the last. His knees continued to buckle, but he was pleased he didn't fall. More progress. Determination burned through his frustration, pushing him forward.

He lifted his hand to press the panel. A glowing bracelet on his wrist caught his eye, sending a chill down his spine. He hadn't noticed it until now. It was a smoldering, dim red; a reminder of something he should be worried about. He ran his right hand across the smooth surface, trying to find a way to remove it, but it melted into his skin like a tattoo. *What the hell have they done?* He dismissed the thought. *Focus.* He'd try again later when his vision improved. Right now, he needed answers, and those would only come after finding out where he was.

His fingers found the switch, and the blinds inched open. A sliver of light seared his vision, making him squeeze his eyes shut, and his head throbbed harder. The Brightness, though overwhelming, helped with the pixilation. The little squares were smoothing out as objects became more defined.

The bed was placed in the center of the space, with a nightstand on either side. His eyes landed on the bedding—satin-striped sheets, a black silk duvet—the exact setup he had at home. The hairs on his arms stood at attention. *Who had given them this information?* Unease thickened in his chest. Whoever they were had reached right into his private world, mapping it here without his permission.

Apart from the tables and bed, the room had no other furniture, not even a lamp.

He opened the blinds fully and looked through the floor-to-ceiling window. He had no idea what he was expecting, but this wasn't it. Beyond his room stretched a patio with flowering potted plants, a hammock swaying between two posts of an awning, a bistro set, and a stone water feature. It was too serene, too staged.

The patio led to a lap pool, its surface shimmering in the light, and beyond that, an endless sea of tall, sun-scorched grass. No roads, no power lines, no buildings. Nothing but emptiness stretching to the horizon. A chill crept over him as he looked left, then right. The same patio repeated itself, like he was trapped in some endless, mirrored reality.

He looked for a way to get outside, but didn't see any doors leading out from the bedroom. However, there were two interior doors, each leading to another room. Through one, the glint of tiles and a sink suggested a bathroom. The other opened into shadows, where the faint hum of an appliance promised the fridge Mel had mentioned.

Walking came more smoothly now. His hands, previously gripping the wall and furniture for support, swung freely at his sides. His legs were still heavier than they should be, and he lacked coordination, but getting to the kitchen and living room wasn't difficult.

The rooms were large and open, with a modern, minimalist design. The ceilings were high, and windows continued out from the bedroom and through the rest of the apartment. On the walls hung a few weighty and abstract pieces of art. They were in blues, reminiscent of water. There was no TV, but a small bookshelf held a variety of titles. The sparse furniture, contemporary yet inviting, was very much to his liking. A detail that unnerved him.

The floor in the new rooms still had the odd, soft give that cushioned each step as he moved through the apartment. The longer he walked on it, the more he found himself enjoying the sensation. He made a mental note to ask about it later. Maybe have it installed at home.

Home! The thought snapped him back to his predicament. Anger simmered under his skin. He pressed the button on his bracelet. "You told me to ask if I needed anything," he yelled, forcing his voice to stay steady. "Well, I need some fucking answers!"

"Hi Josh, it's Mel."

The voice surrounded him, soft yet clear. It wasn't coming from any specific direction or location. He couldn't pinpoint the speakers or the source of the sound. Instead, it echoed from everywhere, wrapping around him and filling the room like a presence, almost like it was coming from inside his brain. His skin crawled. They had to be watching.

"You're adapting very well; much better than our other voyagers."

Voyagers? His fear snagged on the word. *Voyagers to where?*

"You're probably hungry, and it would be a good idea if you eat something before we meet. As I mentioned before, the food will taste strange, and your stomach will be upset for a few minutes. Shannon has prepared a light salad for you. It's in the fridge. We've found this is one of the easier meals to handle after an extraction."

Extraction? What the fuck does that mean? More questions. He forced his face to stay impassive. Any reaction might betray him, and he didn't want them to see any cracks in his composure.

Mel's voice still flowed around him. "Once you've finished eating, I'll meet you outside on the patio."

He hadn't noticed the void in his stomach until now. A deep, gnawing ache pulled at his insides. As he opened the Thermador fridge, the cold air provided a welcome relief against his flushed skin. Next to pitchers filled with pulpy, fresh-squeezed juices was a salad bowl, packed with spinach, blueberries, and goat cheese.

Pulling out the salad and what he assumed was orange juice, he turned his attention to scouring the kitchen for a glass and silverware. With a yank, he pulled open a drawer, causing its contents to jostle as he grabbed a fork made from some sort of wood.

He stared down at the salad, stomach demanding food, though something inside him screamed not to. But he had to eat. If they wanted him dead, he'd be cold by now. He speared a forkful and brought it to his mouth. His taste buds were already firing for familiar flavors. The cold crunch hit his teeth; his tongue, however, curled in protest.

The texture, that of a salad, but had the taste of biting metal laced with gritty earth, chased by a bitter, oily burn of gasoline. His jaw locked, the sharpness overwhelming his senses. A shudder rolled through his body as his stomach threatened to revolt. His mind begged him to spit it out, but he forced it down, throat so tight it was almost impossible to swallow.

A violent cramp tore through his abdomen, his whole body curling forward as if someone had plunged a fist into his gut. The pain was immediate and searing, leaving him gasping for breath. Clutching his middle, he doubled over. He rocked as the agony ripped through him and every nerve in his body screamed. And then, as suddenly as it had come on, the discomfort was gone. He sat there panting, sweat dripping from his forehead.

He waited a minute, not daring to move in case another wave

of pain was behind the first. When none came, he took another cautious bite. Then another. Each mouthful offered a subtle shift, a hint of something delicious. By the time he finished, the layers of flavor had unfolded into something otherworldly.

A soft breeze brushed his skin as he took his last bite. When he turned to the wall of windows, the glass was gone. He stepped outside, where the warmth of the sun somehow refreshed him, but the light was too bright, making him squint. The air energized him, unlike the city air in Seattle.

Sitting at the outdoor table was a woman. It had to be Mel. She looked to be in her mid-forties, maybe a bit taller than him, with a classic beauty that appeared effortless. Wavy, sandy-brown hair spilled over her shoulders, framing her face and drawing attention to the warm smile softening her features. Her floral wrap dress hugged her athletic build, a body kept fit through routine. Aside from a blue bracelet encircling her left wrist, she wore no jewelry, the simplicity only adding to her striking presence.

His hands curled as he walked toward her, but his mind was unflustered.

Why am I calm? I shouldn't be calm, I should be raging.

Every muscle in his body was ready to snap, yet an eerie stillness settled over him as he sat across from her, thoughts subdued.

"Hi, Josh." Her voice was composed, but her cheeks flushed when she made eye contact. "It's a pleasure to meet you. You must have a lot of questions."

"You're not fucking kidding."

Mel smiled and nodded. "We'll have a meeting with all the voyagers tomorrow once you've had more time to recover. You'll get more information then. For now, I'll keep it simple and short."

He stared at her; the sunlight burning the back of his neck as he listened. He wanted to demand answers, to push her until she cracked, but a strange serenity dulled the urge. He fought against it, but the harder he tried, the more the haze settled, numbing his anger into something unreachable.

"We built this facility during the CryoSpora pandemic. Everyone's focus was on the chaos caused by it, so little attention was paid to what we were doing here... in southern Saskatchewan."

"Jesus fuck."

Mel ignored his vulgar interruption. "We're far enough from civilization that no one would've noticed the trucks coming and going, anyway. We have a small army of people all committed to the cause. They built this place and another one where most of them live and keep tabs on our tech. We only have a small staff here. You'll meet your guide, Thalia, soon. And Shannon, our chef. Other than them, I'm the only person you'll be interacting with."

His brain grasped at the words, attempting to process them, but the effort proved futile, like trying to hold on to water. The heat on his skin was getting uncomfortable, but he didn't move. He stared, watching her lips, catching fragments of her explanation as his mind stumbled over itself.

She met his eyes again. "No harm will come to you or your family, Josh. I want you to know that. You have no reason to trust me, but I give you my word. Thalia will come tomorrow to bring you to the meeting."

Her voice was soothing, but it only fueled the growing frustration inside him. He wanted to ask a million things. Demand answers. But his body was exhausted.

Mel stood gracefully. "Rest up. I need to go see what the news is saying about your disappearance. I'll see you tomorrow."

His eyes followed her as she walked toward the next patio. But as she passed the potted plants dividing the two, her form distorted, bending and shifting until she disappeared entirely. His breath caught as he remembered the mirror in the gym exploding into water.

CHAPTER SIX

As morning light filtered through the sheer green curtains, Mel's head pounded, a dull ache pulsing behind her temples. She groaned, pressing her fingers to her forehead in an effort to push away the lingering effects of last night's bottle.

A wave of guilt washed over her. Her professionalism was slipping, and she knew it. This wasn't who she used to be. During med school, she'd prided herself on being the steady one, the type of person her classmates could count on to be the designated driver. But after Lee's death, that discipline crumbled, and grief paved the way for an illness she never thought she'd develop. And now, the pressure of the project threatened to undo fifteen years of sobriety.

They need you to keep it together. The thought stirred a mix of disappointment and determination. She dragged herself out of bed, swallowing against the nausea and making a silent vow: *This can't happen again.*

Under the hot shower, steam cocooned her and relaxed the knots in her muscles. The water streamed down, washing away the fatigue, the self-reproach, and leaving in its place a new clarity. By the time she stepped out, wrapped in a fresh sense of purpose, a glimmer of her old self emerged. She slipped into a blue button-down dress, its soft fabric would be her armor for the day ahead. A mug of black coffee completed her transformation.

"William, can you hear me?" Mel asked, her voice soft as she rubbed the thin, bony back of the seventy-year-old. "William, I need you to try to wake up for me, okay?"

The night had passed without alarms, which was a relief because he was decades older than the others. An introvert by nature, he had quietly built a global empire without ever stepping into the spotlight. He had been chosen for the project to balance the big energy of Josh and Matt. Yet, despite his sharp mind and strong physical health, his age introduced complications no amount of preparation could erase.

His extraction had sent a bolt of fear through her, as his heart hadn't been beating when he'd arrived. It was a miracle only one pulse from the defibrillator dragged him back from the brink.

A groan of awareness escaped from the older man. Encouraged, Mel continued rubbing his back and took out her smelling salts. The irony of such a low-tech solution in such high-tech surroundings made her grin.

William's eyes flew open as he gasped. "Maria... Maria, was passiert?"

A stab of sadness struck Mel, sharp and familiar, as she replied, "You're safe, William. My name is Mel. You've had a medical episode and are under my care in a private hospital."

Her voice was steady, but the echo of her own grief surfaced—memories of calling out for Lee in the first days after his suicide. Her voice hitched as she continued to reassure the old man, hoping he understood enough English to grasp the meaning of her words.

"Wo ist Maria?" he whispered, his voice laced with fear and longing.

With all the calm she could muster, she explained he was in quarantine, which, sadly meant visitors weren't allowed. As the confusion settled in his eyes, he accepted her answer without pressing further. She hated lying.

Although she'd had to insert a catheter the previous night, she hoped he'd be strong enough to walk and use the bathroom by himself within an hour. She opted to withhold any information about his whereabouts until he regained full mobility and lucidity. She wanted that to be as quickly as possible, so the group meeting could happen. Matt and Josh couldn't be left hanging much longer.

Matt had emerged vomiting, but, thankfully, other than that, his arrival had been as smooth as Josh's. Now, as William drifted in and out of consciousness, each passing minute stretched unbearably for Mel as she watched his shallow breathing.

She paced around his room, chewing on her lip, stealing glances at her bracelet to track the time. Just when her mind began to spiral, Monica appeared in the doorway, concerned eyes on Mel.

"Hey." Monica put a hand on Mel's lower back. "Why don't you let me watch him so you can take a break?"

Mel hesitated, fueled by worry and a fierce determination to be there when he woke again. But she was exhausted. With a sigh that caught in her throat, she put her head on Monica's shoulder and wrapped her arms around her. "Thank you."

Once Mel left, Monica settled back against the wall, legs stretched out before her as she opened *Eat Mangoes Naked* by Sark. Sunlight spilled across the pages, and as she read aloud, her voice filled the quiet room, casting a sense of serenity she hoped might reach William.

She wasn't one to indulge in soft emotions, but she had the psychological attunement of an empath, acutely aware of the subtle cues others gave off. Even in his unconscious state, she could sense William's steady presence, a kind soul despite the fog he was trapped in.

Good choice, Mel, she thought. Gratitude rose in her for being paired with someone approachable, someone she might genuinely connect with.

She paused her reading, eyes drifting up to the ceiling, the book resting in her lap as her thoughts shifted to the group dynamics. She prided herself on her non-judgmental approach, yet an instinctive concern stirred in her, thinking of Thalia and Cath, who'd be dealing with Josh and Matt's overblown egos soon enough.

Mel came back before William woke fully. A lingering scent of chlorine and alcohol wafted in with her.

Monica tilted her head to the side and squinted. "Is everything alright?"

Mel smiled. "Yeah, I took a swim to clear my head."

Monica paused before broaching the real question, her tone gentle but firm. "I couldn't help but notice...have you been drinking?"

Mel hesitated, her eyes flickering away before meeting hers again. "What? No. It's just chlorine... the smell, and it does a number on my eyes and skin."

Nodding slowly, Monica's expression softened with understanding, but her tone betrayed her doubt. "Right. Chlorine...It's been a long couple of days. Please be sure to take care of yourself."

Mel's head bobbed in response, acknowledgment flashing in her eyes. "Thanks, Mon. I really appreciate you. I've got it from here. Why don't you wait for us in the dining room? I hope to have him up and moving shortly."

Mel took a seat beside William's bed, her heart aching at the sight of his fragile form. She took his right hand, palm down, and pressed firmly on his thumbnail. The elderly man's eyelids fluttered open, pupils dilated.

"Hi, William. I hope you're feeling well."

"No, not well at all." His voice was faint and fragile, but stern.

"Let's get you propped up a bit." She carefully arranged the bed pillows behind him to keep him upright. "I know you're still groggy, but we need you to try really hard to get moving," she continued, keeping her tone light. "Take it slowly, hold on to walls and furniture. Monica and I will meet you at the breakfast table in the next room once you're ready. There are fresh clothes for you in the closet."

"Who is Monica?"

"I'll explain everything to you when you come out," she replied, offering a reassuring smile as she disconnected his catheter and IV. She hesitated at the door, glancing back, relieved he had slept through most of the effects of the extraction.

Confusion clouded William's mind, but he refused to acknowledge it. Taking a steadying breath, he braced himself and gingerly swung his legs over the side of the bed with determination.

I need answers, he thought. *What happened to me? Why am I in the hospital? Where is Maria? And why didn't Mel speak German?*

His muscles flexed as he attempted to stand. Not quite. He tried again, this time grabbing hold of the headboard to help, his bony fingers straining as if they might snap. Success. He made it across the spacious bedroom to the bathroom using a cautious shuffle, relieved to avoid any mishaps along the way.

When he reached the closet, he burst with relief; everything looked familiar.

Maria must have brought my things.

She would be nearby, worried, of course, but surely they could see each other shortly. Bracing against the door frame, he took a moment to collect himself.

The aroma of freshly brewed coffee filled the sunlit kitchen as William entered, the warmth giving him a semblance of normalcy. He scanned the room, eyes landing on Mel, whose smile seemed genuine. Next to her was a woman he didn't recognize, but something about her expression held a quiet understanding that put him at ease, even if he wouldn't show it.

"You're looking fantastic." Mel rose, gesturing toward the brunette woman beside her. "I'd like you to meet Monica. She'll be your personal guide here, and you'll be spending a lot of time together."

Monica stood, her eyes meeting his as she extended a warm smile. "Hi, William. It's lovely to meet you. Please, come sit with us."

The familiarity of her voice tugged at something in his memory, but he couldn't quite place it. As he joined them at the glass table, his fingers absently fidgeted with the strange red bracelet around his wrist. Its design was unusual. It didn't move, but it wasn't uncomfortable. Nothing like any hospital bands he had ever seen. Quite unsettling.

Mel caught his attention and winked. "That's a new technology we're using here. You're probably wondering why there are no beeping machines in your room. Our bracelets tell me everything I need to know about you."

She held up her own wrist, displaying a blue band. As her fingers swept across its surface, a display materialized with streams of data scrolling past.

He nodded, masking his apprehension with a neutral expression, though his mind buzzed with questions.

"How are you feeling?" Monica asked.

"Confused."

"I imagine that's an understatement." Mel slid her finger over her bracelet, making the display vanish. "You've just been through an experimental procedure with some challenging side effects. We want you to rest. This meeting is only to reassure you that you're safe and well cared for.

"There are others here who've also recently arrived, so I need to check on them, but if you need anything, simply push the button on your bracelet. You'll be able to speak to Monica as if she's right here with you. And remember, take things slowly; we don't want you hurting yourself."

Mel rose, giving William's hand a comforting pat. "Take good care of him for me, Mon." With one last unreadable look, she slipped out through the open windows to the patio.

"Why do you and Mel not speak the German?" His English was stilted, though he was sure Monica would understand him.

"This is a very specialized facility, William." Her voice carried a reassuring steadiness. "The treatments here aren't available anywhere else in the world. I don't want to alarm you, but we're actually in Canada."

"What?" The color drained from his face, but he held himself rigid, determined not to let the panic show.

Monica's bracelet beeped. She silenced it with a quick touch. "I know...it's a lot to take in, and you must have countless questions. But for now, it's best if you focus on getting your strength back.

"We'll keep the windows closed today so you won't be able to go outside. We don't want you falling in the pool." Monica giggled like a little girl as she got up and touched a switch on the wall. Glass slid silently across the open space Mel had exited through.

He caught Monica's subtle shift in demeanor as she activated the windows, sealing the space.

Like a cage, he thought. He kept his expression neutral, though, schooling his reaction.

Monica's tone was professional again. "I'll leave you to rest. Your fridge is stocked, and Shannon, our chef, will bring you lunch and dinner. She'll give you a warning about half an hour before she arrives. There's a bookshelf with a wide variety in your living room. We don't want you to be overstimulated today, so I'm afraid that's your only entertainment for the time being. Rest up and call me if you need anything. I'll be back in a few hours to take you to the group meeting."

Once alone, he remained seated, gripping his chair as he stared at his bracelet. *Canada...How the hell did I end up here?*

CHAPTER SEVEN

JOLTED AWAKE BY AN UNFAMILIAR VOICE, JOSH SHOT UPRIGHT.

"Hi Josh, my name is Thalia," it was saying, the sound coming from everywhere and nowhere at once, chilling in its soft detachment. "I'm your guide and am waiting in your living room to take you to the meeting. I know you need to freshen up, so take your time and come out when you're ready."

He rubbed his eyes, the remnants of exhaustion clinging to him, but beneath the fog, anger simmered. *I thought you told me I had some privacy here.*

The fire in his blood propelled him out of bed. A prickle of curiosity edged through his frustration. *Who else is here, and what kind of game is this?*

Veins bulging in his forearm, he reached for the closet doorknob. With a quick tug, he opened the door—and froze. Before him was a replica of his closet at home, down to the smallest detail. A cold wave of disbelief washed over him, but his anger flared hotter as he looked closer. His suits, perfectly aligned, his T-shirts folded with precision, and even the leather jacket he picked up in Italy hung on a hanger. *Fuck me.*

A shudder rippled through his body. They knew him. They

knew everything. He ran his fingers over the soft cashmere of a sweater he'd bought in Northern India. The memories of the bustling marketplace where he'd haggled with the shopkeeper over eighty-four rupees for sport flooded his mind. Were these his actual clothes painstakingly transported here? Or were they duplicates? A carefully constructed illusion to make him comfortable, or worse, complacent?

He chose a solid gray button-down Luca Faloni linen shirt, left untucked for a more casual air, and form-fitting Alexander McQueen cotton stretch jeans that hugged his legs comfortably. He drew a fortifying breath into his lungs, the familiar fabrics brushing against his skin as he studied his reflection in the mirror. At least he'd look good while he was here.

He was surprised by his lack of consideration for appearance when first meeting Mel. She exuded quiet elegance and intelligence, a combination that stirred something within him that hadn't been there in a long time. That depth was never present in the women he pursued these days, and it only heightened her appeal.

Turning from the mirror, he stepped into the bathroom. It was a study in understated style. Smooth, white tiles reflected the soft glow of recessed lighting overhead. The sink, a floating slab of polished marble, had a sleek chrome faucet matching the brushed steel handles on the cabinets.

He opened the vanity drawer. The sight slapped him in the face—his brand of shampoo, the exact body wash he used, even his preferred Saunders & Long moisturizer all lined up like he'd put them there himself. The sheer level of intrusion made his anger spike again.

A steady breath eased his nerves, for now. He adjusted his collar, smoothed his hair, and checked every detail before striding out to meet Thalia.

Sunlight streamed through the apartment, casting a warm glow on the woman flipping through a National Geographic photo book. Josh paused, struck by the sight of her. Her skin seemed to shimmer in the light, and her dark, expressive eyes sparkled as she smiled.

"Hi, Josh." Her voice was the same buttery texture he'd heard before. "I'm Thalia. I'll be spending a lot of time with you for the next little while as I'll be your guide. I know that doesn't mean anything to you yet, but it will shortly."

Should he be relieved or concerned? Fascination overtook him, drawn to her despite her appearing to be the complete opposite of his girlfriend. Lisa, a tall blonde, had the best set of tits he had ever had the pleasure of burying his face in—and he had buried his face in more than his share of tits. She was a familiar type, the type he had always thought he wanted but couldn't have until money allowed him to have it. However captivating Lisa's sexual appeal, Josh had a persistent feeling of discontent.

Unlike Lisa, who fit a certain stereotype so neatly it sometimes bored him, Thalia was an enigma. She carried an understated beauty worlds apart from the high-maintenance look he'd come to expect from the women in his life. Her long, dark curls highlighted features that defied symmetry, somehow making her all the more captivating. Her small breasts, lemons rather than melons, didn't need a bra, which only added to her quiet self-assurance.

Where Lisa's appeal was surface-level, Thalia's allure came from the spark in her mischievous eyes and the way her smile hinted at secrets she might never share. There was something unguarded about her presence, as if she moved through the world without needing anyone's approval. That confidence pulled him in. And yet something about her made him nervous. He brushed it off as a reaction to his current predicament; a natural response to the strange confines he found himself in.

"What's with all the beautiful women in this place?" he said, covering his apprehension with a smirk. "Are you here to seduce me into giving you all my money? Or to create some sort of scandal? I'm sure you know, scandals have a way of being forgotten quickly."

Thalia's demeanor didn't waver. "You must have a million questions. No, no scandals. Quite the opposite, really. Let's get you to the meeting so you can get some of the answers you're looking for. We can continue our conversation later."

"Well, Josh, this is as far as I go. What's behind this door is going to be quite upsetting to you." Thalia stopped at the end of the hallway and scanned her bracelet on a reader next to the door. "I'll see you afterward. Good luck."

He froze. "Quite upsetting?" he repeated, a flash of irritation mingling with dread. He forced a laugh. "Thanks for the heads-up."

As the door swung open, he hesitated before stepping into the large circular room. Light flooded in from the windows, which wrapped around half the space, casting a surreal glow on the faces appearing through doorways just like his.

What the hell am I walking into?

With clenched jaw and a racing pulse, he strode through the door with feigned confidence. *Who else is here?* He only needed two steps to find out.

Holy shit. How the hell have they pulled this off? He had to admit, he was impressed... and terrified at the same time. He stood motionless as he observed the reactions of the other four men. William Becker's legs gave out beneath him as he fell to his knees, hands over his face, sobbing. Matt Aronowitz rushed to a nearby wastebasket as he retched violently.

An uncomfortable titter escaped his mouth when he saw Joel Berg rocking back and forth, eyes glued to the floor, mumbling something under his breath. The only other person in the room who seemed coherent was Mykle Drexel, doing exactly what Josh was doing. Watching.

His mind went into overdrive. This wasn't about him or his money. This was much bigger. State-sponsored, maybe. No individual would have the means or the need for something like this, at least nobody outside the room he now found himself in.

Still, he was the big fish here, central to whatever scheme was unfolding. Strategic thinking would serve him better—alliances with these men could prove useful.

Never with Aronowitz, he's a pussy. Becker? Old man can't keep his shit together. Fuck that. Berg? Over there looking like Rainman. Don't think so.

That left Drexel. At the same time, he came to the conclusion that Mykle Drexel would be the only one in the room worth speaking to; the CEO was making his way over to him.

"Josh, do you have any idea what's going on?"

"None whatsoever. Last thing I remember, I was finishing a workout and getting ready for a board meeting. Then I'm waking up in this nightmare."

"I was sitting at my desk, going through paperwork. Then, like you, woke up… or whatever you'd call that…here."

"Have you talked with anyone else? I've only met some woman named Mel, who seems to be in charge, and Thalia, who they say is my guide, whatever the fuck that means. They've told me nothing. Said I'd get answers here. Do you have any?"

"No. I haven't been given any information other than we're in Saskatchewan, of all places. I can't fathom who would be able to do this, or how."

"Are they expecting us to talk to each other, try to figure this out? Like some kind of fucked up escape room thing? The others look like they're going to be useless." He cocked his head toward Matt.

Another door opened, and Mel entered.

"Gentlemen, please have a seat." She motioned to the chairs set out in a semi-circle in the center of the room. Her voice cut through the disarray like a sharp blade as she made her way to the front.

Josh hesitated, watching as the others pulled themselves together. Becker wiped his face with shaking hands, sobs fading to sniffles. Aronowitz straightened and took unsteady steps toward the chairs. Berg's rocking stilled, though his gaze remained distant. Drexel followed without hesitation, and Josh fell in behind him as they all took their seats.

"I know you're scared. As I told you all individually, your well-being is our top priority, so please don't think we're here to hurt you. We're also not here to take your money."

Josh had no reason to believe her, but he sighed with relief, anyway. If they weren't after his money, though, what were they after?

"What I'm about to tell you will bring up more questions. I'll explain as much to you as possible, but there'll be some things I can't give you details about just yet. I can assure you, however, all your questions will be answered by the time you leave this facility."

"So, we are leaving this place, yes?" William was still sniffling. "How long will we stay here? When can I speak to my wife?"

"Yes, we're very hopeful you'll get to go home. The timing of that's dependent on how cooperative you all are." Mel made eye contact with Josh, as if singling him out. "Before I get into why you're here, I want to tell you how this location was chosen. As you've been told, we're in Canada. Our founders went to great lengths to find a location as far from civilization as possible, without having extreme temperatures. There's a possibility you could be here for several years. We hope not, but it's po…"

"Several years? Are you kidding me?" Matt had found his voice.

Mel kept talking over him. "…ssible, so they made sure you'll be able to go outdoors year-round. Not too long ago, the winters here were very harsh, but they aren't anymore."

Sweat beaded on Josh's forehead as he shifted in his seat. It would be impossible for them to hide him for that long. Of course, he'd be found. It wasn't like he was on another planet.

Knowing the kidnap clause in his financial directive would activate and mobilize every available resource to find him gave Josh a burst of hope. At any moment, he expected to hear the whir of helicopters slicing through the air above them. He didn't know what drugs Mel was smoking, but if she believed he could be there for several years, she must be on something.

For a moment, he wondered what would happen to Omnicia without him at the helm for an extended period. He shut the thought down, though, as he assumed he'd be out of this place, whatever it was, within a few days.

"I'll tell you a bit about the technology developed for this project," Mel continued. "I'm sure all of you have some top-secret things you're working on, so it shouldn't come as a surprise other wealthy individuals are doing the same. You already know your bracelets give us information about your vitals, but they also prevent you from leaving the facility and harming yourself or others."

Individuals. So *not* state-sponsored. Names of other billionaires swirled in Josh's head. Who had enough money to orchestrate something like this, and why did they choose him and *these* four men? What connection did they have?

"The bracelets allow your guides and me to touch you, but you cannot touch us or each other. Go ahead. Try to touch the person next to you."

Intrigued, but also leery of touching the man beside him, Josh hesitated. Would it be painful? He extended his hand, inching it toward Mykle's arm with cautious deliberation.

Four inches from the other man's arm, his hand seemed to press against something soft and invisible, like an under-inflated balloon. There was a slight resistance before it gently bounced back. He tried moving faster, pressing harder, but nothing changed. The same subtle push-back met him each time.

"You'll feel this same sensation when you reach the boundaries of the property," Mel explained. "It won't ever cause you pain, no matter how hard you try. If you attempt to harm yourself, your bracelet will sense changes in your brain waves, heart rate, and blood pressure, which will trigger alarms. And if you experience pain, it'll also alert us."

She paused to let her words sink in. "The bracelets are also used for communication. No need to speak directly into the device. Press the button and speak normally, as if the person you want to talk to is right beside you."

Mel held up her wrist, displaying the controls on her bracelet. "And yes, we can immobilize you with the touch of a button, so don't get any ideas about trying to outsmart us."

She took a sip of water and looked into the eyes of each man before her. "The entire complex is concealed by an energy field, impenetrable by any technology available today. Anyone flying overhead would see nothing but open grassland. We're fifty miles from the nearest dirt road, so the odds of anyone stumbling upon us are close to none."

The ground shifted beneath Josh's feet, the very foundation of his reality shaken. He ranked as the wealthiest person in the world, spending billions of dollars to develop new technologies in space travel and robotics, but he had never heard of anything like an energy field that rendered entire buildings and their inhabitants invisible. However, a new technology that hadn't been thoroughly tested might have vulnerabilities; this thought gave him another tiny burst of hope.

The technology of the bracelets made more sense to him. Even through his fear and anxiety, the brilliance of it demanded his admiration.

Mel kept talking, her tone collected and steady. "I know you all have questions about how you got here and what an extraction is. I'm a doctor and a scientist, but not the type who understands this technology."

A twinge of frustration sparked in him as she continued with her vague explanation. "What I can tell you is it's a safe, pollution-free way of traveling both long and short distances using gravity waves. Unfortunately, you've all experienced the side effects, but I'm told the developers are working hard to reduce them.

"This system can transport objects too, not just people. That's how we get our supplies delivered. We have a team working around the clock at another facility like this one, ensuring we've everything we need and all our tech is operating smoothly."

Holy shit, thought Josh. The implications of this type of advancement left him stunned, mind racing with possibilities. Maybe he was being enlisted to aid in the dissemination of these groundbreaking technologies. If so, he couldn't help but be enthusiastic. However, the elaborate measures taken to involve him seemed unnecessary. They could've just picked up the damn phone.

"I'm guessing your biggest questions are why you're here and why you? The success of this project depends on keeping some crucial information from you to start off with, and we'll be meeting with you individually to share more, but I'll let you know now what the end goal is." Mel took a breath and another sip of water. "We're here to solve the climate crisis."

"You've gotta be joking." Josh stood up and went to the window. He looked out at the grass swaying in the breeze for a second before turning back to the room. "You think five people can do what millions are trying, but failing to do? Why the hell do you think we're the people to do it?"

"We have a secret weapon we'll be discussing with each of you in private," Mel answered.

Josh tensed, his curiosity and frustration spiking as she continued. "I'm going to stop talking now, and you'll head back to your apartments with your guides. They'll explain more about the facility and, most importantly, the program."

Josh tried to read more into her words as she went on. "You won't be seeing each other again until we're certain you can work together."

She finished with a firm, "I'll see you all again soon." Then she pressed her wristband, and the doors they had entered through swung open once again.

"Josh, we need to figure this out. What should we do?" Mykle whispered.

"Please don't speak to each other on your way out."

Mykle stopped talking.

Josh looked around the room as each man rose from his seat without a word. Surely they, too, had unspoken questions. They looked like schoolboys following their teacher down the hall to the gym, obeying orders and not stepping out of line. He wondered what their internal dialogue was. Were they also questioning their acquiescence?

His head buzzed with more questions than when he'd first arrived. One in particular nagged at him, though it seemed trivial in the scheme of things: Why was he so calm? Sure, he was angry and tense, but shouldn't he be clawing his way out of here? Shouldn't he be shouting, trying to break free? Instead, he was just... sitting there, listening quietly as Mel outlined the details of the strange prison he found himself in. And then there was that word she'd used. Program. *What the hell are they planning to do to us that could take several years?*

CHAPTER EIGHT

As Josh and Thalia moved through the hall toward his apartment, she detailed the facility's layout. Each voyager's quarters branched from similar halls, leading to the main boardroom. A floor below held a medical center, gym, theater, meditation room, and a salt room. All shared spaces would need to be reserved for the time being.

When they reached his quarters, Thalia asked him to follow her outside. By the pool, she pointed out a pair of inconspicuous cameras, assuring him they were strictly for his safety. Beyond the pool, she slowed her pace so he could take the lead. A peculiar, weightless sensation began at his face, drifting down the front of his body. Without comment, he jogged back to the pool's edge, then ran flat-out toward the open field. This time, the air thickened around him, resistance swelling like he'd crashed into an invisible wall of foam. It wasn't solid, but it wouldn't let him pass.

Thalia's laughter trailed behind him. "Every single one of us did the same thing when we first arrived."

A dizzying mix of amazement and dread crept into Josh's

thoughts. The tech was staggering—elegant, seamless, and beyond anything he could have imagined—beneath the wonder, though, was something cold and horrifying. Apprehension took hold as he looked back toward the building. His confinement was a reality now.

A gleaming surface stretched across the length of the property on both sides. It created an illusion of an endless line of pools, their symmetry almost hypnotic. Josh tilted his head, searching for where the mirror met the sky, but it was impossible to tell where one ended and the other began.

"These mirrors are soundproof," Thalia said, sweeping her hand toward the walls, "So you won't be hearing anything from your neighbors."

They made their way back to the patio, where Shannon had arranged a spread of fresh fruits, thinly sliced meats, and cheeses. Besides the food, a bottle of Louis Roederer Cristal, his favorite champagne, was chilling.

Suspicion tugged at him as he surveyed the table. This wasn't hospitality, this was coaxing. A file with his name in elegant script lay beside the dishes.

Thalia eyed the file as she took a seat across from him. "We're aware of your preferences, Josh, but we aim to go beyond your basic needs. We want this environment to satisfy you holistically." Her tone contained warmth that matched the flush rising in her cheeks. "This includes the things people don't always talk about openly."

His eyes narrowed. "Such as?"

She hesitated and reached for the pitcher of ice water. "You'll find...options here for almost every personal need, including physical pleasures. We know sexuality can't simply be shut off."

The bluntness caught him off guard. "So, that's what this is?" He waved the file in the air. "You're asking for my ... preferences? You've invaded every aspect of my life. Surely you know everything there is to know already."

Thalia held his gaze, her face now a bright red. "We don't want you to feel you're giving up those parts of yourself while you're here. We've developed immersive technology that can simulate certain experiences. Intimacy included."

Josh barked out a laugh. "Intimacy? You think I'll trust you with that?"

Thalia winced. "We won't force anything on you, Josh. But it's here, should you choose. There's no agenda beyond making your time bearable."

"Oh, so this isn't some psychological control game? You think I'll just relax into your program? Let you poke around in my brain until I've forgotten who I am?"

"I understand your hesitations. But trust can come only from time, and yes, a little willingness on your part."

"Trust you?" His laughter had no humor in it. "Let's get one thing straight. You don't own my choices. You might get me to stay here, but don't think for a second you've got my compliance. I'll figure out what you're doing, and I'll destroy you."

A flush of heat colored his face. The rapid thud in his veins hinted at an elevated heart rate and rising blood pressure. At that moment, his bracelet glowed bright red, and Thalia's started beeping. She touched her wrist to silence the alarm.

"I'm sorry, Josh. Mel gave me strict instructions to cut the meeting short if any alarms went off. She doesn't want to take any medical risks. If I give you more information about the program now, it could cause a stroke so soon after your extraction."

The sudden spike of adrenaline collided with his exhaustion. Her words blurred as his mind tried to keep up.

"It's been a long day, and you must be overwhelmed. You still have a ton of questions, and I promise to answer more of them tomorrow. Shannon will bring dinner in about two hours. Is there anything else I can provide to make you more comfortable before I go?"

Thalia stood, her hands resting on the back of the chair as she waited for his response.

"Ya, there is. I'd be more comfortable knowing who the hell is running this operation and what the fuck they want from me?"

"I'm so sorry, but I can't answer that right now. It won't be long before you have a better understanding of everything. If you need anything, just ask. I'm looking forward to seeing you in the morning."

With that, Thalia walked straight past Josh's apartment, into the mirrored wall, and disappeared.

She was right. He was overwhelmed. He had just watched the person holding him captive walk through a wall of the most incredible technology he had ever seen, and he didn't even have the energy to care.

Looking at the food made him lose his appetite. Even the sparkle of champagne fell flat. Pushing back from the table, he left the gourmet setup untouched and went inside. The books on the shelves weren't any more appealing than the food. Drained, he made his way to the bedroom, dropped onto the bed, and let sleep take over.

A new voice cut through his uneasy dreams, dragging him back to reality.

"Hi Josh, sorry to wake you, but your dinner's here," the enchanting voice said. "My name's Shannon and I'm outside at your table. I'll wait here for you, but take your time getting up."

It struck Josh as odd the chef would wait around instead of leaving the food. Maybe she was hoping to meet him, a fan eager for a few words. Whatever the reason, after his nap, he woke more energized and figured there might be a chance to get more information out of her especially if she was an admirer.

On his way to the kitchen, a dart of self-awareness hit him.

The hallway mirror reflected a scruffy, unpolished version of himself. It wasn't the image he wanted to present to someone he'd never met. He doubled back to the bathroom, where he combed and gelled his hair, trading his wrinkled clothes for the smooth lines of an Armani suit.

Well, this is going to be easy, Josh laughed to himself as he laid eyes on Shannon.

Sitting at the table was a short, plump, disheveled woman who was probably in her sixties. Her long white hair sat atop her head in a tangled mass, strands jutting out at odd angles. She wore a cooking apron that read, "Food is My Love Language", over her frumpy, hand-sewn frock. On her feet were bright pink Crocs.

When Josh approached, she jumped out of her chair, clapped her hands together, and squealed. "Well, Helloooo!! I am soooo excited to meet you!"

Doing his best to match her excitement, he flashed a smile, teeth gleaming like a used car salesman closing a deal. His hand moved instinctively toward hers before remembering the deflated balloon effect when he'd tried to touch Mykle at the meeting.

"Oh, that's okay." She laughed as his hand bounced off hers. "Don't worry about it. I'm sure everyone will forget in the beginning."

"Please sit." Josh gestured to her seat. "Will you be joining me for dinner?"

"Oh, you're too kind, but no, I've already eaten. I wanted to introduce myself so you know who's preparing your food."

"Well, maybe you could stay and chat with me while I eat." He hoped she was too dumb to suspect ulterior motives. "I'd love the company. I get the feeling I'll be quite lonely in this place."

"Oh no, no you won't, not at all! We're all super nice and friendly, the staff, I mean. No, don't worry about that."

"I'm assuming all conversations will be monitored, isn't that right? I'm guessing you've been told what you can and can't tell me."

"Well, kind of, but not really." Shannon fussed with her apron, retying the waist belt. "We're all here for the same reason, because we believe in the mission, but nobody besides Mel and the founders knows everything about the program, so the rest of us truly can't give you any information about that, so no real need to monitor conversations. We're here to support you and take care of you, so if that means sitting and talking while you eat, then that's what we'll do."

"You mentioned the mission," Josh interrupted. "What can you tell me about that?"

"Didn't Mel tell you? You're going to solve climate change."

"She did. But how? I'm hoping it has something to do with bringing all of this cool tech to market, but if that were the case, you wouldn't have needed to kidnap me. So I'm assuming it has something to do with taking all my money." His voice stayed casual, without a hint of anger, but his fingers curled against his palm, nails pressing into his skin hard enough to leave indents.

"No, nobody's going to take anything from you, but by the end of this, you won't want your money. You don't believe me now, but I've faith in Mel and Thalia that they'll change you, and by doing so, change the world."

Josh let out a laugh from his gut. "You're out of your mind if you think that's going to happen. I don't care how much I'm tortured, I'll never give you psychos anything. And changing the world? Don't you think I've already done that? Just look at what Omincia's done in the past ten years, and you've no idea what I've planned for the next ten."

"C'mon, Josh, you won't be tortured. In fact, I think you'll come to enjoy it here, and as for changing the world, we mean changing it for everyone, not just for people who can afford things from Omnicia. I hope you enjoy your dinner. I need to get going." Shannon brushed imaginary crumbs from her lap and then walked through the mirror.

Well, that didn't go as planned.

A flood of frustration welled up within him as he reflected on his interaction with Shannon. She knew more than she let on. Why didn't he ask who the founders were? Her expression had hardened the moment he claimed Omnicia had changed the world. Or maybe it was when he called her a psycho.

He wondered if all the staff were Omnicia haters, and haters of him by extension. While he imagined most people revered him as a godlike figure, he recognized the growing number of those who loathed him. Maybe that was why he was here. They wanted to destroy his empire. He never understood why so many people hated him; he was only trying to make life easier. People had become so dependent on his company they couldn't imagine life without it.

The steam rising from his duck had all but disappeared, and Josh's stomach growled. His salivary glands exploded as he took a bite of the fatty breast—Shannon was a culinary genius! He devoured the rest of the meal, each bite better than the last.

The day had stretched on endlessly. Josh had no idea what time it had been when he'd first heard Thalia's voice or what the current time might be. He hadn't noticed a single clock anywhere in the facility. When waking, brightness had greeted him, and only now was it starting to get dark. Late June in Saskatchewan meant there were over sixteen hours of daylight.

The world around him faded as he sat at the table for what seemed like hours. His mind was a whirlwind of thoughts as he replayed the events since his arrival. Time became a malleable concept, stretching and contracting as he grappled with the uncertainty of his reality.

His breath came in slow, even measures; he was again surprised by his unexpected stillness. Maybe he was subconsciously enjoying the thought of not being responsible for all his commitments for a while. Years, decades actually, had slipped away since he'd last savored a day unburdened by work obligations. If he never got out of this place, the world would go on without him, he mused. His loved ones would be well taken care of for generations, and Bradley James proved a competent successor for Omnicia. So was he truly that important?

A crack of sound. Mel's voice shattered the silence and ripped Josh from his internal labyrinth. He flinched, his eyes darting around like a startled animal regaining its bearings.

"Josh, I'm sorry to interrupt you. I just wanted to tell you we'll open your blinds fairly early in the morning. There are no alarms, as we think a gradual sunrise is a much less stressful way to wake up. You should try to get a good night's sleep so we can start explaining the program to you tomorrow. We'd like to begin the work as soon as possible."

Program. Work. The words landed heavily, pulling him back to his current situation. Still, his reply was polite. Controlled. "Thanks for the update. I look forward to getting more answers tomorrow."

Even as the words came out of his mouth, he blinked in surprise, stunned by his own agreeableness. He wasn't this pleasant when meeting with his C-suit, being told the stock price was up again. Something always missed the mark with him. Even those he respected weren't immune to his scrutiny, their flaws cataloged in his mind as opportunities for improvement. His sharp opinions flew freely, a constant reminder to everyone his shit-list had plenty of room for more names.

He pushed himself up, leaving the untouched charcuterie, the empty plates, and the full bottle of Champagne behind. In the bathroom, he stood at the sink, toothbrush in hand, moving it back and forth in a slow, mechanical rhythm. The bristles skimmed his teeth, hardly making contact, his mind drifting elsewhere as he stared blankly at the mirror.

His suit dropped to the floor as he changed into the silk Versace pajamas someone had laid out on his bed. He assumed the staff would clean up after him, and the mess outside would be gone by morning.

As he climbed into bed, questions gnawed at him, refusing to let him relax. What were they planning tomorrow? All the friendliness, the luxury—was it a setup, softening him before something horrendous? His thoughts spiraled as his eyes fell shut: torture, manipulation, or something he couldn't even imagine.

CHAPTER NINE

AFTER THE MEETING, BACK IN THE UNEASY QUIET OF MATT'S apartment, Cath's body stiffened at the thought of the conversation they had to have. Maybe she could postpone it. He looked like he'd swallowed something rotten. His face had gone a pale green, and his eyes were squinted like he was fighting to keep down whatever was left in his stomach. She guided him to the bed, watching as he collapsed onto the mattress with a shudder.

"Here." She placed a bucket within his reach. "Just in case." Tucking him in struck her as oddly intimate, as though she were caring for a helpless child rather than a business mogul.

As she adjusted the blanket, Matt's hand reached out, grasping the air before falling back onto the bed. "I forgot…" His voice was distant.

Offering a reassuring smile, she hoped her voice might soothe him. "That's okay. It'll take time to get used to everything. Is there something you need?"

"So many things…" The words trailed off as his eyes closed, his breathing evening out as he sank into sleep.

With sagging shoulders, Cath sighed, relief mingling with the uncertainty that had gripped her since watching the meeting from the theater. She should have been talking to him about what lay ahead, but was grateful she didn't have to explain the program to him just yet.

Mel insisted the guides begin with private conversations, giving them space to break the ice and start building a connection with their voyagers. But Cath's blood nearly burst out of her veins at the thought of it. She had confidence in the bracelets, so it wasn't worry about her safety. Instead, she feared verbal abuse.

Mel might think she could handle it, that she had an innate gift for drawing out people's goodness, but Cath wasn't so sure. Being here alone, expected to make this world leader like and trust her, was terrifying.

She'd heard enough about Matt to know he was supposed to be good-natured and laid-back for a CEO. His employees adored him, and he had a reputation for laughing off criticism. If anything, he came across as fake, since he constantly had a toothy grin plastered across his face. But what if? What if stress and fear brought out something darker in him? What if he became angry?

Her breathing halted, an old anxiety she knew well. She helped people face their vulnerabilities, sure, but her years as a psychedelic facilitator had taught her one thing about herself: she wasn't equipped to manage violent emotions. In every client screening, she'd been careful to weed out anyone with anger issues. She handled fear, sadness, and shame well. But fury? She'd never found the strength to meet it without becoming paralyzed.

She sighed again, running a hand over her face. She understood why Mel thought she and Matt would be a good fit, but it didn't quell her doubts. If he ended up lashing out, she wasn't sure she'd be able to deal with it.

As she pulled Matt's bedroom door closed behind her, she crouched down against it, putting her face in her hands. She refused to cry. Crying was her typical response, not only with sadness, but with all emotions: disappointment, relief, joy. Her hands shook as she drew in several slow, measured breaths to steady her nervous system.

She'd learned a lot about breathing in prison. If her time there had taught her anything, it was how to use her breath to anchor herself in the present moment, finding refuge from the chaos around her. In the confined environment, amidst the clangs of metal doors and the constant shouting, she learned her breath was a tool that grounded and soothed her racing thoughts.

Thankful her work was done for now, she found herself eager to hear about the other women's experiences with their dragons. In a few hours, she'd need to check on Matt again to see if he was still asleep or ready for a conversation. Before then, she hoped to convince Mel to come along; facing it together would be far less daunting.

As she headed to the community room, she imagined being in Matt's shoes, and a wave of empathy flooded her. She couldn't forget the image of him retching at the sight of the others, the humiliation and confusion that must have gripped him. Guilt churned deep within as she reminded herself of the mission's purpose. She despised being the source of someone else's suffering.

When she'd signed onto the project, she'd known they'd be treading a morally gray tightrope—a necessary evil for the greater good, or so she told herself. While she couldn't take away his initial pain, she held to the hope that, if they succeeded, Matt might one day understand. And maybe even forgive her.

The grand common room lay empty when Cath arrived. A bit disappointing, but not surprising. The others were likely doing the difficult work she'd managed to avoid for the time being. *Coward.* She fought the tears welling in her eyes. *No crying.*

The click of the door closing behind her sounded louder in the silence. Daylight flooded the opulent space. In one corner, a chef's kitchen gleamed with stainless steel and polished granite, its professional-grade appliances testifying to the endless resources of the founders. Across the room, plush armchairs and deep sofas gathered around an electric fireplace, creating an inviting nook for relaxation. Or confessions. The walls, painted in cheerful yellow and adorned with vibrant paintings, only deepened the dissonance within her.

She pulled a rom-com from the bookshelf, hoping some mindless fluff might drown out her thoughts. She let herself sink into the navy-blue couch, arranging the shaggy, white pillows behind her. But after reading the first page three times, she still couldn't make the words settle in her mind.

The truth was inescapable. Here, within these lavish walls, Matt and the others were prisoners. Prisoners she was complicit in holding. She thought back to her own time behind bars, when confinement had stolen her youth yet had somehow, impossibly, shaped her future. Now, here she was, a reluctant warden in this gilded cage, with all the comforts but none of the freedom. The irony was raw, the constant push and pull between her past and present humming beneath the surface, reminding her that no amount of beauty or luxury could erase that a prison was still a prison.

Monica startled her back to awareness an hour later. "Hey Cath, how did the chundermonkey do after the meeting?"

Cath smiled as she put her book down. Monica meant well, but her mannerisms were a bit jarring. That was surely the reason Mel had paired her with the German.

"Luckily for me, he went straight to sleep. How was your conversation with William?"

"Not too bad, since he kind of already knows me. Mel didn't want me to tell him about the drugs yet. She wants to be the one to explain that stuff to him. I spoke in generalities, mostly about the facility, yoga, and meditation. He got pretty upset with me when I was trying to leave, though. You'd have freaked out. I was surprised by his negative energy. I had him pegged for a docile old man."

"Why did he get mad at you?"

"Because I was being vague and wouldn't answer his questions."

"That's understandable. I'd be mad too."

"I don't think Mel has increased his PLH as much as the others. I hope she does soon, or my job is going to be much harder than I thought." Monica dug around in the fridge.

"Did you think it was going to be easy?" It wasn't until after she'd said it, Cath realized her comment was unintentionally snarky.

"Well, obviously not. But I'll take all the help I can get." Monica tipped over a bowl of peanut sauce, making a mess. "God damn it."

"I'm sorry. I didn't mean to piss you off. I should have phrased it differently."

"No, don't apologize. I think we're all a bit on edge. I know you didn't mean it how I took it. My bad."

Cath tried to lose herself in her book again, hoping to ignore the silence between her and Monica. But each word blurred as her mind wandered. Monica's chair scraped against the floor, the sharp screech setting Cath's nervous system off. Her fork clattered against the plate, making Cath's grip tighten around the pages. Even the other woman's crunching noises crawled under her skin, every sound amplifying until she couldn't focus at all.

Despite the group's camaraderie, during one-on-one moments with Monica, the atmosphere grew heavy with awkwardness and silent judgment.

When Monica finished eating, she wiped her hands and glanced at Cath. "I think I'm going to try the new VR program. I'm going to the beach. I could use a mini-vacation."

"Which beach are you going to?"

"Manuel Antonio in Costa Rica," Monica replied, her voice softening a little, a rare glimmer of warmth breaking through. "White sand, clear blue water, and monkeys who'll steal your stuff if you're not watching. It's my favorite place. Want to give it a go first?"

The invitation surprised Cath. "Sure, I could use some beach time."

Monica handed her the headset. As Cath slid it on, her vision shifted instantly from the kitchen to a sunlit paradise. The sand stretched before her, the gentle waves rolling in and out, just as Monica described. She found herself transported to a warm, peaceful beach where the air was thick with the scent of salt and sunscreen. She lay back on the sand, letting herself sink into the soft, heated grains. The warmth radiated through her skin, the distant chatter of people, and the occasional sound of monkeys rustling in the palms blended with the soft whisper of the tropical breeze.

This moment, away from the stress and second-guessing, was exactly what she needed. Why hadn't she thought of it? She couldn't remember the last time she'd allowed herself to unwind without guilt creeping in. After a few minutes, she let out a sigh. "This is perfect, Monica."

"Oh, good. I'm excited to try. Can I please have it back now?"

"Of course." Cath removed the device and pressed her lips together, reminding herself to keep the peace.

Thalia returned to her quarters, craving a hot shower after the interaction with Josh. She wanted to scrub away the memory of his laughter, that harsh, biting sound echoing in her mind. It reminded her of another laugh, one she hadn't heard in over a decade. Her husband's. He'd had the same sharp, cutting bark, wielded like a weapon. Laughter like that meant power and control.

Closing her eyes, she let the hot water cascade over her. She wondered how Cath and Monica had fared, but the thought of a conversation right now loomed too large to face. She needed a bit of solitude. For a brief moment, she allowed herself to savor the warmth, the steam curling around her like a safe cocoon. As always, guilt slipped in quietly. Back then, there had been too many people in the household. Too many wives and children. Showers had been a luxury, stolen in hurried bursts.

When the familiar twinge of shame for wastefulness rose, she got out. *Old habits*, she thought, wrapping herself in a towel. It was time to check in with the others.

Her eyebrows shot up when she entered the common area and found Cath and Monica off in their own worlds.

"Hey Cath, how's it going?" She made herself comfortable in the swivel recliner opposite the sofa.

"Pretty good. How about you? How's Josh?"

"Boy, he's angry, but who wouldn't be, right? I was pretty shocked at how well the PLH is working, though. He's angry, but he's relatively calm and non-combative. What about Matt? How did things go with him?"

"He was still sick, so he went to sleep. We didn't talk at all, which I'm relieved about. I should check on him in a bit, but I'm hoping he sleeps through the night."

"That would be nice. How did Monica do?" Thalia glanced over at the woman lying on the floor with a VR headset on. "I'm surprised you guys aren't debriefing. Or did you already?"

"Neither one of us had much to say. She was a bit testy, so this was best." Cath held up her book and waved it around. "She's at the beach."

"Yup, she can get that way when she's stressed. You made the right call. Have you seen Mel at all?"

"No, she's probably with the founders."

"Right, that would make sense."

Thalia looked down and studied her hands for a moment, her fingers tracing a faint scar across her knuckle. It had faded, but the memory of the dish she'd dropped as a teenager still felt vivid, as did the berating from her sister wives that followed. "A woman's hands should always be steady," the oldest had said while she whipped Thalia's appendage with a stick. "Should always be serving." Thalia shook the thought away, reminding herself that now they served by choice.

"Cath, you know I love you, but I think I need to be alone. I'm going to grab some food and take it to my room and hole up for the rest of the night. If Mel comes and needs me, let me know."

"I get it. I think I might do the same. Mel knows where to find us."

Thalia went over to Monica, crouched down, and stroked her head like a cat. Monica shuddered, sat up, and took off the headset.

"I'm so sorry to interrupt you, babe." Thalia was still petting her. "I wanted to tell you I'm going to my room for the night unless you want to talk for a bit."

"Oh, hey." Monica smiled, evidently more relaxed after her beach visit. "Did things go okay with Josh?"

"Yeah, it was better than I expected, but energetically exhausting. And William?"

"About the same."

"I think we're all emotionally spent today. I'm sure we'll feel better tomorrow, and we can talk more. Hope you get some sleep." Thalia stopped petting her friend's head.

"Hey, before you go. Have you given any thought to when we should talk to Mel again about Aya?" Monica kept her voice low.

Thalia wrinkled her nose and bit her bottom lip. "I don't know. She was pretty adamant the last time we brought it up. I think we should wait to see how they do with the MDMA and mushrooms first."

"Ah, fuck her!" Monica's hand flew over her mouth, and she lowered her voice again. "She thinks she knows everything. She might know more about the other drugs, but I know way more than she does about Ayahuasca. She's a fool to rule it out."

"I agree with you, Mon." Thalia resumed the petting to cool her down. "I just don't think now's a good time. Everyone's totally stressed, and we've no idea how the dragons are going to react when we tell them about the drugs. We should wait a bit."

"Ugh, fine. But we have to do it at some stage. Why does she get to call all the shots? We all have as much riding on this as she does. She's playing God with our lives."

"Girl, chill. I think you need to go back to the beach for a while. You sound like you need a Snickers." Thalia laughed, trying to lighten the mood.

Monica stood and went over to Cath. "I'm sorry I was a pill earlier. I'm going back to the beach when I get to my room. I promise to be better tomorrow."

"No worries, it's been a day."

"Get some sleep, guys," Monica said as she left with the headset.

Thalia plunked herself back down in front of Cath. "I'm sorry if you overheard any of that."

"I heard everything." Cath didn't look up from her book. "You know this whole thing wouldn't exist without Mel, right? I think she deserves a little more respect. If you have a problem with her, you should talk to her."

"You're right. I will. I think she'll receive it better from me than from Monica."

"Yeah, no shit. She can be pretty abrasive."

"Yup, but we all know she means well. She was never really taught social cues. I try really hard to give her the benefit of the doubt."

"Well, neither were either of us, and we don't behave that way."

"Everyone deals with trauma differently. We of all people know that." Thalia put her hand on Cath's shin. "I love you. You can always talk to me about anything. I hope you sleep well."

"Uh-huh. Love you too."

CHAPTER TEN

No alarm prompted Josh to wake up. Instead, a blend of rhythmic waves and the hum of crystal singing bowls seeped into his senses. Slender beams of light filtered through the blinds, casting patterns on the walls, while the music slowly faded. For a second, he forgot where he was.

His mind wandered to a memory of hearing the same type of music. His sister Marne had somehow convinced him to hire a sound healer during a family vacation on his private island. Josh hadn't been able to make time for more than one session, though; Omnicia's transportation network had suffered a system failure, and he'd spent days buried in his laptop.

He remembered the vibrations of bowls, gongs, and drums the night he'd been able to attend the sound bath. For an hour, it had allowed him to disconnect. He'd liked it. Told Marne he'd try it again someday. *Someday.* That word held no promise here.

As the blinds slid open, bathing the room in morning light, his first instinct was to reach for his phone. It was his link to everything, his means of control. But, of course, it wasn't there. Lisa wasn't there either. She was always by his side before the chaos of the day began. He'd dive into his phone, sort through emails, calls, and crises. If there was a crisis, which there typically was, he'd go straight to his desk in the den to immerse himself in work.

Occasionally, in the absence of urgent matters, he'd make time for breakfast with her before they went their separate ways—she to the gym, and he to the office downtown. Even during those shared moments, Josh's mind was focused on work, and they exchanged little more than glances over screens.

Now, lying in a strange bed, fear curled in his stomach. What did they expect him to do here? The urge to act, to do something, made him itch, but for the first time since childhood, a complete sense of powerlessness gripped him.

As the music ended, his present reality snapped back into focus. He swung his legs over the side of the bed and rubbed his eyes. He'd slept surprisingly well, waking with a clarity he hadn't felt in years. Strangely awake, with a sharp energy running through him, he studied the room. His eyes consumed every detail, looking for something to ground him, but found nothing.

Shaking off his angst, he made his way to the kitchen, unaware that he was humming. On the counter sat the espresso machine from home, its polished surface catching the morning light. Somehow, it had escaped his attention yesterday. He punched the buttons, preparing his usual double, non-fat, extra-hot cappuccino, the familiar routine keeping him steady. He carried the steaming mug out to the patio, where, as he'd expected, breakfast was waiting.

He took a sip of coffee. Its warmth settled, but didn't soothe. The comfort was superficial, doing little to relieve his restlessness. As he finished his last sip, Thalia's voice cut into his thoughts.

"Good morning, Josh. When you're finished, would you mind changing into something comfortable you can move freely in? I'll be there soon so we can talk and get started. Let's meet out by the pool."

A rush of adrenaline shot his heart into overdrive. Not enough to set off alarms, he hoped. "Sure."

Wanting more answers, he wasted no time. A hot shower chased away his remaining agitation. While shaving, he caught himself staring in the mirror, wondering if anyone besides three women would ever see his face again. In the closet, his fingers hovered over tailored pants before settling on a pair of knit joggers—a compromise between comfort and style. He slipped on a tight-fitting, dry-weave T-shirt, aiming for an air of effortless ease, the kind he'd seen in Thalia yesterday.

Reaching the pool, he found her there already, waiting. The water glinted in the Saskatchewan sun, mimicking the sparkle in her eyes as she looked up to greet him.

"Good morning. Come have a seat." Smiling her perfect smile from her yoga mat, she motioned to the second mat laid out for him.

Josh lowered himself to the ground with a magnetic pull of attraction toward the woman before him. He found the aura surrounding her impossible to resist. He wondered if she sensed his attraction to her.

"Okay, let's get to work! Each day, after breakfast, we'll meet out here for yoga and meditation. I'll start gently so I can assess how your body moves and how comfortable you are with the poses." She had her hands resting on her knees, palms facing up. "As far as meditation goes, we'll start slowly with that as well. A lot of people get frustrated with themselves when they're first learning because they can't clear their minds. I want you to know there's no wrong way to meditate, and thoughts will undoubtedly come up. Try to acknowledge them, thank them, and let them pass like clouds through the sky."

Josh had tried to meditate in the past at his sister's request. She insisted his life was way too stressful, and he needed to "chill out a bit". The endeavor hadn't been very successful. He couldn't sit still for over ten minutes, and Thalia was right; thoughts about work were constantly popping into his head. He couldn't help but think about the endless tasks waiting for him. Each moment was wasted time.

"Oh, my God." He rolled back onto his mat and laughed. "This is some sort of fucked up intervention, isn't it? Marne did this, right? You somehow got all our family members together and got them to agree to this... Brilliant!"

"How'd you feel if it was?"

"Pretty fucking pissed off. She knows I don't have time for this shit."

"What shit?"

"This self-help, woo-woo, meditation bullshit. She's a hippy-dippy, crystal-loving, be in the now, peace, love, and rainbows kind of person. She has the time and money to be in the now because I work my ass off to fund her sound bathing ass." Josh threw air quotes around "be in the now".

"If she did set this whole thing up, which I'm not saying she did, could you possibly try to see it as someone who loves you very much trying to help you?"

"I see what you're trying to do, and that mind-fuck stuff won't work on me. All the yoga and meditation in the world isn't somehow going to get me to love my family more, work less, and be more 'mindful' of my actions."

"I can understand why you feel that way, but I think you'll be quite surprised by what happens here."

"Since you mentioned it," he shot back, "what exactly *is* going to happen here?"

Thalia paused for a moment as she closed her eyes. After a long exhale, she opened them and looked straight at him. "We're going to change the world."

"For fuck's sake, Thalia, you know that wasn't the question. Just fucking tell me what you're going to do to me besides stretch my body and clear my mind."

"Okay."

The Saskatchewan sun was already beating down on them, making Josh's face dewy. Thalia suggested they roll up their pants and sit with their legs dangling in the pool while they talked. The water, so refreshing, tempted him to strip naked and jump in.

Why not? What could they possibly do to me?

With a shrug, he stood, peeled off his clothes, and dove headfirst into the pool, the water shocking against his skin. When he surfaced, slicking back his mop of brown hair, he caught sight of Thalia watching him, a small smirk playing on her lips.

"Nice move," she said, laughing. "I'd join you if I could, but we all agreed to keep our clothes on around voyagers, no matter what. You're more than welcome to be naked whenever and wherever you wish. In fact, I think it's a great idea. People are way too uptight about nudity, in my opinion."

Josh hadn't expected her reaction, though, and wasn't quite sure what he had been hoping for. Maybe he simply wanted to push the boundaries to see where they were.

He grasped the side of the pool and put his arms up on the cement next to Thalia. "Okay, now that I'm comfortable, you can go ahead and tell me about this program."

She leaned back and looked up at the blue sky, likely organizing her thoughts.

After a moment, she looked at Josh and spoke. "I'll tell you as much as I can, but there's a lot I don't know and a lot I'm not allowed to discuss with you. You can ask me as many questions as you like, but I'm not able to answer them all. I'll start by telling you all the staff members are here voluntarily, without pay, and we live here with you 24/7. We don't get to leave unless the mission is accomplished, so we want nothing more than for the program to succeed. If it doesn't, none of us, including you, will ever get to go home."

"What the actual fuck? So you're a prisoner here, too, but you volunteered for it? And what do you mean, we might never go home? Mel said it might take a couple of years. She never said anything about the possibility of dying here."

Moments ago, he had been lighthearted and playful, but now he seethed with anger. He hoisted himself out of the pool, grabbed a towel off the bench, and wrapped his lower body with it.

He let out a guttural, "Fuck," then added, "What kind of sickos are you people?"

When he finished screaming, he heard the low hum of a small prop plane. He glanced around, looking for something to reflect the sun. Finding nothing by the pool, he ran inside and grabbed the mirror from the hallway. He ran back just as the plane flew overhead. Angling the mirror perfectly, he shot a beam of light directly at the aircraft. About fifty feet up, it refracted into tiny beams, none strong enough to catch the attention of someone in a plane thousands of feet above.

"They can't see us, Josh. I don't understand how the technology works, but it does. And no one on the ground is going to wander into us either. You're not going to be saved, no matter how hard or how long they look."

For the first time since waking up in the facility, the brutal truth hit him; no one was coming for him. His legs gave out, and he crumpled to the ground, naked, the towel left behind when he'd rushed inside.

He had never been an emotional person. Couldn't even remember the last time he shed a tear before arriving here— maybe when he was seven and his golden retriever was struck by a car and killed. Now tears streamed down his face uncontrollably.

"How in God's name did they convince you this was a good idea? You seem like such a nice person."

"Mel recruited all of us. None of us has significant others, children, siblings, or living parents, so there isn't anyone to miss us. We told our friends we were going to live in an ashram in

India. Occasionally, we can get letters to them, postmarked from Varanasi." Thalia was looking at the sky again.

"We're all kinda hippies, so nobody questioned it. Mel was impeccable with her research on us; she monitored our social media posts for years to ensure we fit the profile of people who could be convinced this project could and would work."

Thalia paused briefly as Josh stood and wrapped the towel around himself again. He had stopped crying.

"Once she deemed us good candidates, she befriended us. As we became better and better friends, she started asking hypothetical questions about seemingly impossible things like kidnapping billionaires. Then one day, three years into our friendships, she dropped the bomb. She told us who she was and what she was doing. She showed us some of the tech and asked if we were willing to live our beliefs. I don't know if there were others who said no to her. I don't want to think about what would've happened to them if they had."

Josh's head throbbed. He attempted to understand what Thalia was saying, but he was in disbelief. Disbelief anyone would agree to such a huge ask, and disbelief that plans had been in the works since before he became a household name.

"So, if Mel recruited you, who recruited her? Who's funding all of this?"

"I'm sorry, Josh, I don't have the answers to those questions." Thalia blinked repeatedly. "All Mel's told us is that there are two very wealthy men behind everything who want to see the priorities of the 0.1% and world governments change. They've spent billions on the project so far and have billions left to spend. They're devoting everything they have to this. They believe it's the planet and humanity's best chance for survival. We, the staff, agree with them."

He didn't like her answer. They were probably people he knew; they might even be friends of his. "Mel said we wouldn't see the other voyagers again until you know we can work together. How the hell are you going to know that?"

"The timing of everything here is completely dependent on your progress. Nobody'll see each other again until Mel believes everyone is 100% ready. That means, if you reach certain milestones quickly, you'll have to wait for the others to get to the same point."

"What are the milestones? A perfect downward dog and enlightenment?"

"Mel hasn't given us specifics. All we know is we have to gain your full trust."

"Wow." Josh shook his head. "I can understand why you think we might all die here. I'm telling you right now, there'll never be a day when I trust people who are holding me against my will, no matter how beautiful they are, how amazing the food is, or how cool the technology is."

"I understand why you feel that way. We all foresee this being a long process, and no one expects you to change overnight. We hope knowing how dedicated we all are to this will help you grasp the consequences of not doing what's asked of you. Everyone, including myself, wants nothing more than to go home."

A flush rose up his neck as he realized his bare skin was still exposed. His movements turned hurried and clumsy as he scrambled to pull on his clothes, inwardly cursing himself for ever stripping down in the first place. Thalia clearly wasn't like other women who swooned over him, and now he only felt foolish.

"So it sounds like I basically have two choices. One, die here with the rest of you, or two, give you all my money and hope the others do too, so we can all go home and live in a world where I presume you'll distribute the wealth according to your collective moral compass. Since I have no desire to die here, please show me what to sign so we can all get the fuck out of here."

"I'm afraid it isn't quite that simple, Josh. I told you, we won't take your money. That isn't what this is about. There's nothing you can sign to get this over with. The only way home is full cooperation. Naturally, you're going to be resistant, we expect that. You're going to have questions throughout the program, and we'll answer them if we can, but eventually, you *will* have to trust us."

Thalia's gaze stayed fixed, like she was studying his soul. His jaw tightened, and he held her stare, refusing to look away. Friction built in his muscles as his anger simmered.

"I know this has been a lot. I'll leave you alone. Mel and I will come back after lunch to tell you more about the work you'll be doing."

"Good."

Thalia rose from the pool and walked toward the shimmering wall. With a single step, she vanished through it, leaving Josh to his anxiety. *What work? What are they going to make me do?*

CHAPTER ELEVEN

THOUGH HIS BODY HAD RECOVERED FROM THE EXTRACTION, A storm brewed in Josh's mind, swimming had always been his escape. Since childhood, the cadence of his strokes had brought clarity to his thoughts. Today, he plunged into the pool, hoping the repetition would steady him, but every stroke only seemed to sharpen his rage.

He sliced through the water, grappling with the reality of his captivity. Hands reaching forward as if lunging toward freedom, while his mind raced with strategies. As he pushed himself harder, he considered his options, looking for ways to outsmart them. He'd have to make alliances, no matter how much he hated the idea. Shannon seemed like an obvious start. Maybe he could sway her with promises of wealth, dangling luxuries she'd never even dreamed of in front of her.

On the other hand, there was the tech. The unbelievable system keeping him in and others out was likely untested, its weaknesses still waiting to be discovered. He'd have to be careful with his exploration of it, knowing the ever-present cameras would track his every move. He kept coming back to the people. They were the real vulnerabilities.

What about Thalia? If he managed to earn her trust, perhaps manipulate her emotions over time, he might have a chance. But he'd need patience. It wouldn't happen overnight. This was a long game—weeks, maybe months of careful moves. *Fuck.*

With a final stroke, he reached the pool's edge, chest heaving. Water dripped down his face as he hauled himself out. He headed straight for the shower, leaving trails of water throughout the apartment.

Emerging from the steamy bathroom, he scanned the closet, opting for a plain, loose-fitting T-shirt and Bermuda shorts, aiming for a look that said "regular guy" rather than "pompous billionaire".

He examined his reflection, forcing a controlled smile. It wasn't genuine, just a mask. One he'd wear until it was time to act. He'd play nice, cooperate, nod along, and bide his time, all the while gathering every piece of information he could. Whatever vulnerabilities they had would become his leverage. And when he found the right moment, he'd turn the tables.

"Hellllooooo, hi Josh, it's me, Shannon. I have your lunch here for you." Shannon's matronly voice came from outside, not from his bracelet.

Josh dabbed pomade in his hair, smoothing it just enough to keep it neat but not too polished. He ran his fingers through once more, then headed to the table, his steps unhurried and casual.

"Hey Shannon, it's nice to see you again. You're looking lovely today. Something smells delicious. What is it?"

He sounded inauthentic. He'd need to tone it down a bit if he didn't want Shannon to suspect anything.

"Oh, thank you, Josh. That's very kind of you." Shannon blushed as she proudly described the Caribbean seafood stew with coconut milk. "I hope you like it."

"Wow, that sounds amazing. I can't wait to dig in! Will you be joining me?" Shit, he did it again.

"Sure, I can sit with you while you eat, and then Mel and Thalia can join us when you're done."

He planned to slip into casual conversation with her, acting as though he had a genuine curiosity about her life. He'd need to find the right balance; not so eager as to raise suspicion, but warm enough that she'd believe he wanted to get to know her.

"From my limited time here, I can tell you're a genius with spices. Where did you learn to cook like this?"

"Oh, thank you, that means so much to me." Shannon beamed at him. "I used to own a small farm-to-table fusion restaurant on Lake Union in Seattle called Lion's Main."

"No way!" This time, the reaction was authentic. "I used to eat there all the time. I was sad when I heard it closed, but I don't remember seeing you there. Wasn't the owner that tall guy with the handlebar mustache... No?"

"Yes, that was Steve, my late husband. We were unstoppable together - he was the face of the business; he loved interacting with guests, especially our regulars. I pretty much stayed in the kitchen. I wasn't comfortable making small talk, never thought I presented very well." Shannon gestured with her hands, moving them from head to torso on either side of her body as if to say, "Not much to look at here."

"I'm sorry to hear Steve passed. Is that why the restaurant closed?" Josh asked with a hint of real empathy.

"I guess you could say that, but it took a few years. It wasn't the same without him, even though I found a front-end manager who filled his shoes the best she could. Our regulars sure did miss him. Thankfully, they kept coming back for the food. I did my best to keep the place running, but my heart wasn't in it without him, so when Mel told me about the big plan, I wasn't too sad to call it quits."

"I didn't realize so much time has passed since I last saw Steve. I guess when Omnicia got really big, I stopped going to my favorite spots and had food delivered." He looked up at the sky, briefly pausing, then sighing. "I miss my anonymity. I mean, don't get me wrong, I'm not complaining about my life, but there are definitely things I'd change if I could... oh shit, here I am going on about myself when you already know all about me and I want to get to know you. So, are you originally from Seattle?"

Shannon's eyes lit up. "No. We ended up there in our twenties. We were from Gillette, Wyoming, far too small for our dreams. My parents owned a diner there; Steve worked as a server, and I was on the line in the back. We fell in love, saved as much as we could, and set out in our Volkswagen bus. Had no idea where we were going; we just had to get out of Gillette. We drove until we hit the ocean, well... what we thought was the ocean. Turned out to be the Puget Sound. We didn't know shit about geography."

Josh joined in with Shannon's laughter.

"We thought we'd discovered paradise," she continued. "We'd never seen such a beautiful place. After getting jobs at decent establishments, we could afford a pretty nice apartment in Queen Anne overlooking the Space Needle. That was back when normal people could afford to live in Seattle. Man, if we had arrived today, I'm sure we'd be homeless..." Shannon looked away. "Anyhoo, we both worked our way into management positions and learned how to run a business. About ten years later, we had saved enough to open our little restaurant."

Shannon paused, a distant expression crossing her face as she seemed to drift into her memory. Josh remained attentive, nodding slightly to encourage her. His patience paid off when she resumed her story, clearly convinced he was invested in every word.

"Wow, what a scary time that was! We knew most restaurants fail within their first three years, but we didn't want to keep working for someone else for the rest of our lives, so we risked it all, and it paid off. Lion's Main became our life. It was lucky we worked together, or Steve and I would never have seen each other. It was exhausting, but we loved every minute of it."

Shannon's bracelet chirped, and she bit her bottom lip. "Oops, I think we've been talking too much. You'd better eat up because the others will be here soon."

Josh downed the delicious, now lukewarm stew, and was tempted to lick the bowl. If things went well and Shannon cooperated with him, he'd offer her the position of his personal chef. He wondered if it was a coincidence they were both from the same city and he had been somewhat of a regular at her restaurant years ago.

As Josh finished his lunch, Mel and Thalia appeared from the mirror.

CHAPTER TWELVE

"HI JOSH. IT'S NICE TO SEE YOU AGAIN. I'M GLAD YOU'VE FULLY recovered from your extraction. Some of the others aren't fairing quite as well." Mel pulled out a chair and took a seat with Shannon and Josh.

Thalia flopped herself into the hammock, still within earshot. Josh didn't know where to look. He reckoned he'd have a better chance of seducing Thalia than Mel, so he didn't want Thalia to see his attraction to her boss.

Mel got down to business. "Thalia has briefed me on everything the two of you already covered, so I'll try not to repeat what you know. You're welcome to ask questions as they come up, but as we've said, there are certain things we're not at liberty to discuss with you at this time."

She looked up, paused, and smiled at Josh as she flipped through a binder. Her smile was captivating, but he managed to look away before his cheeks flushed.

"You'll get more information as you move through the program. Before I explain what that entails, I want to go over everyone's role here. Shannon's pretty easy. She's our amazing chef, and for now, she's also helping with housekeeping. Once everyone's settled in, we'll expect you to do things for yourself, so eventually, she'll be teaching you how to cook and you'll be expected to clean your own space."

He couldn't remember the last time he'd touched a dish or thought about making a bed. Employees handled all that—along with any mess he left in his wake. He'd grown comfortably lazy around his home, tossing clothes on the floor, leaving empty glasses wherever he pleased. Why worry? Someone else would be there to pick it up.

"So, once I'm expected to do my own cleaning, what type of punishment will there be if I don't? You've repeatedly told me I won't be harmed, so I'm assuming it'll be some kind of deprivation or mental torture."

Mel laughed. "Sure, you could say it's mental punishment, but really, it'll just be you having to live in your own filth. We don't care if your apartment is clean, so it's up to you how you want to live. But if you don't cook, you'll go hungry, and if you don't do your laundry, you'll have to wear dirty clothes."

Amused at his own thoughts, Josh let out a short, breathy snicker that was more exhale than sound. This was the program? Getting him to be a good boy and take care of himself like the plebes. Did they think somehow he'd realize he wasn't better than everyone and would want to give his wealth away? He couldn't believe the exorbitant amount of money spent to get him to clean his room. A bunch of women taking a stand against the patriarchy; getting rich, entitled men to do housework—what a fucking joke.

But what will the founders get out of it? Why would they spend billions to get me to do laundry?

Mel was still talking.

"As you've heard me say before, but with no context, Thalia is your guide. I'll tell you what that means in a bit. The most important aspect of *my* role here is keeping you safe. Thalia will be doing the most work with you and will keep me updated on your progress."

Perfect.

"You and I will have frequent one-on-one meetings, but you'll see me the least. I'm the only one here, besides Shannon, who's working with all the voyagers, so I don't have as much time to devote to each person. Now, I want to tell you about what has been happening to you since you got here. You probably couldn't put your finger on it, but you know something's off."

Josh leaned forward, ready to finally get some fucking answers.

"One of the other functions of your bracelet is to administer a drug into your system. Since your arrival, you've been receiving micro-doses of a new phenethylamine, similar to MDMA, I developed for this program. One of the pleasant side effects is everything tastes incredible."

Shannon piped up with a smile on her face. "And here you thought I was a culinary genius."

The two other women laughed while Josh sat frozen, unamused and frankly a bit scared.

"The main reason we're using this drug is it allows you to let your guard down and be more relaxed," said Mel. "You might've been surprised you haven't been trying very hard to figure out a way out of here, and you're quite calm despite your circumstances."

She was right. The realization cut through the dull acceptance that had settled over him since his arrival. He'd been going along with everything, barely questioning, barely resisting. How had he fallen into compliance this easily? His mind raced, piecing together every moment he'd simply nodded, followed, and kept quiet. Of course, he was being drugged. A mix of anger and disbelief stewed within him. Anger at himself for not fighting harder, for letting himself sink into this strange passivity.

I guess it's better than torture.

"This dose of the drug we're calling PLH will help you with the work you'll be doing with Thalia," Mel said. "Not only will she be doing yoga and meditations with you, she'll also introduce holotropic breathwork when she feels you're ready. The PLH will help you go much deeper and will allow you to get into an altered state faster."

The last time Josh remembered being in an altered state had occurred in his second year of college, when his buddy Jay had convinced him to take mushrooms before a Nirvana concert. It hadn't gone well, and Josh had a complete freak-out during the show. The experience was so traumatizing that he'd sworn to never touch drugs again, and he hadn't. Who the hell were they to override his decision?

"We'll wean you off the PLH as you get more comfortable and are able to attain this state without it. Once you're completely off it for at least a week, we'll start your real journeys. We'll introduce you to full doses of MDMA as well as psilocybin, also known as magic mushrooms. Thalia will be with you the entire time you're voyaging and will help you integrate what you learn. She'll be your therapist, if you will."

"Therapy is for people who are depressed or anxious." Josh almost spat the words at Mel. "I am neither of those. What exactly do you think this therapy is going to do for me? And you can go fuck yourselves if you think I'm taking mushrooms."

Thalia took over from Mel. "We believe therapy is beneficial for everyone, Josh, but specifically in your case, we believe this can cure you of your illness."

"What illness?" He shot back, pissed off now. "I am the healthiest guy I know. There's absolutely nothing wrong with me."

"If one monkey hoarded all the bananas while the rest of his troupe starved, scientists would conclude the monkey was sick," Mel said in a condescending voice. "Humans are the only animals who hoard wealth while others die; we think that's an illness."

"We want you to get better, Josh." Thalia swung her legs over the side of the hammock so she could make eye contact. "When an alcoholic or drug addict is forced into rehab, they're typically uncooperative, but when they come out clean, they're incredibly grateful to be well. This is our hope for you and the other voyagers."

"Riiight." His voice dripped with sarcasm as he extended the word. "So you expect me to thank you for kidnapping and drugging me? Am I getting that straight? And then, once your therapy starts working, I'm going to give all my money away because I'll have seen the error of my ways and I'll realize what a bad person I've been. You're all fucking delusional!"

Mel and Thalia's bracelets were beeping, alerting them to Josh's spiking blood pressure. They silenced the alarms as he kept ranting.

"I will get out of here, whether it's me finding some flaw in your technology or the outside world figuring it out first. I know you're all committed to dying here, but I also hope you're willing to go to jail for the rest of your lives, because that's what's much more likely to happen. Speaking of needing therapy, have you all taken a good, hard look at yourselves?"

Heat crept up his neck, spreading to his face as his skin flushed red.

"Josh, of course, we expected this reaction from you and the others. Don't think for a second the other voyagers are saying, 'Hey, what a great idea! I'll do whatever you want me to do," Thalia said.

"As we've told you, we all 100% believe in the tech keeping you hidden." Mel's voice was quiet but firm. "We've all tried as hard as we could to compromise the systems, and none of us has come close. If somehow, someone is able to figure out a way around it and we're all sent to prison, we'll take comfort knowing we did everything in our power to make the world a better place and live with the consequences. We don't expect this to be easy for anyone, voyager or staff, but we hope once you come to terms with the fact you're not going to be rescued, you'll start cooperating, as it's your only chance of going home."

A knot formed in Josh's stomach. Half of him was in full resistance mode, wanting to tell them all to shove it, while the other half recognized the tech far surpassed anything he'd ever seen. Perhaps they were right; he might not be saved.

He turned over the idea of cooperation, then imagined rescue arriving before their plan reached fruition. If that happened, this drug-induced "therapy" might expose parts of him his captors could twist into weapons, splashing his secrets across the media, even from behind bars.

He tried to think of skeletons that could be in his closet, but nothing came to mind. The world already knew more about him than he cared to admit - the whole scandal when they found out about Lisa marked a low point in his life, and he regretted some of his choices surrounding his reaction. He couldn't come up with anything else that would harm him if it got out.

"Okay, so now what?" He sounded like a CEO again. "Do you expect me to be nice and pretend what's going on here is normal? Do you expect me to jump out of bed in the morning, excited about being drugged and doing yoga?"

"No, Josh," said Thalia. "We don't expect anything of you. Your response to all of this is completely up to you. You can choose to be angry and hostile for as long as you want, but that'll mean spending more time here than is necessary. We'll do everything we can to make you comfortable with us and the process if you allow us to."

Mel continued Thalia's thoughts. We'll certainly make suggestions we think will move you through the program the quickest, but nothing is compulsory."

"Why are you forcing us to take the PLH, but won't make us do the other drugs?"

"It's very important you have the right mindset when voyaging with psychedelics." It was Thalia's turn again. "If you aren't in the right headspace going into a session, it can make for a pretty bad trip."

"Believe it or not, Josh, we're all here to help you. We care about your happiness and well-being." Mel stood up. "I think we're done for the day. I need to go check on William."

CHAPTER THIRTEEN

MEL'S FINGERS TREMBLED. SHE BIT HER NAILS AS SHE WALKED AWAY from the conversation with Josh. It had gone better than expected, but her relief was fleeting. Her mind was drifting to what lay ahead, the sheer magnitude of responsibility stretching before her.

Slipping into her apartment, she poured herself a glass of wine, watching the light catch the ruby liquid. The first sip was a balm to her anxiety, soothing her nerves. Yet, she knew it wouldn't last. The thought crossed her mind to take a small dose of PLH to steady herself, but she dismissed it almost immediately.

What would the founders think if they found out?

She took another sip, the familiar comfort tempting her to lean on it again. But she fought it, determined to prove she could stand on her own without a crutch.

She couldn't decide if the thought of talking with William or facing Monica filled her with more dread. Her entrance yesterday had gone unnoticed, as quiet and unremarkable as her exit. She'd stood just beyond their line of sight, blending into the shadowed corner, shocked by what she heard coming out of Monica's mouth.

The moment Mel had heard her name, something in her had stilled, instinctively keeping her silent. When turning to leave, her footsteps were as soft as her breathing, carrying her out of the room and back down the hall without a soul aware she'd ever been there.

Exhaling, she set down the glass, her frayed nerves had been coaxed into submission. She called Monica and asked to meet her outside William's apartment.

"You good?" she asked as she approached Monica in the hallway.

"Yup, let's get this over with."

As she braced for the difficult conversation with William, she couldn't help but wonder if her relationship with Monica was as strong as she thought it was. The memory of that moment still stung. Monica's words echoed in her mind like a bruise that hadn't healed.

She had always considered Monica a friend, not just a colleague, but someone she could rely on in this chaotic mission. Part of Mel wanted to confront her, demand an explanation. But another part knew it would only complicate the already fragile situation. She had to compose herself. The project depended on it.

The two women found William sitting in the sun, reading "War and Peace". The summer breeze caught the pages, making them flutter. So lost in the narrative that he startled when Mel said "hello".

He looked up, scowled, and muttered, "Verdammte verrückte Schlampen."

Mel understood enough German to know it meant, "Damned crazy bitches".

"So much for a docile old man," Monica said under her breath.

"Hi William, I hope you're feeling much better today," Mel said as they took a seat at the table. She didn't wait for him to respond. "I'm sorry it's taken us so long to come and speak with you. I can understand why you don't like us very much."

Mel's grasp of the German language was limited, but the icy edge to his voice required no translation. Plastering on a smile, she stuck with her pre-planned script about the program's goals. With each word, she tiptoed around the crux of the work, knowing the psychedelic part of the therapy would be a major issue for him.

"It's not like talk therapy." She leaned forward, sure to make eye contact with him. "There's very little talking involved. It's more of an internal journey. Imagine... instead of dissecting issues for months, or even years, with a therapist, you have a powerful experience in just a few days that helps you see things from a different perspective. It's a shortcut to understanding yourself and your place in the world without having to tell anyone anything if you don't want to."

William became visibly agitated as his eyes narrowed to tiny slits. "So let me make sure I understanding you, since I clearly have a language disadvantage." His accent was thick as he stammered. "You expect me to cooperate in a scheme where I am drugged on a regular basis in order for me to go to my wife?"

Mel attempted to answer, but William didn't miss a beat. "You are all crazy, and I will take my chances, thank you very much. I am sure there is a very huge search for me and you will see prison before any drugs pass through my lips."

"Your response is completely understandable." Mel pitied the older man, but it was essential he grasp the seriousness of the situation. "We noticed you haven't been out to test the perimeter yet. Why don't you come with me so you can see for yourself how impenetrable it is?"

"Sure, a little tour will be just the thing. Yes, show to me all the wonderful technology so we can come back and go on a fantastic trip together." The anger in William's broken English was unmistakable. "I am not going anywhere with you. I will not do anything you tell me to do, for that matter. I will sit here until I feel like it. Maybe I will not eat anything until I get sick and you will have to take me somewhere. I have plenty of options."

"You're correct, William," Mel said as she and Monica stood up to leave. "We won't make you do anything, but we hope you'll come around sooner rather than later. Please feel free to do whatever you wish in your quarters. I am upping your dose of PLH, and we'll see how things go." Mel tapped the screen on her bracelet. "Shannon will continue to cook for you and will give you half an hour's advanced notice before she brings your meals. If you need anything, just ask. If we don't hear from you within two days, I'll come and check on you."

As they exited through the shimmering barrier, Mel couldn't get rid of the tightness in her chest. She hadn't missed the shock in William's eyes when she mentioned the increased dose, nor the resentment that shadowed his face. As she glanced back, she caught a glimpse of him, headed to the perimeter.

Only moments after they'd left, a sharp, high-pitched alarm blared from her bracelet. Mel's stomach dropped.

"Shit." She grabbed Monica's arm. "Get back there. I'll be right behind you."

She took off down the hallway, her feet hardly touching the ground as she raced to the elevator that would take her to the medical center. Her pulse hammered in her ears, her mind racing through worst-case scenarios. The blurred walls around her didn't register as she grabbed an eighteen-gauge syringe.

Breathless, she returned to William's quarters to find him on the ground, Monica propping him up from behind.

"William!" She couldn't hear her own voice over the pounding in her ears as she rushed to his side, watching his gasping, uneven breaths. His skin had turned a pale blue, and his tongue hung out of his mouth like an old dog. It was all she could do to keep her mind from flashing back to finding Lee lying lifeless on their bed.

Without hesitation, she plunged the needle into his thigh, exhaling only when she saw his eyes flutter open and his breathing starting to regulate.

"You're okay, William," she said, her voice wavering despite her best effort to sound composed. "Focus on your breathing. You're safe."

Behind him, Monica swayed gently as she held him.

He looked at Mel, confusion evident in his eyes. Guilt was already rising in her body when he managed a raspy, "Thank you... I don't know what happened." A lump formed in her throat, an apology stuck below it.

"You had a close call, but we're here to help you," Monica said, still swaying.

"Let's get you into bed." Mel glanced at Monica as they deactivated their bracelets' protection mechanism, allowing William to hold on to them as they lifted him off the ground.

He seemed to age in their arms, no longer the fit older man with full control of his faculties. Supporting him on either side, they guided him, hands stabilizing his faltering steps as they made their way to his bedroom.

As he eased onto the bed, Mel fluffed the pillows and tucked them carefully behind his back, her fingers pressing and adjusting until they cradled him just right.

When William turned to her, his voice was low and weary, but still had hints of confusion and distrust in it. "What did you do to me?"

"You had a reaction to the PLH. I think it's because you haven't been eating, and your system metabolized it too quickly. This was my fault, and I am truly sorry."

Muttering something in German, he shook his head and sank

back against the pillows. Mel's guilt deepened as he struggled to get comfortable.

"Please rest." Mel's voice lacked its usual authority. "Shannon will leave food for you in the kitchen when you're ready. Take it slowly, okay?"

As she and Monica left William's room, the image of him, worn and slumped against Monica, stayed with her.

"Are we doing the right thing?" Mel's question was more for herself than for Monica.

CHAPTER FOURTEEN

MONICA LET OUT A QUICK BREATH AS THEY MADE THEIR WAY toward the community room, her exhale sharp and audible. "Jeeesus, that was intense!"

Mel's own adrenaline was still surging. "Fuck." She slammed her hand against the wall, causing the photographs to vibrate. "Fuck, fuck, fuck, fuck, fuck!"

Filled with guilt, worry, and dread, she thought about what the founders would say when they found out about the incident. Even though they had already left for the second facility to oversee operations there, she'd have to tell them. Hiding the truth wasn't an option, not if she wanted to live with herself. But the idea of facing their judgment crept into her mind like a demon, filling her head with doubts about her competence and the safety of the PLH.

She couldn't deny how much it had helped stabilize the voyagers these past few days; taking them off it now smacked of recklessness. But after this, there'd be questions. Questions about the drug, about her choices, and about whether she was in over her head.

Thalia opened the door. "What happened? I heard some fucks and a thud."

Mel trembled as she collapsed onto the sofa. Her body quivered with the aftershocks of the ordeal. She put her left index and middle finger on the pulse of her neck. Inhaling deeply, she counted the beats—one, two, three, four, five, six—before exhaling slowly, matching her breath to the steady cadence of her heartbeat. She did this for ten cycles until her nervous system began to regulate.

Monica went to the kitchen and prepared Tulsi tea. "Here you go. This should help." Monica handed one of the mugs to Mel and another to Thalia.

"Thank you, sweetie. Yes, it will."

"What happened?" Thalia asked again.

The memory of William's pained expression replayed on an endless loop in Mel's mind, his flash of terror seared into her thoughts. The realization of what she'd almost done settled in her gut and made her want to vomit. Guilt consumed her, its tendrils digging into her confidence. Its insidious voice whispered, "Am I really capable of leading this thing?"

Her failure to properly administer the correct dosage of the drug not only put William's health at risk but also posed a significant threat to the success of the entire operation. If he'd died, it would've set the project back months while the founders researched and targeted another dragon. She didn't want to dwell on what might have happened.

As she recounted the events to Thalia, her voice faltered, exposing the vulnerability she desperately tried to hide. Unaccustomed to sharing her own emotions, Mel considered it an admission of weakness in herself, though didn't see it as such in her clients. Her thoughts flashed back to the overheard conversation between Thalia and Monica. The whispered doubts about her leadership. What would they say now?

Thalia's hand on her shoulder, and Monica's empathetic eyes, offered a sliver of comfort. So did the tea. Although it dulled the edges of her self-recrimination, she wished for something stronger.

But she couldn't dwell on self-doubt. The project's success hinged on convincing William to cooperate, a task that now seemed infinitely more daunting. The trust she had hoped to build with him lay shattered, replaced by fear and resentment.

Thalia whispered, "Wow," as she wrapped her arm around Mel's waist and pulled her close.

"Yeah, a great way to start, eh?" Mel said through the side of her mouth.

"We all knew there'd be unexpected setbacks, especially at the beginning," Monica said. "I'm sure the founders expected it, too. Overall, I think we're off to a pretty freaking great start."

Mel appreciated Monica's bluntness. It was part of what made her so effective. She spoke with a directness that sliced through pretense, never dressing up the truth. But that sharp honesty hit differently when it wasn't meant to be heard. Mel fought to keep her emotions in check, masking the sting of Monica's overheard words. She couldn't afford to let infighting jeopardize the project.

"The extractions went as well as we could've hoped. And so far, none of the voyagers have shown any violent tendencies," Thalia added.

Monica met Mel's eyes. "The founders will understand. You need to shake this off so we can get back to work. You still have to talk with Matt. Once that's done, you can take the rest of the day to relax. Hopefully, you'll have a week or so to recoup before the dragons are ready to start voyaging."

"You're both right. I'm trying really hard to swallow my ego." Mel sighed as she downed the rest of her tea. "I better call Cath and get Matt over with before I lose my nerve."

She moved through the motions of hugging each woman, her embrace with Monica stiff and fleeting. "Thanks, girls. I love you."

Pressing a button on her wristband, she asked Cath to meet her outside Matt's apartment.

In the narrow corridor between Matt and Josh's patios, hidden by the mirrored walls, Cath stood with her arms wrapped around herself. Mel hesitated before approaching, unsure if she should share what had happened with William. She chose not to, deciding Cath already carried enough anxiety. Instead, she pulled her into a hug, whispering, "We've got this."

Cath's grip lingered a moment longer than usual before she gave a slight dip of her head.

Glancing at her bracelet, Mel noted a subtle shift in Matt's brain waves. He was awake, though probably sluggish. She tapped the blue band and told him they were waiting outside.

When he finally emerged, his movements were heavy, like he was dragging himself through quicksand. Mel's trained eyes didn't miss the pallor of his face or the way his shoulders drooped. The improvement from the day before was minimal, but at least he wasn't doubled over with nausea. He downed a glass of water in one long swallow, as if the rush of cold liquid might scrub away the remnants of whatever nightmare he'd endured.

"Good afternoon, Matt, how are you doing today?" asked Cath as he took a seat next to her.

"Afternoon...already? I guess I needed the sleep. I'm quite a bit better. Thank you for asking."

Mel's relief was genuine, though tempered by the memory of William's terror. "That's great to hear," she said, forcing a smile. "We have a lot to go over, but I don't want to overwhelm you. If at any point you start feeling sick, just say the word and we'll pause. There's no rush."

"Okay." Matt's response was almost inaudible as his eyes darted briefly to the endless expanse of yellow fields before dropping back to his lap. He sat hunched over, gripping the water glass like it was the only solid thing in his shifting world.

Mel cleared her throat, launching back into the details she'd already shared with the other men. She kept a keen eye on his reactions, searching his face for the telltale green shade that might signal a hasty exit. He sat rigidly in his chair with the water glass in hand at all times, quietly sipping as he heard what lay in store for him. Now and then, his gaze drifted back to the horizon, but mostly he stared into his lap, as though he couldn't face the reality she was laying out for him.

"Matt?" Cath's voice interrupted Mel. "Are you following this? I want to make sure you understand what's being said."

"Uh-huh." He didn't lift his head, didn't meet their eyes. The flatness of his tone made Mel cry inside. This wasn't the reaction she'd expected. He seemed detached, almost numb.

Cath raised her eyebrows in silent question when Mel looked at her. She had no doubt Cath shared her uncertainty—unsure whether Matt was in shock or simply refusing to process what they were telling him.

Mel leaned forward, her voice softer but insistent. "Matt, can you tell me what you've understood about the program so far? I need confirmation you comprehend the magnitude of what we're saying."

"Yup, I got it." He still wouldn't look at her. His voice was dull, each word detached as he stared at his hands. "You're going to... I mean, you *are* drugging me and more drugs... and I've no option other than to take them and I am stuck here forever if I don't do what you tell me to do and even if I do and the others don't I'll still be stuck here forever and I won't be harmed and I'll be cooking and cleaning and..."

Mel interrupted his unraveling monologue. "It sounds like you heard everything. Can you tell us how you feel about it?"

"Not great."

"Hmm." Mel nodded and looked at Cath. "Okay, I think I'm

going to leave the two of you now, so Cath can show you a few things and answer more questions."

Mel got up, petted Cath on the shoulder, and walked through the mirror.

🍩

Cath sat in silence for a minute, considering the best approach for the somewhat catatonic man in front of her. She was grateful Matt wasn't agitated, but was worried about his emotionless state.

"Hey Matt, let's go inside so I can show you your VR headset. I think you'll enjoy it. I'll leave this on the table inside for you, and you can fill it out when you're ready. It's pretty straightforward." She left the papers asking about his preferences unexplained.

"Okay."

When they arrived in the living room, she took down a white box off the top of the bookshelf.

"This is probably going to be your best friend for a while," she said as she took out the headset and handed it to him. "You control everything with your eyes. There are some brain games, movies, music, and meditation apps. The forest bathing is my favorite, but there are other nature programs as well. When you've filled out the questionnaire, we should be able to get some other programs designed for you, even *porn*." She whispered the last word.

Taking the headset from him, she put it back in its box. She hesitated, unsure how to bridge the gap between small talk and the heavier topics waiting to be addressed. Nervous energy thrummed beneath her skin as she ran her hand along the shelf, pretending to read the spines of the books.

"These might give you a better sense of what we're doing here." She gestured toward the titles on psychedelic-assisted therapy. Her voice quivered, so she covered it with a bright, forced smile, pulling out a slim paperback with a frayed cover from the shelf below. "And if you haven't read this one yet, I highly recommend it. 'Ishmael' by Daniel Quinn. It's one of my favorites." She turned the book over in her hands before passing it to him.

Matt took the book from her, his expression unreadable. Her heart pounded as she searched for any flicker of interest, something to indicate he wasn't completely shutting her out. Her nerves made her gestures more animated than they should be, like she could compensate for the friction in the room by feigning excitement.

"Over here," she continued, waving her hand toward a stack of notebooks. "These are for journaling. Sometimes it helps to put your thoughts down on paper. And if that feels like too much, there are adult coloring books. They're great for relaxing. It can be surprisingly therapeutic."

She picked up a set of colored pens, holding them out to him with an almost theatrical flourish. "You can use these. There's a color for every mood."

He said nothing, but gave a nod. Her nervousness escalated. Was he annoyed? Was he humoring her? Was he even paying attention? It was impossible to tell. Pushing down her uncertainty, she motioned for him to follow her into the bedroom, trying to keep the momentum going.

Warm sunlight poured through the window, casting a golden hue throughout the room. The air, though, was still tinged with the stale, acrid smell of vomit. Her nose crinkled, but she forced herself to ignore it, her focus on the task at hand.

"Here's something cool." She pointed to a recessed panel in the ceiling and pressed a button on the bedside table. The roof began to slide back, revealing an eight-by-ten-foot opening directly above the bed. She examined his face, hoping for any sign of curiosity. "On a clear night, you can see all the stars. It's one of my favorite features of the facility." She held her breath, waiting for his reaction. Any reaction.

His eyes glazed over, and he fidgeted with his hands as she

continued. "Stargazing can be very therapeutic, and it's nice to get some fresh air while you're sleeping. You can even have it open if it's raining or snowing, as the energy field will repel the moisture."

Nothing.

"I think that's about it, besides the floor—you might have wondered about that. It's a new material that's easy to clean, and it prevents you from hurting yourself if you fall; once you're doing full doses of MDMA and psilocybin, your balance can be affected. It also integrates with the VR experience."

He trailed behind her in silence, the strain between them almost suffocating. She forced herself to keep talking, pointing out the features of his apartment, but her voice was too bright, too forced. His eyes skimmed over what she showed him, unfocused, while his body angled away as if to escape. Overwhelm radiated off him.

He didn't care about the gadgets or the roof. She saw it in the way his eyes darted past everything, landing nowhere. His distant, glassy look worried Cath. Was he listening at all? She pushed on, trying to fill the silence. She couldn't escape the sense she was intruding: not just in his space, but in his thoughts.

The truth was, she didn't want to be here either. Her own doubts were pressing on her chest. Would she ever be able to reach him? Was she the right person for this job? Mel seemed to think so, but right now...ever since he'd arrived, she wasn't so sure.

Matt's silence was a chasm. He was somewhere far away, thinking about something or someone he'd left behind. When he wiped his damp palms on his jeans, she caught a flash of emotion on his face. Fear? Sadness? It was hard to tell, but the rawness of it stabbed her heart. He wasn't here with her. She didn't know his boyfriend's name, but his presence was unmistakable, lingering in the pauses of Matt's speech and the way his focus seemed to drift, as though someone else occupied the room.

Matt's jaw clenched, and his breath hitched, possibly about to say something, but then he swallowed the words back down. She saw his struggle; the questions clawing at him. He looked down at his hands again, which were fidgeting with the book he was still carrying.

He turned to Cath with a startling look in his eyes. "Alright, that's enough." His voice shattered the brittle air. "I'd like you to leave now."

She blinked, taken aback by the abruptness of his words. "Sure, yes… yes, of course." Her heart was pounding in her ears as she stammered. Trying to keep her voice steady, she took a step back. "I'll leave you alone until you ask for me. Your fridge will be stocked, and Shannon will bring meals for you. I'll make sure she doesn't bother you."

Her words tumbled out. "I hope to see you sooner rather than later. Goodbye for now." She gave him a hesitant smile, but he didn't return it.

As she left the room, she looked back to see him drop heavily onto the couch, his head falling into his hands. The door closed behind her, and she exhaled shakily, pressing her back against the wall outside. Her nerves buzzed like static, and she swallowed the lump in her throat, wishing she'd found something better to say.

CHAPTER FIFTEEN

JOSH RAN A HAND THROUGH HIS HAIR, RELIEVED TO BE ALONE AGAIN. Although he was outside, the space felt oppressive and airless. At least now he could think. He needed a plan, something that didn't involve blind cooperation.

Swimming had always been his way to untangle his thoughts, to find clarity in the chaos. He rifled through the closet, searching for another pair of swim trunks, but as he did, he had an idea. It was bold, maybe ridiculous, yet he couldn't get it out of his head.

A grin tugged at his lips as he tossed aside his clothes. *Why bother?* The women were trapped there, too, weren't they? He wasn't stupid; he'd spent enough time in front of a mirror to know the effect his body had on people. Muscles built by years of disciplined workouts, the kind of physique that drew attention whether he wanted it or not. Who was he trying to fool? He always wanted it.

If these women were stuck there as long as he was, they would have their own needs, too. And if seducing one, or two, or all of them, gave him an edge, why not play that card? It wasn't a great plan, but in the absence of any others, it was still his best option for the time being.

The water comforted him as he dove in. The cool rush against his skin momentarily quieted the storm in his head. He sliced through the water, each stroke punctuated by a surge of fury. In his mind, he scoffed at the absurdity of it all. These women thought they could turn him into some kind of puppet, high on their concoctions, tripping over himself to hand them his fortune. As if mind-altering substances held the key to unlocking his philanthropic spirit, turning a hardened businessman into their own personal Robin Hood.

His muscles burned, but he pushed harder, welcoming the sensation. It was a rebellion in its own right; a reminder of his strength and control. They wanted to mold him, to strip away his defenses with their drugs and pretty hair. He imagined himself, slumped and glassy-eyed, reduced to a shadow of who he really was, throwing money at whatever cause they deemed worthy. The thought made his blood boil, igniting a hot coil of defiance in his core.

They won't break me, he vowed, slamming his hand into the water as if striking the very notion itself. *I'm not their pawn.* Whatever twisted game they thought they were playing, he'd make damn sure he'd be the one to win it.

The notion that Marne might be involved in some way persisted, stubbornly clinging to his thoughts. She was always on his case about giving back, badgering him to put his money toward fixing Earth instead of investing in space travel. It would be like her to get tangled up in something like this, all for the sake of some grand, misguided crusade.

The swim had done little to quiet his mind, though his muscles had relaxed. Climbing out of the pool, he grabbed a towel and dried off. He made his way to the kitchen, absentmindedly popping grapes into his mouth as he leaned against the counter, staring out at the mirrored wall.

He'd seen the women pass through it and assumed their blue bracelets were somehow the key. He hadn't touched it yet, hadn't tested it. Did it have the same strange, elastic resistance as the perimeter barrier?

His eyes narrowed. *What if I smashed it?* The idea thrilled him for a moment, imagining the chaos that would ensue if it shattered. There were cameras outside… he didn't care. Let them watch.

Frustration boiling over, he stormed outside and grabbed one of the heavy metal chairs from the patio. It scraped against the concrete, the legs leaving thin, white marks as he dragged it to the mirror. With a deep grunt, he swung it hard, like a caveman wielding his club. The impact sent a shock up his arms, but the wall absorbed the blow without so much as a ripple. Instead of rebounding, as he expected, the chair slipped out of his grip and slid to the ground, almost comically gentle.

He stared at it, stunned. *What the hell?* It was as if the wall had sucked the force out of the swing. It must be the same technology as the perimeter. He wondered if his bracelet extended its properties to whatever he was holding?

Sucking in his cheeks, he picked up the chair again, this time heaving it at the wall with all his strength, releasing at the peak of his swing. It hit the surface like a wet noodle, slapping against the mirror before sliding to the ground in silence. The only sound was the metallic clatter as it landed on the patio.

He marched back inside, the cool air of the kitchen doing little to douse the heat of his frustration. Drawer after drawer rattled as he yanked them open, searching for a sharp knife. Bamboo clattered against the drawers' edges, but nothing useful surfaced. No sharp objects, just biodegradable cutlery.

A dark laugh escaped him. They were treating him like a child in a padded room. Undeterred, he grabbed a wooden fork and pressed it against his palm, testing it. The tines held firm, but didn't pierce his skin.

In a frenzy, he rifled through the drawers again, gathering forks and snapping the prongs off halfway to the base. From the fridge, he retrieved an elastic band holding a bunch of asparagus and used it to bind the forks together.

He jammed the bundle between the drawer and the counter and leaned against it. His chest expanded to brace himself. *This is gonna hurt.*

But that was the whole point. He raised his left hand, knuckles white from the pressure of his clenched fist, and brought his wrist down hard onto the jagged points. Pain shot through his arm as the tines bit into his skin. The forks flew out of the drawer, scattering across the floor.

He looked down at his arm. Blood was pooling around four small puncture holes. A strange satisfaction washed over him. It wasn't much, but it was proof. Proof he wasn't entirely under their control.

"Josh, it's Mel. What's going on? I got a notification your hand is bleeding. I'll be there in just a minute."

"No. No, don't come, it's nothing. I just cut myself with some silverware." Although in quite a bit of pain, he didn't want to admit it to Mel.

"That would have taken some planning. Why are you trying to hurt yourself?"

"To see if I can." His tone was testy. "And I'll keep thinking up more ways to do it."

"We've done everything we can think of to keep you safe, but if you do get injured, we have a full medical facility here, so don't think it's a ticket out of here. Do you need a bandage? There are some under the sink in your bathroom. Let me know if you need anything more than that. Oh, and you shouldn't be wanting to hurt yourself, so I'll need to increase your PLH."

He ran his wrist under cool water, watching the blood swirl away in thin, pink spirals. The sting made him feel alive. He slapped on a bandage and went to the living room. Spotting the box with the headset, he took it off the shelf. He had the latest VR model from Omnicia at home, but this looked very different.

He slipped it over his head. Transformation was immediate; it molded to his face, feather-light, as if it weren't there at all. The surrounding room melted away, and in an instant, he was standing on a sun-soaked beach, the waves rolling in with a gentle hiss. He blinked, startled by the vividness. And it wasn't just visual. He tasted the salt in the air, felt the sun warming his skin. He turned his head, watching the palm trees sway in the breeze, their fronds casting dappled shadows on the sand.

No way, he thought, crouching down to the ground. The sensation of the sand beneath his hands sent a shiver through him. It was warm and fine, slipping between his fingers like real grains. He pressed his palms flat, half-expecting his hand to pass through the illusion, but the sand held.

He stood, heart pounding with a strange mix of awe and fear. At the edge of the water, he dipped his toes in. The chill bit into his skin. He couldn't help but laugh in disbelief. *This is impossible.* He splashed water onto his legs; the droplets trailing down to his ankles.

"How the fuck have they done this?" It wasn't just advanced VR; this was something beyond anything he'd ever experienced. His mind spun with possibilities, calculations. *This tech could make a fortune. It could change everything.*

Four icons hovered in front of him: games, movies, nature, and meditations. He assumed the beach belonged to the nature app. He focused on the nature icon, and a new menu popped up: forest, beach, mountain, meadow, desert, and jungle. His eyes lingered on "forest" until a sub-menu appeared. He settled on "bamboo".

For a moment, nothing happened. Then, as he turned away from the ocean, the surrounding landscape shifted. The golden dunes shrank, the horizon morphing before his eyes. The sand gave way to thick, towering bamboo sprouting from the earth. A wooden boardwalk snaked through the grove, inviting him in. The sound of the waves was replaced by the melodic clacking of bamboo.

The sound reminded him of the wind chimes that hung from the porch of his grandmother's cabin near Leavenworth. The summers he'd spent there had been an escape from the chaos of his childhood. In a world constantly shifting beneath his feet, his Nana had been his anchor. For a moment, he could almost feel her arms around him, the smell of pine and campfire smoke mixing with her rose-scented lotion.

Focus. He shook his head to clear the memory. He eyed the boardwalk warily, wondering if he'd slam into a wall if he followed it. His curiosity won out against caution. He stepped onto the wooden path, the solid planks pressing against the soles of his bare feet. Reaching out, he brushed his hand along the smooth, cool surface of a bamboo shoot, half-expecting it to dissolve into pixels. But it didn't. It felt impossibly real.

He continued down the trail, the creaking of the bamboo blending into the rustle of overhead leaves. The farther he walked, the more the lines between reality and illusion blurred. As a kid, he'd fantasized about the holodeck from Star Trek: a small space, where you stepped into any environment as if it were real. This was that fantasy brought to life. He forgot entirely about his captivity; the strange barriers that trapped him were no longer taking up space in his brain.

After an hour of exploring, his stomach growled, snapping him back to reality. Reluctantly, he pulled the headset off, the room around him coming back into focus, his mind reeling from the experience.

In the kitchen, he slapped together a giant sandwich of Iberico ham and Delice de Bourgogne cheese, savoring each bite. As he ate, he leafed through the questionnaire Thalia had given him, rolling his eyes at the food and drink preferences section. *They already know everything I like*, he thought as he skipped ahead to hobbies and interests.

A bitter laugh slipped out. He couldn't remember the last time he'd done something purely for himself, something not tied to Omnicia. Work had swallowed every piece of him, even his so-called vacations. What *did* he like to do? He paused, trying to think back. He liked the pottery class he'd taken in college on a whim. The sensation of wet clay oozing through his fingers, the satisfaction of shaping something imperfect, only to squash it and start fresh. He scribbled "pottery" on the page.

The next section made him smirk, imagining what kind of sexual experiences the headset could offer. His mind spun with possibilities, and a wicked grin spread across his face as he filled out the page with surprising ease. "What icon would that be under?" He laughed, picturing it under the nature icon.

CHAPTER SIXTEEN

MEL TAPPED THE SCREEN ON HER BRACELET TO CHECK WILLIAM'S vitals. His pulse and breathing patterns had stabilized, a welcome change from yesterday's chaotic readings. Relief rushed through her, though it was quickly eclipsed by her continued anxiety. Repairing the damage she'd caused was her only focus now, not knowing if it was even possible.

She headed to his quarters unannounced. Through the open sliding door, she caught sight of him moving around the kitchen. He looked... better. More steady on his feet, more alert.

As she approached his outdoor bistro table, the scent of fresh coffee mingled with the fragrance of the cut flowers in the center. A colorful array of fruit, arranged in the shape of a rainbow, was on display. Shannon's touch. Mel couldn't help but smile. The motherly chef had a way of bringing comfort to people in difficult situations.

William spotted her and paused, his expression guarded but less hostile than yesterday. He motioned to the empty seat, then joined her without a word. She lowered herself into the chair, crossing one leg over the other and letting her hands rest lightly in her lap. She kept her posture loose, though her insides were in turmoil.

"Good morning, William." Did he hear her nerves or sincerity? "I'm glad to see you up and about."

He studied her, saying nothing at first. She could almost see the calculations running behind his eyes.

Shannon arrived carrying a platter of bacon and eggs. "Hey there." Her voice, like honey, was a sweet and calming balm to the discord. "I hope you're feeling better today."

She set the food in front of him, making small talk as she poured him a cup of coffee. Mel caught the subtle shift in William's body language, softening ever so slightly in response to Shannon's easy demeanor.

"Thank you." His tone was curt as he narrowed his eyes, glaring at Mel. "I am still here, am I not? How could you think I would be better?"

The iciness in his voice was unmistakable. Mel's stomach twisted. He was still shaken, and any hope of building trust quickly had been shattered by yesterday's events.

Shannon, unruffled, sat down across from him. "I know yesterday was awful for everyone. It's okay if you're still unsettled by it. It's totally understandable, but we're here to help."

William leaned back, folding his arms. "Help? You think you will help me? I do not know how you can say that with a face so straight. I thought I would die." His words, not only biting, were laced with disbelief. "You drugged me. Nearly killed me."

Mel swallowed, forcing herself to look him in the eye. "You're right. I miscalculated." Her voice cracked despite her best efforts to control it. "I'm deeply sorry for what happened. It wasn't supposed to be like that. I was trying to make your adjustment to being here easier."

William muttered under his breath and pushed the plate of food away.

Shannon gave him a sympathetic smile, unfazed by his rebuff.

"No one's going to force you to do anything, William. We hope in time, you'll see the benefits of what we're doing here. I know no one has had the chance to show you all the wonderful things we have available to you."

"That is funny. Are you not forcing me to be here and already drugging me? You show me whatever it is you want to show me, but it will not get me to agree to this scheme of yours. I never take drugs in all my life, and certainly will not start now."

Shannon maintained her cheer. "I can see why this is going to be difficult for you. Maybe if you allow Monica to do things without drugs, like meditation and breathwork, that might be enough for Mel. Maybe she won't make you take the drugs."

Mel's eyes widened as she looked at Shannon. She had no right to put her on the spot like that. Was she intentionally setting her up to be the bad guy? Did she feel the same way about her as Monica did? The entire project hinged on the psychedelic part of the therapy. Sure, breathwork and meditation were a great way to achieve results, but the drugs would be much more effective and take far less time.

William looked into the distance as he spoke. "I make a deal with you. I cooperate with you and Monica, but not drugs. I do whatever meditations and breathworks you want me to do if you will let me speak to my wife. If I do not speak to her, I do nothing you ask of me."

Mel allowed a moment of stillness before responding. "William, I know how much you love your wife and know she must be out of her mind with worry, but how could we possibly allow you to speak to her without jeopardizing the entire program?"

William shrugged. "That is not my problem to solve. From what you've said to me, the program will not go far anyway if I do not participate, so it is your choice, is it not?"

"You're correct. If you don't participate, the program fails, but what I don't think you understand is if you don't, you'll still never see your wife again. I'm sure you don't believe we could remain hidden for that long, but I assure you, the technology keeping you here is fail-proof."

"I will take my chances." William removed himself from the table and walked into the kitchen.

Mel didn't try to stop him. She'd lost this round, so her attention turned to Shannon. "I'm not quite sure why you said that. I'm trying my best not to feel undermined."

"Oh, no, no, that wasn't my intention at all. Oh my gosh, I'm so sorry. No, I was trying to... to make him feel we're listening to him. Maybe if we let him adjust in stages, we can slowly introduce the big, bad stuff when he's more comfortable."

Mel tapped her fingers on the arm of her chair as she contemplated what Shannon had said. "Ummm. Huh...yup, I think you're definitely on to something. I have to remind myself these men aren't clients who've come to me for help. And I have to remind myself this is going to take time, which we have, so no need to rush. Thank you, Shannon. I'm sorry. But please, next time if something like this comes up, talk to me first and not in front of a voyager."

"Oh, yes. Of course. I... it just came out. I'm the one who's sorry." Shannon got up and brushed off her lap. "I need to start prepping lunch."

Mel stayed at the table, thoughts ruminating. Convincing William about drugs was probably going to be harder than with Josh and Matt, but the thought of what the founders might do if he didn't cooperate made her sick. After all the work the two men had done on themselves, it didn't erase their capacity for ruthlessness.

If William didn't fall in line, they wouldn't hesitate to use other tactics. They were willing to kidnap family members and film their terror to use as leverage. Bile rose in her throat at the idea. It wasn't a line she was willing to cross. That wasn't who she was. She'd built her entire career on connection and empathy, not coercion and threats. If she couldn't get through to him, the founders would do it their way, and it wouldn't be her call anymore.

If she failed to bring him on board, she couldn't stomach the lengths they'd go to. That was why she had to succeed on her terms. Maybe Shannon's plan was the best way for now. It might be the way to get through to him because losing William wasn't an option. He was chosen for a reason.

He had a way of pulling strings in places that mattered, in regions like Bangladesh and India, where pollution was rampant, where climate change wasn't some distant threat but a daily reality. He'd built his empire quietly, cultivating relationships with world leaders and industry giants, all of whom trusted him on a level that made him invaluable.

She believed William would be the anchor for the others. He cared more about the planet than Josh or Matt ever had, so he might be able to convince them of the necessity to save it. The project's success depended on his cooperation, and she'd almost lost him already.

The look of panic on his face was still etched in her mind. It hadn't just shaken him; it had shattered her own confidence. *What the hell was I thinking?* She asked herself for the hundredth time.

Still, she couldn't bring herself to scrap PLH altogether. She believed in it, even if she was clinging to that belief by her fingertips. If she got his dosage right, it might help crack his tough exterior. Beneath the stoic businessman was a man who loved his wife with a fierceness she couldn't help but admire. Reaching that part of him was the key.

CHAPTER SEVENTEEN

"Cath, I can't seem to close the blinds. Could you please come and help me?"

Matt's voice made Cath jump, a flutter of anxiety taking hold in her solar plexus. She still wasn't sure how to handle him, a man who seemed both fragile and impenetrable at the same time.

He's asking for help. That's something, she reassured herself, but the thought didn't relieve her nerves. The last thing she wanted was to push him too hard and send him spiraling further into himself.

"I'm sorry, Matt." Her words had to strike the perfect balance between confident and caring. "The blinds open for everyone at the same time each morning and can't be overridden except by Mel. I know she wants you to get up, so I doubt she'd override them today. Is there anything else I can help with?"

She waited, bracing herself for the irritated response she expected. The silence stretched on, and she winced, imagining him stewing in frustration.

"No."

The single word came back flat. She let out a slow breath.

Then his voice again, quieter this time. "Cath, I changed my mind. I'd like to use the salt room if it's available."

Relief mingled with surprise. She'd been expecting more resistance, not a request for something so tranquil. "Let me check...yup, no one's reserved it today. It's available anytime you're ready. Just let me know when you want to go."

"Now."

She hesitated. "Don't you want to eat breakfast first?"

"No."

The way he shut her down stung. She was unsure whether to press or let it go. *You're supposed to build rapport, Cath.* He wasn't giving her much to work with, though. "Umm, okay then. I'll come get you in about ten minutes."

"Thanks." There was no appreciation in his voice.

When she arrived at his apartment, she saw him slumped on the couch, looking utterly lost, his VR set dangling from his hand. He didn't look up as she approached. She plastered on a smile.

"Hey Matt. Ready to go?"

He rose slowly, pulling a pillow to his chest with his free hand. His intentions for the day were clear.

They walked down the corridor in silence. She glanced at him, searching his face for any sign of connection, but his eyes were vacant, fixed on a point far away. Although she tried to make small talk about the photographs hanging on the walls, but by the time they reached the elevator, she was talking to herself.

As they made their way through the lower level, she forced herself to keep talking, pointing out the theater and the gym as they passed. It was all filler.

When they reached the door to the salt room, she forced a fake, cheerful voice. "Here we are! There's a bathroom and a water fountain in the back. No food allowed, so if you get hungry, call me and I'll take you back."

Matt nodded, stepping past her into the dimly lit room. He ran his hand along the smooth wall of pink Himalayan salt blocks.

Faux stalactites hung from the ceiling; pillars of chunky, irregular blocks of yellow and pink salt. He stared up at them, then down at the pink salt sand floor.

He shuddered. She was glad he had thought to bring a robe with him. He pulled it tightly around himself as he maneuvered one of the chaise loungers behind a pillar, clearly trying to position it strategically, shielding it from view if anyone were to enter.

"Do you have any questions?" she asked.

"No. Thank you. I'll call you when I'm ready to leave."

"Okay, enjoy your time."

She exited, fully aware of Matt's plan, but didn't have the heart to tell him he couldn't. She wanted him to see her as an ally so she could start building trust with him. One day of sleeping wouldn't derail the program.

As the door clicked shut, she paused. *What are you doing?* She bit down on her lip, debating whether to leave him be. Every instinct told her to back off, to give him space. But another voice, Mel's no doubt, whispered in her head: *This is an opportunity. You better take it.*

With a quiet exhale, she opened the door and stepped back inside, squinting as her eyes adjusted to the dim light. She found Matt curled up on the lounger, his shoulders hunched inward as though he were trying to fold himself into a smaller shape, one that might disappear entirely.

She edged a foot forward, unsure if she should commit. One hand held on to the back of a nearby chair, needing to anchor herself before daring to close the distance.

"Mind if I join you for a bit?" Her voice was softer than she'd intended, and she worried he hadn't heard her.

Matt's eyes flicked open, narrowing, but he didn't say no. He gave a slight nod, so she perched on the chaise next to him, keeping her body angled away, trying not to crowd him.

"I noticed you brought the headset. Were you thinking of using it?"

Matt let out a dry laugh. "No. It's just a prop." He ran a hand through his hair. "You knew that, though, didn't you?"

The bitterness in his voice stabbed her heart. She nodded. "Yeah, I figured. But I didn't want to call you out on it."

Matt didn't respond right away. Instead, he looked away, staring at the far wall, the rigidity in his face melting into something softer. "I dreamed of him."

His words came out low and indistinct, forcing her to strain to catch them. "Do you want to talk about it?" she asked.

A muscle twitched in his jaw before he nodded. "I was back at Burning Man." His eyes remained distant. "It was when we met. He was bartending at the Pleasure Dairy, cracking jokes and making everyone laugh. He didn't recognize me with my dust shroud on. It was the only time I felt like I could breathe, you know?"

Her throat tightened at the raw honesty of his words. "It sounds like you could really be yourself around him."

Matt's eyes snapped back to hers, sharp, accusatory. "Yeah. And now I'm stuck here, in this place where everyone wants something from me again."

Cath nodded as she tried to keep her tears at bay. She felt his emotions as her own. "I understand why you feel that way, but maybe talking about him will make this place a little less... suffocating. At least for now."

Matt's lips parted as he sighed. When he spoke again, his voice carried a warmth she hadn't heard in it before. "I've been going to Burning Man for years. For one week, I can lose myself in the crowd, blend in completely. It's like...shedding my skin."

He looked at her sideways, as if expecting her to laugh. When she didn't, he pressed on. "The costumes, the music, the lights. It's all an escape. I can be whoever I want."

"That sounds freeing."

"Yeah." Matt breathed out. "Last year, everything changed for me. I met *him*. They had these ridiculous udder-shaped liquor dispensers. He was having a blast. People flocked to him like moths. He had this way about him... magnetic, you know?"

His face lit up as he spoke, an unguarded look she had yet to see from him. "He sounds pretty special."

"He is." Matt's voice was softer now. "At first, we were just friends. He didn't know who I was—didn't care. He'd listen, really listen, in a way no one else ever had. I didn't have to pretend with him. For the first time, I could just... be."

She kept nodding. "That kind of connection isn't easy to find."

"No. It's not." He paused and looked down at his hands. "After the burn, we kept in touch. I had a lot of business in New York, so he'd stay with me whenever I was in town. And when I wasn't, I'd fly him out to the Valley. It was easy with him. We'd spend whole days talking, or not talking at all. I didn't need to perform, didn't feel like I had to be the version of Matt everyone else expected. He *got* me." His voice trailed off as he blinked repeatedly.

She stayed quiet, letting him compose his thoughts, hoping he was comfortable enough to keep talking.

Matt hesitated, his fingers tightening around his pillow. "I've never brought anyone home before," he said. "Not a boyfriend, at least."

Cath tilted her head, an unspoken invitation to continue.

"My family... they're good people, you know? Loving, generous. They'd give you the shirt off their back if you needed it. But they're also religious. Really religious." He sighed and leaned back. "They've never said anything outright. But I know how they feel. They don't have to say it."

Cath still said nothing, sensing there was more he needed to get out.

"I was going to bring Travis home for Thanksgiving this year," Matt said, voice faltering. "It's a big deal. I'd finally worked up the courage. I want them to see how happy he makes me. I thought...

maybe if they met him, if they saw us together... maybe they'd see... me." His shoulders sagged. "But now I'm stuck here. And Travis..." His voice trailed off.

Cath leaned forward. "It sounds like you've been carrying this alone for a long time."

"Yeah. I thought this year would be different. But instead, I'm trapped in this...this place." He gestured at the surrounding walls. "And I don't know if he's okay. I don't even know if he thinks I still care."

"He loves you. That doesn't go away just because you aren't there." Cath kept her voice soft.

The silence between them was pregnant, but she didn't try to fill it. She could see the grief in every line of his face, the anguish of being ripped away from the one person who'd made him whole. She wished she had the right words, but there weren't any.

Matt dropped his head into his hands. "I just want to see him. I need to know he's okay."

Her chest ached from his pain, but she knew she couldn't promise him that. "I wish I could do that for you. But I can't. All I can do is try to make this a little less unbearable for you. If you let me."

He didn't answer, but he didn't tell her to leave either. It was a small victory. She didn't say anything else. She sat there, a silent companion in the dim light, hoping maybe she had finally made some progress.

CHAPTER EIGHTEEN

THE SOFT, RHYTHMIC TAPPING OF RAIN AGAINST THE WINDOWS pulled Josh from sleep. He lay still for a moment, certain he'd heard music, but the room was silent now. For the third morning in a row, he woke feeling... good. It was strange, unsettling even, to be so well-rested, his shoulders loose and unburdened. The constant demands and ceaseless pressures of the past decade were gone. He wasn't sure if he hated or loved the sensation of having nothing to do.

Steam filled the bathroom, fogging up the mirror as he stood under the scalding spray. He lingered, letting the heat wash over his skin, tingling and alive. The water, hotter than he'd normally tolerate, ran over him, cleansing in a way he hadn't realized he needed.

He stepped out, wrapping a towel snugly around his waist. His reflection was a blur in the mirror, but he still couldn't resist wiping away the moisture to check his face. A little stubble on his jawline, but his skin was glowing. He rubbed his chin with his thumb and forefinger. "Still got it."

The gray flooring muffled his footsteps as he padded to the kitchen. The rain had stopped, and the glass in the windows was missing again, though he couldn't pinpoint when it had returned during the night. Had it happened when he was lost in the VR forest?

The familiar hiss of steam and the earthy, rich aroma of his cappuccino filled the kitchen. He savored the scent for a moment before taking his first sip. *Perfect.* With his mug in hand, he strolled outside. On the patio, a colorful breakfast awaited: fresh berries, flaky croissants, and a bowl of Greek yogurt topped with honey. The setup looked like something out of a luxury hotel, down to the folded linen napkins.

But, as he reached for a blueberry, a flash of self-consciousness hit him, sitting there bare-chested, still dripping from his shower. *What the hell am I doing?* Yesterday, he'd have lounged on the patio, fully aware of his own appeal, daring anyone to look away. But now, the thought of the women seeing him like this sent a jolt of embarrassment through him.

He swore under his breath and hurried back inside, the towel clinging damply to his hips. Setting his mug down, he yanked open the closet. He pulled on a pair of fitted jeans and a black t-shirt, something simple but intentional. He examined himself in the mirror, running a hand through his hair to smooth it down. The man staring back at him looked composed and confident, like someone ready to outsmart anyone in the room.

His experience with the headset the day before had been a revelation. Not just because of its realism, but because of the potential he saw. The tech was groundbreaking, unlike anything he'd ever encountered. The fortune he'd make if Omnicia got involved was staggering. The sheer scope of its market potential made his pulse race with excitement. This was a game-changer, and for the first time since arriving, something other than anger or fear stirred within him.

The realization he might actually want to play along, but on his own terms, of course, struck him with clarity. He wasn't going to tip his hand yet. Let them believe he was still a reluctant prisoner. He'd bide his time, get a better sense of what the tech could do. If he played this right, he could walk away with a massive cut of whatever profits this place was set to generate.

His plan for the day: explore the VR menus in more depth, and see if there were any hidden gems he hadn't discovered yet. For the first time since his extraction, he found himself eager to start the day, now that he had a different purpose. He was thinking like an investor now, scouting an opportunity. And if he had any hope of being taken seriously when the time came, he couldn't be parading around like an arrogant playboy.

Josh went through all the menus and sub-menus but couldn't find anything remotely sexual. He had to admit his disappointment.

He landed on the nature icon again and selected "Mountain". The sub-menu had a list of familiar names like Kilimanjaro, K2, Rainier, and Everest, along with some generic titles like Rolling Hills, Easy Hike to Alpine Lake, and Moderate Hike to Endless Views. In his youth, he'd had somewhat of a fixation on Mt. Everest and had hoped to one day summit. However, by the time he'd had enough money for the climb, he didn't have the time.

After opening the Everest tab, he found another sub-menu: Basecamp, Camp One, Camp Two, Camp Three, Camp Four, and Summit. He selected Basecamp and was awed as the dunes behind the home screen beach morphed into spectacular snow-covered peaks. His foot landed on a jagged rock, but instead of the sharp bite he expected, the impact was cushioned. He looked down. Sturdy hiking boots hugged his feet. The leather gleamed, laces threaded tightly. He flexed his fingers, meeting resistance. Gloves, creasing with the motion.

Incredible!

As he navigated the trail, his mind buzzed with a flurry of questions. What would happen if he fell into a crevasse? How did the furniture not get in the way as he hiked? The incongruity of the situation baffled his mind.

The path wound its way uphill, narrowing as it snaked through the rugged terrain. Small stone cairns marked the path, silently leading him deeper into the wilderness. His every step ground into the gravel, the satisfying crunch his constant companion. The sun beat down, and beads of sweat clung to his hairline. His mouth grew dry, lips cracking with thirst. Each breath scraped against his throat, grit clinging to every inhale.

He yanked off the headset. The jarring shift from the Himalayas to the sterile apartment left him momentarily dazed. He wiped the sweat from his brow, muttering to himself. "It'll be a major pain in the ass if I have to keep stopping for water."

The windows had returned. He stared at them, amused. *They must be making sure I don't go walking off the floor and straight into the pool.*

After quenching his thirst, he slipped the headset back on and once again found himself surrounded by towering mountain peaks. The air felt colder now, thin and biting. He trudged onward until the sprawl of Basecamp came into view.

Red and yellow shelters dotted the jagged landscape, bright streaks against the muted backdrop of white and gray. Colorful prayer flags swayed and snapped in the wind. Sherpas and climbers bustled around him as they checked gear and pitched tents. Focused on their tasks, they paid him no attention.

He pushed on, determined to explore every inch, but soon hunger caused his stomach to ache and his legs burned with each step. He needed a break.

There was no lunch waiting for him, but he immediately heard Shannon's voice. "Ah, there you are. Are you ready to eat?"

"Yes, please. And if possible, could I please get an extra-large portion of whatever you've made for me? I've overdone it a bit."

"Yes, absolutely. I should be there in about fifteen minutes. You might want to find a quick snack if you're that hungry. See you soon."

He found some crackers while he waited. Talking with someone didn't sound awful, so he planned to ask her to stay while he ate.

"Yoo-hoo, lunch is served."

He made a beeline for the table when he heard Shannon's call. "Oh man, this looks great," he said, plopping himself in front of an enormous bowl of chicken carbonara. "I'd love it if you stayed to keep me company for a while, if you have time."

"Yes, of course. I'd love to, thank you."

"I'm so sorry, I'm starving. Please excuse my manners." He knew he looked like a barbarian as he shoveled the pasta into his mouth. "Is it okay if we talk after I finish eating?"

"Oh, yes, for sure. Please take your time. I've already delivered lunch to the others."

When he had devoured every bite, Josh sat back, sighed, and rubbed his belly. "It can't all be because of the drugs. I do think you're a culinary genius. But I already knew that from your restaurant, didn't I?"

"Aww, thank you, Josh, you're too kind. So, did you have an enjoyable morning?"

"I had an amazing morning. I'm beginning to understand why I'm here now. The tech is mind-blowing, and I can't wait to get it into mass production," he replied with excitement.

"Oh, were you playing with the headset, by any chance?"

"Yes, and wow! I started at the beach and then climbed up to Everest Basecamp, all in one morning. It was exhilarating. It really is the most incredible thing I've ever seen—and I've seen a lot of things."

"That's fabulous, Josh. I get it, we all use the headsets a lot.

They keep us from getting cabin fever. I haven't made it to base camp yet. It's a bit too hard for me, but I'm working on it."

He leaned back, feigning casual interest. "What's up with the windows? Sometimes they're there, sometimes they're not?"

"They open automatically during the day if the temperature is in a certain range, but you can close them using the wall switch." Shannon pulled at a loose thread in her apron. "They seal automatically when you activate the headset. It's all part of the system to keep the special floor in play. Without it, most of the programs can't function properly."

"Understandable."

"Shoot, I've got to go. Dinner isn't going to make itself."

As Shannon stood to leave, he handed her his questionnaire. "Thanks for the chat. Please let Thalia and Mel know I just need a bit of time to wrap my head around everything. But I'm feeling... better about it all."

"Will do." Shannon flashed a smile before disappearing.

For the next few days, Josh immersed himself in the VR programs. He navigated digital worlds like a conqueror, scouting new lands, dissecting every experience, and mentally cataloging what worked and what didn't. There were moments where the line between virtual and reality blurred, and he found himself seduced by the illusion of control and freedom it offered.

The more he explored, the more ideas flooded his mind. He envisioned how Omnicia's product line could integrate seamlessly with this technology, creating a bridge between physical experiences and virtual enhancements. He imagined the possibilities: the untapped market, the potential partnerships, the unimaginable profits.

Shannon brought his meals three times a day, and with each visit, their conversations became a bit more relaxed, almost friendly. Her company was a strange comfort. She had no agenda, no angle, just simple, unforced human interaction. It had been years since he'd connected with someone this way, without the usual power dynamics, hidden motives, or sexual tension.

Still, beneath it all, he was on edge. He was being lulled into a false sense of security. They wanted him compliant. But he wasn't fooled.

CHAPTER NINETEEN

"Excuse me, does any of you play chess?"

Mel almost dropped her spoon. Thalia choked on her toast. Monica raised an eyebrow, and for a second, the entire room held its breath. It was William's voice, heard for the first time in days.

"I use the headset, but I do not like it."

Monica's response came quickly. "Hi William, it's Monica. I love to play chess. I can bring a board to your quarters as soon as I'm done with breakfast."

The strain in Mel's body released with a slow, quiet breath. Was this the beginning of a breakthrough with William? She couldn't help but cling to a sliver of hope. Monica had a gift, a way of coaxing the most impenetrable people into opening up, similar to cracking a shell without damaging the insides.

She glanced at Monica, who had already risen. Her friend could be blunt, even harsh at times, but there was no denying her skill when it came to her work. She had seen Monica's uncanny ability to read people, to dig out their truths with gentle persistence, time and time again.

Even so, the memory of that overheard conversation was still a splinter in her heart. The words she wasn't meant to hear still stung. They replayed in her mind at the most inconvenient times, chipping away at the confidence she had in their bond and in herself. *It's just the way she is*, she tried to remind herself. Monica's sharp edges weren't out of malice. And yet, the betrayal struck her as personal, even if it wasn't meant to be.

Swallowing her emotions, she offered Monica a supportive smile. "Good luck," she said as Monica retrieved the chessboard.

Monica found William seated outside, focused intently on a mandala coloring book. As he shaded the intricate pattern with a colored pen, each stroke appeared to be a study in focus and control. A sense of peace seemed to emanate from the very core of his being, in stark contrast to the turbulent emotions she had witnessed in him before.

The PLH must be working, she thought.

"Wow, that's beautiful. I love the colors you've chosen," she said, sitting down next to him.

"Thank you," William said with a smile. "I find this helps with the stress, and as you can imagine, I am having much stress."

"Yes, I get it. I do a lot of coloring too. Sometimes I do it as a meditation to clear my head."

Arranging the pieces on the board with an easy rhythm, her words flowed like a gentle stream, the conversation slipping into the comfort of an old habit. While she gave him plenty of space, there was a subtle nudge in her questions, a quiet encouragement to engage. Eager to connect but wary of pushing too hard.

"Mel tells me you meditate regularly. How long have you been practicing?" She tried to keep her expression open, but her heart thudded, the sound pounding in her ears as if it might escape. This was about building rapport, but the connection was delicate, especially given the circumstances.

William's stare was hard and fixed, perhaps assessing her sincerity. She sensed his wariness, though his muscles appeared relaxed.

"I was fortunate," he said in his low, gruff voice, that was somehow smoother than she expected. "My parents were spiritual people. Ahead of their times. They schooled me about mindfulness and meditation *before* it was fashionable."

She leaned in, keeping her movements unthreatening. The edge in his tone faded. The wall between them lowered a just fraction.

"I meditated often before the career took my time." A wistful smile tugged at his lips. "It is funny, yes? The more busy I got, the more I need it, but the less I do it."

"Funny how we tend to avoid the very things that could help us the most." She was guilty of it, too.

"My wife, Maria, she is the one who pointed me back," he said, his voice growing softer. "I try to finish my last big project before I retire. It was too much. I think I was not nice to be around. She told me I lost my... I don't know the right word in English. Middle? No, not right. Center. She has always been smarter than me." He chuckled, a genuine laugh that seemed to surprise him.

Monica's heart softened at the sound, and she decided to share a piece of herself, too, hoping it might deepen the connection. "I know what you mean. My upbringing was, shall we say, unconventional? I grew up in a commune in Denmark. It was a bubble. When it disbanded, I had to face the real world without any of the tools I thought I had. It was a shock, to say the least."

"That was quite an adjustment, yes?"

"It was. I had to find my own version of balance. It wasn't easy trying to reconcile two very different worlds. I felt lost. I tried to cling to routines I understood, but they felt inadequate. The emotional upheaval was unbearable. I needed something to ground me, and that's when I turned back to my spirituality."

She paused and looked at him to see if there was any interest in what she was sharing. "I found my renewed purpose in the most unexpected place. A luxury Ayahuasca retreat in Costa Rica."

She felt an inner light brighten as she spoke of Ayahuasca, and her hands were as descriptive as her words. At first, they fluttered near her chest, rapid then hesitant, reflecting the initial chaos of the experience. Then, her palms flew upwards, fingers spread wide, as if reaching for the vastness she encountered under the influence of the mother vine. Her forehead furrowed in concentration as she described intense visions, hands swirling in complex motions. Finally, they settled, palms facing upward and open. Her fingers came together in clasped hands, signifying a newfound wholeness and the sense of regaining her footing in the world.

William nodded along, but his agreement felt more like a reflex than a genuine conviction, as if the idea of indigenous medicine transforming a psyche was a step too far. For all his politeness, his eyes held a quiet, calculated doubt. Despite his upbringing, she assumed he preferred logic and reason to the mystical and unexplainable.

When he finally declared, "Checkmate," William's lips curved into a brief, satisfied smile. A quiet triumph coursed through her, not from the game, but from the way he was letting his guard down.

As he gathered the chess pieces, he seemed more at ease. Perhaps a glimpse of the man he was outside of this place. She hoped it was the fragile beginning of trust she could weave into a relationship.

"You played well. I'd love to play again tomorrow," she said.

"I would like that. Yes, please," he replied, the genuine warmth in his voice surprising her.

After mulling over ways to deepen their connection, Monica proposed a twist to the game as she set up the board the next day.

"Let's play with a new rule today. Every time one of us captures a piece, we get to ask the other a question. But nothing about work or the program. And if you don't like the question, you can ask for a different one. Deal?"

William studied her face for a moment, then gave a small nod. "Deal. Though based on yesterday's game, I expect I'll be doing most of the questioning."

She grinned. He didn't know she'd been holding back, that she'd let him win on purpose. She'd spent years playing chess with her father. Today, she'd give him a real challenge. She'd ease into it, though, wanting to build trust over simply winning.

They played in silence for the first few moves, the clinking of pieces the only sound between them. Then Monica captured a pawn. "Alright, first question. How did you meet your wife?"

"Maria." His face lit up with joy. "We met by accident. Quite literally."

"Go on."

"I was working at the Ritter Sport chocolate factory in Waldenbuch. Every day after work, I would stop at the local pub for a beer. One day, before I go inside, a young woman charges down the sidewalk with groceries. She tripped right in front of me. Eggs flying everywhere. One of them is on my shoe."

Monica laughed. "What did you do?"

"I froze for a moment. She was crying, trying to say sorry and clean the mess. When I bend down to help, a chocolate bar falls from my pocket and hit her on the head." William's eyes crinkled with the memory.

Monica leaned forward.

"We both start laughing. I take her to the tavern and we talk for a long time. It felt like we knew each other our whole lives."

Monica placed her hand over her heart. "Sounds like fate."

"I think yes. She always said so."

Monica took another pawn. "What's the best part about being married to her?"

The question seemed to catch him off guard. He paused, as if weighing whether to answer, before he spoke. "She is the only person who knows me inside."

"That's a rare gift." Monica's vision blurred. "Not many people get that kind of love."

"I know." William took Monica's pawn. "Your turn. Tell me about your family."

The ask touched a vulnerable spot she often kept hidden. "Both of my parents are gone. And I never married or had kids. After leaving the commune, I didn't know how to fit into the so-called 'real world'. I couldn't understand the obsession with 9-to-5 jobs."

"So, what did you do?"

Monica shrugged while she moved her bishop. "I flitted around, took whatever job I could find: restaurant work, cleaning houses, yoga instructor. None of it paid well, but I scraped by. By the time I landed in Costa Rica, I'd never stayed in one place long enough to build any kind of romantic relationship."

"You have never been in love?"

"Not really." She brushed a stray strand of hair behind her ear. "I had deep friendships with my coworkers. People who shared my interests, my worldview. But that's all they were, friendships.

The game continued, but they lost track of whose turn it was to ask a question, the conversation flowing so easily, it didn't seem to matter.

"You have tricked me. You are a good player." William deftly maneuvered his queen into position. "Check."

"You haven't seen anything yet. I've been going easy on you." Her teasing tone coaxed a smile from her opponent.

He made the final move, declaring, "Checkmate," and then

leaned back with a look of satisfaction. "Stay for dinner?" He seemed hesitant, maybe afraid she'd say no.

"Why don't we cook together? We can make something that reminds you of home."

Monica set off to the pantry. When she returned, she had the ingredients for curry wurst and potato salad. To drink, she brought several large bottles of Gaffel Kolsch.

The lines on his forehead softened as the evening unfolded, each emptied bottle loosening his expression. She kept her own drinking minimal, carefully pouring just enough into her glass to seem like she was keeping pace.

"You're quite the beer enthusiast." She topped up his glass while leaving her own untouched.

"Of course. It is in my blood. A German who does not drink beer is a rare thing indeed."

She leaned back in her chair. "Tell me more about your parents' spirituality and your upbringing."

A shadow passed over his face, and she wondered if she'd pushed too far. But William surprised her.

"Yes, they were Baha'i faith. It was not easy for them. During the Nazis, they had to pretend to be Protestant. By the time I came, it was better, so they could be Baha'i again."

She listened without interrupting. His eyes looked distant, like they were peering into the past. "As a boy, I was more interested in causing trouble than in listening to my parents' teachings, but I thought meditation was normal. Something everyone did. I did not connect it to their beliefs."

"So you didn't believe the same things they did?"

"You could say so. Only in college I started questioning why people believe what they do. I looked at many religions...

Buddhism, Christianity, and even atheism. Nothing stayed with me. Nothing until I met Maria."

"What does she believe?"

"Maria." Saying her name brought warmth to his face. "She showed me Science of Mind. It is practical, not dogmatic. The law of attraction, you know it? It made sense to me. I control my own reality. It helped me build everything."

Monica bobbed her head, digesting his words. "I can see why that philosophy would resonate with you. You've certainly done a good job shaping your reality."

The mood shifted as William's expression darkened. "But there is one thing I cannot shape."

"What's that?"

He hesitated before answering, his voice quieter. "Time. It slips through my fingers. I am worried now about dying."

The honesty of his words nearly made her weep, grateful he felt comfortable sharing. She gave him space to continue.

"I do not dwell on it, but it sometimes... sometimes, I do not sleep. One day soon, I will not be here. Where will I be? I do not know. Yes, sometimes I do not sleep."

"Hmm, me too. There are a lot of things that keep me awake. But talking about them helps. Thank you for talking with me."

The conversation flowed without barriers. William shared stories of travel and the early days of his business. She offered anecdotes from her time in Costa Rica. They laughed over stories of strange clients and shared their favorite meditation techniques. The hours slipped away unnoticed.

The darkness outside finally registered in Monica's awareness, and the ache in her back reminded her how long she'd been sitting. "William, this has been a wonderful evening, but I should probably get going. I need to be up for my sunrise meditation."

She stood to leave. "Before I go, I want to make a small request. Would you consider letting me come by during the day for some yoga and meditation? Nothing intense. Just a way to help you feel less cooped up, to stretch a bit, and maybe introduce you to a new way of meditating."

William regarded her with a thoughtful expression. "Yes, I think that will be all right. But do not think this is instead of our chess games. I would like a rematch."

The knot in her stomach was gone. "Deal."

CHAPTER TWENTY

"HEY MEL, I THINK I AM READY TO HAVE A SIT-DOWN WITH YOU."

Cath and Thalia were playing cards while Mel read on the sofa. Thalia looked over at Mel with a mischievous smile.

"Hi Josh, it's Thalia. Great to hear from you. Unfortunately, Mel's occupied at the moment, but I can tell her you'd like to see her as soon as possible. I'm guessing it'll be at least a few hours."

"Ya, sure, thanks."

Cath and Thalia laughed. Mel couldn't help but join in. It had been her idea to make him wait when he finally reached out. *Of course, he's pissed.* Mel bit her lip, trying to hide her smile. He wasn't used to being ignored, wasn't used to anyone telling him no. In his world, people rearranged their schedules to accommodate him; they bent over backward to secure a moment of his time.

Thalia turned to Cath and smirked. Her voice carried a hint of satisfaction. "Did you hear how pissy he sounded?"

The corners of Cath's mouth twitched, mirroring Thalia's. "Yup, sounds like he might need some coaching on that."

Mel's heart raced as she wondered how he'd react to being

forced to wait. For now, though, she couldn't help but revel in the moment, relishing the camaraderie shared between her friends.

She wanted him to understand who held the power, and she was unwavering in her resolve to assert her dominance. For the project to succeed, it was crucial for Josh to understand who the authority lay with, to recognize that she was the one steering the ship.

But it wasn't just about asserting dominance. It was about creating a ripple of uncertainty, making him question his place, having him wonder if the other men had already started cooperating while he held out. She needed that edge to keep him off balance and engaged. If he thought he was behind, it might drive him to lean into the program rather than resist it.

Although there were no cameras in his apartment, she had been monitoring his VR activities. She was pleased he had been using it as she worked with tech support to get programs developed based on his questionnaire. She'd been a bit shocked to see he'd filled out the section on sexual preferences. Neither of the other men had touched it, but Josh had. She wondered about the mental gymnastics he'd gone through in order to trust them enough with such personal details.

Josh skimmed the titles on his bookshelf, his fingers hovering over the spines, tapping each one before moving to the next. It was the first time in years he'd had to look for something to do. He pulled *Ishmael* from the shelf, laughing to himself at the absurdity of reading a book about a captive, telepathic gorilla while he was being held in a high-tech prison.

Settling into a lounger by the pool, he flipped open the first page, squinting at the bright reflection of the water dancing across the text. The story started slowly, but soon he found himself pulled into its strange narrative. Ishmael, the gorilla, was challenging everything he'd been taught to believe. The book poked holes in the idea humans were the apex of evolution, dissecting mankind's arrogance.

He let out a low whistle, half in disbelief. *This damn gorilla is making a lot of sense.* The book's critique of civilization's mythology—its blind faith in endless growth, its delusions of supremacy—hit closer to home than he was comfortable admitting.

He didn't realize how absorbed he'd become until Mel's voice shattered the quiet.

"Hi Josh, is it okay if I head your way now?"

He wanted to make her wait out of spite, but decided against it. If he intended to be cooperative, he should stop being so petty.

"Ya, sure, anytime," he responded politely.

A few minutes later, Mel strode into his space, her presence commanding attention as she balanced a binder and a laptop in her arms. With her hair pulled back into a casual ponytail and a pair of red polka-dot glasses perched on her nose, she exuded an air of intelligence laced with a playful charm.

"How have things been going?" Mel pulled up a seat next to him.

"Better than I'd expect for being kidnapped a week ago. I can't wait to get home and start marketing this tech!"

"I'm glad to hear that. We're all pretty excited to get home and see where all of this can make a difference."

Mel set the laptop on the table, but kept the binder in her hands.

"First things first. I wanted to tell you we should have your personal programs ready soon. It can be a bit of a sensitive subject, so I won't say too much except that while the technology is incredibly advanced, other than superficial touching, you won't really be able to do anything other than watch."

As heat crept up his neck into his cheeks, Josh willed the color to dissipate, fearing Mel might catch the telltale flush. The last thing he wanted was for her bracelet to alert her to his heightened arousal; the thought of her knowing such intimate details about his innermost desires turned him on, but also made him uncomfortable.

"Great," he muttered. "Let's move on now. I want to know what to expect as far as the drugs go."

Mel handed him the binder.

"This'll give you all the information—sometimes reading about things is more beneficial than having it explained. Though I'm happy to come talk to you about it when you've read through it."

He leafed through the pages. The contents are organized into chapters: Holotropic Breathwork, MDMA, and Psilocybin.

Mel continued.

"In each section, you'll find information about the different effects of the drugs, what to expect when you're working with them, and several medical studies showing how they're being used in therapeutic settings. I understand you don't think you need therapy, but these modalities have a way of showing us what we need to know about ourselves."

Josh, quite certain he knew everything there was to know about himself, still couldn't understand what they were hoping for. He continued to sift through the binder as Mel carried on.

"It isn't anything like talk therapy; you won't be sitting around chatting with Thalia. You'll be going on very deep, personal journeys inside your consciousness. You don't have to say anything at all, but Thalia will always be there if you want to process any of your thoughts out loud. We highly recommend writing down anything that comes up, whether you talk about it or not."

She opened her laptop and turned it toward him, revealing a calendar. As she moved, light played in the strands of her hair, illuminating warm highlights that framed her face. Heat billowed up his neck again, spreading to his ears, as he glanced at her, wondering if she'd caught his reaction. He half hoped she had.

"These medicines speak differently to people during different parts of the day, so there'll be times when you're up all night or up very early in the morning. This calendar is fluid and will change based on several factors. You can access the most recent copy on your VR home screen. If you're overwhelmed at any stage, let us know. This isn't going to be quick, and it certainly isn't going to be easy."

Despite her professional demeanor, she had an unexpected openness. He couldn't put his finger on what exactly, but something about her, beyond the obvious intelligence and attractiveness, sparked curiosity within him.

He scanned the calendar and saw entries stating things like "full-day, MDMA," and "half-day breathwork" and "R&R".

Mel was still talking.

"I'll mostly be hands-off, working behind the scenes to monitor your progress. Your bracelet will provide feedback about your brain activity and vitals, and of course, Thalia will keep me updated on your mental progress. You and I'll sit down at least weekly to debrief. Do you have any questions?"

Josh was disappointed he wouldn't have the opportunity to spend as much time as he had hoped with her, but Thalia… she wasn't a bad consolation prize. "So what do I have to do for you to let me work with the other men?"

"It isn't about *doing* anything. It's completely about the way you *feel*. We aren't going to tell you what we're looking for, because we don't want you just saying what you think we want to hear."

She explained that although he didn't have to tell Thalia or herself what came up while in an altered state, she encouraged him to, so they could help him understand and integrate the new knowledge into his life.

"We won't know if you're ready to move into the next phase unless you talk to us."

"Well, that's not cryptic at all," he said, not bothering to hide any of the irritation he felt. "That would be like me telling an employee I want a full report by Monday, but not telling them what I want the report to be on. I'm not a mind reader."

"I realize how it must sound, but we believe in the process and are hopeful that once you begin, you'll have a better understanding. It's difficult to explain when you have no prior experience."

"Okey dokey, if you say so. I can't wait to get started."

"Good." She was clearly unfazed by his sarcasm. "Thalia will be here after breakfast tomorrow. And just a heads up, Shannon is going to stop cooking and cleaning for you in a few days. However, she will walk you through the basics and cook alongside you until you're comfortable handling meals on your own. Some drugs require a certain diet before and after, so she'll be made aware of your schedule and will keep it in mind. Enjoy the rest of your day, and good luck with Thalia."

Josh leaned back on the lounger again after Mel left. He scanned the information in the binder. The MDMA sounded intriguing; he had to admit it didn't sound like what he expected. It wouldn't be some wild trip or loss of control, but something more personal. A drug designed to strip away defenses and fear. To evoke trust and vulnerability. *But that's the problem*, he thought. Vulnerability wasn't something he did. And what if it was a trap?

The psilocybin section made his skin crawl. A shiver ran through him as he remembered a college night gone sideways: vivid, hallucinatory nightmares that had left him spiraling for hours, terrified of his own reflection, questioning what was real. He'd sworn off drugs after that.

Setting the binder aside, he pushed the button on his wristband. "Thalia, I need to talk."

When she appeared through the mirror moments later, his heart quickened. The way her dark curls bounced on her shoulders, the way her presence felt warm, contrasted with Mel's sharp edge. There was something disarming about her; the kind of woman who didn't need to try to be beautiful. She just was.

He cleared his throat, shoving the attraction aside. He couldn't allow himself to be sidetracked by the way her shirt hugged her breasts.

"Look." His voice came out harsher than intended, a shield he'd instinctively raised around himself. "I've read through the binder. I get the basics of what you're asking me to do, and while I can see why you think MDMA might be useful, the mushrooms are a hard no from me. I had a bad experience before, and I don't want a repeat."

He examined her face for any signs of judgment, but only found compassion. It made him uncomfortable.

Pushing on, the words spilled out in a rush. "I don't know what you expect from me doing these drugs, but I've accepted that if I don't cooperate, I'm stuck here forever. I get that now. The technology—ya, I believe it. I don't see any way out, so I'm willing to move forward with whatever this is. But let's get things straight: I'm not doing it willingly. I'm not about to pour my heart out to you or anyone else. I'll play along, but don't expect me to crack my soul open and share my deepest, darkest secrets. That's not who I am."

Thalia didn't flinch. She dipped her head slightly. It said she'd already known this about him.

He hesitated, thrown off by the lack of resistance. "Mel said the more I engage with you, the faster I'll be ready to collaborate with the others. So that's what I'm doing. I'm here, talking to you, and I'm ready to get on with it. But let's not pretend this is anything other than what it is. I'm cooperating because I want to get out of here, not because I want to do this."

The silence was taut as he waited for her response. He expected some kind of lecture. Instead, she smiled, as if she'd seen right through him.

"I appreciate your honesty, Josh." Her voice was clear, but gentle. "And I promise I won't ask you to do anything you're not ready for. We'll take it one step at a time, and if there's something you don't want to do, you can say no."

It was such a simple statement, but it caught him off guard. He wasn't expecting to have 'no' offered as an option. He blinked, disarmed.

"Good." He looked away and back at the binder. "Then I guess we'll see what happens tomorrow."

He wasn't sure what unsettled him more: the idea of opening himself up to this process or the realization that, somewhere deep down, a small part of him might be curious about what he'd find out.

"Mel has done extensive prep work, so she knows exactly what doses to administer, and I know she's going to start slowly to help you adjust. All we ask of you right now is to keep an open mind and try not to resist the process. You don't agree right now, but this whole thing is for your benefit as well as ours. If you really commit to this, we think you'll be surprised by what you learn."

Thalia smiled, leaned forward, and clasped her hands on the table in front of her.

"Josh, we're so impressed with how you're handling all of this. We really didn't expect any of you to be so cooperative already, so, as far as we're concerned, you're already making incredible progress. We know what's coming would be a bit scary for anyone, but we'll do our best to help you with your fears. I'll be with you every step of the way and promise nothing bad will happen to you."

Her comment about not expecting any of them to be so

cooperative already had him wondering. "Have the others already started the program?"

"I'm sorry, Josh, you know I'm not at liberty to discuss that with you. If you don't have any other questions, I'll leave you in peace and see you bright and early tomorrow."

CHAPTER TWENTY-ONE

THALIA PRACTICALLY BOUNCED INTO THE ROOM FOR THE WEEKLY guide meeting. Her energy was infectious, but Mel noticed her friend pulling it back, toning down her excitement as she glanced at Monica and Cath. Despite Josh's surprising cooperation, Thalia was sensitive enough to recognize the struggles her colleagues were facing.

Mel filled her lungs to center herself as she led them through a brief meditation, inviting everyone to settle into stillness. When the moment felt right, she opened her eyes.

"Now, Monica, why don't you start us off?"

Monica's voice was steady as she gave her update. "I'm optimistic. William and I've made a lot of progress. He's still opposed to any drugs, but he's agreed to meditate with me and is open to learning breathwork techniques."

Thank God for your patience, girl, Mel thought. She had worried that William's skepticism and near-death death would stall the project indefinitely, but Monica's persistence was paying off. "I'm so glad you know how to play chess. You've really opened him up."

Mel turned her attention to Thalia. "Okay, your turn."

Thalia tried unsuccessfully to hide her enthusiasm. "I'll be starting the program with Josh tomorrow. Well, kind of. We'll do breathwork until Mel has weaned him off the PLH enough to do MDMA. We aren't telling him, though. We're hoping for a placebo effect, keeping him compliant without it."

Mel gave her an encouraging smile. She remembered the first time she met Thalia at the TAPS psychedelic therapy training program. She'd been one of the most promising students Mel had ever mentored—passionate, dedicated, and unafraid to challenge the status quo. Thalia's commitment ran deep, rooted in her underground practice.

Thalia's bravery had always been a source of admiration. She willingly risked everything for her beliefs, even when it meant operating illegally. Not to mention her courage to heal her own wounds from a religion that nearly broke her, she had fought for her freedom in ways most people couldn't even comprehend. Mel knew some scars still lingered in quiet corners of Thalia's mind, but she'd rebuilt herself, piece by piece. And now, she stood on her own terms, her work helping others find the strength she'd found in herself.

"Good luck tomorrow." Turning from Thalia to Cath, Mel softened her expression. "Cath, it's your turn. We know Matt is struggling. None of us thinks this is a reflection of your abilities. We're here to support you."

Cath looked like a tiny axolotl, trying to smile, but failing. "There's not much to report. He's depressed. He spends most of his time in bed, hardly eating. Just enough to keep us from force-feeding him. He's not open to trying anything, not even nature walks or meditation on the headset." She wiped her eyes.

Her emotions weren't a sign of weakness, but a testament to her deep empathy. Mel had seen it firsthand when she was training the younger woman to be a facilitator; when Cath had held space for her with a gentleness Mel had rarely experienced.

Cath's tears weren't just sadness; they were born of

compassion, of a love for the people she worked with. Mel knew how hard she'd fought to become the woman she was today. The foster care system had tried to break her spirit, bouncing her from home to home until she'd aged out at eighteen. Her parents, lost to a pain-killer addiction after a horrific car accident, had never gotten clean, never tried to reconnect with their daughter.

And yet, Mel thought, *look at her now.* Cath's resilience had always astounded her. They had been introduced by a mutual friend, Terry, who ran a holistic health center. Terry called Cath a "healer in the making," and Mel had seen why almost immediately. Despite her traumatic past—her own addiction that led her to prison after a drug-fueled car crash that took a life— Cath found a way to transform her pain. She'd told Mel that prison was where she realized she was responsible for everything in her life. Not necessarily at fault, but responsible. The distinction had taken her years to internalize, but once she did, she dedicated her life to helping others understand the difference.

Mel squeezed Cath's hand. "I'm going to increase Matt's PLH. If he still refuses to engage after that, the two of us will have a conversation with him."

Cath bit her lip as she fought back tears.

"You're doing everything right, Cath. He just needs more time. You'll find a way in. I believe in you."

As the women got up to leave for their separate rooms, Mel pulled Thalia aside. "Can I talk to you for a minute in private?"

"Sure, of course. What's up?"

Mel waited for the door to close behind Cath and Monica. "This is difficult for me, but I can't let it take up any more space in my head."

"Shit. What did I do?"

"I'm actually taking the slightly easier path by talking with you rather than Monica."

"Oh...kay?" Thalia drew out the word as if it were a question.

"There's no easy way to say this... I overheard your conversation the other day."

"Which convers... Oh. Oh shit." Thalia poured herself a glass of water and chugged it, as if it would wash away what had been said.

"I get it. We were all under incredible stress the day of the emergencies, but I want to make sure we're all on the same page and I'm not being undermined."

Thalia sucked on her lip and took another swallow.

Mel looked at the water glass and wished she could share a bottle of wine with Thalia. It would make the conversation easier.

"I thought we were all aligned on this." She tried to keep her voice from cracking. "We decided Ayahuasca wasn't right for the program. It's not just the group ceremonial aspect, which would be impossible until much, much, further down the line, when the men are already co-operating with each other, but we don't have a shaman. We don't have anyone who truly understands the medicine in the way it was intended to be used."

Thalia's eyes darted away. "I think Monica would disagree with you on that."

"It's about respect. I don't want us to fall into the trap of cultural appropriation. We can't co-opt something sacred just because it's convenient for us. I know Monica believes everyone should have access to it, and I know she has led ceremonies, but I'm not comfortable with her leading a group journey. I have to be able to make some unilateral decisions. We're not going to agree on everything."

"I hear you, Mel. I do." Thalia's tone carried a hint of defiance that Mel couldn't ignore. The words seemed like an agreement on the surface, but the way her friend avoided eye contact told a different story.

"I need us all rowing in the same direction, Thalia," Mel said, almost pleading. "The project can't succeed if we're pulling against each other."

Thalia nodded, her smile tight. "You have my full cooperation, Mel. But you're going to have to have this conversation with Monica at some point, too."

"I know you're right, but I don't have the strength for it right now. I just really need to know I can still count on you."

"Of course you can."

"Thank you. Get some sleep. You have a big day tomorrow."

When the door shut behind Thalia, Mel shook out her hands and arms, trying to release stiffness. She wanted to believe Thalia's assurances, but doubt burrowed deep into her psyche.

CHAPTER TWENTY-TWO

Wrapped in anxiety, Josh read the section in the binder about holotropic breathwork in its entirety. It seemed pretty straightforward, but he still didn't understand how it would get him into an altered state. If it did, he worried it might bring up some dark part of his past he didn't even remember.

Sleep refused to come. He sprawled across the bed, the soft, ambient music unable to mask the hum of his thoughts. He couldn't shut off his mind. How quickly he'd fallen in line had surprised him the most. Was it the PLH dulling his resistance, or the dawning realization that escape wasn't an option? Either way, the fight in him had quieted, leaving only resignation.

It occurred to him that he hadn't thought about missing Lisa or the boys and only entertained passing thoughts about Omnicia. He hadn't once considered how much money they'd be spending trying to find him. He found his lack of reflection on these subjects quite disturbing; what did it say about him?

As the blinds cracked open with the first light, Josh told Shannon he'd make his own breakfast. The thought of small talk made him itch.

He shoveled yogurt and blueberries into his mouth; the

sweetness lost on him as he observed Thalia arrange mats and blankets by the pool. The sight sent a shockwave of nerves through him. He gripped the counter, steadying himself against a tremor.

The dishes clattered as he attacked them, scrubbing them harder than necessary, as if scrubbing away his own fear. When the sink was empty and spotless, he grabbed a pen and notebook, squeezing the pen so tightly it left an imprint on his palm.

Stepping outside, he found the morning air crisp. His heart hammered in his chest. Thalia looked up, her face bright with anticipation, eyes gleaming like she was about to share a secret that would change his life. He couldn't return her smile.

"Good morning. Mel told me you didn't sleep well, so I won't be concerned if you fall asleep in our session today. How are you doing with things?" Thalia looked like a messenger of God as she spoke, the sunlight at her back creating a halo around her.

He hated that they knew everything about him. "I'm tired and cranky and don't want to be here."

"I understand. For the first time, we're going to take things slowly. A true holotropic session is usually several hours to an all-day event."

Thalia finished setting up the space and pushed play on her music device.

"We're going to start with an easy yoga Nidra session and a quick body scan meditation to get you relaxed. Then we'll break for lunch, and you can take a nap or go for a swim if you want. This afternoon, we'll do a short breathwork session. So let's get started."

Thalia's electric energy radiated from her. With a voice matching her angelic appearance, she guided him through a series of postures designed to open his body and quiet his mind. They began with "broken wing," where he extended one arm out to the side, stretching his chest and shoulder. Next, they moved into "pigeon," his leg folded beneath him, creating a deep hip opening.

Finally, she led him into *"savasana,"* corpse pose, where he lay flat on his back. Her voice, now a soothing whisper, painted a soundscape of relaxation. He closed his eyes, letting tension melt away with each exhale.

"Great work, Josh. Now we'll transition into the body scan."

Thalia passed an eye mask to him. The smooth fabric was cool against his skin as he slipped it over his eyes. Returning to his supine position on the mat, he surrendered to the darkness.

"Okay, I want you to close your eyes and focus on your breath—deep breath in through your nose, and a long exhalation out through your mouth. As you keep breathing deeply, in through the nose and out through the mouth, I want you to notice your belly expanding on the inhale and relaxing your whole body on the exhale."

Breathing in sync with him, she offered instructions. It was as if she recognized her own need to surrender to the moment and relax.

"If you're comfortable with it, on the exhale, you can make an 'aaahhh' sound. A few more of these breaths and we'll start the body scan. Each time I mention a body part, I want you to bring all your attention to it and imagine you're breathing in and out from that place. I also want you to imagine you're being bathed in golden, nurturing light, and with every exhale, stress and fear are leaving your body."

She guided him through his entire body, from his toes to his third eye in the middle of his forehead.

"Now, I want you to draw in energy through your feet and up through your body to the top of your head with every inhale. And with every exhale, the energy moves in the opposite direction from the top of your head to the soles of your feet, cleansing everything that isn't needed in a wave through your body."

The notion of breathing in and out from different body parts was entirely foreign to him. Unlike the gentle rhythm of deep breathing, this instruction conjured images of invisible currents and internal landscapes, concepts his mind struggled to grasp.

He tried. He genuinely did. He closed his eyes tighter, straining to sense this nebulous "energy" pooling at his feet. He imagined himself coaxing it upwards, picturing it as a warm, gentle current flowing through his legs and torso. But it was like chasing wisps of smoke, elusive and impossible to grasp. His mind, accustomed to the logic and analysis of the business world, balked at the idea of manipulating something so intangible.

Frustration clouded his thoughts. Was he failing? Was there something inherently wrong with him that prevented him from connecting to his body? But then, a faint sensation emerged. A tingle, almost like pins and needles, crept up his legs. He held his breath for a second, afraid to disrupt it. Was this it? Was this the elusive "energy" Thalia spoke of? He continued his deep breaths, focusing on the faint warmth, allowing it to spread inch by inch through his body.

"Good. Keep the wave going as we move into the meditation. It isn't uncommon for people to fall asleep. It's totally okay. You'll wake up refreshed and energized."

She began the meditation by asking him to imagine he was standing at the top of a cliff, overlooking a beach and the ocean. A wooden staircase led down to the sand, and she wanted him to envision walking down to her count. She counted backward. Slowly. From twelve to one. Once at the sand, she asked him to pay attention to the sound of the water and the gentle salt breeze on his face.

"Take a moment to enjoy the beauty of nature. Maybe there are some birds, or maybe there are a few fish jumping. Notice. Are there clouds in the sky? Just notice."

He had never tried visualization. Despite hearing about its benefits for athletes and performers, he didn't think it would do anything for him personally.

"Notice if there's anyone else with you on the beach. Just notice."

To his amazement, Nathan and Brock, his sons, came into view. As they approached, they smiled, nodded, and continued walking right past him. Thalia's voice, a steady guide, said he only needed to notice; he didn't need to do anything.

The meditation ended with him climbing back up the stairs. Ten, eleven, twelve, and finally back to the pool where his body lay.

"When you're ready, you can take off your eye mask and write down anything you felt or saw."

He reached for his pen. Accustomed to jotting quick notes and leaving his admin to craft them into full sentences, he now found himself scribbling furiously, the pen darting across the page in a race to keep up with the flood of thoughts spilling out of him. After what seemed like ages, he stopped and realized he had written two pages.

"That seemed to go well. How are you feeling now?" Thalia asked.

"Surprisingly surprised. And less tired and cranky."

"That's wonderful! Is there anything you'd like to talk about? Do you have any questions? This is a judgment-free zone. I'm here to help you process what comes up, that's all. You don't have to tell me anything if you don't want to, but you might progress faster if you do."

"No, I don't think so."

He wouldn't share these thoughts with anyone.

"So, are you a witch or something?"

Thalia nearly spit out her lunch and burst into laughter.

"What would make you say something like that, Josh?"

"I'm just wondering how you knew I'd see people on the beach at the exact moment I saw people?"

"Oh, good. So you did see someone or someones. Don't worry, I don't have magical powers. You only saw them because I planted the seed in your brain. The power of suggestion is very strong in guided meditations. In the breathwork session, there'll be no suggestions, so you'll go wherever your mind thinks it should go. We've reason to believe the PLH is really going to help you let go and go deep."

"So if you aren't guiding me, what exactly is going to happen?"

She walked him through the entire process, but her words drifted, muffled and distorted. His nerves were getting the better of him.

"I won't be saying much, just reminding you how to breathe. The music will be your guide." Her voice was so full of confidence it irritated him. "We'll start with light, rhythmic drumming, gradually building in intensity as your breathing deepens. The rhythm will help push you into an altered state. Then once you're there, the music will shift into something softer, more heart-opening. At the end, it'll transition into a meditative flow to bring you back."

He stared out at the pool. How could music have that much power over him? He kept his face neutral, fighting the urge to cross his arms like a petulant child.

"You might get sensations in your body, like tingling and numbness. It's normal to have the urge to move or have emotional outbursts. Whatever comes up, don't resist it. Let it flow through you."

He forced a laugh, the sound flat, even to his own ears. "Well, that doesn't sound too difficult. I think I can manage to breathe for an hour or two."

"I'm sure you'll be surprised by it. I'm going to go do my own meditation now. I'll see you in a couple of hours."

As soon as she left, Josh dove headfirst into the pool, a deluge of restless energy propelling him forward. The moment his body cut through the surface, the rigidness in his shoulders loosened. He pushed off the edge, kicking hard, his strokes powerful and fast. Counting laps proved impossible, though. His mind slipped into its own current, drifting away from the pool and back to thoughts of Brock and Nathan.

He wasn't the kind of guy who bought into this woo-woo, subconscious nonsense, but he couldn't ignore the nagging suspicion his mind was trying to dig up something he wasn't ready to face. Guilt maybe? For not missing them as much as he thought he should? And why *wasn't* he missing them?

He worried about his sons, but for different reasons. Nathan, the carefree golden child, had inherited the fearless, outgoing spirit of their mother, Pam. He lived for adventure, chasing big waves across the globe, with little interest in the business degree he was supposedly pursuing. Brock, on the other hand, was a different beast entirely. He was uptight and driven, a disciplined overachiever who excelled academically but never seemed to enjoy himself.

He imagined Nathan coasting through life, never holding a steady job, relying on his trust fund forever. Brock would undoubtedly have a brilliant career, but would likely be alone, isolated by his own ambition. The realization stung. But what could he do now? He gave them everything they wanted, didn't he? Whatever they asked for, they got.

Pam always fought with him about how he spoiled the boys. Not that it was all they fought about. She had initiated the divorce, timing it to coincide with Omnicia's IPO—a move he'd taken as calculated, proof she resented that the company had always come first. And she wasn't wrong. It always did, always. The bitterness between them only deepened when he moved on to Lisa. Pam had accused him of cheating long before their marriage ended. She'd been right about that, too.

Cutting through the water with a final stroke, he surfaced for air. He had no idea how long he'd been swimming. Lost in the churn of his own mind, he was unaware of Thalia standing at the side of the pool.

"Time to get back to work." She winked as she held out a towel for him.

He dried off and pulled on fresh clothes. Each step toward Thalia was slow, like climbing Everest. She waited with a serene smile, but the butterflies in his gut flapped wildly, more like vampire bats than anything delicate. He couldn't let her see his nervousness, so instead he slipped on the mask of the aloof businessman, untouched by fear, that he had worn for years.

He crossed his arms, half hoping the session would fail spectacularly so he'd have a reason to write it off as bullshit, but another part clung to the possibility of finding something, anything, that might help him get home.

Trying to delay the inevitable, he fussed with the blankets and pillows, shifting them over and over. Thalia's gentle nudge to lie down carried the weight of a command. With a frustrated huff, he finally settled, pulling the eye mask down to shut her out. The music started, and his hand moved to his stomach as she guided him into circular breathing, each inhale and exhale melting into one another without a pause.

"Match the length of your inhale to your exhale." Her voice was smooth. "You might feel like you're about to hyperventilate. That's normal. Just keep going."

He did as she asked, though his breath came jagged at first, scraping against the inside of his chest. Then the rhythm picked up, and so did his breath. Faster, deeper, until pins and needles danced along his fingers. His hands cramped, curling themselves into claws.

In a sudden burst, he erupted into uncontrollable laughter, catching both himself and Thalia off guard. He sat up abruptly, tearing the eye mask off his face.

"I've no idea what that was about," he said, looking at Thalia questioningly.

"You don't have to understand what it's about. Let whatever happens, happen. You're doing really well."

She restarted the music as he messed with the pillows again and lay back down. This time, his muscles relaxed more quickly, and the strange sensations in his body were less uncomfortable. He followed her instructions to deepen and quicken his breaths. And then ... nothing.

He had no idea how long he spent engulfed in nothingness; he couldn't feel his body, couldn't hear anything. Two hours later, or maybe it was two minutes, Thalia's voice directed him to slow his breathing and to take a brief pause at the top and bottom of each breath. Awareness and thoughts oozed back like tar. His hand instinctively reached for his pounding heart, a silent thanks for the return of his senses. He started wiggling his fingers and toes, then proceeded to lift his arms and legs one at a time, releasing a long, drawn-out sigh as he removed the eye mask.

After a few blinks to adjust to the brightness, he reached for his notebook. The pen rested oddly in his hand, almost weightless, and seemed to move on its own. He didn't think. He just wrote. His fingers were guided by something beyond conscious thought. Words spilled onto the page, his pen scratching furiously across the paper with a life of its own.

When he finally paused, he stared at the page, bewildered. The writing, not his: letters wide and long, the strokes smooth and continuous. He couldn't remember forming those sentences, and yet there they were, spilling out in a scrawl he didn't recognize as his own.

Thalia gently broke the silence after a few minutes of him staring. "Welcome back, Josh. How are you doing?"

"Um, I'm not too sure. I don't understand what happened or who wrote all of this," he said, holding the notebook up for her to see.

"That's a valid answer. There's no way to prepare someone for this, as everyone's experience is different. And each time you do it, it'll be different. Do you want to talk about anything?"

"No, I don't think I do. I think I want to be alone now, please."

Thalia left him sitting by the pool, staring at the pages that looked like a message from another world. A chill crept up his spine as he read one line over and over, something he couldn't remember writing, but that stared back at him with an eerie clarity:

"What have I done?"

CHAPTER TWENTY-THREE

Shannon's voice pulled Josh out of a deep, dream-filled sleep. He blinked, disoriented. He hadn't made it to the bedroom after his session with Thalia, and it took a minute to realize he was on the couch.

A plate of sea bass with mango salsa waited for him on the table, the aroma teasing his senses awake. He ate on autopilot, hardly tasting what he swallowed, his mind turning back to his notebook. He flipped it open, expecting the familiar sharp, strokes of his own handwriting.

His fingers traced the round, looping letters, the ink smudged from his left hand. No jagged edges. It was his, but it wasn't. The script floated in erratic patterns, lines ignored, words bleeding into each other, unanchored by punctuation.

He scanned the first line, then the next. He remembered the act of writing, the frantic movement of his pen across the page, but the writing itself was like someone else had borrowed his hand.

After seeing his sons on the beach, Josh had written what could only be described as an unhinged apology to them.

I let you down I wasn't there not the way you needed me to be I am so sorry thought I was doing the right thing chasing a future for all of us forgot what truly mattered lost in the desert of my ambition I do love you both of you fierce and bright a love that burns a love I know I haven't shown enough of proud of who you are like your mom strong here I stand a failure of a father ashamed so ashamed ashamed I missed so much the comfort I couldn't give you you and your mother deserved so much more a love that held you close a support that never faltered if I could tell you I love you now I would shout it let the whole world know I would hold you tight both of you the past is dust and I must rise to earn you back to earn the love I carelessly threw away I am so sorry sorry for the pain I caused you the guilt is unbearable it will fuel me to be better to be who you deserve can you forgive me what have I done

Josh wept. He hadn't seen either of his children for over two months, though they were both out of school for the summer. The last time he was with Nathan, they'd gotten into an argument that ended with Josh calling him a worthless piece of shit. He couldn't remember the last interaction he had with Brock.

He leaned back in his chair, staring blankly at the blurred pages, his mind drifting to the past. The sea bass turned bitter in his mouth, soured by a flood of memories. Memories that should have been sweet. Memories of family.

Pam had been there from the start, through every long night and missed holiday. She'd shouldered the brunt of his ambitions, absorbing his fury when things fell apart and offering her steady patience when the weight of the world bore down on him. He pictured her sitting across from him in their tiny first apartment, nodding along as he ranted about the idiots at work, fingers drumming on her mug, eyes alert, absorbing every word.

She'd been his confidante, his sounding board, his partner in a way he'd never acknowledged. Some of Omnicia's most innovative projects had stemmed from her ideas. Ideas he'd claimed as his own without hesitation. He had rewarded her with a dismissal of her contributions, an unspoken betrayal that now sat heavy on his conscience.

Then there was Lisa. He remembered the first time he'd seen her: stunning, poised, like a trophy promising a new kind of validation. The thrill of superficial attraction had masked the emptiness beneath it. Lisa was a polished ornament on his arm, eager to reap the benefits of his success, but uninterested in the man behind the empire. He knew what she was—vapid, a beautiful shell. And he didn't love her. Not really. She was an accessory, a status symbol he paraded around like a prized possession. The unspoken agreement between them was transactional at best: she loved the lifestyle he afforded her, and he tolerated the unfulfilling relationship as a distraction from everything he'd left unresolved with Pam.

He pushed the plate away, the food now tasteless. A realization seeped into the corners of his mind: He had traded something real for something empty, and for what? To feed an ego as shallow as his relationship with Lisa.

Through his tears, he had an overwhelming urge to call his sister Marne. She was the only person left in the world he trusted with the real Josh.

She was three years younger than he was. After high school, she left to join an off-grid community in Arizona, where she lived with a group that her parents were convinced was a cult. They couldn't fathom why anyone would willingly choose to live in tents, bathe in rivers, and grow their own food. Marne had always been the rebel. She had rejected the world's standards, while Josh had been laser-focused on conquering them. Their lives couldn't have diverged more sharply, yet they shared a bond that transcended their differences.

He never wanted her to change. Her indifference to money and status was something he envied, a trait that let her see the heart of a person rather than their wallet. Around her, the facades he carried in his world of power and wealth fell away, leaving him exposed. He knew without a doubt that if he lost everything, she'd still love him.

The suspicion that she somehow had a hand in this program still lingered. It felt like something she'd want for him—the ultimate intervention, wrapped in her unshakable belief he could use a deeper kind of healing. He had avoided therapy his whole life, dismissing it as something other people needed. Now he was beginning to question that certainty.

CHAPTER TWENTY-FOUR

Scenes of his parents and Marne filled Josh's restless dreams. He was absent, though, like watching a movie. Then Thalia and daylight ripped him from the shadows of his mind.

"Good morning, Josh. I'll be there in an hour to start our session."

He pushed himself out of bed, almost grateful to have something tangible to focus on. He moved through his morning routine on autopilot, stuffing granola into his mouth without tasting it. His mind spun around the edges of what happened yesterday, replaying fragments of the session he couldn't quite grasp. *How do you describe nothing?*

"Are you ready for me, Josh?" Thalia's voice broke through his reverie.

"Ready as I'll ever be." He wasn't sure if he meant it.

A thin veneer of poise covered him, but beneath the surface, he kicked frantically like a duck. He had the urge to tell her about it, to get it out before it swallowed him whole.

His fingers worked the hem of his shirt, rubbing the stitching, before opening his notebook. He couldn't look at her as he spoke. "I...I looked at what I wrote yesterday. It's pretty clear I'm a shitty father. A shitty husband. Brother. Son. It's all right here." He tapped the page with a shaking hand. "I don't really understand what happened yesterday, but I'm sure you do."

Forcing his eyes up, he expected judgment. Instead, he found softness.

"Thank you, Josh. Thank you for trusting me with this. I know it wasn't easy. And, for what it's worth, the fact you went so deep on your first try is incredible. It takes most people weeks, even months, to reach that level of release. And you're willing to talk about it now, too? That's huge."

Oddly, he felt relief. His fingers stilled, no longer tugging at his shirt.

"I think you might be ready for a session with MDMA, but I'll have to speak to Mel about it. Your PLH will have to be reduced in preparation, and I don't know if she'll agree to that just yet. She might want you to continue with breathwork for a while so you can get used to expanded states before adding another variable. But I believe if family and close personal relationships are what's coming up for you, MDMA is perfectly suited for that type of work."

The conversation hadn't gone how Josh had imagined. He had half expected her to make him lie down on the couch and tell him yes, he's a shit person, and this is how he needs to fix himself. He thought she'd probe him about his childhood to figure out what trauma had occurred to make him into the monster she surely thought he was.

They set up the mats and blankets in silence.

"Okay, I think we're ready. It'll be like yesterday. Start with yoga and a body scan." Thalia's voice held a tempered authority.

It wasn't lost on him that she was easing him into this, like coaxing a skittish animal closer, not wanting to spook him before the deeper work began. He followed her lead, sinking into now familiar stretches, muscles lengthening and releasing knots. For a moment, the sensation of his body moving moored him to the present.

But the vampire bats were back. Was it excitement? Fear? He couldn't tell. All he knew was he craved that elusive sense of nothingness he'd tasted the day before, the fleeting escape from the endless churn of his thoughts.

Thalia seemed to sense his turmoil, her voice cutting through his inner chaos. "I want to remind you that no two experiences will ever be the same. Today, I want you to allow whatever happens to happen. I know I keep saying that, but I can't stress it enough. Don't fight any feelings and don't try to figure out what anything means while you're in it."

The music began softly, its rhythm syncing with the beat of his heart. He closed his eyes and focused on her voice, following the rhythm she set, breathing deeper and faster. He couldn't get enough oxygen, as he tried to force air into a space that had grown too small. Fighting the urge to gulp, Thalia's prompts kept him steady, guiding him through the mounting urge to panic.

Soon, a tingling wave spread up his limbs. It was a buzzing, electric sensation that demanded movement. His fingers twitched, then his arms. Without thinking, he started shaking them out, like he was shaking free from invisible chains. The agitation spread, rippling down through his legs until his entire body trembled, an unstoppable vibration as though something trapped inside him was desperate to get out.

And then it broke free.

A scream tore from his throat, raw and primal, echoing off the mirrored walls. It wasn't the controlled yell of a man venting frustration. It was the howl of a wounded animal. Tears poured down his face. Before arriving here, he hadn't allowed himself this kind of release. It stunned him.

He tried to pull himself back together, but it was too late. This wasn't a version of himself he recognized anymore. This wasn't the confident, ruthless CEO who dominated boardrooms and shut down competitors with a smirk. The armor he'd spent years building, the facade of power and invincibility, had cracked, exposing a soft, vulnerable core he had hidden even from himself. He lay there, convulsing with sobs, as if he were a child.

Thalia's peaceful energy was a beacon in the chaos. But he couldn't look at her. He wasn't ready to confront what she might see.

"Allow it, Josh, don't fight it," he heard her say, just loud enough for him to hear.

His sobbing subsided, and his breathing became more rhythmic as he followed her gentle reminders. She guided him back to a familiar physical state, with his mind returning to the present like a tethered balloon.

"I want you to focus on your heartbeat now, Josh. I want you to see if you can get it to slow down."

He hadn't realized his heart rate had spiked, but now that she mentioned it, he became aware of it thumping throughout his body.

"Open your eyes whenever you're ready," she instructed.

He pulled the eye mask up. Sunlight stabbed through his vision. Embarrassment lodged inside him as he wiped his cheeks with the back of his hand. He wanted her gone. Regaining his composure felt impossible with her watching.

She stayed quiet, watching him with an expression he couldn't read.

"Josh." He almost didn't hear her when she finally spoke. "Would you like to talk about anything, or would you prefer some space?"

"Space." The one word was a struggle.

She nodded, her face softening in a way that made his eyes wet again. "I understand. I'll leave you alone, but if you feel like talking, you know how to reach me." She hesitated for a second, as if considering saying something more, but then rose from her mat and walked away.

The reality of what happened slammed into him like a freight train as he dropped his head into his hands, fingers gripping his scalp. He'd lost control. Completely. He wasn't sure he could reconcile the screaming, sobbing man with the one who'd built Omnicia, who made million-dollar decisions before his morning coffee, who commanded rooms full of executives without breaking a sweat.

He grabbed the pen and notebook without thinking, scribbling frantically again, with no sense of time. Here, with no empire to rule, the truth was slipping out. And what scared him most was the tiny, traitorous part of him that felt relieved.

CHAPTER TWENTY-FIVE

Josh sat on the mat long after Thalia left. He had no words for what had happened during the session. He recalled no concrete thoughts. Just raw emotion. The kind that bypassed the brain and tore through his heart. It was completely different from the nothingness the day before.

He forced himself up, making his way to the shower by way of the pool, stopping to stare down at his reflection. He wasn't sure he recognized the man looking back at him.

Hot water pounded his back, but instead of clarity, it only amplified the disorientation. He scrubbed his skin harder, trying to wash away the remnants of whatever had clawed its way out of him. What the hell was happening to him? He wasn't the type to cry, let alone scream, yet something buried deep had erupted. And now, in its aftermath, a barren emptiness remained. Cleaned out, but not cleansed.

Maybe he could relieve the discomfort of not knowing himself with something familiar. He slipped on the headset, hoping for a distraction. The main screen blinked to life, and his eyes settled on a new icon labeled "Josh".

He navigated to the sub-menu. Two options appeared:

"Pottery" and "X-Rated". The absurd juxtaposition made him bark out a laugh. He laughed again when he realized he was more curious about making a clay pot than about diving into a virtual sex program.

A fully equipped studio materialized around him, detailed and tactile. Towering shelves crammed with glazed vases and bowls; a supply wall packed with tools like throwing sticks; and two massive windows that framed a tranquil lake edged by dense pines. At the room's center, a worktable complete with a wheel and sink.

In one smooth, satisfying motion, he cut a chunk of clay off the brick he had hefted onto the table. He slammed the slab down on the workbench, relishing the impact, a visceral release of stress. The sound of clay meeting wood cut through his thoughts, leaving only the next motion.

He settled at the wheel, dipping his hands into a bowl of water. As he began to shape the clay, his mind melted into the flow of the moment. He couldn't remember the last time he had been so absorbed in something purely for the sake of doing it.

Ideas sparked as the wheel spun. This tech wasn't just a toy. It was a revolution waiting to happen. He envisioned classrooms with students sculpting, painting, or dissecting without material costs. Med schools offering realistic practice sessions without risk. And the business implications for Omnicia? He imagined the zeros in his bank statement lining up.

The sensation of wet clay slipping through his fingers transported him back to his college days, a time when he'd finally found a place where he belonged. It was heaven compared to high school. In public school, he was overweight and seething with anger. He lashed out at everyone, whether they deserved it or not. He was the bully who shoved weaker kids into lockers, the loudmouth who disrupted classes so he could watch the teachers squirm. Despite the chaos he caused, his sharp mind carried him through. Nobody understood him, least of all himself.

It wasn't until his parents' divorce in his final year that something cracked open inside him. His father, an abusive alcoholic, had been the source of most of Josh's rage. He'd seen his dad put his mom in the hospital more than once. The image of her black-and-blue face was burned into his memory forever. His mother, though terrified, had always tried to protect him, shielding her children even when it meant taking the brunt of the abuse. When his father left, lured away by another woman, the household let out a collective sigh of relief.

Freed from the fear that gripped his home, he found himself channeling his anger into workouts instead of his classmates. His body changed. The layers of fat melted away, and muscles carved new shapes beneath his skin. By the time he entered college, the kid who'd once used his weight as a shield was now flaunting a six-pack and collecting phone numbers like trophies. He loved the newfound attention, but more importantly, he found a space where his intellect was valued. For the first time, his actions aligned with the vision of the person he wanted to become.

Pam came into his life during his sophomore year. From the start, she struck him as different. He'd never known anyone so genuinely kind. He used to tease her about it, saying she was too nice for her own good. But her niceness wasn't naivety; it came from a well of empathy shaped by her own difficult childhood and her volunteer work at a women's shelter. When Josh opened up about his father, she didn't flinch or judge. She simply listened, holding his pain with a quiet strength that made him feel seen, maybe for the first time in his life.

They eloped in their final year, a spur-of-the-moment decision they knew was right. They flew to Mexico over winter break and got married on a quiet stretch of beach in Todos Santos. No friends, no family. Just the two of them and the sound of the ocean. Pam got pregnant not long after, giving birth to Brock while he juggled his first year of business school.

Their tiny one-bedroom apartment was always a mess, toys

strewn everywhere, textbooks piled on the kitchen table. But they were happy, blissfully so. Pam, despite her family's wealth, wanted nothing from them. She craved a life built on love and struggle, not cushioned by money.

After earning his MBA and Nathan's birth, Josh took a job at his father-in-law's company. Jack had built the aerospace business from the ground up, turning it into one of the biggest parts suppliers in the world. Josh admired his savvy, but had no respect for the man otherwise. Jack was domineering, belittled his employees, and was infamous for his temper. Holes in the office walls told stories of more than one outburst.

Josh soaked up everything he could about running a global enterprise while secretly mapping out his own vision for Omnicia. The moment he'd saved enough for his family to survive for two years, he handed Jack his resignation.

Most people thought he was reckless for walking away from a business he was poised to inherit. But Pam wasn't most people. Her smile that day was pure relief. She trusted his drive and intelligence to turn his dreams into reality.

The early years were a blur of sleepless nights and relentless hustle. The boys were little and wanted their dad around, but he hardly had enough time to eat, let alone play. Sixteen-hour workdays were the norm, weekends indistinguishable from weekdays. Pam missed him, but she understood. At night, lying in bed, they'd whisper about the future where Omnicia ran itself, and the four of them could jet-set about on luxury vacations.

His hands were still working the clay, the wet slip gliding through his fingers like the past sliding away. His mind wandered to the year the company went public. It was the moment everything fell apart. Pam filed for divorce. He hadn't seen it coming; he was too blinded by the adrenaline of launching his company onto the global stage and his affair with Lisa.

The years that followed Omnicia's meteoric rise brought a gradual fading of his friendships. One by one, his college buddies stopped calling, unable to compete with his single-minded focus on the company. He hadn't realized how isolated he'd become until this quiet moment here, in this bizarre sanctuary, forced him to confront it.

The vase he was shaping wobbled before collapsing in on itself. He stared at the crumpled clay. It was laughable that even here, in a virtual world, he couldn't escape the consequences of his choices.

He took the ruined piece as a cue to end the session, switching off the headset and pulling it from his face. He instinctively glanced down, expecting his hands to be slick with wet clay, needing a good rinse. But they were dry. Spotless. Would this technology ever stop blowing his mind? Next time, he'd make a point to explore what the developers had created for him under the "X-rated" icon.

CHAPTER TWENTY-SIX

Monica arrived at William's quarters with a smile plastered to her face, but beneath it, nerves bubbled like a shaken soda can. She knew William was a seasoned meditator, an expert by any measure. What could she, with her eclectic mix of training and unconventional practices, possibly offer this man? Still, she couldn't let him see her doubts.

"Good morning, William. How are you today?" She dug around in her overstuffed Ikea bag, trying to hide her jitters.

He looked up from the table, his expression somewhere far away, his thoughts on Maria, no doubt. "Hello. I am fine, thank you."

She didn't believe him. His eyes were rimmed with redness, the kind that comes from crying when you think no one's watching. Shannon's beautifully prepared breakfast plate lay untouched.

"I probably brought too much stuff," she said with a self-conscious laugh, swinging the heavy bag off her shoulder. "But I want you to be as comfortable as possible. I can get everything set up if you need to do anything before we get started."

"Thank you, yes, I will be just a moment." His politeness was a thin veil over the storm that must be raging inside.

As he retreated, she got to work, but her mind wouldn't shut up. Was she good enough for this? She unfolded a thick, woven mat with a satisfying whoosh, the geometric patterns catching the morning sun. She layered the mat with a bright yellow blanket. It was a piece she'd had since the commune, something comforting and familiar. Maybe it would offer him a sliver of that comfort, too. The pillow she placed at the top was soft and perfectly worn in. Creating a space that felt inviting and safe was her top priority.

Next to the mat, she set out two embroidered meditation cushions. In between them, she arranged a circle of smooth, polished stones. They were grounding tools, but also talismans of sorts. She'd collected them over the years, each one imbued with memories of places she'd traveled, Ayahuasca ceremonies she'd led, and people she'd helped. Maybe they'd lend their energy to William, too.

She looked up as he made his way back to her. His steps seemed heavier than before, like the weight of his grief had settled deeper into his bones. She patted the pillow across from her, forcing another smile.

"I know you usually meditate with mantras, so this is going to be quite different from what you're used to. We're going to start with a breathing exercise and then go straight into the guided meditation. After the breathing, you're welcome to continue sitting, or you can lie down if you're more comfortable. The entire session will take about an hour and a half. Do you have any questions?"

"No. I will do as you say."

"Okay, here we go," Monica said as she started the music. "I want you to squeeze the muscles in your perineum and slowly breathe in through your nose as you squeeze the muscles in each of your centers as your breath moves up through your body."

William raised an eyebrow, but followed her instructions. His posture, upright and rigid, was like a soldier bracing for battle.

"As you bring your breath up through your body, I want you to focus. Gather all of your energy up with the breath until all your air and energy is at the top of your head, then hold it…hold it."

She surveyed his face, noting a slight twitch as his forehead furrowed in concentration. His chest expanded as he filled his lungs. She could almost see the current of energy he was visualizing and almost feel the static electricity building in his body.

"Now, exhale forcefully through your mouth. Let it all go and relax. Just relax."

The exhale left his lips in a gust, a release that almost looked painful. She repeated the exercise twenty times, attuned to the subtle shifts in his energy. Each inhale seemed to draw him further inward, and each exhale unraveled his apprehension.

"Would you like to lie down before the meditation starts?" The tremor in his hands was noticeable.

"No. I will remain seated."

Shifting gears, she guided him into the meditation, her voice a low murmur. She asked him to imagine he was floating up. Up past the trees, up past the clouds, up past the Earth. Looking down at the planet shrinking into nothing as he continued to float away, moving further and further into darkness.

The change in his breathing came first, growing so faint it was as if he were no longer connected to his physical form. His shoulders no longer stiff, but slumped. His face smoothed out, the lines of distress and grief dissolving as he drifted deeper into the meditation. She knew he was in the void that held everything and nothing at the same time.

It always amazed her, this part. The surrender, the leap into the unknown. She knew his energy had shifted the moment he let go. It wasn't easy to reach this state, especially for someone who was being held against his will. But here he was, unmoored.

She took her time bringing him back, aware of how disorienting it could be to return after touching that place. Softening her voice further, she coaxed him gently, grounding him with each word, until she saw movement behind his eyelids. He blinked as his unfocused gaze drifted out over the endless Saskatchewan prairie.

Careful not to intrude, she waited. Only when his eyes seemed to sharpen did she speak. "How was that?"

He didn't respond right away. With glistening eyes, he took a deep, shuddering breath, his chest heaving as though he'd resurfaced after being underwater.

"I would like to speak with you and Mel."

Surprised by the request, she didn't know if she should be hopeful or worried. She touched her bracelet and asked Mel to join them. As the trio settled around the outdoor table, William spoke.

"You women know what you are doing. I have never experienced this. Never have I had such a clear meditation before. I have a message I would like to share with you."

Monica and Mel looked at each other in amazement as William shared his vision. He spoke of humanity—all people, past, present, and future—being surrounded, every day, by the source of all things. He said the source was available to every person equally, but most people were so caught up in daily living that they didn't know it was there.

"When I was in my meditation, the noise of life was gone. Everyone was gone. I was alone in the source, and I could feel my connection to it, and I could access its power."

His vision had explained to him that altered states were like fire in the process of human evolution. When the first humans harnessed it, most were afraid. The ones who remained afraid died out as the ones who controlled it multiplied and evolved. William drew a parallel with meditation and psychedelics.

"Those who learn to reach the source will grow, and those who stay afraid will die out as humanity changes. I know there are answers there, in the blackness. I think I understand why you want us to take the drugs, but I want to offer another way. At least for me, because I have much practice with meditation."

The women sat stunned.

"I want to ask that you make an exception. I am an old man. While I can see the potential of drugs, I do not want them for myself. I have to be clear. I am afraid. I will cooperate with you as I can, if you will please spare me from the drugs. I think you would agree...I can make progress without them."

Mel dipped her chin in a series of small, thoughtful bobs. Her eyes cast downward as she contemplated what William had asked.

"William, I can't tell you how grateful I am you asked to speak with me. I know I speak for Monica as well when I say we're both in awe and quite surprised by your experience. If you could please be patient with me while I give your request the consideration it deserves. Please keep working with Monica, and I'll have an answer for you in a couple of days."

CHAPTER TWENTY-SEVEN

"Hey Shannon, I was wondering if you might help me cook dinner for Mel and Thalia tonight?" Josh rifled through his fridge, looking for a snack as he contacted Shannon. "Of course, you're welcome too if you have time, but you probably have to help the others with dinner, so I don't want you to feel pressure to stay."

"That's a wonderful idea, Josh," Shannon replied. "I'd be happy to cook with you. I'll let Thalia and Mel know the plan."

"Great, see you soon." He finally found the pineapple spears he was searching for.

He sat at the dining table, re-reading his scribbles. He still couldn't understand what he had written after the breathwork session; *the badger and the squirrel are not friends, but the squirrel needs the badger, but does the badger need the squirrel? The badger and the wolf are not friends. Am I the badger or am I the wolf? Maybe I'm the squirrel? Who's the wolf?*

Shannon's voice startled him. "Hi Josh, Thalia, and Mel want to cook with us too, so we'll be there in just a few minutes."

"Oh, okay, sounds great."

He darted into his bedroom. Flinging the closet open, he sifted through hangers in search of something that struck the right balance between casual and calculated. He needed an outfit to make him look laid back, but still showed his physique.

He settled on a fitted navy t-shirt that clung to his biceps and a pair of tailored jeans that accentuated his prized possession. Staring at the mirror, he scrutinized his reflection, willing his face into a mask of indifference. Thalia and Mel each exerted a compelling force on him. Flirting with both of them wouldn't be difficult. Jealousy, a powerful tool.

The truth was, total cooperation still scared him. He needed to keep his escape options open, just in case. If there was one thing he knew how to do, it was play people against each other. He'd seen the way both their faces blushed when speaking with him.

When he opened the door, his confidence wavered. Shannon was in front, her presence was solid and maternal. She gave him a small smile, but it didn't register. His attention was on Thalia and Mel.

Thalia was stunning. Her asymmetric dress clung to all the right places, effortless and bold. The stretchy, garnet fabric hugged her curves, moving with her like a second skin. Her eyes sparkled with playful challenge.

Mel, on the other hand, had chosen a long, flowing, floral print skirt with a slit that allowed her legs to peek out. Her emerald blouse, with its deep V-neck, showcased the graceful lines of her collarbone. A breezy confidence seemed to suggest she wasn't trying at all. Her face was bare, no makeup, but she didn't need any since her skin glowed naturally.

Josh swallowed, hoping no alarms would go off as Shannon pushed her way into his apartment.

"Since you're a beginner," she said as she unpacked ingredients onto the counter, "we'll whip up something simple. But trust me, it's going to blow your mind."

The kitchen buzzed with activity as they dove into the tasks Shannon assigned. Mel cut the chicken into manageable chunks, while Thalia and Shannon diced vegetables. Josh fell in line, grabbing plates and cutlery for the table.

He found himself surprisingly relaxed. It felt almost... normal. For a moment, he pretended he wasn't in this strange, isolated bubble.

He set the table, but it was apparent his arrangement lacked experience.

Thalia smirked, shaking her head as she adjusted a fork. "You'd think a billionaire would know how to set a table."

Leaning in close, his voice dropped to a lower register. "I'm better with my hands when it comes to other things."

She snorted, and he couldn't ignore the gleam in her eyes. He held her gaze for a beat longer, watching her reaction, pleased when she bit her lip.

Turning his attention to Mel, he couldn't resist commenting on her ability to handle the kitchen's heat, his voice laced with sexual suggestion. He let the innuendo linger, daring her to react.

She didn't miss a beat. She glanced over her shoulder, one eyebrow lifted and a playful curve to her lips. "Careful, Josh. You're not the only one who knows how to raise the temperature."

A hint of something deeper sparked in her eyes, but she kept her tone casual as she turned back to her task. Thalia shot her a quick, knowing glance. Josh didn't miss it. Was it some sort of agreement between them? The attraction was clear, but there was an underlying current he hadn't anticipated.

This is a game, he reminded himself. *And you're just getting started.*

For now, the flirtation counted as a win. He'd stirred the pot just enough and seen the interest he was hoping for. But as the laughter died down and the food sizzled, he couldn't ignore the realization that he may not be the only one playing a game here.

Ten minutes later, Shannon plated the dish, adding a dollop of the feta tzatziki Mel had whipped up. She stepped back and took a moment, visibly pleased with how everything came together. The scent of harissa chicken and fresh herbs filled the room as the women took their seats.

"I was saving this for graduation day," Josh said as he returned from the fridge with the bottle of Louis Roederer and four champagne flutes. "But screw it. There's clearly enough money around here that another bottle will magically appear when we're ready. Now, let's pretend like we aren't being held captive in a high-tech prison, and see if we can get to know each other."

The women laughed as they held their glasses up to be filled. Thalia shot a questioning glance at Mel, as if asking a silent question, but Mel ignored her. Josh caught the exchange, but said nothing.

"I'm assuming you all know everything there is to know about me, so tonight is about me getting to know you better," Josh said as he lifted his glass to the trio, took a sip, and leaned back in his chair.

"You already know me pretty well," said Shannon, "and I'm guessing you've had quite a bit of time to talk to Thalia, so why not start with Mel?"

"Sounds like a plan," he said. "Mel, how the hell did you get roped into this?"

Mel looked at her bracelet, pretending it was a watch. "Hmm, I don't think we have time for that story, so I'll give you the Cliffs Notes version."

The other two women chuckled, but Josh didn't crack a smile.

"I got into psychedelics after my husband's suicide. We had tried so hard to find a cure for his PTSD after the war, but the American government..." Mel blinked back tears. "You don't need to know that whole story, I'm sorry. It just upsets me so much that he could have been helped, and so many more people could be helped. But I'll move on. I'm sure you don't want to hear about my trauma."

She blew her nose on her napkin. "Let's see, I was a doctor before I was a psychedelic therapist. And before that, I was an activist fighting for a maximum wage. I never believed raising the minimum wage alone could fix inequality, not when CEOs were making thousands of times more than their lowest-paid workers. So yeah, the founders knew exactly how I felt about billionaires."

Josh's grip on his fork tightened, her words lodging under his skin. A maximum wage? Fuck her. Years of sacrifice, singular ambition, and sleepless nights had built his empire. How dare she think he didn't deserve his success? Yet he clamped his jaw shut and stabbed at his chicken with unnecessary force, his knife scraping against the plate.

"Okay, I'm sorry for your loss, truly," he said after a moment, cutting her off mid-sentence. "So tell me more about MDMA and PTSD. Since I don't have PTSD, how is it you think this drug is somehow going to fundamentally change me?"

"Well, this is how I see things," said Mel, "and some might disagree with me, but it's what I believe. I think every human being has gone through some sort of trauma. I don't want to minimize severe PTSD from things like war and physical abuse, but I truly believe nobody gets through life without at least a bit of it. Not only that, but society has programmed everyone alive— MDMA helps people find aspects of themselves that have been buried by said programming."

"So now you're telling me not only do I have PTSD and trauma, but I've also been programmed." He sneered. "If you're right, I've gotta admit—they did a hell of a job. I'm trying hard to get on board with all of this, but only because I don't see any other options at this point. You'll have to excuse me if I'm irritated, but the fact remains: No matter how lovely you all are as people and no matter how cool the toys are, I'm still a prisoner. There's nothing wrong with me that needs to be fixed by you!"

Thalia, who had been mostly silent, jumped in. "How about this, Josh? Instead of thinking of it as us trying to fix you, maybe try to see it as a learning experience. Yes, it's being forced on you, but if you try to change your mindset and see it as an opportunity, you might allow yourself to take part more freely."

Thalia took a sip of champagne as Mel took the lead again.

"We understand you don't want to be here and you think we're all nuts, but like you said, you don't have much of a choice. You really only have two: continue to work with Thalia, or we all enjoy our VR programs in the comfort of our rooms for the rest of our lives. I can tell you, we all pray you choose the first option."

He pushed away from the table and walked out to the barrier without looking back. The endless grassland stretched before him, its golden expanse undisturbed, as if mocking his captivity with its serene indifference. He pressed a hand against the invisible wall, encountering slight resistance but no real connection. His eyes scanned the horizon, desperate for a sign of life. Two weeks without any indication that anyone was searching for him.

Did they think he was dead? Would anyone care if he was? He bit his cheek, forcing down the welling panic in his chest. He couldn't allow himself to go there.

His mind raced, a jumble of what-ifs and worst-case scenarios. He pictured himself walking out, a free man, only to find the empire he'd built reduced to ashes.

CHAPTER TWENTY-EIGHT

JOSH'S MOOD TURNED SOUR. HIS WHOLE BODY BECAME ONE EXPOSED nerve as he weaned off the PLH. The drug had dulled his sharper edges, and now every emotion, every thought, rang louder, amplified to an almost unbearable degree. He was irritated. Even the smallest noise made him want to lash out. His head throbbed with cluster headaches, and an unwelcome heat spread through his body, igniting a familiar, insistent desire. Sexual frustration mingled with restlessness, creating a swirl of sensations that left him half-crazed.

He'd told the staff to leave him alone. What he needed was space. A buffer from their overly cheerful voices. No interactions, not like this. Just an escape. VR.

After his experiences with the other programs, his expectations for the X-rated one were high. If the tech was as advanced as it seemed, it would be the distraction he needed.

With a cynical laugh, he stripped off his clothes and picked up the headset. He still didn't trust that there weren't any cameras hidden in his apartment, but he couldn't bring himself to care. If they wanted a show, they'd get one.

Sliding the headset on, he awaited his wildest fantasies coming to life. If the program were half as realistic as the others, he'd be feeling the touch of hands on his skin and the pressure of lips on his shaft. He pressed the start button, anticipation racing through his veins.

After selecting "girl-on-girl" from the sub-menu, the beach home screen changed very little. The shimmering sweep of golden sand melted into the endless blue of the sea. A few yards from him, two women reclined on a striped blanket, their skin bronzed and glistening under the sun. The brunette, her hair a cascade of dark waves, traced lazy circles around the redhead's nipple.

Fire pooled in his groin as he approached. He introduced himself, though the women gave no indication they'd heard him. They remained absorbed in each other; the redhead arching her back, lips parting in a soft sigh as the brunette's fingers played across her skin. Unbothered by their indifference, Josh settled beside them. He reached out, his hand hovering for a moment before he cupped a firm, sun-warmed breast.

The women were still oblivious to his presence, but he didn't care. He let his hand slide down the redhead's abdomen to the curve of her hip. She moaned, but it wasn't for him. Curiosity piqued, he tried more assertive touches, experimenting to see if the program would adapt. He caressed their bodies, even tried to insert himself, but it was though he were a ghost. The sensation of their skin against his was tantalizingly realistic, yet his advances had no effect on the scene playing out before him.

The women carried on, enraptured by each other. The brunette's tongue moved down the inner thigh of the redhead, as Josh remained the invisible observer. With a frustrated sigh, he leaned back, resigned. *Fine*, he thought. If he couldn't join them, he'd enjoy the show. He gripped himself, the heat of the sun adding to the heat in his flesh, and gave in to the scene's eroticism, letting the sounds of their pleasure pull him into his own release.

He tossed the headset aside. The program had been a letdown, yet he still couldn't deny the technology's staggering potential. It was light-years ahead of anything he'd seen. The immersion, the tactile realism. It all left him in awe. But awe didn't quiet the anger boiling in him again.

Mopping the sweat from his brow, he settled on the sofa. How had it come to this? He'd have thrown himself into a partnership with the founders, whoever the hell they were, if they'd just asked. Hell, he would've leveraged Omnicia's resources to help them bring this tech to market without hesitation. But that wasn't what this was about.

The familiar ache of a cluster headache was back, a reminder of the withdrawal symptoms from the PLH. He stared out the window, watching the clouds drift over the prairie. The technologies he'd seen so far would revolutionize transportation, medicine, education, and so much more. The extraction mechanism alone could render fossil fuel vehicles obsolete. The founders didn't need him for this. They already had the tools to change the world. So why the elaborate ruse? Why the drugs and manipulation?

His thoughts spun endlessly, pulling him into loops of doubt and mistrust. How much were the others cooperating? If he chose to play along and they didn't, would that seal his fate? Still, cooperation seemed to be his only shot at freedom, and possibly a way to stake his claim on the technology he couldn't stop thinking about. Resistance seemed pointless.

Days crawled by, blurring together in a haze of withdrawal and anger. Every morning, he awoke with an irritability no amount of swimming or VR distractions could dispel. He avoided the women entirely—wouldn't even allow Thalia in for yoga—uncertain of himself and what he might say. It wasn't until the fourth day that something clicked—or maybe snapped. He couldn't stay in limbo forever. He needed to do something, so he invited Thalia for lunch.

A small space of peace opened up as she settled into her chair across from him. Her serene presence drew him in. When she spoke, outlining the plans for his MDMA session, he listened with intensity. He nodded along, absorbing every detail, every reassurance she offered.

Her exit left a vacuum Shannon soon filled, bringing with her a dinner that was heavier than usual. Pasta and bread, loaded with carbs in preparation for his journey the next day. He hadn't realized how ravenous he was until the first bite. He ate slowly, savoring the simple pleasure of it, as the layers of anxiety peeled away.

With Shannon, everything flowed effortlessly, uncomplicated. There was no underlying pressure, no need for a mental chess game. He let himself relax into the conversation, his guard dropping in a way it never did with Mel or Thalia.

The easy flow of their banter slipped into a more intimate rhythm after his plate was empty. It was only when the topic shifted to the VR programs a trace of awkwardness crept in. But he had a burning question.

"I would've thought with such powerful technology it might've been, shall we say, more interactive?"

Shannon nodded with understanding.

"I get why you're asking, and yes, I think they could make it better, but the developers had to follow Mel's instructions. She made it clear it couldn't be too realistic."

"Why not?"

"She knows you need sexual release, but she didn't want to take the risk you'd use the program while under the influence. Sex could be ruined for you if you engaged while on some of these drugs." Shannon spoke without a hint of discomfort.

"I don't understand how being on drugs can ruin sex?"

She described how MDMA heightened every sensation,

transforming a sexual encounter into something unnaturally intense. Colors seem brighter, textures more sumptuous, and the most subtle touch electrifying.

"Once you've experienced it, you'll want it that way every time. We don't want you going home and only desiring to be intimate while on drugs."

"I'm so glad you're looking out for my best interests."

Shannon chuckled. He knew she could tell his sarcasm wasn't hostile. She then asked what his thoughts were about the next day.

"I read the information Mel gave me, but reading about something can't really prepare you for how it'll feel, can it? I'm assuming you've done it before. What was it like for you?"

"The first time, I was so scared. I had no idea what to expect since I'd never done anything other than pot. 'The War on Drugs'... you know, those ads with the eggs in the frying pan... really did a number on me." Shannon let out a belly laugh.

"Yup, I remember those," he said with a grin. "That whole campaign scared the crap out of me, too."

"Well, Mel calmed my nerves with facts about how safe it is, especially when done with the right mindset and in the right setting. There's nothing to be afraid of with MDMA. I can't really describe how it feels, other than being wrapped in a blanket of love."

"Doesn't sound terrible."

After a brief pause, Shannon continued. "Have you ever heard of the book, 'Love is Letting Go of Fear'? That's what MDMA does. It breaks down all of your fears, so you have only love for yourself and others. It allows you to face things you might've been so afraid to deal with that your subconscious has been hiding them from you. Those things, the ones you didn't know you needed to face, are what often come up."

CHAPTER TWENTY-NINE

Josh's breath came in short, quick bursts, matching the anxious tempo of his pulse. The once comforting nightly music seemed to be lost in the pounding of his own heart. He had about four hours before Thalia arrived. Needing to burn off his nervous energy, he settled on a hike.

The Samaria Gorge stretched out before him. As he set off on the unfamiliar trail, he allowed himself to be swallowed by the towering cliffs; looming overhead, their ancient faces were weathered by time and the elements. Hours blurred as he navigated the labyrinthine pathways, his footsteps steady against the earth. Lost in his thoughts, he didn't register the sound of Thalia's voice at first. Then, when the sound fractured his stillness, it sent something twisting in his gut.

"Hey Josh, sorry to interrupt, but I'm going to come start setting up. Please finish what you're doing and get ready for our session."

He snapped back to reality, and bats danced in his stomach once again. No matter how much he thought he was prepared, the weight of the moment was undeniable. He pulled the headset off and used the toilet. Cold water sluiced over his fingers and splashed over his face as he tried to wash away his tension. His reflection was a portrait of apprehension.

Steeling himself against the rising tide of nerves, he forced one foot in front of the other, each step a march towards the unknown.

Outside, a breeze threaded fingers through his hair. Thalia gestured to the empty chair next to her and asked him to sit.

"How are you feeling?" she asked, but didn't hesitate long enough for him to answer. "I'm guessing you're pretty nervous, and that's normal. We'll get you as comfortable as possible before the MDMA kicks in. Some people get hot, some get chilly, so we'll have blankets available if you choose to be outside. You might get nauseated. I have a bucket here for you, so you won't need to run to the bathroom."

Thalia then reached for the basket she had set on the table.

"I have some items here if you'd like something to hold on to. I like to have something smooth to rub."

She took a small wooden hummingbird out of the basket, rubbed the part between the wings with her thumb, and handed it to Josh. She took a few other items out and placed them on the table. The collection included several polished rocks, a couple of small plush toy animals, and other wooden items. Josh put down the hummingbird, picked up an egg-shaped purple crystal, and rolled it between his palms.

"I like this one."

"That's amethyst. Great choice. It's a natural stress reliever, and it helps open your third eye as well as opens your heart. It's a beautiful compliment to MDMA."

He kept rubbing the stone as Thalia continued to set his expectations. He didn't believe a word she said about the purple egg, but he liked how it rolled in his hands. She asked him to speak up at any time if something annoyed him, including her music choices. If anything distracted him, he should let her know so she could address it.

She asked him to keep the eye mask on as much as possible. Although he had a notebook to write in, she explained the act of removing the mask might interrupt his flow, so she invited him to ask her to write things down for him.

"It's best if you try to work things out on your own, but I'm here if you need me. We won't be speaking very much at all, Josh. After about an hour, I'll assess how you're doing, and I might give you a booster dose. If you vomit, then we'll definitely do the booster. Does all of this make sense? Do you have any questions?"

"I don't have any expectations for the day. I guess my only question is, what are you and the founders hoping for? What do I need to do to be ready to meet with the others again?"

"That's a good question, but I can't answer it. Mel hasn't actually told us what she's looking for. She doesn't want anything to influence your experience. This has to be about you and what you need to learn from the medicine. The medicine knows what you need. I'm sorry. I know that isn't what you wanted to hear."

He wondered how the others were faring with the program. Were they cooperating, resisting, or grappling somewhere in between? And what did they think about him? Did they think he'd never bend, so why should they? If they were cooperating, what were they discovering about themselves? And when they came together again, would they share those truths or guard them with their lives?

Deciding he'd be most comfortable in his bed, his fingers played with the hem of his shirt as Thalia built a nest for herself with blankets and pillows at his bedside. He tried to keep his expression neutral as apprehension coiled tighter in his gut.

She caught his eye and smiled, a gentle, knowing look. "Please take off your shoes and stand facing me. I like to begin each journey with a cleansing ritual. It's a way to clear the space and set an intention. I cleanse everyone I work with before we start. All I ask is that you keep an open mind."

"An open mind... that's kinda what I'm afraid of."

Her smile didn't waver. She picked up a large eagle feather and a bundle of sage wrapped with twine. As she lit the herb, she blew on it until a thin plume of smoke curled into the air, filling the room with a sharp, earthy scent. It reminded him of the smell of sagebrush in Eastern Washington, where his family had camped in his childhood. Moments of simplicity he hadn't thought about in years.

"Hold your arms out to your sides." Thalia's instructions were firm.

He obeyed, trying to ignore the tremor in his hands as smoke billowed around him. She wafted the feather over the front of his body, moving in a pattern from top to bottom. The fragrant smoke enveloped him.

She began to pray, invoking the four directions.

"To the East, where the sun rises and new beginnings emerge, I offer my gratitude for the light and inspiration you bring to my life."

When she finished the East, she asked him to turn around and lift one foot at a time, so she could cleanse each foot while praying to the South.

"To the South, where warmth and growth reside, I honor the energy and vitality that fuels my journey."

She then cleansed his back with the West.

"To the West, where the sun sets and darkness falls, I embrace the lessons of reflection and transformation that come with the night."

Finally, she waved the smoke over his head and prayed to the North.

"To the North, the place of wisdom and stability, I seek your guidance and protection as I navigate the path ahead. I stand at the center, in balance and harmony with all directions, grateful for the interconnectedness of life. May this journey be one of insight, healing, and connection. Aho."

Once cleansed, she instructed him to sit on the side of the bed with his feet on the floor. She presented him a capsule in a small crystal dish with a glass of water. Before taking the pill, she asked him to repeat after her, either in his head or out loud:

"Grant me guidance, insight, and protection as I embark on this journey.

May my mind and spirit find clarity and healing, and may I be open to lessons and experiences that come my way.

May I navigate this path with a heart full of gratitude and respect for the mysteries of the Universe. Amen."

He said, "Amen," then swallowed the pill, pulled the mask over his eyes, and lay back on the bed. She started music, the kind she often used during their meditation sessions, and reminded him it would take about forty-five minutes before the effects set in. For now, she suggested, he try to relax and clear his mind.

His clarity surprised him, realizing his curiosity outweighed his fear. From all the reading he had done about MDMA, he knew the experience wouldn't be anything like his mushroom trip back in college. But he still didn't know what to expect.

After an hour, something changed, but if asked to describe it, he wouldn't have words. With every exhalation, he couldn't help but make a "hmmm" sound, similar to the sound one might make as they eased themselves into a beach chair on the first day of vacation. That sensation would be the closest he could come to describing it: total relaxation and happiness.

His mind drifted back to his adolescence. He was the observer, watching himself spit in Chris Morisson's face while pinning him to the ground. Chris, a nerd with few friends, had never done anything to him, but Josh had never needed reasons to torment his classmates.

He'd spent his adult life burying memories of his bad behavior as a teen. The way he'd conducted himself back then left an undercurrent of shame whenever he considered how his actions had affected other people's lives. School reunions? He'd avoided them like the plague, even before he became famous. The idea of facing those he'd hurt was unbearable. Revisiting those years reopened a wound, dragging him down a path often ending at the bottom of a bottle.

Lying on the bed in a state of bliss, Josh reviewed scene after scene from his early school years. Tears spilled down his cheeks as compassion welled inside him. It wasn't just compassion for the kids he'd tormented, but also for himself; the scared, angry boy who didn't know how to deal with his own emotions. He finally saw how deeply his father's abuse had twisted his view of the world and formed his beliefs about himself.

The tears didn't stop. He was overcome, gutted by it all. For years, he'd carried the guilt like a scar, a constant, silent reminder of his cruelty. He knew now those violent outbursts weren't who he really was. They were an extension of the darkness passed down by his father. The insults, the raised fists, the unrelenting criticism—he'd absorbed it all, like a sponge soaking up poison. He saw how he'd convinced himself he was unlovable, unworthy. Whenever love did show up, he'd ruined it without understanding why.

In an instant, he recognized his father's influence didn't have to define him. He had the power to rewrite his own narrative, to break free from the cycle of pain and embrace a different path. With each tear that fell, he forgave himself for the hurt he had caused, both to others and to himself.

He cried for the love he never received from his dad. He cried for his mom and Marne. And finally, he cried for the man he had become; desperate for approval from those incapable of giving it.

Several hours passed with bouts of tears and periods of laughter. The only interaction he had with Thalia was when she asked if he was okay, during one particularly difficult memory that had him sobbing so hard it was tough to breathe.

Hours into his journey, he sat up and asked to move outside. Night had fallen, and he yearned to see the entire sky full of stars, beyond what the retractable roof offered. Thalia positioned one of the poolside chaise-loungers at the far end of the property and outfitted it with pillows and blankets.

As the lingering effects of the drug continued to weave through his body and thoughts, he remained keenly aware of his expanded state. He was thankful Thalia had disabled her bracelet while guiding him to the chair, allowing him to hold on to her.

Once settled, she let him know she'd be reading by the pool if he needed her. He was glad she would be leaving him alone.

An hour later, he knew the effects of the drug were wearing off, and his hunger was growing. Shannon brought in some soup and explained she didn't want to upset his stomach with anything too heavy. Once convinced he had come down enough, Thalia asked if he wanted to talk about his experience.

"No, not really, but I'm beginning to understand what this is all about. That wasn't at all what I was expecting, though I don't think I had any expectations. If you don't mind, I think I'll do some writing and then go to bed."

"I'm proud of you, Josh," she said before leaving him alone with his notebook. "If we were in the real world, I'd give you a hug. Pay attention to your dreams tonight. They might hold more answers for you."

The silence after she left was welcome. He opened the retractable roof and stared up at the sky, scattered with stars. Propping himself against the headboard, he began scribbling. The pen moved faster than his conscious mind once again. His eyes grew heavy, but he didn't stop. He couldn't, not until the pen finally slipped from his fingers.

He drifted off with the notebook still open on his lap, a single question scrawled on the last page: What if I can't change who I've become?

CHAPTER THIRTY

THE DRAWN BLINDS COULDN'T HIDE THE ANGLE OF THE SUN. IT WAS clearly past morning when Josh opened his eyes.

"Good afternoon Josh. How are you doing?" Mel's voice. Somehow comforting.

Until Mel asked, Josh hadn't considered how he felt. "Well, um, not fantastic, I guess. I have a bit of a headache. I'm dizzy, and my jaw hurts."

"Those are common side effects, nothing to worry about. On your table, along with the food Shannon has prepared for you, you'll find a small dish with some supplements. Magnesium will help with your jaw and there's also 5-HTP. Some people feel a bit out of sorts after MDMA because it depletes your serotonin, so the 5-HTP could help. You might be more depressed than usual and unmotivated for a day or two. Thalia will check in tomorrow to see if you want to do yoga and meditations, other than that we'll leave you alone for a couple of days. Oh, and Josh?"

"Um Hm?"

"I want to tell you how proud we are. We know this isn't easy for you."

Before coming to the facility, he hadn't heard those words from anyone since being married to Pam.

For two days, he pulled back. Alone, his tangled maze of thoughts was his only company. His only sense of time came from watching the light shift across the walls. Each sunrise brought hope he'd snap out of his funk, but by sunset, the shadows seemed to stretch longer and creep into his mind.

On the third day, Mel and Thalia interrupted his self-imposed isolation, arriving with a tray of sandwiches and smiles that clashed with his stormy mood. They spoke lightly at first, easing him in, but then Mel brought up mushrooms, the next step. The word alone sent a shiver through his body, the muscles in his back flexing involuntarily.

The mere mention of mushrooms released a rush of memories he'd buried. The first, and only, time he'd tried them was a nightmare. He'd been lured in by the promise of a good time, a chance to let loose and laugh with friends. Instead, he found himself spiraling into the most terrifying hours of his life. In the dim, pulsing lights of the Crocodile, a small venue packed with sweaty bodies and the volatile mix of angst, frustration, and longing of Nirvana's music, the walls had begun to close in on him.

Faces in the crowd, friends who'd been laughing moments before, warped into grotesque figures. They leered at him, their mouths stretching too wide, their eyes empty pits that swallowed the room's dim light. The sound of guitars twisted into a low, droning hum that vibrated through his bones, filling his chest with a crushing sense of existential dread. He couldn't breathe. The ceiling rippled as if it were a living thing, inhaling and stealing the air from the room and from his lungs. Minutes felt like hours, stretching and folding in on themselves, trapping him in a loop of panic.

A tremor passed through him, the memory slamming into him with force.

"Josh." Thalia's voice soothed the chaos in his head. "I get it. Your experience sounds horrifying. But that was a different thing altogether. You were thrown into it without guidance, without support. The setting makes a big difference, too. This isn't going to be like that. I'll be here with you every step of the way."

He wanted to believe her. He needed to believe her.

As dawn broke, he ate a simple breakfast, the oatmeal doing nothing to settle his stomach. An edge of panic crept in. He pushed back from the table and threw himself into the pool, the cold water shocking his system into temporary silence. As he swam, each stroke was a silent scream to quiet the noise in his head. The water muted everything, giving him a moment of peace. He wished he could stay under forever.

When he surfaced, sucking in air, Thalia was looking down at him with her familiar, serene smile. Her stillness settled his nerves. He needed it more than he wanted to admit.

"You may want to start outside," she said, looking down at him. "A lot of people are more comfortable in a natural setting when using mushrooms. Forest bathing on the headset might also be nice."

The tightness in his body remained, but he appreciated that she was giving him options. It came across as a choice, even if he knew it wasn't. He pulled himself out of the pool, shivering from nerves and the morning air. Thalia set up blankets and pillows as she waited for him to dress.

She sat on the lounger next to the one she'd prepared for him, inviting him to sit when he came out of his apartment.

"Start with the eye mask on, though feel free to take it off if you want to when the visuals begin. This experience will probably change several times. Sometimes you'll want to move, other times you'll want to lie still. You might want to talk, or you might not say a word."

"Remember..." She paused, holding eye contact. "Allow whatever arises to surface without resistance. Let it flow out of you in whatever form it takes."

His breath hitched.

"Try not to judge things as they unfold," she continued. "Listen to your body and honor the instincts that guide you. I'll be here to ensure your safety every step of the way."

The reassurance that he was safe, that someone would be there for him, was something he hadn't realized he needed so deeply. He nodded, unable to find his voice. He wanted to tell her he was scared, but the words stuck in his throat. Pursing his lips, he looked away, trying to swallow down the emotions threatening to choke him.

Following the ritual of smudging and prayer, Thalia gave him a piece of rich, dark chocolate.

"This has two grams of mushrooms in it. We don't want to overwhelm you on your first experience, but we don't want to give you so little that nothing happens. We'll see how you do with this and might try a bit more next time. You'll be working with mushrooms a lot more than MDMA because they don't have the same issues with overuse."

The chocolate melted on his tongue. He'd expected it to taste mushroomy, but it was surprisingly sweet. He scribbled in his notebook, each line coming faster and faster. The words blurred, losing meaning as a strange sensation rippled through his brain.

Setting the notebook aside, he pulled the eye mask over his face. He reclined and settled in. The sun warmed his arms, but the rest of the world slipped away. The music Thalia chose cradled him in gentle tones, carrying him far away.

For a long time—he didn't know how long—he didn't move. Time ceased to exist as his thoughts spun like a cyclone. Faces and fragments of memories flashed before him: Brock's disappointed frown, Nathan's carefree laugh, Pam's tear-streaked cheeks. Emotions he'd pushed down for years bubbled to the surface. The fabric of his mask became soaked, but Thalia stayed silent.

When he finally moved, it was with the trembling uncertainty of a newborn foal. His breathing was shallow as he pulled off the mask. "I... I need the bathroom."

Thalia was beside him in an instant. "Of course." She guided him inside with the practiced care of someone who'd done this countless times before. "Do you want to talk about anything?" she asked as they stepped into his apartment.

"Not yet, thanks."

He caught his reflection in the bathroom mirror and froze. His face warped before his eyes, like he was looking into the distorted glass of a carnival funhouse. The sight made him gag. He turned away as flashes of the Nirvana concert flooded back into his mind. It was the same overwhelming sense of wrongness. The impression that reality was twisting.

Once he'd relieved himself, he lingered by the sink, staring down at the smooth porcelain. He hated the thought of returning to silence. Talking about it might help untangle the storm in his head.

Back outside, he pulled out a chair at the table, the cool metal grounding him for a fleeting moment, and told Thalia he'd changed his mind. She didn't press him, didn't fill in the space with words. She just waited.

No sound came out as he opened his mouth. A single tear tracked down his face, followed by another, then another, until they fell in a steady stream. He didn't hide. For the first time in forever, he let himself feel something.

"How did you know I needed this?" he asked, while wiping away the tears. "I certainly didn't know."

He described his trip to Thalia. In the beginning, fear had consumed him as he moved from total darkness into strange colors and shapes that meant nothing to him, but somehow made him anxious. Soon, a giant spider with large fangs loomed before him, triggering a surge of terror. As it approached, wings grew from his back, and he took flight in the form of a hummingbird. Flying over the spider, he realized it was tiny and he could eat it if he wanted to, but pity welled in his heart, and he left it untouched.

While in flight, erratic swoops and dives sent him plummeting earthward. As he lost control, his body lurched unsteadily with each descent. Falling, the fear of death gripped him, but each time his mother's hands caught him and lifted him back up. He suddenly realized there were two hummingbirds, but neither of them was him. They were falling, falling, falling, and he couldn't catch them. They were tumbling down into the darkness, and he knew he should help them, but his hands were busy building a pyramid. Every time his hands lifted a block into place, it disintegrated. He built the pyramid for eons, but he never completed it; it kept turning to dust.

Thalia sat quietly, listening without interruption. When he went silent except for sobbing, she asked if it would be okay if she rubbed his back. He nodded.

"Do you understand what the images were telling you, Josh?"

"My mom was always there to protect me from my dad, but I've always been mad at her for allowing him to hit her and for not leaving him," he sobbed.

Josh had never realized that he blamed his mom for his father's behavior. He now had nothing but empathy for her and understood how much strength and resilience she had. His understanding of forgiveness for his father was also beginning to grow. He couldn't hurt him now, and Josh only hurt himself by continuing to make him into a monster.

He also now understood the hell he'd gone through had prepared him to overcome obstacles in his adult life. Though he wished those lessons hadn't been learned the hard way, gratitude for the experiences replaced his anger.

"I think I can figure out forgiveness, but I don't know how to forgive myself. I've deprived my kids of their father, as I was deprived of my own. I never meant to do that to them. Nothing I've achieved means anything if I don't have my kids."

Thalia didn't ask questions, but suggested he write as much as he could with the experience fresh in his mind. When his pen stopped, she asked if he wanted to return to the lounger or try the headset.

"I think I'll try the headset."

He selected the beach program, needing to be still, rather than moving. The sun made his skin tingle as he sank into the soft, golden sand. He settled close enough to the water for the gentle waves to kiss his toes. A humpback whale breached in the distance, its massive form arcing gracefully against the sky. It stirred awe in him, a feeling he hadn't had in ages.

A sea turtle emerged from the crystalline waters. Its ancient shell glistened like a polished stone as it lumbered up the shore, not far from him. A swell of love and gratitude overwhelmed his heart.

As the turtle turned toward him, its mouth opened, and for a surreal moment, he thought it might speak. But instead of words, a torrent of plastic bottles spilled out, choking the magnificent creature. Josh's delight was shattered in horror as the animal's eyes pleaded for help with each labored breath.

Panicked, he leaped to his feet, sprinting across the sand to the struggling turtle. He clawed at the bottles, desperate to clear them away, but no matter how many he pulled free, more kept coming. His hands fumbled uselessly; the task was insurmountable. The creature's eyes dulled as its body withered under the unrelenting sun, until nothing remained but a mound of plastic.

The sea, once a pristine Caribbean blue, darkened and thickened, churning with garbage. Wave after wave crashed onto the shore, each one louder and more full of debris. He turned and ran, his feet sinking into the sand, making him stumble, as he tried to escape. The mountain of garbage coming from the water consumed everything in its path and engulfed him, pressing against his chest, robbing him of air.

Then he remembered he could fly. His wings engaged as he shot up and out of the nightmare. As he looked down, the blue planet before his eyes turned brown. As he grew tired, he spotted another blue planet in the distance. Too far away; he'd never make it there. He tumbled again, but no hands reached out to catch him. As he fell, thousands of other hummingbirds plummeted into oblivion alongside him.

Falling to his knees, Josh ripped off the headset, startled to see Thalia sitting across from him.

"Oh, you're still here? Aren't you tired?"

Thalia smiled and asked why he thought she'd be tired.

"It feels like I've been doing this for days. Don't you need to sleep?"

"No, it's only been about five hours so far," she replied softly. "That's the thing about psilocybin. It does some interesting things with time."

"I think I need to vomit." Josh held his hand over his mouth and took off towards the bathroom.

He didn't quite make it to the toilet. With an unsteady gait, he stumbled and fell. Like a helpless child, he puked all over the floor. Thalia helped him into bed and retracted the roof so he could see the stars.

Sinking into bed, he surrendered, weightlessly floating on a cloud. He cried as stars fell down on him like diamonds. An intense love overcame him. It was something he'd only experienced twice before—the days his sons were born. It was a love, pure and untouched by cynicism or ambition.

CHAPTER THIRTY-ONE

:Subject: Important News Regarding Matt

Mel,

Peepl's board had an emergency meeting this morning. Brooke says they're taking steps to remove Matt as CEO as quickly as possible. They're also looking into legal options to remove him as executive chair of the board. It's going to be very messy since he's still the controlling shareholder, but in light of current circumstances, they hope there will be some leeway. If this happens, it's unclear how Matt's net worth will be affected. I think we should share this information with him. It might light a fire under him to agree to the program. Brooke will keep us updated if there are any further developments. Let me know if you have questions.

Sincerely, Joel

MEL PRESSED HER PALMS TO THE DESK, EXHALING IN A LONG, controlled stream. *Okay, this isn't terrible, but it's not great either.*

Matt was a brick wall, and Cath's attempts to chip away at him had mostly amounted to nothing. With Josh making surprising progress and William beginning to open up in his own guarded way, Matt remained their greatest hurdle. Without him, they couldn't move to the next phase of the program.

She touched her bracelet. "Hey, Cath, can you please come to my office?"

"Yeah, sure, I'll be right there."

The soft knock at the door interrupted her thoughts. "Come in."

Cath peeked through the door before entering. "Everything okay?"

"Yeah, yeah, sure. Well, not really. Tea?" Mel gestured to a steaming mug on the desk.

Cath took the mug, wrapping her hands around it as she sat.

"There's something I need to talk to you about before I get into the developments with Matt." Mel folded her arms across her chest. "It's been bothering me, and I need to talk to someone about it."

Cath set her mug on the desk. "Okay…"

"I overheard Thalia and Monica talking. It sounds like I don't have Monica's total support."

Cath's mouth opened, but no words came out.

"You knew, didn't you?" Mel said quietly.

"I heard them."

"And you didn't tell me?"

"I thought it would do more harm than good," Cath said carefully. "I was trying to avoid more conflict."

Heat prickled at the back of Mel's neck. "Avoid conflict? By keeping me in the dark while Monica undermines me?"

"Mel, you're the reason we're here. This project wouldn't exist without you. Monica knows that too. You can't let one comment shake you."

"I'm trying to hold all of this together, and if even one person isn't fully behind me…" she trailed off, shaking her head.

Cath's face softened. "I should have told you. I should have trusted you to handle it."

Mel looked away, staring out the window. "Thanks for admitting that. I'm still figuring out what to do about Monica, but for now, you and I need to discuss Matt."

Cath sipped her tea while Mel told her about the email.

"I don't know what else to do with him," Cath said. "He's so closed off. Every time I try to connect, it's like he pulls back even more. I don't know if he regrets talking to me in the salt room, or if it's something else."

Mel leaned forward and rested her elbows on the desk. Sunlight streamed through the blinds, slashing her desk with stripes that looked too much like bars. "He's definitely depressed, and that has nothing to do with you. But if we don't reach him soon, I'm afraid we'll lose him entirely."

Cath stared at her cup, her finger tracing along the rim. "It's like every step I take toward him, he takes two steps back. And now with this news…"

"He has so much potential, Cath. If we can just…" Mel willed herself to keep the frustration out of her voice as her hands shot into the air. "If we can just get through to him. He could contribute so much. Not just to the project, but to the world."

"But how?"

Compassion softened Cath's eyes. Mel held steady, her expression firm. They both sought the same outcome, but their approaches were distinct.

"We need to frame this differently," Mel said after a long pause. "He needs to see the drugs as a way forward, his salvation, not a punishment."

Cath straightened in her chair. "Yup, that's it. He needs to recognize how precarious his situation is. We need to strip it down to the facts. Make him face reality. He has to see it."

There was no malice in their plan. They'd paint a clear picture of the consequences of his continued resistance. He'd lose his company and everything he had worked so hard for if he didn't start cooperating with them.

They were ready to speak to him. His readiness to hear what they had to say was another question altogether.

Matt lay sprawled on the sofa in mismatched pajamas when they arrived. Uninvited light cast harsh shadows on his unshaven face, while his hair, usually flat and plastered to his head, stood on end like a cartoon character. Beneath his bloodshot eyes, dark circles appeared like bruises.

A sour scent filled the women's noses. A pungent cocktail of body odor and grief. He flinched, caught in the spotlight of their arrival. He didn't look at them. His eyes, dull and distant, remained fixed on the floor. His shame was undisguised and acrid.

The conversation Cath and Mel had rehearsed dissolved in the stale air. The meeting they had braced for seemed insignificant. Matt's unfiltered appearance was a gut punch. A reminder that even the most capable of humans can crumble.

"Matt, we have some news from the outside world." Mel tried to infuse her voice with compassion, but she wasn't as good at it as Cath. "Let's sit outside and get some fresh air."

Cath made coffee and offered it to Matt as if it were a truce flag.

Matt grunted, taking a sip. "Talk."

He listened as the women broke the news that Peepl aimed to remove him as CEO as soon as possible.

"They want me out?" His voice, usually commanding when discussing corporate affairs, was now a strained whisper.

Cath leaned forward, empathy emanating from her body. "Not want, Matt. Need. This isn't personal, it's business."

"Not personal? It's *my* company, *my* creation. My sweat and very soul built the damn thing. It's personal."

Mel cleared her throat. "There's still time, Matt. There's still a narrow window. It wasn't in our plans to tell you about the other participants' progress, but in light of the circumstances, we can make an exception."

"Everyone else has been cooperating." Cath fidgeted with a napkin on the table. "We can get you caught up. Once everyone is working together, we think you'll be able to go home pretty quickly."

Matt let out a bitter laugh, shaking his head. "Cooperating? Sure. Josh has to have an angle. You think he's cooperating? Ha, not a chance. And the old men, you're kidding, right? There's no way. I don't believe you for a second."

Mel exchanged a look with Cath and let her keep talking.

Cath leaned forward. "Matt, I know it's hard to believe. You're not wrong to think that way, but we aren't lying to you. Josh fought us, too. It's not like he wanted to do this, but he could see there were no other alternatives. And now, he's actually embracing it. And the others, too. It isn't easy for them. It's messy and ugly, but they're engaging with the program."

"Engaging. So I'm the problem. The outlier. The failure." He set his coffee cup down and stared at the pool. "Whatever. Fine. Do what you need to do with me. But don't expect me to *engage*, or trust any of you."

CHAPTER THIRTY-TWO

THE SMELL OF BURNT TOAST AND COFFEE PERMEATED CATH'S apartment. She paced around the kitchen, taking sips of the piping-hot beverage, mentally rehearsing the events that would take place later in the day. Her thoughts were a maelstrom of preparation and doubt.

She had rationalized their actions from the start: The mission was too important to let righteousness stand in the way. She knew what they were doing would be seen by many as immoral, but she had hoped more would see them as heroes. If she were looking in from the outside now, she wouldn't know what side she'd be on. In the beginning, it wasn't even a question, but now that she saw Matt as a human and not some movie villain, she was starting to wonder if they had gone too far.

She squared her shoulders and headed down the hall with determination. She would meet the day head-on.

As she entered Mel's office, the familiar smell of chamomile greeted her. Tea would have been a smarter option. Coffee gave her the jitters, and she wished she'd made a better choice.

"Come in, sit. Would you like some tea?" Mel said as Cath sat in the chair opposite her desk.

"Yes, please. I think that's a good idea."

Mel's office was small, with little room for anything but the desk, two chairs, and a mini-fridge and microwave. Cath wished it were bigger. It was claustrophobic.

"How are you coping with everything?" Mel asked as she reached for Cath's hand in a motherly way.

She hesitated, not wanting to admit she was torn, that she wasn't sure if what they were doing was right. "I'd be lying if I said I wasn't nervous."

"Is there anything I can do to make you less anxious?"

"Thanks." Cath squeezed Mel's hand. "I can't think of anything. I guess knowing you'll be watching helps a lot."

"You've got this, Cath. I have complete trust in your abilities."

"Thanks. I wish I did."

Cath stepped out of Mel's office, her nerves still tight, but her heart a shade lighter. Mel had that effect. She was steady and grounding, always reminding her their work had purpose even when the path ahead seemed impossible.

Once in the community room, she set about collecting everything she needed for Matt's tea ceremony and session. Others relied on the convenience of chocolate to deliver the mushrooms, but she believed in the ceremony. She thought it allowed the voyager to connect with the medicine in a deeper way by engaging more of his senses.

Here we go, you got this. She finished putting everything into a basket and headed toward Matt's. When he opened the door, her breath caught. He was freshly showered, clean-shaven, and his damp hair was neatly combed. His transformation was striking. Though shadows lingered beneath his eyes and weariness clung to him like a second skin, there was a sharpness to him she hadn't seen since his arrival.

"Wow. I almost didn't recognize you!"

He nodded without a word, stepping aside to let her in. She clung to optimism, hoping his change in appearance was the beginning of a shift. Maybe, just maybe, he'd be more cooperative in the days ahead.

There hadn't been time to wean Matt off the PLH, so Mel was beginning with psilocybin rather than MDMA. There were no contraindications with psilocybin, and they wanted to get him started on the program as quickly as possible. The idea didn't thrill Cath, since this would be Matt's first exposure to any type of mind-altering drug. She had hoped to start him gently with MDMA, which almost always produced a positive experience, rather than risk an unpleasant trip with mushrooms his first time out.

She understood the importance of mindset when it came to voyaging with mushrooms. A clear and centered mind elevated the experience, while negativity could easily spiral into a bad trip. Although he didn't show it, she knew Matt was angry, and anger was the worst emotion to bring to a mushroom ceremony. She tried to shake her racing thoughts, but they clung to her like a stubborn vine, twisting and constricting.

Her hands trembled as she set out the elements of the ceremony: teapot, teacup, lemon, honey, mushrooms. Her fingers hovered over the spoon before deciding on its exact placement, as if every detail held the power to determine the session's outcome.

She glanced toward Matt. His face gave little away, but his shoulders seemed less hunched than usual. Was it progress or wishful thinking?

She cleared her throat. "Why don't you get your pillows and blankets set up on a lounger beyond the pool? I think the fresh air will help you have a better experience."

As he set up his spot, she stole a moment to center herself. She looked at the sky. It was both a comfort and a reminder of the enormity of what they were doing here. When everything was ready, she motioned for him to join her again.

"Alright, to begin, tear the mushrooms into small pieces and put them in the cup."

He wordlessly did as he was asked. Her heartbeat hammered in her chest. When he finished, she slid the lemon toward him.

"Now, squeeze this into the cup. The acid will help break down the psilocybin and convert it to psilocin. It'll bring on the effects a bit quicker, and it should help with nausea."

He didn't respond, but followed her instructions. A twitch ran through his fingers. She was grateful he was holding it together, for now.

"I want you to be as prepared as possible for whatever comes up." She filled the silence while the mushrooms steeped in the lemon juice. "Everyone's experience is different, so I can't tell you what you'll feel. It might be emotional, physical, or you might want to talk. The most important thing is to let go of any expectations. Don't fight what comes up. Observe it, allow it, and trust that your body, mind, and the medicine all know what they're doing."

She finished by reminding him she'd be there to guide, support, and keep him safe throughout the experience. "Do you have any questions before we get started?"

He paused for a second. "No."

"Okay then, pour the hot water into the cup and add the honey."

He reached for the teapot, tilting it carefully to pour the steaming water over the torn mushrooms. They floated to the top before sinking beneath the surface again. The swirling steam mimicked the emotions Cath knew were twisting within both of them. As he scooped honey into the brew, they both watched it dissolve in slow ribbons.

They sat in silence with the tea cooling between them. Cath

clasped her hands in her lap, nails pressing into her palms to keep herself grounded.

She broke the quiet. "Before you drink, I'd like you to set an intention for the session. It doesn't have to be complicated. Just think about what you'd like to gain or understand today."

Her words hung in the air. She waited, hoping for a response.

"My only intention is to make it through the day." Matt's jaw clenched, and his fingers curled tightly.

"I understand this is difficult for you, Matt. Please try to stay open to the possibility of a life-changing event. The more relaxed you can get, the better your experience will be. I'll set my own intention for you."

Closing her eyes, she placed her right hand over her heart, the gesture heavy with irony. Telling him to relax while tension gripped her tighter than ever was laughable. He sat in silence as her lips moved with no sound. When she finished, she asked him to drink the tea.

"Please drink it slowly. As you drink, try to think about things that bring you joy and hold that feeling in your heart."

After he consumed the last of the golden liquid, she encouraged him to lie back on the lounger and place a mask over his eyes. Settling nearby, she guided him through a short, heart-opening meditation while soft, binaural beats played on her portable speaker.

For two hours, he lay silent, motionless except for the steady rise and fall of his chest. She kept a close eye on him; her nerves were taut with anticipation, monitoring every subtle shift in his breathing for signs of change. But he remained in stillness, nothing giving way.

Then, without warning, his body erupted in violent convulsions. His muscles jerked as if an unseen force had seized control, contorting him into unnatural angles. Waves of agony ripped through him, his form wracked with torment as he tried to gain control.

"I have to pee." His voice was sharp and demanding.

The abruptness of his tone startled Cath as he ripped off the mask and flung the blankets to the ground, his movements frantic.

"Okay, I'll walk you to the bathroom." She hesitated, but decided to deactivate her bracelet. His convulsions had looked so intense she feared he might collapse. She wanted him to be able to hold on to her for stability if necessary.

"No, I'll go alone."

She followed behind at a slight distance, hoping she wouldn't annoy him. As he passed the pool, he stopped and pulled down his pants.

"No, not here, Matt. Let's keep going inside." She put one hand on his shoulder and the other lightly on his waist to guide him away from the pool.

"Fuck you, I'm going swimming."

In an instant, he turned, his eyes wild and unfocused. He shoved her with a sudden burst of strength, catching her completely off guard. Her feet slipped out from under her, and her head hit the concrete with a crack.

Matt thrashed wildly in the water, his arms flailing against invisible torment as Mel burst through the mirror.

She hadn't expected mayhem. Between bites of her sandwich and sips of merlot, she had casually been checking the monitor displaying his patio. Nothing out of the ordinary; a quiet reassurance that all was well. But the piercing alert from Cath's bracelet had shattered her peace, yanking her from her book and into action. The sight of his violent struggle now made her heart pound as she raced to his pool.

"FUCK!"

She urgently called for Thalia to come and attend to Cath while she jumped in the pool to help Matt.

Thalia arrived to chaos. Limbs flailed in the pool like a shark's feeding frenzy, while Cath lay crumpled on the ground nearby. She dropped to her knees beside her, quickly assessing her condition. Cath's eyes fluttered open, face pale but showing no immediate signs of severe injury.

"Cath, can you hear me? Stay with me," Thalia said, guiding her to sit up.

As Cath coughed and winced, Thalia glanced toward the pool, a look of horror on her face. Matt had Mel's head forced under the water, her struggles weakening.

"Thalia, help Mel!" Cath rasped.

"No, no, no, no!" screamed Thalia as she dove into the water, pulling the lifeless woman from Matt's grip, up the stairs, and onto the concrete.

She immediately began CPR and called for Shannon and Monica. "C'mon, Mel," she cried as she did chest compressions. "Oh my God, this isn't happening!"

Confusion and despair greeted Monica and Shannon when they arrived. Thalia, still doing compressions while wailing at the sky. Cath was rocking back and forth by the side of the pool, while holding her head in both hands, crying softly. Matt, half-clothed and soaking wet, was repeatedly throwing himself at the barrier, yelling something about being God.

Monica rushed to Thalia's side and held her as she sobbed over Mel's blue body. Thalia clutched at her friend's back as she convulsed in tears. Shannon crouched next to Cath and stroked her hair.

"It's okay. It's okay, I'm here. I'm here."

CHAPTER THIRTY-THREE

CATH TRIED THREE TIMES TO ENTER HER CODE INTO THE PAD ON Mel's desk.

She couldn't remember how they'd all gotten to Mel's office. She couldn't recall who had taken care of Matt, or what happened to Mel's body.

Finally, she got the code right. When Mykle's face appeared on the screen, a fresh wave of nausea rolled through her. She gripped the side of the desk, barely managing to stay upright.

"What's going on? Where's Mel?" The crease between Mykle's eyebrows deepened.

Cath opened her mouth, but the words clung to the back of her throat. She fought to steady herself, but when Joel joined the call, it pushed her to a breaking point. "There's been an accident." Her voice cracked as her vision blurred. "We don't know what to do. Mel's dead."

The words crushed her, and she folded forward, her forehead nearly touching the desk.

"Jesus Christ..." Mykle dragged a hand through his hair. "What happened?"

Shannon's voice broke the stillness, trembling but clear, as she recounted the events by the pool. Cath didn't hear much of what she said. She stared at the screen, but Mel's terrified face was all she could see.

By the time Joel asked the women to stay in the office while he and Mykle spoke privately, she wasn't sure how she was still standing. She moved in a dream state, climbing into Mel's chair and curling into herself. The leather, too big and too cold, swallowed her whole. She pressed her knees to her chest and stared at the room, where the others were each unraveling in their own ways. Thalia paced in front of the blinds, her nails in her mouth, while Shannon and Monica sat against the wall, clutching hands as if letting go would make the rest of the world collapse.

Minutes stretched into eternities before Mykle's voice filled the room again. "Joel will be there tomorrow morning at 7:30, and I'll be there as soon as I can. Say nothing to the men until we arrive."

"What if Matt wakes up and starts asking questions?" Thalia said from across the room.

"Let's hope he doesn't, but if he does, please go and be with him. We trust you'll help him understand this wasn't his fault. None of you is at fault. You all know that, right?" Mykle's voice, typically unapologetically brusque, was now low and comforting.

None of the women responded, but even in her fog, Cath knew it wasn't true. It was all her fault.

"I can't imagine how you're all feeling." Joel picked up where Mykle left off. "But please know, we will take care of you. Once we're there, we can all figure out how to move forward. You won't get any sleep tonight, so please stay with each other if you can. I'll let you know as soon as I've recovered enough from my extraction to meet you in the community room."

Only bits of the conversation registered in Cath's mind. The words bounced around in her head like ping-pong balls. Say nothing. Be with each other. None of this was your fault.

When Mykle and Joel's faces disappeared, she stayed curled in the chair, unable to move. Tears burned her eyes as Monica crouched beside her, gently rubbing her back. She didn't have the strength to tell her not to touch her.

Shannon's voice again. "I'm going to the kitchen to make us some soup. I don't feel much like eating, but it'll take my mind off things. You're all welcome to help me chop vegetables, or just sit with me. I think Joel's right... I don't think anyone should be alone tonight."

Monica put her arms around Cath and pulled her off the chair. They all followed Shannon, wordlessly converging in the communal area.

Cath sank into the sofa beside Thalia, slipping her cold hand into her friend's. She stared into the yawning void before her, trying to hold back a tide of tears. Thalia's fingers curled protectively around hers.

Across the room, Monica's knife hit the cutting board with a steady thunk, the sound grating against Cath's nerves. Monica was carrying on as if nothing was wrong. She wanted to scream at her. Her chest ached with the effort of holding it all in.

"I remember the first time I met Mel." Monica's voice. "I had just moved to the US from Costa Rica and was trying to find my tribe, which wasn't easy for someone who'd never lived in a normal society. I found a plant medicine group that Mel had started. I think she was using it as a recruiting tool."

Shannon paused her own chopping and placed a hand on Monica's back. Cath could see the encouragement in Shannon's touch, the way it urged the other woman to keep talking.

"Mel became my first and only friend for a while." Monica's voice again. "She was like the sister I never had. Always there for me...letting me crash on her couch until I could get my own place. She let me cry on her shoulder when I didn't understand why the world was so cruel, and most of all, she loved me every single day."

Sobs broke through Monica's words as Shannon pressed a

tissue into her palm. Cath's emotions wavered between empathy and something harder to name. Was Monica's grief genuine? Her own tears spilled over, sliding down her cheeks.

"I know, honey," Shannon said, wrapping Monica in her arms. "She was our family."

Cath's voice emerged in a whisper. "This is so messed up."

Thalia's grip tightened around her hand.

"She was everything to me." Cath's voice cracked as the tears came harder. "She saw into my soul and knew who I was when *I* didn't even know. And look what I've done." The words poured out of her, each one a jagged shard of grief cutting into her.

Shannon put the pot of soup on the burner to simmer, then crossed the room to sit across from Cath and Thalia. Monica moved to the center, sitting on a meditation pillow with her eyes closed, as if searching for Mel's presence.

The firelight flickered, casting long shadows that danced across the room as Shannon leaned forward, her elbows resting on her knees. Her fingers twisted around each other as she spoke.

"The day Mel told me about the dragon project…" She paused to collect herself. "She invited me on a hike. One of her favorite trails: the Commonwealth Basin in the Cascades. It was beautiful, of course, but there was something off with her. Like she was carrying something too big to hold alone."

Monica was the only one looking at Shannon. The others seemed to be listening in their own way.

"It was so Mel, you know? She didn't just want to tell me. She wanted the trees and the wind to bear witness. She stopped us at this little clearing by a stream, where the only sounds were the water and the birds. She turned to me, and I knew it wasn't about the hike."

"What did she say?" Thalia's voice was so soft, Shannon almost didn't hear her.

"She told me the story of how she and Brooke met and how Brooke introduced her to Joel and Mykle. And how they grilled her with hypotheticals like, would she give someone mind-altering drugs without their consent if it was for their higher good? She said it was like being tested. Not only on her ethics, but her whole character."

"How did she answer that question?" Thalia asked.

"She said it was unethical." Shannon quietly laughed along with the others, though there was no joy in the sound. "She said it was clear they weren't only looking for someone qualified, they were looking for someone they could trust implicitly."

Monica shook her head. "And she still agreed to work with them. I wonder how they hooked her?"

"Well, they obviously did. When she told me what their actual plan was, I literally gasped and asked her what her answer had been. I hoped it was no. When she said she'd accepted, I nearly fell over! I asked her what would have happened if she'd said no." Shannon paused. "She said they didn't have a plan for that."

"I always wondered what Mel would have done if any of us had said no to her. I wonder if there was anyone who did?" Thalia's questions didn't seem directed at anyone.

Shannon smiled through her tears. "I couldn't imagine why anyone would say yes to such a thing."

Keeping the story going, Shannon explained why Mel had agreed, despite her contempt for billionaires. The idea anyone could justify spending half a billion dollars on a yacht while people slept in tents on the streets below their offices was something she couldn't fathom. Prioritizing space exploration over solving Earth's crises, many of which she blamed on the ultra-rich, disgusted her to the core. She'd hoped the project would mark the beginning of the end for such excess in society.

But more than that, Mel's faith in psychedelics had driven her decision. She believed in their power to heal trauma and addiction and envisioned a world where those who needed them most, like the people in those tents, had access to them in therapeutic settings.

Then Joel and Mykle gave Mel a glimpse of the technology.

"Mel did it to me, too," said Shannon. "She whipped out a headset from her hiking pack and told me to put it on. The developers had made one program that didn't need the floor. She had me sit on a log to experience it."

All the women knew what was coming, but they let Shannon continue with her story.

"As I sat there, my surroundings changed to a beautiful room with a bay window looking out over fields of wildflowers. I was sitting in a comfortable chair, watching birds outside. I couldn't believe how real it was. And then it got better! A beautiful, fluffy orange cat sauntered in and jumped on my lap. I could feel the vibration of his purrs as he snuggled with me. He was so soft and real."

"I named him Grady White, after the boats, because he purred like a motorboat," Cath whispered with a tiny laugh at the end.

Shannon smiled at her. "Well, obviously, none of us could say no to Grady White."

CHAPTER THIRTY-FOUR

Sorrow saturated the room. Tissues littered the floor, abandoned after a night of quiet sobs and aching silences. Blankets and pillows, dragged from bedrooms, formed beds where Shannon and Monica lay curled together. The air was heavy with the weight of what they'd lost.

Cath leaned on the sofa, her knees pulled to her chest, arms wrapped tightly around them. Across from her, Thalia sat cross-legged on the rug, her head bowed as if the floor might offer answers. No one spoke. Cath was sure they were all blaming her, even if they didn't have the guts to say it.

When the door opened, no one looked up but her. Joel stepped in, his expression shadowed with exhaustion. His presence felt intrusive, like a splash of cold water reminding Cath that the world outside this room still existed. He was speaking, but his words didn't reach her. Something about a difficult time, we're here for you, blah blah blah. Her mind was full of fragments: Matt's wild eyes, Mel's lifeless body, her fault.

"Cath, I know it's unimaginable to think about speaking with Matt. You must have so many emotions, but we need to be ready with a plan when he wakes up. He hasn't called for you yet, has he?"

His words, directed at her, pulled her back to the present. She wasn't ready. The idea of facing Matt was too much. Her throat was raw. "He hasn't."

"Good, but we don't have much time till he does. Are you able to talk to me about it? Should we go somewhere else, or would you be more comfortable here?"

The idea of leaving the room made her sick to her stomach. "Here's fine."

Joel leaned forward, his expression earnest but unreadable. "You know better than I do how much he'll remember. Is there a chance he won't remember what happened?"

"Unlikely."

Joel's lips pinched as he leaned back. "Alright then. Do you have a sense of how he'll feel about it? Has he made enough progress that he'll be upset, or will he see it as a victory of sorts?"

"He didn't dislike Mel... he isn't a monster. He's going to be beside himself with guilt." Cath looked at the ground as she whispered.

"And you know this isn't your fault in any way, right?" Joel made sure she made eye contact with him.

"It's all my fault!" She broke down and wept. "What was I thinking, setting up by the pool? How could I be that stupid? And why did I think it was okay to deactivate my bracelet? I know better than that."

"Oh, Cath, honey, no." Shannon moved to sit next to her distraught friend, pulling Cath's head into her chest and hugging her tightly. "This wasn't your fault. Nobody blames you."

"I blame me!" Her wail tore through the room, a sound of anguish and uncontainable sorrow.

The room was silent, except for Cath's sobs. Nobody spoke until she started speaking again.

"This is something I'll have to deal with on my own. Matt's what's important right now, so I need to pull myself together."

"No, you won't have to deal with it on your own," Thalia said as she, too, hugged her friend. "We're all here—none of us will deal with this alone."

Monica and Shannon nodded in support.

Thalia squeezed Cath's hand before rising and pacing the room. She bit her nails with a contemplative look. "How could this have happened? Shouldn't Mel's bracelet have prevented Matt from being able to hold her down? We checked, and her bracelet was still activated."

Joel's eyes shifted downward. A lone tear welled in the corner of his eye and spilled over, leaving a wet trail down his cheek. "I'm truly sorry. There are no right words to express how deeply regretful we are. Our failure to test the bracelets in water was a colossal oversight. We take full responsibility for what happened to Mel, and I can't apologize enough for the pain it has caused everyone."

Cath couldn't stand to look at him. His words sounded genuine, but she wondered how many times he'd rehearsed them. She still blamed herself, even with this revelation.

"It's nobody's fault," whispered Monica as she moved to the sofa to soothe Cath. "Sometimes shitty things happen to good people."

"Please don't...just don't." Cath angled her body away from Monica. "It's my fault."

"Cath, what the fuck happened?" came Matt's panicked voice. "Cath, please tell me I just had a bad trip."

"Oh God," Cath whimpered as she tried to gain her composure.

"Look at me," Joel said in a firm but compassionate voice. "I understand this conversation with Matt is going to be really hard. I want you to know you're not alone in this. You don't have to carry the burden of Mel's death by yourself. Say whatever you need to say to make it clear to him, and to you, neither of you is at fault for this."

Cath's body ached as she sat among the others, their quiet support wrapped around her like a too-heavy blanket. Their warmth that usually comforted her now, stifling. She glanced at Monica, her hands neatly folded in her lap. So calm. How was she so steady when the ground beneath them was shaking?

She bit the inside of her cheek, guilt nipping at her for questioning Monica. Of course, she cared. They all did. But a small voice in the back of her mind kept telling her something was off. She pressed her fingers into her thigh, trying to push the thought away.

It's the grief, she told herself. The exhaustion. None of this made sense, and her brain was searching for a culprit. But still, when she met Monica's eyes, she had to look away.

Joel's voice again. "Are you ready, Cath?"

She nodded automatically but didn't stand. Her mind said "up", but her body was unwilling to obey. She looked down at the marks her nails made on her legs.

"Here I go." She forced herself to her feet.

The other women reached for her as she left. Their gestures should've comforted her, but instead, they came across as expectations, binding her to something she wasn't sure she believed in anymore. Mel was dead. That wouldn't change even if they solved the climate crisis.

Walking toward the door, the whispers in her head grew louder, a murmur of thoughts she couldn't quite decipher. There was no time to unravel their meaning now. Her focus had to be on Matt and what she was going to say when she faced him.

CHAPTER THIRTY-FIVE

CATH WIPED HER PALMS AGAINST HER PANTS AND PUT HER THUMB and finger up to her nose as she paused behind the mirror. She closed her eyes and began alternate nostril breathing. In through the right, out through the left. In through the left, out through the right. The rhythm steadied her enough to will herself forward.

Stepping onto Matt's patio, she fought the magnetic urge to look at the pool. She couldn't break down again. She had to keep it together. She kept her focus on Matt, who was walking in circles and talking to himself in his kitchen.

He frantically ran out to meet her when he noticed her standing outside. "Where's Mel? What happened to her?"

"Let's go inside and sit down, okay, Matt," she said with a hitch in her voice.

She sat on the edge of the sofa as Matt continued to wear a path into the floor. "What do you remember?"

"I remember everything." His voice was so small. "At first, it was nice. Warm. I saw my parents. When I was a kid. My dad holding onto my bike, my mom hugging me when the training wheels came off. I could smell her perfume. Smell her homemade lasagna."

Cath didn't say anything, knowing too much encouragement might make him retreat. She tried to make her body small and nonthreatening.

"Then I saw my brother. Summer days, racing bikes. Me and my friends, building forts in the trees behind the house. Ice-cream truck."

"What happened next?" She tried to nudge him.

Matt's whole body froze, as if bracing for an incoming blow. "Then it all shifted. The joy, the memories, all gone. I saw myself alone. All alone. My friends were gone. My family was gone. I was in Times Square, packed with people, but no one was looking at anyone else. Just screens. Heads down."

Cath's heart ached at the tremor in his voice. "That must have felt awful." She was trying to sound comforting, but was failing.

"It was my fault." His tone was flat. "Peepl was supposed to bring the world together. All it's done is rip them apart. It's not only the screens. It's the way people talk now, or should I say *don't* talk. Every interaction has been flattened into this fakeness." His voice cracked. "It's not real. None of it's real."

He fell silent, staring at the ground. She resisted the urge to reach for his hand.

"I saw Travis, too." His eyes were distant. "He was there, but I couldn't reach him. It was like he wasn't real, either. Then I ran. I ran and ran and ran. I'm the god who created this dystopian nightmare. My dream has made the world inhuman. My guilt and shame boiled up and then... I wish we'd stayed inside."

"There are a lot of things I wish," Cath said under her breath, trying not to cry.

A subtle tremor began in his hands. Her bracelet sensed it too, beeping in acknowledgment. Without a word, Matt bolted to the bathroom. The sounds of retching echoed through the otherwise silent apartment. She willed herself to check on him.

"Matt, it's okay. You don't have to relive it. Please come back when you're ready."

She reached for a box of tissues above the bathroom sink. Her grip faltered, nearly sending the box tumbling. She carried it to the living room, where she dropped onto the sofa. A mandala coloring book sat on the table beside where she put the tissue box. The intricate patterns on the cover blurred through tears.

She wanted to scream, to rage against the unfairness of it all, to find someone or something to blame. But as her fingers absently traced the mandala's spirals, her fury dulled, giving way to memories of another death.

She was back in that cramped living room, standing before the family of the man she killed. Just out of prison, barely piecing herself back together, she had knocked on their door with hands that wouldn't stop shaking. Their faces, now sharp in her memory. The eyes of grief, the mother clutching her rosary.

She'd been ready for their anger. She had braced herself for their hatred, prepared to absorb every harsh word they threw at her, because she deserved it. But when the door opened, what she found wasn't rage. It was kindness. Forgiveness. They had pulled her into their arms, holding her like she was one of their own, as she choked on apologies that rang hollow in the face of their grace.

She closed her eyes now. She could never understand how they offered her such absolution. Now, as she waited for Matt, it dawned on her; it was her turn to forgive. Not only him, but herself as well.

Minutes ticked by, each one lengthening into an unbearable eternity. The sound of the toilet flushing interrupted her thoughts. Matt emerged, his face pale and drawn, eyes filled with a thousand unspoken apologies. He slumped into the chair opposite her, burying his face in his hands.

She gathered the will to speak. "It's okay, Matt. You don't have to talk if you don't want to. We can just sit here until you're ready."

She closed her eyes again, focusing on her breathing.

"Is she dead?" His right hand clamped over his left and squeezed.

"Yes."

He cradled his head in his hands as his fingernails dug into his scalp. "How can you stand to be in the same room as me?"

"It wasn't your fault, Matt."

"I held her head under the water and killed her. How can you possibly say it wasn't my fault? And now, I'm a murderer. You people have turned me into a murderer."

She waited for his sobbing to subside. "If it was anyone's fault, it was mine. We never should have been out by the pool, and I never should have deactivated my bracelet." Cath held a tissue to her eyes.

"What's going to happen now?"

"I don't know yet. The founders are here, but we haven't had a chance to talk about the project. I'll let you know as soon as I have any information."

"We're all going to die here, aren't we?" Matt's whisper was lost as he ran back to the bathroom.

CHAPTER THIRTY-SIX

"WHAT A MESS." JOEL BROKE THE QUIET, HIS VOICE RAW WITH emotion and exhaustion. He stared at the endless swath of grassland beyond Mykle's patio, hoping it would offer some answers. "We need to make sure the women have time to grieve properly. Mel deserves that. She gave everything to this project, and to us."

Mykle, his face still pallid from the aftereffects of extraction, reclined with a blanket draped over his legs. He looked physically present, but emotionally distant. He shifted, rubbing his temple.

"Agreed. But how? Do we bury her here? If Brooke buys a casket, people will ask questions."

"No casket. Blankets will have to do. I'll ask Brooke to send shovels."

Mykle nodded. "Do you think any of the women can take over for her?"

Joel rubbed the back of his neck and shook his head. "None of them has medical training. That's going to be a problem if there's another emergency. The PLH seems to be dialed in now, but... Mel was their rock. Hell, she was ours, too. How do we replace that?"

"We don't." Mykle rested his chin in his hand. "We can't."

"Well, we can't just send everyone home. The program's too far along. Dismantling it now would be dangerous."

Mykle leaned back in his chair, the lines on his face deepening as he rubbed the bridge of his nose. "It would be reckless."

"Josh's progress is promising, but promising doesn't mean permanent. And the other two? They're not even close." Tracing the rim of his untouched coffee mug, Joel sat in contemplation. "It's about self-preservation. You know as well as I do, if they walk out of here now, they'll come after us."

"And they won't stop." Mykle's tone was sharper now. "We're not dealing with ordinary people here. The resources they'd use... private investigators, hackers, hell, even hit-men. The works. They'd stop at nothing to find out who did this to them. I know I wouldn't."

"I'm sure revenge would consume them."

"We're talking blackmail. Threats. They'd ruin us, Joel. Destroy everything. Hell, they might come after our families. Who's to say they wouldn't cross that line? We would."

"We knew there were risks. From the beginning, we knew."

Mykle ran a hand through his hair. "Knowing doesn't make it easier."

With a sigh, Joel leaned forward and rested his elbows on his knees. "No, it doesn't. But we can't allow this to fail. Not now. Not when we've come this far."

"We can't leave them here forever." Mykle expressed the unspoken fear they both had. His voice, typically booming with confidence, now held a tremor of uncertainty.

For a moment, the only sounds were the rustle of wind through the grass and the distant call of birds. Mykle was right. Confining the men indefinitely wasn't a viable solution. Not realistically. They needed a plan. Joel's mind raced through contingencies, searching for a solution that wasn't a Hail Mary.

He looked at the ground. "True. Maybe we should allow the

women to continue doing what they've been doing. They possess enough knowledge about the other substances to carry on with the work. I just don't know if they're mentally prepared to keep going."

"I don't think we should discuss the project with them, at least not until Mel's been buried. We need to let them grieve."

Joel rose from his chair. Mykle's pallor hadn't improved, and the uneven rise and fall of his chest drew Joel's attention. He crossed the patio and brought his friend back a glass of water. He remained standing as Mykle took the glass.

"I know the women need time, but how much? I don't know what's reasonable. We owe them that, but not at the cost of the project." Joel rocked back and forth. "Grief has a way of festering if it doesn't have direction. And at least one of us has to get back to the other facility. Brooke can't stay there forever."

Mykle looked at his bracelet. "Shit. It's been over an hour. We better go check on them. See if Cath's back from Matt's yet."

"Are you okay?" Joel put a hand on Cath's shoulder as she stood outside the community room, gulping for air.

"Better than ever," she replied, her tone dripping with sarcasm.

"I'm sorry. I didn't mean it that way. I apologize."

"No, I'm sorry. I know you didn't."

"Are you ready to go in, or do you want to take some time out here?" asked Mykle.

"I'm fine, let's go."

Cath almost broke down again when she saw the nest of pillows and blankets where Monica and Shannon lay entwined with Thalia. The shadows beneath their closed eyes were long and dark. Thalia's forehead held the creases of distress that Cath bore as well.

Her eyes lingered on Monica the longest. What thoughts was she having? Was she glad Mel was gone?

Stop it, that's not fair. Monica had been like a sister to her. They all had. But the whispers in her mind still pestered her.

"Let them rest." She said it more to herself than she did to Joel or Mykle.

She forced her feet to move back toward the door, the men trailing behind her. The cool air of the hallway helped erase the oppressive heaviness of the room they'd left. She shivered, unsure if it was from the chill or the doubts that were taking root inside her. The colorful photographs on the walls seemed to mock her anguish as they made their way to Joel's quarters.

His apartment echoed. It was the kind of space that existed out of necessity rather than intention. The bare walls and utilitarian furniture kept Cath shivering. She settled into a chair at the bistro table, its metal frame unyielding against her back. Mykle sat across from her, his face a study in exhaustion.

Joel rummaged through the cupboards as she sat silently, hands clasped, nails biting into her palms.

'How did things go with Matt?" Joel's voice, tinged with empathy that almost undid her, drifted over his shoulder as he filled the kettle.

"As well as could be expected." Her voice was flat and strained. "He has a ton of guilt, and his mind was replaying the scene in a loop. I tried to assure him it wasn't his fault, but..." She shook her head. "I don't know if he actually heard me. He's terrified. Terrified of being trapped here forever. He thinks it'll be his fault if that happens, and it's adding to his guilt."

Mykle scratched at his salt-and-pepper hair. "I don't want to discuss the future of the project with the men until we've given Mel a proper burial."

"I think that's a good idea." Her fingers curled around the warm mug Joel placed in front of her. The thought of discussing the logistics of everything dragged on her like wading through wet cement.

Joel took his seat beside her. "I'm sorry to burden you with this conversation, but did you notice any issues with Mel?"

Her head pulled back in a small but sharp motion, while her eyes searched his face for clarity. "Huh? What do you mean? The thing with Monica?"

"Hmm, I don't know about the thing with Monica. Maybe we need to talk about that, too. No, I meant...did you... was she drinking? Her teeth were black from red wine when...well, we were just wondering."

"What? No. Of course not."

Joel scratched his head. "Umm hmm. Well, we won't mention anything to the others, but we wanted you to know, in case it helps. In case it might make you feel better to know... this really wasn't your fault, Cath. There were so many things that contributed."

"Stop. Just stop." She wiped away the tears that were falling again. "I wish you would stop telling me it wasn't my fault. I don't care how many other things contributed. It wouldn't have happened if not for my actions."

Mykle cleared his throat. "Maybe if we switch topics for a bit."

Her head tipped in agreement.

"We said we wouldn't talk logistics, but maybe it'll help take your mind off things. We're going to need one of you to step up. After what you've been through, we'd never ask it of you, so..." Mykle paused. "How do you feel about Thalia?"

Her lips parted, but no sound came out. She looked at the faces of both men, expectant and waiting for an answer. *What, you don't think I'm capable? Fuck you.*

"Umm, I ... well, yeah sure, I guess. I think we'd all need to talk about it first."

CHAPTER THIRTY-SEVEN

THE MIDDAY PRAIRIE SUN BORE DOWN INCESSANTLY, A HEAT SO oppressive it seemed to dry the air in Cath's lungs. She stood inside the community room, staring out at the two figures in the distance. Thalia and Monica were digging. The dirt they heaved from the ground fell with muffled thuds. They moved as though each shovelful of soil unearthed more of their pain.

She lingered in the kitchen, unable to join them. Her legs barely held her weight. She wrapped her arms around herself, the ache in her heart intensifying as she thought of Mel. Only days ago, she was the unshakable center of their world. Her quiet, unassuming leadership had been their anchor. Now, Cath drifted, untethered in a sea of emotions.

Shannon still slept in the nest of blankets and pillows, her chest rising and falling with uneven breaths. Cath looked at her and wondered if she too couldn't bear the thought of digging the grave. She looked at her own hands, pale and trembling. How could they bury her? How could she carry on without her?

"Cath, honey?" Shannon's voice broke through her thoughts, gentle but hoarse. "Are you okay?"

She forced a nod, but her throat was too tight to speak. She gestured toward the garden outside. "I—I need to get the flowers."

Before Shannon could respond, Cath slipped out onto the patio. The potted garden Mel had cherished burst with color: fuchsias, gladiolas, marigolds, roses. Their vibrant blooms seemed almost cruel, thriving while Mel was gone.

Her hands moved mechanically as she clipped stems, arranging them into a bouquet. With each snip, her mind wandered back to the day Mel invited her to join the project. A sense of purpose had filled her then, a conviction that they were creating something extraordinary.

But now? That conviction was gone, replaced by an ache so big she didn't think the world could hold it. The flowers in her hand blurred as her thoughts spiraled. What was it all for? Was their grand idea worth the cost of Mel's life? Matt's life? Hers?

She froze, scissors hovering over a particularly beautiful gladiola. She couldn't bring herself to cut it. Mel loved these flowers. She often joked they were as dramatic as she was. The thought made her cheeks wet again.

Another memory surfaced: The day Mel confided in her about her doubts. "I hate that we're forcing this on them," Mel had said, her voice low, as though afraid the others might hear. "But maybe it's the only way. If we can change them, we can change everything."

At the time, Cath eagerly reassured her. But now, standing here with a bouquet for her funeral, she wasn't convinced. What if they weren't changing anything? What if they were just breaking people? Killing people.

She looked at the flowers in her hands, her grip tightening until the stems broke. A bead of sweat rolled down her temple, stinging as it reached her eye. She blinked it away, but the sting only made her tears flow faster.

In her peripheral vision, she saw Mykle and Joel enter the community room. Their presence reminded her of everything she didn't want to face. The billionaires. The project. The future. The impossibility of leaving now.

Could she leave? Would they let her? Would she have the nerve to ask? No. Not yet.

"Cath?" Joel's voice called her back to reality. He was standing a few feet away. Mykle was behind him, still looking pale and unsteady.

"We're ready," Joel said softly.

She nodded, though her feet needed convincing to move. She followed them out to where Thalia and Monica had left a mound of dirt.

The open grave yawned before them, a jagged wound in the earth. Thalia and Monica stood beside it, their faces streaked with tears and dirt.

Cath took her place beside Shannon, who reached for her hand. It was comforting. These women had become her family. They had shared everything—laughter, tears, dreams. Bonded by a mission so extreme they could tell no one else about it. And yet, she felt distant from them, especially Monica.

How could she have said those things about Mel? Maybe that was why Mel had been drinking.

Cath looked at Monica, standing stiff and solemn, eyes fixed on the grave with tears spilling down her face. How could she doubt Monica? They had been through so much together. They had loved Mel together.

Her thoughts battled for space as Joel and Mykle lowered Mel's body into the grave. The shroud of sheets and her cherished blanket, hand-knit in greens by her mom, seemed impossibly small. The cocoon couldn't possibly contain the woman who had been larger than life.

Monica spoke first, her voice trembling. "Mel was a force of nature, and her spirit will live in all of us. It will live on in the world we're creating because of her. Let's remember her laughter and the unwavering friendship she gifted us."

Thalia scattered yellow daisy petals onto the shroud. "In Pachamama's embrace, we know you are loved. May your spirit find comfort in the earth, part of the eternal ebb and flow of life. The ripples you created in the world will continue to spread, and your spirit will weave itself into the fabric of our lives, forever present in our thoughts and actions."

Cath leaned on Shannon, hands around each other's backs. She swallowed hard, wanting to speak, to say something meaningful, but the words wouldn't come. Instead, she clung to Shannon, letting her tears speak for her.

They took turns adding handfuls of dirt; the soil crumbled through their fingers, hinting at the impermanence of life. Cath hesitated when it was her turn. She kneeled by the grave; the bouquet vibrating in her grasp.

"Mel," she whispered, her voice breaking. "You gave me life. You gave me everything. May your journey be as brilliant and extraordinary as the life you lived. I love you."

Thalia and Monica picked up their shovels to fill in the hole. The thud of dirt, a somber metronome of grief.

When the dirt was filled in, Cath topped the grave with the flowers she'd picked. The group stood in silence, each lost in their own thoughts. Cath stared at the mound of earth. It was as if she were burying more than Mel. She was burying her certainty, her purpose, her place in this fractured family.

As they turned to leave, she looked back one last time. The gladiolas stood out against the dirt, their colors defiant in the face of death. She wished she had the same defiance, the same strength. But all she felt was doubt pressing down on her like the prairie sun.

CHAPTER THIRTY-EIGHT

THE AROMA OF TOASTED ALMONDS AND CHARRED PEPPERS WAFTED through the room as Shannon stirred a pot on the stove. Thalia sat in the living room, a steaming cup of chamomile tea cradled between her hands, staring at the ripples in the liquid as if they held answers.

Mel's absence was a gaping wound in the room. The silence was stifling, but no one dared to break it. Thalia looked out at the mound where her friend was buried as she reached for a tissue to wipe her eyes. The pain was sharp, but beneath it another truth pressed against her heart. They couldn't let Mel's death be in vain. They couldn't let it stall the project. It wasn't what Mel would have wanted.

The tea was too hot, but she sipped it anyway, watching the others. Cath's fingers traced absent patterns on the arm of the sofa, while Monica leaned back and crossed her arms over her chest. She was grateful for Shannon's determination to do something—anything—normal. But normal drifted out of reach, impossibly distant now.

She wanted to say something to fill the void, but she couldn't

formulate a coherent sentence. Joel's voice shattered the silence
for her.

He cleared his throat, a jagged sound like a stone breaking
glass. "Please forgive me. I know nobody wants to talk about this
right now, but we need to start thinking about the project."

Thalia straightened in her seat, her grip tightening on her
mug. The words weren't unexpected, but they still struck her like
a blow. Joel's eyes swept over the group, pausing briefly on each
face. Shannon's knife faltered on the cutting board, the chopping
ceasing as she turned to listen.

"I'm really sorry," Joel continued. "I'd like nothing more than to
give you all the time you need to grieve Mel, but the reality is, we
can't keep Matt, Josh, and William in the dark much longer."

The room seemed to inhale. Thalia felt an unspoken resistance
from the others. For a moment, she shared it, the ache of loss and
the desire to stay in this suspended moment of mourning. But the
pragmatist in her wouldn't allow it.

"We understand. Nothing about this was expected." Thalia
didn't know who to look at. "I don't think there's any benefit to
having separate meetings with the men. Why not include them in
the exploration of options?"

Confusion was evident on the others' faces as her words hung
in the stillness. She set down her tea and leaned forward.

"What I mean," she said hesitantly, "is that we should allow
them to be part of the conversation. Let them brainstorm together
ways to move forward. If they understand that Mel's death could
prolong their captivity, possibly indefinitely, it might make them
more inclined to cooperate. They might be more invested if they
help establish the direction we take."

Monica's brows knit together while Cath looked away, but
Thalia saw a hint of understanding in Joel's eyes, so she pressed on.

"Mel believed in this project. Fuck. She gave her life for it." Her
voice faltered at Mel's name. "She believed we could create real

change. If we lose momentum now, everything she sacrificed for could fall apart. I know we're all devastated, but if we can make the men believe this isn't something happening *to* them—that they have a say in it—maybe it'll shift their mindset."

The room was silent again, but this time it was filled with contemplation. Monica was the first to speak. "We brought them here to change the world. Why not let them do it? Maybe they don't need the drugs to be decent humans. Let them talk to each other and see what happens."

"There doesn't seem to be much harm in trying that," Mykle said reluctantly. "Maybe we haven't been giving them enough credit. You're right, maybe they don't need the drugs, or maybe they've already learned enough."

Joel steepled his fingers, considering her suggestion. His lips parted slightly before he spoke. "It's an intriguing idea. I can see how it might encourage collaboration if they feel some ownership. But..." He paused and looked at Mykle before continuing. "Do you think they're ready for that? These are men who've spent their lives running the show. They're not exactly known for playing nice with others. They might just end up fighting over how to proceed."

"No, I don't think they're ready." Thalia leaned back. "But that's the point. If they don't start seeing each other as allies, we won't get anywhere. This could be the push they need to start working together."

"Thalia, are you comfortable taking the lead?"

Joel's question took her off guard. "Umm, if by taking the lead, you mean facilitating the meeting, then yes, but if you mean taking over for Mel, then probably not."

"Uh, yes... just the meeting. Obviously, we can't replace Mel."

"We're going to need to agree on some parameters ahead of time, so we know when we can trust them," said Monica. "They might solve climate change, but where does that leave us if they want us behind bars for the rest of our lives?"

"I think we'll get a sense of things as we go along." Thalia smiled a tiny smile. "I don't think we can set any expectations since anything could happen. Why don't we all agree we all have to consent to any plans involving the outside world in any way? Let's play it by ear and see what happens."

"Okay then," said Mykle. "Let's bring everyone together tomorrow and tell them about Mel. I don't think we need to tell them how she died. Matt can tell them if he wants to, but I don't see an upside to us sharing that detail. Thalia, we trust you'll handle it with grace."

"C'mon everyone, let's eat." Shannon's voice lacked its usual enthusiasm as she put the final dish on the table.

The clatter of chairs spoke louder than anything else until Shannon raised her glass. "To Mel..." Her voice sounded hoarse from crying. "May we do you proud."

"To Mel," murmured the group.

CHAPTER THIRTY-NINE

GOLDEN LIGHT BATHED THE BOARDROOM, YET THALIA REMAINED untouched by its warmth. She pressed a hand to her chest and closed her eyes, willing herself to steady.

They had agreed the other women would observe from the theater room, a precaution to avoid awkward questions about the absence of guides for Joel and Mykle. But standing here alone, she felt exposed. She looked at the camera on the ceiling, hoping to draw strength, knowing her friends were watching downstairs.

She allowed her belly to expand with an intake of air, inhaling the herbal scent of lavender wafting from a diffuser in the corner as the five men entered from their separate doorways and took seats set out in front of her. Matt hunched forward, avoiding eye contact. Josh leaned back in his chair, one ankle crossed over his knee, while William rested his hands on the arms of his chair, eyes fixed on her with suspicion. Joel and Mykle flanked them, their presence stoic.

The men in front of her wouldn't understand. Why would they? They didn't know Mel. She was a villain in their world. But to Thalia, losing her was losing a kindred spirit.

Her voice stumbled as she addressed the men. "I...we have some terrible news to share with you."

Josh and William sat upright. Matt didn't move a hair.

Her past whispered to her. Different rooms, different men. Back on the ranch, when she was a girl dressed as a woman, she'd learned how to speak without saying anything, to bow her head and parrot whatever kept the peace. Her existence stripped of agency. Even now, the specter of that life shaped her doubts. Could she make these powerful men listen to her? Could she compel them to act?

"There's been an accident. Mel... is...um...Mel is dead."

The reality of her words rippled through the room. Matt's shoulders trembled as he tried and failed to hold back tears. Josh's hands gripped the armrests of his chair, his knuckles pale and taut. His face hardened, but the muscles in his jaw quivered as if fighting against a scream. William leaned his head back, eyes shut, his mouth pressed into a thin, trembling line. Joel dropped his head into his hands while Mykle turned and looked out the window.

She stood motionless, her hands clasped in front of her. Her words hung unanswered. She braced herself for someone to respond. She prayed she had the strength to answer their questions without breaking down.

The air was thick with emotions. Shock, despair, and anger. Beneath their reactions, she sensed the undertow of selfishness, their thoughts already shifting to what Mel's death meant for them.

"What's going to happen to us?" asked Josh. "Is the project scrapped now? Can we go home?"

Of course, that's your first question. "No, the project isn't scrapped, but we'll be changing course. It'll be up to the five of you to come up with a plan... up to you to figure out a way home."

"How did she die?"

Thalia had expected the question, but had hoped it would have been asked first to show some humanity. "I'm sorry, Josh, I'm not at liberty to say."

"Is the plan still involving drugs?" asked William.

"That'll be up to you, but we're still looking for the same results, with or without them."

"And what exactly are those results?" asked Josh. "Are you finally going to tell us what you expect from us?"

"That's a fair question." She paused to gather her composure and looked toward the camera again, hoping to get some silent encouragement. "There are only two main objectives. First, you must solve climate change. Originally, we were hoping for much more—we wanted you to solve other big problems, like inequality and war as well, but we need to be realistic and focus on the most important goal."

"Why is climate change the most important issue?" asked Mykle, though he knew the answer.

"Because none of the other problems will need solving if we don't have a planet to live on," said Thalia.

Josh leaned back in his chair. "That's not true. If we can colonize Mars, which is what I'm trying to do, then solving climate change isn't as important."

Her jaw locked so firmly that a dull ache spread through her temples. Josh's audacity landed like a personal insult. Mars wasn't a solution; it was an evasion. Like abandoning a house with a small fire on the stove without attempting to extinguish the flames. Did he really believe swapping one set of problems for another constituted progress?

She envisioned generations of displaced people, struggling to survive on a barren world while Earth withered away. An escape plan… ha; more like a callous abdication of responsibility. A billionaire's fantasy masquerading as a solution. And she refused to let it go unchallenged.

"Josh, help me understand your reasoning. Instead of fixing the mess you and your other rich friends have made here, in this beautiful world, you want to relocate billions of people to another planet that has even fewer resources? How does that make any sense at all?"

"We need a safety net if Earth is already too far gone," Josh replied.

"Earth is not already too far gone, and thinking like that only makes it worse," interjected Joel. "Thalia's right. It's people like us who've created the mess we're in with our greed and unsustainable desire for unfettered growth. We should be responsible for fixing it."

"Sounds like *you* made a lot of progress," said Josh with a smirk. "How'd you like the mushrooms?"

Joel shot him an icy look.

William's thick accent cut through the room. "Enough. I do not care who agrees about climate change or space travel. I care only about going home to Maria, and I want to know how I do that. What is the second objective?"

"The second objective might be harder than the first." Thalia's eyes met Josh's. "We need to know once you have an actionable plan, you'll follow through with it. Not only that, but you won't hold us responsible for your captivity, so we can go back to our normal lives without fear."

"Fuck." Josh muttered under his breath before raising his voice. "And just how will you assess that?"

"We all trust our guts implicitly."

Josh slouched in his chair with his arms crossed like a schoolboy and mumbled under his breath again, this time more quietly. "Fucking women. Our fate rests on their feelings."

"Excuse me, Josh? Do you have something you want to say?" Thalia sounded like a grade school teacher trying to rein in an unruly child.

"No."

"Good." She took a sip of water to compose herself. "You've all seen the technologies used to bring and keep you here. You'll be incorporating them into your plans, but we need to know it won't get into the wrong hands."

The EmergEx mechanism would either revolutionize the world or devastate it if not used wisely. Her voice wavered as she emphasized the need to incorporate the tools responsibly, urging them to approach their plan with the assumption that global cooperation would follow.

"Don't let politics and borders inhibit your thinking."

The sharpness of Matt's voice startled everyone. "If you want this plan to be actionable, then we have to take politics into account."

"No, Matt, you don't. Once we're satisfied your solution will work, we'll send out a video to the world's media. We'll evaluate the response of major players and then make a judgment call." She knew what she said next would be a bombshell.

"This facility has room for twenty more people. There's also a second facility that can hold thirty-five. We can bring more of your peers as well as political and religious leaders. It would then be your job to convince them to implement your plan... or continue down the road to mass human extinction."

"You've got to be fucking kidding me." Josh's tone was biting. Heads of government can be replaced within days. If this is what the entire plan hinges on, we're all screwed."

Thalia dipped her chin. "I get your concerns, but we have to try. Realistically, we think we'd have two days to deliver our message and get a consensus before the world is thrown into chaos. We hope your plan is so airtight that there won't be anyone in the world who can take issue with it, and all of this will be moot."

"In your fucking dreams." Josh's laugh sounded malevolent.

"Yes, Josh, in our fucking dreams. We're putting all our faith in the five of you. You clearly know how to get shit done. You have almost unlimited resources, and you all have big-picture thinking.

I hope you see this as an opportunity to be saviors of humanity rather than a punishment."

"So, just so I understand," said William, raising his hand. "We do not have to do the drugs?"

"No. But we strongly encourage it. We believe you'll think more creatively in expanded states of consciousness. It might take less time to come up with your solution, and you might work together better as a team if you continue with the meditations, breathwork, and yes, drugs."

Thalia draped a soft blanket over her lap as she sank into one of the leather recliners in the theater room. She looked at her friends, all trying to focus on the present moment and not let their sadness overwhelm them. Shannon passed around a bowl of popcorn as Monica built a nest of blankets and pillows on the recliner next to Thalia. Cath sat on the other side of her, arms crossed tightly, the muscles in her jaw flexing and releasing.

The big screen in front of them showed what was happening in the room Thalia had just left. The men sat staring at each other, all seeming to wait for someone else to speak first.

"Do you think they'll actually get to work?" Shannon said with a piece of popcorn pressed to her lips.

Thalia shrugged. "They might. Or they might talk about what's been happening to them since they last saw each other. I mean, we're letting them talk about whatever they want, so who knows what's going to happen?"

Monica let out a humorless laugh. "With Josh and Matt in the same room? I'm betting on fireworks."

Cath exhaled sharply. "I don't care what they talk about. You're all acting like nothing happened."

Her voice trailed off, but Thalia knew where her thoughts

were going. "Oh, Cath, hon. No, we're just trying to deal with reality as best we can."

"Well, the reality is you and Monica were talking behind her back. I can barely stand to be in the same room as you two. And by the way, she heard you. That's probably why she was drinking."

Shannon gave Monica and Thalia a shocked look.

"Fuck this. I'm going to my room." Her recliner snapped upright with a thud as Cath shoved herself to her feet.

The door slammed shut behind her. Thalia jumped from her seat and ran after her, but the elevator doors closed before she could reach it.

"I didn't catch up to her." Out of breath, Thalia sank back into her seat. "I think we should leave her alone for a while. I'll talk to her later. Shan, I can talk to you later too if you want, but let's focus on the men for now, okay?"

William looked at each man, making direct eye contact before asking the room, "Did you take the drugs?"

"I did," answered Joel.

"So did I." Mykle looked at Joel and dipped his head.

"Ya, me too." Josh looked at the ground.

"I did not," said William matter-of-factly. "I am glad I did not give in to their demands. It looks like now I will not have to."

"I actually learned a lot with my experiences." Joel looked at William. "Even under duress, I can see why they wanted us to take them."

"I have to admit, my experiences were pretty profound too." Josh lifted his head, glad to hear he wasn't the only one. "I might ask to do them again, depending on how things go here with all of you. Thalia's right. They might help us think in ways we wouldn't without them."

"I wouldn't trust a word they say." Matt sounded angry. "We're still their prisoners and they can do whatever they want with us. I'll never touch the shit again, not after what happened."

William lifted his right eyebrow. "What do you mean? What happened? Did you have a bad trip?"

"Yes. A very bad trip. She tried to help me in the pool, but I didn't know it was her. I thought she was a demon and I..." Matt didn't make eye contact with anyone as a tear slid down his cheek. "I held her under."

The moment Matt's words landed, the air in the room seemed to vanish. The news yanked the very oxygen from Josh's lungs. For a moment, the room wasn't just silent, it was a vacuum. Every sound—Matt's voice, the scrape of a chair, even their collective breaths—seemed swallowed by his confession.

Josh slumped in his chair. His acerbic wit, his armor, his go-to defense in uncomfortable situations, was nowhere to be found. He looked around the room and found William staring at Matt, his face slack. The man looked as if he'd been frozen in mid-emotion, caught between shock and disbelief. Joel and Mykle were no better.

The gravity of Matt's revelation was immobilizing. Images of Mel flashed through Josh's mind. The fire in her eyes when he challenged her, the warmth in her laugh when she let her guard down. And now she was gone. Matt killed her.

It took a minute to find his voice. "Are you...serious?" His speech, normally full of bravado, was full of trepidation. "They're never going to let us out of here! You murdered her!"

"I didn't fucking murder her, you asshole," Matt fired back, his face darkening with rage. "It was entirely their fault. They're the ones who put me in that position."

"You held her head underwater until she stopped breathing. Sounds like murder to me!"

Matt's hands curled into balls at his side, his voice rising with each word. "Fuck you, Josh. They're the ones who made this happen. You think you're so fucking righteous? It could just as easily have been you."

"Look, just stop." Mykle's voice was booming. "It doesn't matter what happened. Right now, all I care about is getting home, and bickering won't help."

William and Joel nodded in agreement.

"We need to set aside our differences and get to work." Mykle tried to gain control of the room. "Can we please all agree to focus on the task at hand?"

Josh glared at Matt and nodded his head.

"Whatever." Matt folded his arms across his chest.

Mykle got up from the table and went to the whiteboard in front of them. He picked up a black marker and wrote "climate change" at the top. Underneath, he started writing a list of words: water, weather, fire, plastic, emissions, fossil fuels, recycling, melting ice caps, livestock, and deforestation.

"What's all that?" asked Matt.

"I thought we might tackle each component. Maybe brainstorm a different aspect of it each day," answered Mykle.

"I think we should start with a general overview." Josh had found his composure again, but remained agitated. "Decide how the money is going to work first and then figure out how to spend it. We need to know what we have to work with before we do anything."

"Money shouldn't be the driving force." Matt threw out his comments to no one in particular. "We need to solve the problem as if we have unlimited resources. If we can come up with a viable solution, the world will have to contribute. Thalia made it pretty clear they'll get others involved if necessary."

"Money is *always* the driving force." Josh laughed with contempt. "We, of all people, know that better than anyone."

A smirk curled at Matt's lips. He dipped his head, eyes flashing like polished obsidian, "Well, well, well," he said, each word laced with mock reverence. "Seems the Almighty Himself has graced us with His divine pronouncements." He raised an eyebrow, the words like barbs dipped in honey. "So, should we prostrate ourselves? Craft hymns and sonnets to His celestial wisdom? Perhaps offer burnt offerings or virgin sacrifices?"

"Oh, fuck off, Matt." Infuriated again, Josh's face flushed. "Do you want to get to work, or would you rather waste time with your theatrics?"

Joel sat back and rolled his eyes.

"I want to talk about money." Josh sounded like a demanding CEO again. "I think we need Thalia to come back and clarify where it's coming from. It's unclear to me if they expect us to contribute everything we have or if we'll all put a certain amount into a pot?"

Matt scoffed. "Why the hell does it matter?" His voice rose, thick with disdain. "We shouldn't be thinking with any constraints. It isn't up to us to come up with the money. All we've been asked to do is solve the problem. Once we do that, they need to figure out the rest."

Josh's eyes narrowed. "I'm asking practical questions. Something you might want to try instead of running your mouth."

Leaning forward, Matt hissed, "This isn't about you, or how much control you think you have, you asshole. We're here to solve a problem."

His laugh was cold as Josh replied, "Right, because you're an expert at solving problems. Seems your little app has done more harm than good in the world."

Matt's face darkened. "Better than your sham of a corporation. All you've ever done is line your pockets and pat yourself on the back for it."

William, until then, the silent observer of the insults hurled between Matt and Josh, spoke when their voices became so loud the windows nearly rattled. "Enough." His voice a low rumble like a thunderstorm beginning to build. "We are here to solve, not squabble. We are each a piece of the puzzle, yet you bicker like children over spilled blocks. Why don't the two of you go to your rooms, and the three adults will sort this out?"

Josh, startled by the German's outburst, fell silent. The agitation between him and Matt still sizzled, though briefly dispelled.

Joel addressed the group. "We're a rudderless ship," he said, voice low but laden with authority. "We're lost in a sea of self-righteous fury while the world drowns. You would think five of the smartest men on the planet would be able to put aside their differences for a few days and work together, especially since our very lives depend on it."

Silence filled the room again. In the stillness, the consequences of their futility seemed to press down on them, suffocating their pride.

"So, what do we do now?" Matt mumbled.

"I can just see it…" Josh addressed the room itself, rather than any of the men within it. "We come up with an airtight plan and think we're going home, then whammo, the bitches tell us it'll cost too much and we need to figure something else out."

CHAPTER FORTY

JOSH'S FINGERS DRUMMED AN ERRATIC BEAT ON THE TABLE AS HE chewed the inside of his cheek. The antipathy in the room seeped into his muscles, creating a posture stiff with frustration. Matt's voice rose another octave. The argument spiraled from heated to outright hostile, but neither of them would back down.

When Thalia entered the room, her presence didn't register, drowned out by the chaos of their debate. Then her voice cut through. "Guys, I think it's a good idea to break for the day."

Her tone had a sharp edge. She must have been caught in the same exhaustion Josh was drowning in. He didn't know how much longer he could stand being trapped with men who shared nothing but resentment and distrust; the battle of egos clashing beneath a thin veneer of cooperation.

"Josh?" Her voice broke into his spiraling thoughts. "Can I make you dinner?"

"Ya, sure. I guess I'm in trouble. Am I going to get a scolding over spaghetti?"

Matt was the last to leave, besides him and Thalia. As he walked by, he cast a pointed look that Josh deliberately ignored.

Thalia's lips twitched into a faint smile, though her eyes

remained serious. "No. No scolding. Just food. And maybe a conversation that doesn't end in shouting."

"Why not?"

"I'll grab ingredients and meet you at your apartment in half an hour."

By the time Thalia arrived, arms laden with bags, Josh had managed to pull his apartment into a semblance of order. Dirty clothes were hidden in the closet, dishes hastily rinsed and stacked in the sink. He was wiping down the table when she walked in.

"Trying to impress me?" she teased, setting the bags on the counter.

Without waiting for an answer, she opened a bottle of wine, pouring two glasses. Accepting a glass wordlessly, Josh walked out to the pool to look at the sky. His eyes traced the clouds as if they were a map of escape routes. He didn't turn back until he heard the sound of chopping.

"You stopped the meeting because of me." It was half question, half statement.

She looked at him, knife pausing in the air. "I called it because it was clear you weren't getting anywhere. Nobody was ready to focus. We should've given you time to digest Mel's death before plunging you into that."

He took a sip from his soon-to-be-empty glass. "So, what's the plan, then?"

"We don't have one, Josh. We're leaving it up to you to figure out. But I wanted to check in with you, alone. That wasn't you in there. Well, at least not the Josh I've been getting to know lately. It was the old you. What's going on?"

"Hmm... let's see... what's going on with me?" He tapped his finger against his lips. "I'm being held against my will. I haven't seen my family for weeks. I have no idea what's happening to my company, and I'm expected to solve the world's biggest problem alongside a murderer. Does that give you an idea of what's going on with me?"

"So, nothing you mentioned is new other than the situation with Matt. Do you want to talk about that?" Thalia said as she sat at the table.

"What's there to talk about other than the elephant in the room?" Josh responded, sitting next to her.

"Which is?"

"How, in God's name, could you allow us to go home as if nothing had happened, even if we come up with a solution? Mel is dead. How's that going to be explained?" His voice rose, each word striking like a hammer.

"Okay, so your anger isn't really directed at Matt; it's with us."

He didn't know how she could stay so composed when her friend had just been killed.

"Look, I don't need you to therapize me, Thalia. I was willing to cooperate when I thought there was a real chance of going home, but now, why the fuck would I continue this charade?"

"Josh, we all loved Mel like she was our family, but when we signed on to the project, we all agreed—whatever happens, the outcome is all that truly matters ."

Thalia's chair scraped back against the concrete, the legs protesting with a metallic rasp as she rose with the slow grace of an unfolding flower. As she paced, her eyes darted everywhere but at him. And then, as abruptly as she had risen, she stopped, sat back down, and met his gaze.

"There's no reason for us to keep you here once you solve the problem. All of us, including Mel, spent a long time engineering our exit from the world in such a way that if we never go back, we won't be missed. None of us has to go back to the lives we left if we do get out of here. We can live anonymously, with only each other, for support. If any of you mention Mel or us to the media, we can go to the second facility at any time. We'd rather not, though."

He narrowed his eyes, causing his forehead to wrinkle as he tried to solve the puzzle in his mind.

"I don't understand," he said, rubbing his forehead. "If we solve climate change, we'll be the biggest heroes this world has ever known. None of you expect to revel in that glory?"

"No. It's all yours."

He couldn't wrap his head around how the women could be so indifferent to admiration, so uninterested in taking credit. It was a concept that challenged his deeply ingrained belief that success was measured by recognition, the pursuit of prestige, and, of course, money. His competitive nature had shaped him into a person who constantly sought validation and thrived on the acknowledgment of his achievements. The notion that others might not crave the same left him utterly bewildered.

"I'm so glad you understand you'll all be champions of the world once you solve climate change. We'd hoped all five of you would come around to this conclusion and be glad to work together," Thalia said as she checked on dinner.

As she worked in the kitchen, he tuned out the clatter of pots and the aroma of roasting vegetables. He lost himself in the yellow grass, shifting and bending as the wind swept through it in waves. He was comforted by its resilience, the quiet surrender to forces beyond its control.

For ten years, he'd moved like a force of nature himself, commanding a whirlwind of power and ambition. The world had danced at his feet, a grand stage built on his brilliance and drive. He'd thrived on the adulation, letting it fuel his every move, but now that energy gnawed at him from the inside like a parasite.

The thrill of success had soured. Behind the power and the carefully crafted image, an emerging truth was haunting him. He was tired. Tired of the endless parade of sycophants, of empty conversations, and of all the superficial bullshit. He finally admitted to himself he didn't crave more; he craved meaning. Something real.

The heaviest weight, though, came from the truths he'd avoided for too long. For years, he'd been protected from the full force of the world's criticism, shielded by teams of publicists and layers of spin. But the truth had a way of seeping in. Millions of people despised him not just for his wealth and influence, but for what he represented. Omnicia, his life's work, had become a global symbol of greed and destruction.

The accusations that Omnicia... that he... had ravaged the environment, plundered resources, and contributed to the planet's slow demise were impossible to ignore now. And the allegations didn't stop there. Whispers of a corporate monopoly, the tendrils of Omnicia entwining around small businesses, suffocating them in the ruthless pursuit of dominance. The truth that his empire was a predatory force, annihilating the dreams and livelihoods of the small enterprises that once thrived, was now a demon that followed him everywhere.

He watched the grass sway. Part of him wished the wind would sweep him away.

"Do all of you hate us?" he asked, as Thalia returned from the kitchen with two plates.

"What? Why would you ask that?"

He laughed nervously. "Because you kidnapped us and think we destroyed the world."

"Hate is a very strong word, Josh. We think you're all brilliant, but the shadows twisted your dreams into something destructive. We want your talents to be used for the good of all, not only the privileged few."

They ate in silence while he chewed on his thoughts. When he finished the meal, he sat back and sighed.

"I get it." He looked through her, not at her. "You not only want us to clean our rooms, you want us to clean the whole house."

Thalia smiled, but didn't interrupt.

"I think another day with MDMA might help me deal with Matt a bit better. Could we set that up for tomorrow?"

"Unfortunately, there can be lasting side effects with overuse of MDMA, and we only want you to use it once a month at the maximum. I think if we meditate on your intention, another mushroom journey could be very beneficial. Would you be okay with that?"

"A month? I don't intend to be here in a month. Shit… I liked the MDMA experience a lot better than the mushrooms, but I guess shrooms it is. At least I know what to expect this time."

Thalia winked. "Don't count on it."

CHAPTER FORTY-ONE

AFTER MEL'S DEATH, IT WAS AS THOUGH AN ENTIRE LIFETIME HAD
passed since Josh had fallen asleep under the glittering sky full of
diamonds. Yet, the echoes of his last journey, the messages
received, were burned in his memory. As he lay in bed, he
replayed every moment of the experience in his head.

He had to admit, the idea of taking mushrooms again scared
him, especially after what happened with Matt.

How is Thalia so unshaken by it? He couldn't believe the women
would let any of them touch mushrooms again. Despite his
worries, he fell into a deep sleep.

His morning unfolded with quiet intention. A small breakfast of
granola and berries fueled a two-hour swim. By the time Thalia
arrived, he felt relaxed, centered, and ready to face whatever came
next.

"How do you know if it's God or yourself creating the
experience?" he asked as Thalia prepared her blankets on the floor
next to his bed.

"How do you know they're different?" she replied without hesitation.

He'd always considered himself a pragmatist, uninterested in religion or spirituality. Raised in a household devoid of faith, he viewed the idea of God as little more than an abstract concept offering comfort to those who needed it, but holding no relevance in his own life. The Christian God his childhood friends spoke of was supposed to be loving. If that were true, why would such a God allow famines, wars, and suffering? Why would such a God stand by as his father's fists rained down on his mother?

The dissonance between the world he knew and the divine love others preached had hardened his indifference into disdain. But now, his experiences here had cracked something open inside him, and for the first time, he saw the world differently. What once appeared to be a chaotic mess of random events now seemed intricately linked. People's lives were like threads woven together in a tapestry, seemingly connected by some invisible force, maybe God, with each moment and every living thing bound in ways unseen.

The memory of the hummingbirds replayed over and over in his mind, their tiny bodies falling together, experiencing the same thing. For the first time, he saw himself not as the man above the fray, orchestrating the world, but as one among many. All are bound by a shared humanity, shared needs, and the shared experience of living on a finite planet. It was a realization that made him feel both small and, at the same time, responsible for something bigger than himself.

He pondered the nature of a higher power, wondering if it was a conscious being, or a cosmic energy braided into the very fabric of existence. Questions of morality, purpose, and the origin of life swirled as he waited for Thalia to prepare the space. For now, he'd embrace the uncertainty.

"I'm going to give you a higher dose today. We'll start with two grams again and see how you're handling it in a couple of hours, and then another gram or two if you're tolerating it well. I've got a bucket here for you, so you don't have to rush to the bathroom if you get sick," Thalia said as she finished setting up.

"Why the higher dose? Aren't you afraid after what happened with Matt?"

Her lips parted for a quick response, but she hesitated. Her fingers found the satin trim of her blanket and began rubbing it between them. "That was... a freak accident." Her voice cracked. She looked away, adjusting the eye mask she'd laid out for him, as if needing to look busy.

He studied her. Her serenity felt forced. "You don't sound convinced."

Her shoulders straightened as she turned to face him. "I'm taking precautions. The windows will stay in place, so you won't be leaving the apartment until I decide it's safe. And I won't be disabling my bracelet this time. Not under any circumstances."

"Not exactly reassuring, Thalia."

"I'm not trying to reassure you. To answer your question, though, I want you to go really deep this time. That's the reason for the higher dose."

"I think I went pretty fucking deep last time, but okay, you're the expert."

After the ceremonial smudging and calling in of the four directions, Josh said a silent prayer to a God he wasn't sure existed and pulled his eye mask down.

Vivid images came to him, as real as memories. He saw himself cradling grandchildren, yet to be born, surrounded by his sons, their faces lit with happiness. Their wives stood beside them, forming a circle. He had an overwhelming sense of unconditional love, both being received and given. Radiant geometric shapes developed, weaving themselves into the faces and forms of his family. Each pattern seemed to bind them together in ways that defied explanation. It left him awestruck and humbled.

"How are you feeling, Josh?" whispered Thalia two hours later.

"Mmmmm, pretty darn good."

"Excellent. I'll give you the booster now and shouldn't have to interrupt you again."

He didn't hesitate to eat the second piece of chocolate, letting it melt on his tongue as he settled into a profound sense of gratitude.

After the booster, he drifted back into his alternate reality. The scene burst into focus—a dream that had been painted in bold, impossible colors. He stood at the bank of a tranquil lake. The sound of laughter echoing as his grandkids, now small children, chased each other through the shallow, clear water.

The air was thick with the sweet, earthy perfume of blossoms and pine. Dappled shadows danced along the shore, cast by the branches of trees circling the lake. Nearby, a family of deer grazed, unbothered by the laughter. The children shrieked with glee as they tried to catch fish with their bare hands.

He stood rooted on the sunlit beach, taking it all in. Joy overwhelmed him; so intense it bordered on pain. He struggled to recall any moment in his life that matched it. For the first time, he glimpsed the wonder of true happiness. He'd spent his whole life chasing it, only to realize he'd been pursuing the wrong things. That was it... he was chasing *things*. Things didn't matter.

Though he knew the glowing sky, the shimmering trees, and giddy grandchildren weren't real, it didn't matter. This feeling was his for now, and he let himself savor every second of it.

Gradually, the idyllic scene shifted, subtle at first, like a distant storm on the horizon. The laughter dimmed, replaced by an eerie silence broken only by the faint hum of something unplaceable. The lake's crystal-clear water darkened, its surface quivering in fear.

He looked to the forest. The towering trees, which stood as

silent sentinels of peace, now seemed restless, their needles rustling with a shiver not caused by any breeze. Shadows grew deeper, stretching unnaturally long across the forest floor. The family of deer froze in place, their ears twitching, wide eyes fixed on some unseen threat. He stood at the edge of a world teetering between beauty and dread.

The perfection he'd experienced moments ago gave way to a new reality. Herds of animals came crashing out of the trees as his skin burned with heat. Thousands and thousands of creatures, throwing themselves into the lake until the water broke over its banks and flooded the forest.

Josh, caught in a torrent of water and hooves, scrambled to gain traction. He reached out for a tree branch, hoping it would stop him, but the tree, along with the others around him, was knocked down by giant machines, cutting vast swathes through the forest.

When the water stilled, he blinked and found himself sitting at his desk within the sterile walls of his office. Random figures came and went in a blur as his phone rang incessantly. His hands hovered over a keyboard. Something urgent pressed at the edges of his mind, an unnamed responsibility clawing for his attention.

He tried to log on to the computer, his fingers pounding out combinations of letters and numbers that refused to align. A cold sweat prickled at his brow as the error message flashed again and again. His hands grew damp, slipping as he pressed harder and harder, desperate to gain access to whatever he'd forgotten.

Suddenly, the screen flickered, and bold red letters appeared: GAME OVER.

He froze. The office closed in around him; the walls leaning inward, the ringing phone now an oppressive scream.

The stark contrast between the peace of the lake and the chaos of his office hit him like a punch to the gut. He had everything: wealth, power, influence... and yet he was empty. His persistent pursuit of more—more money, more control, more validation—

had built walls around him, cutting him off from the simplicity of what mattered. Love and connection, the beauty of just *being*, all of it had slipped from his grasp in the frantic climb to power.

The world snapped into focus with startling clarity. If he didn't change, he'd remain trapped in this endless loop, always chasing and never arriving, mistaking accumulation for meaning.

The vision dissolved, much like the fragments of a dream slipping away upon waking as the medicine wore off. His limbs grew heavy, dragging him back to reality with the inexorable pull of gravity. He clutched at the memory of fleeting euphoria, a desperate attempt to hold on to the impossible bliss he'd briefly grasped.

"Thalia?"

"Yes, Josh, I'm here. Do you need something?"

"I think I'm ready to get up and eat."

Removing the tear-soaked face mask, Josh swung his legs over the side of the bed and paused. A wave of nausea swept through his body, then dissipated. He gingerly lifted his tired body into a standing position and nearly fell over.

"Careful," said Thalia as if she were talking to a child. "Take it slowly."

"Umm hmm," Josh mumbled on his way to the bathroom.

Thalia had fresh fruit with cheese and nuts set out on the table when he arrived in the kitchen. They sat in silence while he nibbled. She waited in patient stillness for him to begin the conversation he seemed poised to share.

"That felt a lot like MDMA, but different. I don't know how to describe it, but I somehow felt whole." He paused. He was still hesitant to share his innermost reflections. "Well, until I didn't. But somehow I'm...hmm...maybe hopeful is the right word?"

Thalia sat listening, quietly nodding as he continued.

"I finally understand money can't buy happiness." A short, breathy sound slipped out, not quite a laugh. "Everyone always says that, but I don't think most people believe it. I didn't. And now I understand why people like me never have enough."

Tears streamed down his cheeks, carving a path through the facade he'd spent decades perfecting. The image of the richest, smartest man in the world was cracking with truths he could no longer avoid. Beneath the surface of his corporate persona, fears he'd spent a lifetime burying were inching their way to the surface.

Who was he really? The question was a pit threatening to swallow him whole.

He wiped his face and thought about the men he'd been thrown into this strange world with. Could they set aside their differences? Build something deep and meaningful together? Whatever came next, he wasn't willing to give up, not on himself and not on them.

CHAPTER FORTY-TWO

As Josh stepped into the conference room, the charged silence was immediate. Four pairs of eyes locked onto him, each filled with varying degrees of curiosity, frustration, and, in Matt's case, hostility.

Thalia's earlier conversation with him ran in his head as he took a seat. She'd told him Matt had a difficult time the day before, his guilt so suffocating that it rendered him useless. Every suggestion, every idea, had bounced off him as if he were wrapped in an armor of self-loathing. By the time he'd excused himself and retreated to his room, the group was too fractured to make any progress.

Looking at Matt now, Josh noted the dark circles under his eyes and the friction radiating from his jaw.

Matt's voice cut through the room like a blade. "I can't believe you'd do that."

Josh blinked, caught off guard by the venom in his tone. He tried to keep his expression neutral. "Do what?"

"Mushrooms. After what happened. Why in God's name would you do that again, since they'll let us out if we solve the problem? We don't have to do the drugs anymore."

His response required delicacy, avoiding anything that might upset Matt further. "I completely understand why you'd ask that... After what happened, I didn't think there was a chance in hell they'd let us out, no matter what we did. That's why I was being such a dick the last time we were together. I want to apologize for that."

The other men exchanged glances of astonishment. Josh Latham apologizing for being an asshole? That was a first.

Josh made eye contact with each man before speaking again. "I spoke with Thalia." His voice was less demanding than usual. "She made it clear. They'll let us go home, even after what happened." He looked at Matt, hoping his expression conveyed sympathy, not anger or hate.

The room remained silent as he tugged at the hem of his shirt.

"Why *wouldn't* we want to solve climate change?" He leaned in, searching their faces for agreement. "I mean, think about it. We've been handed an incredible opportunity. We could fix this."

Matt's chair squeaked as he shifted. William crossed his arms but didn't speak. Joel and Mykle exchanged a quick glance, but said nothing.

Josh continued. "Look, I know we didn't sign up for this. But honestly, what if this is it? What if this is our chance to leave behind something that actually matters?"

Still, no one responded. He rested his elbows on the table. "I get it. It's uncomfortable. For years, we've been in control. Of our companies, our lives, everything. But this? This is bigger than any of us. We all have more money and power than we know what to do with. We think we've somehow benefited society enough to justify our greed and the damage we've done to both the planet and humanity. Well... we're wrong. We are very, very wrong."

Matt's voice was tinged with skepticism. "And you believe them? That they'll let us go?"

"I do. And even if they don't, what's the alternative? Sit here, fighting each other, waiting for nothing to happen? I, for one, am going to put all of my effort into figuring this out."

"Hmmm." William was the only one to make a sound.

"At first, I thought it was a way to make more money and be the greatest savior the world has ever known." Josh was on a roll. "Yup, you might say I had a God complex. I'm sure I'm not the only one. Now, after being here and yes, doing drugs, I want to do this because it's the right thing to do. And because I want to get well. The women are right, we're sick. I want to be happy. I'm not saying it's going to be easy. Hell, I don't know if we can do it. But what I do know is this: Sitting here, doing nothing, guarantees failure. If we fail, we're stuck here. And frankly, I can't live with that."

"And what about the trust they talked about?" William shook his head.

"Yeah. That's the other thing. They have to trust we'll never mention Mel, never mention this facility, and never mention them. And they have to trust we care enough to follow through on the plan."

William interrupted. "Why would they ever trust us? I think we are back to not going home."

"Because they want this to work. They want nothing more than for us to go home and fix the planet. They want out of here, too. They don't want to be stuck here for the rest of their lives, either."

"But that doesn't answer the question of how we get them to trust us," said Matt flatly.

From their seats in the theater, the women strained to catch every word. Thalia picked at her nails as she listened to Josh. She was proud of the new man she saw. But the men were right to question how the women would know if they could trust them?

Since Mel's death, they hadn't spoken about the subject, mostly because Cath spent most of her time in her room.

She was here now, but had been unwilling to talk. Thalia tried to catch her attention, to at least smile at her, but Cath's eyes were on the screen.

Monica seemed to read Thalia's mind. "Matt has a valid point. How can they get us to trust them?"

"Believe it or not, I already do trust Josh." The truth of it surprised her. It wasn't something she'd fully realized until the words left her mouth.

"So what would we want from Matt and William, then?" asked Shannon.

They sat, contemplating the elusive concept of trust. Each of them had spent years honing their empathic ability to read the subtleties of body language, the quiet shifts in energy that spoke louder than words. Intuition had always been their guide, but would it be strong enough for something so important?

Thalia searched the others' faces. They were all asking the same question, though no one voiced it: How would they know if the men had changed—and how could they make them change in the first place?

"Why don't we offer them a one-and-done option?" Thalia finally broke the silence. "What if we can get them to agree to an Ayahuasca ceremony? That might be enough to shift them. We can have Brooke get it for us."

Monica smiled.

Cath shook her head and glared at Thalia and Monica. "Seriously? You're still on that?"

Shannon looked confused. "I'm obviously out of the loop here. Can someone please fill me in?"

"Before the dragons arrived, Thalia and Monica tried to convince Mel to include Aya in the protocol. She was very clear she wouldn't use it under any circumstances." Cath motioned towards Thalia and Monica. "These two wouldn't drop it. I heard them say some pretty awful things about Mel over it, too."

"Even if I disagree with Mel, which I'm not sure I do," said Shannon, "what makes you think you could get the men to agree to it, especially after what's happened? I mean, Matt's traumatized. Why would he say yes to Ayahuasca?"

Cath crossed her arms in defiance. "There's no way I'm asking Matt to do it."

"Cath, I'm really sorry about what you heard between me and Thalia. I regretted saying what I said immediately after it came out of my mouth. You know I can be bullheaded, and I have no filter. That doesn't excuse what I said, though." Monica reached for Cath's hand, but she brushed it away.

"Hear us out," said Thalia. "Obviously, we disagree with Mel. Monica's spent most of her adult life working with Aya. Mel had very little experience with it. The cultural appropriation thing, well, that's subjective, and there are no right answers. What we want you to consider, like really give it some thought…if getting the men to do Ayahuasca allows them to work together and solve the problem, then why wouldn't we try? Everything… I mean, everything we've done here is morally shady. Why is this one thing off the table?"

Shannon sucked her bottom lip and nodded.

"I know this isn't easy, but I think it's the right thing to do." Thalia reached over and squeezed Cath's hand. "I think I can convince Josh, and I think he can convince the others."

"Fuck each and every one of you." Cath pulled her hand away from Thalia. "I'm so done. Do *not* come after me. Do not knock on my door. The only time I want to hear from any of you is if we're getting out of this place. I want nothing to do with this. Oh, and by the way, Monica, it was more about her not having faith in you leading a ceremony than it was about cultural appropriation."

"Cath…please…don't…" Thalia's words bounced off her as Cath stormed out of the room.

CHAPTER FORTY-THREE

JOSH SAT AT THE TABLE, HIS FINGERS DRUMMING AGAINST THE polished wood when the sound of Thalia clearing her throat snapped him to attention. She stepped into the room, her presence commanding without effort.

The atmosphere was heavy with failure; hours spent talking in circles and getting nowhere. The men were spinning their wheels while the world outside waited for something to change.

"I think it would be a good time for you to take a lunch break. Let's meet back here in about two hours. We'll give you a twenty-minute warning before we'd like you to come back," Thalia said to the group.

Josh's chair scraped against the floor as he stood, ready to follow the other men, who had scattered. Before he made it to his door, Thalia intercepted him.

"Josh, can I have a minute?"

He tried to read her face. It wasn't frustration or disapproval he found; instead, it was closer to gratitude.

"Thank you, Josh. I know that conversation must have been difficult for you. I think you made a difference. There's something I need to ask you. Would you mind joining me for lunch?"

He laughed. "Sure. At least this time, I know I'm not in trouble."

As Josh stepped into Thalia's apartment, a sense of comfort welcomed him. The layout of the rooms was almost identical to his own, the way the sun sliced through the hallway, the windows, but everything in it was undeniably hers. The walls, a riot of color, had tapestries woven with stories hung beside mismatched paintings bursting with life.

"You've made this place...yours." His eyes rested on a wall-hanging depicting Buddha seated in the lotus position.

She smiled as she reached for some plates. "I like being surrounded by things that have meaning. Everything in here has a story."

He nodded as he studied the furniture. Plush and inviting, the armchairs and couches were worlds away from the sleek, angular designs of his home. A worn velvet armchair, its fabric softened by years of use, beckoned from the corner. For a moment, he imagined himself sinking into it with a glass of wine and a book, something he hadn't done for decades.

"It's alive in here."

"Alive is good." She lit a candle on the counter. The subtle scent of sandalwood mingled with citrus. "I've always felt a home should reflect the person living in it. Don't you?"

He shrugged. "Never thought about it. My spaces tend to reflect function and minimalism more than anything."

"That's probably why they don't feel like home."

Her words held a quiet truth that caught him off guard, but he didn't respond.

Thalia pulled a few items out of the fridge and assembled tofu curry wraps while he thumbed through the book titled

"Consciousness Medicine" by Francoise Bourzat, which he found on the coffee table.

"That's a great book. You're welcome to take it with you when you leave if you'd like," she said as she put a plate of food on the table for him.

"Uh, thanks."

"So, the reason I wanted to talk to you is we have an idea we're hoping you'll help us with."

Taking a big bite from his wrap, he looked at her as if to say, "Go on."

She drew a long breath in through her nose. "Please hear me out before you form an opinion."

"Oh...kay." The food stuck in his throat as he swallowed.

"We think if you can convince the others to do a group Ayahuasca ceremony, it might be enough to shift them."

He choked on his lunch. "You've got to be fucking kidding me!"

"I know. It sounds ludicrous, but we believe it's our best shot. If you explain to them one ceremony with it can sometimes be as effective as multiple sessions with the other substances, they might understand this could be the quickest way home."

"Matt and William don't know how much the MDMA and mushrooms can shift them. How am I supposed to explain that to them?"

"By *showing* them. By showing them who you are now."

"There's no way Matt and William would agree. I think Joel and Mykle are more open to it, but the other two, uh-uh, no way."

"Maybe," she conceded. "But this isn't just about getting them to heal themselves. It's about getting us to trust them. It's about what happens when someone lets go. Ayahuasca has a way of forcing people to face the parts of themselves they usually hide. If they're willing to do that, together, in front of us, it'll show they're serious about changing. That they're not just saying what we want to hear so they can go back to their own lives."

Josh looked at the ceiling, his skepticism unshaken. "And what if they don't want to change? If they just refuse?"

"Then we'll know that too. But at least we'll have tried. We'll have given them every opportunity we can think of. And if they do open up, it could change everything."

Josh ate the rest of his lunch in silent contemplation.

"Why do you want me to talk to them?" he said, breaking the stillness. "Why can't you do it?"

"You're one of them. As much as you might not like each other, you can all relate. They know who you were in the corporate world, and they can clearly see you're a different person now. It'll have a lot more impact coming from you."

He leaned back in the chair; the velvet cradled him like a mother's gentle hands. Running his fingers through his hair, he filled his cheeks with air and let out a muted hum as he exhaled.

"I can try, but you better have a Plan B and you're going to have to coach me on what to say. I don't know shit about dealing with other people's trauma, and I'm expecting Matt to be apoplectic when he hears this idea. I have no idea what William's reaction will be, but I don't think it'll be pleasant."

"Uh- huh, yep. I know. With Matt, it'll be crucial to tell him you understand how difficult it'll be for him. You have to let him speak about what happened and show empathy without judgment. Validating his emotions with an understanding of his fears will hopefully go a long way. After that, it'll be important to explain the positive aspects of the ceremony and how it could potentially be the key that unlocks everyone's freedom."

He rose and collected their dishes to take to the sink. On his way back, he paused by the window, hands on his hips and his mind on Matt. He hadn't given much thought to how he must feel after what happened to Mel. He hadn't given much thought to anyone's feelings, for that matter, including his own.

He stared out the window as if he might find answers there. He didn't want to admit to himself or anyone that he was grieving for Mel. How could he be, after everything she'd done to him? But grief was there, creeping in. Wasn't it too soon for Stockholm syndrome? Though that would explain it, wouldn't it? A neat, clinical explanation. But deep down, he knew it wasn't that simple.

He moved through a sea of contradictions, struggling to make sense of his emotions. And yet, despite everything, her death felt like losing a piece of himself; his new self. There she was, entwined within the fabric of his recent experiences. Experiences he now admitted had changed everything about him.

But Thalia was there too. He yearned to tell her everything, but a primal fear held him back. He chose to stay silent. Instead, he pictured the conversation he'd have with the others. They wouldn't understand. He didn't know if they'd hear him through their own anger and fear.

He'd spent most of his life ignoring the feelings of others. It wasn't a conscious decision; it was more of a reflexive shield he'd built around himself. An invisible wall of detachment. But the past few weeks had cracked that wall, letting emotions crash in like a tidal wave. The idea of letting himself feel was terrifying, yet he was beginning to understand the toll of keeping everything locked away.

"What do we do about William?" His question was as much to himself as it was to Thalia.

"I'm hoping that by listening to your conversation with Matt, he'll realize this might be his only option."

"Interesting. I hope you're right. What if William reacts before Matt?"

"I'd suggest starting the entire conversation by addressing Matt."

CHAPTER FORTY-FOUR

JOSH ARRIVED BEFORE EVERYONE ELSE. HIS FINGERS FOUND THE HEM of his shirt again, fidgeting with nervous energy. He leaned on the table at the front of the room while he waited.

This self-doubt wasn't a sensation he was accustomed to. He was the most confident person he knew, but he had never dealt with something like this. Used to commanding a room full of shareholders while he spoke in numbers and graphs, talking about himself, the real him, was nothing short of terrifying.

Would Matt listen to his apology? Would he believe it? Josh wasn't sure if he would if the roles were reversed. The thought twisted tighter in his gut as he rehearsed words that sounded emptier each time he tried to form them in his mind.

The sound of footsteps broke his spiraling thoughts. Matt entered first, dragging his chair out and dropping into it with a casual defiance that spoke volumes. He tilted it back on two legs, balancing precariously as his fingers tapped a sharp staccato that punctuated the hostility between them. His eyes narrowed, locking on Josh with unspoken accusations.

Clearing his throat, William took the seat next to Matt. He settled in without expression. Soon, Mykle and Joel followed.

They exchanged a brief look that said they felt the static in the air. Without a word, they sat in front of him.

Josh's lips twitched, aiming for a smile, but it faltered mid-flight, twisting into a grimace before vanishing altogether. He anchored himself, grounding his feet and inhaling through his nose.

"You're probably wondering what I'm doing up here. I'll sit down soon, but I wanted to get your attention before any conversations began. I...uh... hmm... okay, now I feel a bit foolish."

A bead of sweat threatened to roll down his face. He hoped the others didn't interpret the moisture as fear. Nervous energy propelled him to his seat. He perched like a coiled spring on his chair, muscles taut, as the other men stared at him quizzically.

"Sorry," he said as he got settled. "I'm a bit nervous, which I'm not accustomed to, so here goes... I kind of made an apology before lunch, but I want to specifically apologize to Matt."

Were these men, Matt in particular, capable of forgiveness? His heart hammered against his ribs.

Matt crossed his arms and narrowed his eyes further. "Seriously?"

Josh shifted his weight. The disbelief in Matt's face cut through him, and for a moment, Josh's confidence was lacking. But he pressed forward. "Look, I know we've had our differences, but what I said to you about Mel's death was incredibly insensitive, and I truly apologize for that."

Matt didn't budge. His arms stayed firmly crossed, eyes boring into Josh. "Okay," he said flatly, his tone offering no absolution, only a challenge.

The skepticism radiating off Matt was undisguised.

"I was taken off guard and reacted without thinking. I'm guessing none of us has gotten where we are in life by being empathetic." Josh looked around at the men, not sure what he was hoping to see in their faces. "I'm learning. I can't imagine how you feel, and being locked up here can only be making it worse." He paused before continuing. "I think if we have any hope of getting out of here, we need to get to know each other as people and start thinking like a team."

"Ah, let me guess..." William's face twisted into a sneer. "You want us to play some... how do you say it... trusting games? Like falling into each other's arms or telling two truths and one lie. Of course, you, with your American optimism, would think a heart-to-heart could solve our problems." William snorted. "A simple apology won't magically change the situation."

Unphased by the Germans' dry sarcasm, Josh continued to speak directly to Matt. "As I was saying earlier, I think we have an amazing opportunity here. We either get serious about it, or we might as well all go back to our apartments and play with VR for the rest of our lives. Matt, if you're willing to forgive me, not only for what I've said here, but for everything, I'd love to work with you. I'd love to work with all of you. We were chosen for a reason... because we're smart enough to succeed. I'm excited to see what we can do together."

His words hung heavy with implication. His hands became clammy as he waited for Matt's reaction. The silence stretched, pulling tighter at the pressure in the room. Matt's jaw, clenched so tightly it looked like it might crack, began to relax. Josh caught the faintest shift in his posture and a flicker of something less hostile in his eyes.

Matt dipped his head, his lips pressed into a thin line, but the gesture spoke volumes. Not forgiveness, but acknowledgment. Their eyes met in an unspoken truce.

"This does not solve the women's trust issue." William's voice cut through the fragile peace.

Josh flinched. William's sharp tone made the tension in the room bubble back to the surface. He bobbed his head, forcing himself to stay level-headed.

"You're probably right, William. I beg you... all of you, to keep an open mind and don't jump to any hasty decisions when you hear what I'm about to say."

His palms rested on the table, fingers splayed, bracing for balance. He scanned the men's faces—Matt's lingering skepticism, William's cool scrutiny, and glimmers of curiosity from Joel and Mykle. He looked each one in the eye, demanding a connection; seeking assurance they'd be fully present, attuned to his words. When he spoke, his voice was less demanding than his gaze. It was a voice even he was unfamiliar with.

"I've spent my whole life running from my past, from my fears, from myself. My father, well, he drank. He drank a lot. And when he wasn't drinking—and when he was—he was angry. And when he was angry..." He looked at his hands. "Let's say he didn't just yell. And then Pam. She was the first person who ever showed me what love without conditions felt like. She saw something in me I didn't know was there. And...and I betrayed her."

"Lisa," Matt mumbled the name.

"Not only Lisa." Josh's eyes were still on his hands. "I let ambition consume me. The boardrooms, the deals, the power. It all felt safer than feeling anything real. I thought if I worked hard enough, achieved enough, I could drown out the noise."

"That is not exactly unusual." William's voice was low.

"No, it's not. But here's the thing, it's also not sustainable." He let out a humorless laugh. "I missed birthdays, anniversaries, entire chapters of my boy's lives. And for what? Another comma in my net worth?"

Matt uncrossed his arms. "So what's your point, Josh? Why are you telling us all this now?"

"I want you to know me. I want you to know me as a real person, not just what you hear about on the news. And I want you to trust me."

"There is that word again," William muttered under his breath.

Josh smiled at William with a small upward movement of his chin, acknowledging the older man's skepticism. "None of you has any reason to trust me, I get that, but we must start trusting each other before we can expect the women to trust us. I want to tell you about my experiences here that have profoundly changed the way I think about things and have, I believe, allowed Mel and Thalia to have some assurances about my motives."

Matt's knuckles whitened as he gripped the arms of his chair at the mention of Mel's name. He squeezed his eyes shut. A grimace contorted his face, twisting his features into a mask of pain. Seeing him wince, Josh's heart sank, knowing he had inadvertently created a gap that required another apology.

"I'm sorry, Matt."

"Look," interrupted Mykle, "I don't know that it would be beneficial to hear about your trips, especially not for Matt. Is there a way you can get to your point?"

"I won't beat around the bush then. Matt, think of this as fighting fire with fire. Ayahuasca... a group ceremony."

Mykle couldn't contain his anger as his wide eyes met Joel's. The women had completely blindsided them, and the audacity of their decision boiled under his skin. It wasn't as if Josh had come up with that idea on his own.

Ayahuasca? A group ceremony? He gave no thought to the apprehension radiating from the other men. His focus sharpened on the women's betrayal. They knew better. At least Mel had. Her voice echoed in his memory, resolute during their discussions. "It's too risky," she'd said. "Ayahuasca isn't just another tool in the kit. It's way more powerful, and it demands respect."

She'd told them it was like a mushroom trip on steroids, and psychotic breaks were possible. And because she believed in following cultural traditions, she didn't think it was appropriate for the project due to its group nature. Her concern was rooted in the very real danger that a voyager experiencing a breakdown could jeopardize not only their own safety, but the entire group's. A single unraveling might ripple through the delicate shared experience, disrupting the collective journey and potentially pulling the others into the chaos.

Psychotic breaks were rare, but not unprecedented, and managing them was a daunting task. Mel's insistence on excluding the medicine was more than caution, though. It was an attestation to her deep care for the dragons' well-being and her commitment to their safety.

Mykle's mind raced, desperately searching for a way to navigate this unexpected turn of events. His palm was wet on his forehead as he rubbed his temple. He was at a loss for words, his confident voice silenced by the shock.

The realization that he and Joel had no way of privately conversing with the women without arousing suspicion only added to his growing anxiety. He looked at Joel, trying not to draw attention, but Joel looked as lost as he felt.

"I'm sorry, what?" Mykle's voice was laced with confusion. He was now stuck in this bizarre situation, and Josh, instead of offering a clear plan, was talking about Ayahuasca.

"The women believe it could be a one-and-done experience. It'll go a long way in getting them to trust us, and it could help us figure out the problem," Josh replied.

"Why would it work better than MDMA and mushrooms? And why a group ceremony rather than us doing it independently with our guides?" Mykle had absolutely no desire to take drugs with the other men.

When Brooke had approached him and Joel with her plan, he had been skeptical of psychedelic-assisted therapy, but seeing the data and experiencing it firsthand was a revelation. He had no doubt it had profound effects in a short amount of time, but a group Ayahuasca ceremony was pushing his limits.

"Thalia said it's much more potent than the other drugs, and it has a way of really connecting people to...what did she say...

Pachamama, I think? Basically, she believes it'll give us a different perspective on nature—a better understanding of our place in the universe." Josh sounded like he was asking a question rather than making a statement. "And as far as doing it as a group, she says Monica is the only one who's trained to do a ceremony, and in a group she says there's a chance our consciousnesses...is that even a word... might somehow come together."

Mykle could tell from the other men's puzzled looks that they had similar questions.

"Look, I don't understand or believe half of what she told me." Josh got up and took a few steps before spinning on his heel and walking back. "But I do believe her when she says it'll help us gain their trust, so that's why I'm asking you to agree to this. I just don't see any other way to get out of this place."

"What if it does not work?" asked William.

Josh bit his bottom lip and shook his head. "Look. If anyone has a better idea, I'd love to hear it." He sat down, put his elbows on the table, and ran his hands through his hair. "I'm not trying to make things worse here. I'm just try..."

Matt interrupted. The corner of his eyes was wet as he spoke. "I...I don't think I can do it."

"Think of it like we're in an airplane that's about to crash. We have parachutes. It's going to be terrifying to jump, but it's a hell of a lot better than the other option." Josh made eye contact with each man again.

William leaned back in his chair, his speech faltering as he searched for the words in English. "I cannot see how a mystical experience is going to solve the problems."

Josh acknowledged the old man with a smile. "I get it, William. It's a leap of faith, and I'm not asking you to believe in the mystical. I'm asking you to believe this might garner their trust and the possibility that a shared experience might break down the walls dividing us."

Mykle wasn't convinced. "How do we know this won't make things worse?"

"I wish I had all the answers." Josh rested his head in his hands. "But the reality is, we're stuck in a situation with limited options."

Matt spoke up again. "I'm too scared. The thought of losing control again terrifies me."

"Matt, we're all scared. You have every reason to be more frightened than the rest of us. It's okay to be scared. I'd think there's something wrong with you if you weren't, but aren't you more afraid of never getting back to your life?" asked Josh.

Matt sat there, hands trembling, as he absorbed Josh's words. He closed his eyes and wiggled his jaw.

"How long are our companies going to wait for us? They're probably moving on already. Or at least trying to figure out how. Can they wait another month... or year? I doubt it. I want something left for me to go back to. And I want to see my kids." Josh was looking only at Matt.

He opened his eyes and met Josh's. Determination flashed amidst fear as he took a breath. "You're right, Josh. I'm scared. Who wouldn't be? But I can't let it take over. I've got way too much to lose."

Josh let out a breath and looked at the German, who was leaning back in his chair, a sardonic smile playing on his lips.

"So, are we all going to hold hands and sing Kumbaya now?" William said, with dry humor. "I told the women I would not do the drugs. I will meditate while you do."

Impressed by how Josh had convinced Matt to agree to the ceremony, Mykle now felt ready to confront his own fears about it. Who knows, the plan might work.

"William, we're about the same age. Never in my wildest dreams did I ever think I'd be taking drugs. Honestly, I've thought of them as an evil force in society with nothing good to offer anyone. I didn't know Josh personally before coming to this place, but I think I knew enough about him to realize he isn't acting here. I do think he's changed. And I think the women see it too and trust him." Mykle was more shocked by what came out of his own mouth than the others seemed to be.

Joel, who had been silent the whole time, finally spoke. "If Josh thinks the women will trust us if we do this, then I think it's worth considering. Like he said, we don't have too many other options." He stood up and walked over to the window as he finished his thought. "I'll do it."

"I'll do it too." Mykle looked at William. "It's one time. Nobody needs to know but us. You're the last piece. Can we please all go home?"

William rose and crossed the room to where Joel stood. He shook his head as he stared out the window. "Fein."

CHAPTER FORTY-FIVE

THE CEREMONIAL FIRE BURNED BRIGHTLY IN THE CENTER OF THE clearing. It cast flickering shadows that danced upon the ground like apparitions. The flames seemed to possess a wisdom of their own, whispering secrets to those who dared to listen. Surrounding the fire in a semi-circle were five mats covered with blankets, each with an empty bucket beside it.

An altar stood at the forefront of the fire; a low flat stone, the foundation. It was weathered and worn, grounding it in the essence of the natural world. Monica placed herbs and flowers on it. Sprigs of sacred plants, like sage and Palo Santo, smoldered. Their aroma cleansed the air and prepared the space for the journey that was about to unfold.

A small ornate bowl rested on the stone, cradling the heart of the ceremony—the Ayahuasca brew. Its dark, earthy liquid seemed to hold the wisdom of generations as it shimmered with a faint luminescence that hinted at the otherworldly nature of the journey it promised.

As moonlight filtered through the clouds, it bathed the landscape in a soft, silvery glow. The entire altar became a living, breathing entity as the light sparkled on it, witnessing the connection between nature, spirit, and the transformative power of the ceremony.

The crackling flames danced wildly, throwing patterns of light and dark on the men's faces as they took their places beside the blazing fire. Their eyes reflected a blend of curiosity and fear. Nobody spoke. The stillness was broken only by the distant hoot of an owl and the occasional pop of a log.

Draped in flowing white linen, Monica stepped in front of the altar. With a reverence born of ancient rituals, she closed her eyes and inhaled. The stars whispered their secrets into her lungs. She used a handmade, wooden Melina spoon to pour a measure of the thick liquid into a small clay cup. Holding it to the sky, she said a soft prayer only she and the heavens heard. She then raised it to her lips.

"Pachamama, Madre Ayahuasca," she sang after imbibing, "Keeper of the unseen, weaver of visions, I call upon your spirit tonight. Guide these seekers on their journeys, reveal hidden truths, mend fractured souls. Bless them with your boundless wisdom."

She dipped her fingers in a clay bowl filled with water, which reflected the cosmos above.

She called on Pachamama as she poured a handful of liquid onto the earth as an offering. From a braided bag, she retrieved her quena, its wooden body cool against her palm. She lifted it to her mouth and brought forth an icaro; a song woven from moonlight and starlight, the whispers of leaves and secrets of the river. It snaked through the air like a bridge between worlds as it invited the unseen to witness the ceremony.

She moved around the altar, singing and dancing as she traced celestial patterns in the dust. Her chants were older than time. Each guttural sound reverberated in the bones of the earth. It was a language that transcended words like a communion with the ancestors. She pleaded for protection and guidance.

She paused with an inner fire burning deep within her. She met the men's anxious eyes with a voice filled with promise.

"Tonight, we walk the razor's edge between worlds," she announced. "We confront shadows and embrace light. We journey into the heart of ourselves. We seek guidance for transformation. Mother Ayahuasca awaits you. Are you ready?"

The ceremony had begun.

One by one, she called the men up to the altar. For each voyager, she wove a unique icaro in the Shipibo language, which drew on their fears and yearnings. She mirrored their inner landscapes in sound.

Matt approached her with a measured stride. The sound of the crackling fire and a distant frog added to the melody of Monica's song. With hands clenched by his sides, he met her with surprising resolve. Monica held out a small clay cup. Its surface was dull, even in the firelight.

"Matt," she said, her voice low and calming, "the mother offers her guidance. Are you ready to receive?"

Matt signaled his agreement by inclining his head. She dipped the wooden spoon into the bowl on the altar and poured the deep amber brew into Matt's cup. As Matt brought it to his mouth, Monica sang to him—a melody soft and mournful. It conveyed both regret for past hurts and a pledge for future restoration.

As the bitter brew landed on his tongue, he shuddered at the wave of nausea that rolled through him. The icaro swelled as it leaped into a joyous chant, urging him to release and surrender to the journey. Matt returned to his spot next to Mykle and closed his eyes. The world dissolved into the rhythm of the music.

Mykle, then Josh, then Joel, and finally William had their song sung to them and drank the pungent liquid. After administering the last dose, Monica raised her quena once more and sent an icaro into the night. She called the unseen guardians and pleaded for protection and safe passage. Then silence descended, thick and expectant.

The voyagers lay nestled on their mats with eyes closed and soft breaths. Their journey had begun. They were guided by the whispers of the golden grass blowing in the gentle summer breeze and the potent wisdom of the mother vine.

With each breath and each heartbeat, they stepped into the void. With their eyes closed and their bodies relaxed, their minds opened. The men had surrendered themselves to the journey. It remained to be seen whether they'd find comfort, revelation, or a confrontation with their own demons.

CHAPTER FORTY-SIX

THALIA SAT OUTSIDE THE SEMI-CIRCLE, WATCHING AND WAITING. She crossed her legs at the ankles. The silky-smooth fabric of her meditation cushion was soft against her exposed thighs. Her back was straight as she methodically fingered her Mala beads. The popping of the fire swallowed her muffled cough.

Other than her hands, she sat perfectly still. Though relief bloomed in her heart that the men had agreed, it was overshadowed by a torrent of anxieties. Visions of the men writhing in fear, trapped in a psychedelic nightmare, sent a cold ripple of anxiety through her blood. Even if they endured it, a niggling doubt persisted. Could a single experience, however profound, bridge the chasm between their egos and the monumental task of saving the planet? She squeezed her beads tighter, a silent prayer for the men and for the future of the Earth pulsating with each touch.

The low reverberation of Monica's drum as she danced around the fire filled Thalia's chest as the men waited for the medicine to come on. Her eyes monitored their faces, watching for signs of the shift. Tiny tremors began to run through their closed eyelids. Were they visions they saw? Battles fought, victories won? Or was it fear of the unknown lurking in the quiet space between breaths?

Matt hastily grabbed the orange bucket beside him and stumbled away from the fire. Thalia followed behind him, careful to give him space, but near enough to assist if necessary.

As he crumpled to his knees, a searing pain ignited in Matt's gut. A serpent hatched from an egg beneath his diaphragm, its scales glistening with bile. It writhed through his insides, coiling around his stomach as it made its way up through his ribs. Pressing against his lungs, it searched for his heart, and when it found it, it squeezed. The merciless constriction crushed his organ until it burst into a thousand shards of light, which shot out of his chest and filled the sky.

The serpent slithered a path through his sternum, up his throat, and out of his mouth, dragging with it a flood of black tar that coated his teeth and tongue. He heaved into his bucket.

The tar moved. It formed legs. Thousands upon thousands of tiny twitching limbs. Ants crawled up and out, skittering across his hands and arms, before completely swarming his body. Some poured into his ears, others crawled into his nose. And they didn't just crawl, they burrowed; slipping into his pores, digging into muscle and memory.

They whispered to him. "You trained them to scroll past extinction. You made distraction and hate more addictive than action."

The visions they showed him were screens filled with filters and influencers. The algorithms he wrote buried deforestation beneath engagement metrics. Rage won. Lies spread faster than facts.

Just as he reached the edge of madness, they stopped. Then—a shift.

The bodies of the ants grew, swelling as they lifted him with a reverence he didn't understand. With coordinated movements, they marched with him on their backs across a post-apocalyptic landscape—tree stumps like gravestones, riverbeds cracked dry— until they returned him to the fire.

He curled into himself, sobbing as he watched them build cities out of mud beside him. Each ant's actions perfectly coordinated with the others as they toiled as a team. They were a force that couldn't be ignored. A single ant was insignificant, a speck of life easily crushed. But together, they could accomplish incredible feats.

Each insect, so small, so inconsequential, yet so vital to the whole. Maybe Josh was right. Maybe their differences, their pasts, were just that—the past. Maybe what mattered now was the future. A future they could only build together.

He reached for the bucket. More black tar.

Monica set her drum aside and reached for her bundle of Chacapa leaves, their stems bound tight with twine. The leaves rustled like rain as she stepped toward Matt's trembling form. She shook the bundle in rhythm over him. Her voice followed, chanting in the language of the Shipibo-Konibo people of the Peruvian Amazon:

The river flows with one heart. Our paths woven together in moonlight.

The children of mother river, the children of father fire, water, man, mountain, and mother, all one breath.

A single song, a single heart, bathed in moonlight.

When Monica concluded the chant, she continued to dance with the Chakapa, stopping at each reclined man to shake the leaves over him.

As the bundle rattled over William, he sat bolt upright and

began to moan. His body undulating as he hummed louder and louder, hands reaching to the sky as if he were grasping at the brilliant stars. His humming turned into an anguished wail, and tears streamed down his face.

He was ten again, barefoot in a field, chasing butterflies with his sister. The sun and sky, warm and infinite. As he laughed, the field blackened. The grass withered beneath his feet. He ran, but the field stretched into a factory floor. His childhood home became a smokestack.

Shooting into the sky in the form of a golden dragon, he soared over a pristine river valley. For a breath, he was free. Then the stench hit him.

Below, the blue river curdled to brown sludge. Fish floated belly-up in thick, glistening heaps. Factories bearing his name squatted on either bank, vomiting waste into the water.

He roared and turned away, only to find miles of land stripped bare. Forests replaced with factories. Children coughing in smog. Oceans clogged with discarded clothing.

He plummeted as his wings detached from his body. Naked and shivering, he landed in a wasteland. Mountains of cast-off garments towered around him, blocking the sun. The ground trembled with the cries of people he'd never met but whose suffering had bought his comfort.

With a roar, he ignited the mountains of waste. In the fire's wake, rebirth emerged: People helping one another, children playing in fields of daisies, and parents planting trees that grew into forests. They were naked, free of shame, anger, or privilege; all equal, as if Eden had been restored.

Overcome by the intense effects of the Ayahuasca, a wave of nausea swept over him. Black tar in his bucket was a cathartic release of his prior life.

Monica's chanting became strong and fast:

Darkness dances within our blood. With one breath, we forgive man and spirit. With one fire, we cleanse our shared breath.

In one river, we flow as one. Tree, water and man, one heartbeat. Darkness transformed, life reborn in light.

Energy rushed through Joel as the Chakapa bounced above him. The rhythm resonated in his chest.

But his body wasn't his own. His cells thrummed like overloaded circuits, pulsing with code instead of blood. Neurons fired in stuttering loops, caught in recursive patterns—if/then, yes/no, more/more/more.

His breath came in jagged bursts, out of sync with the rhythm. He tried to steady himself, but his lungs were controlled by a program; his entire body a simulation.

He reached for the ground and found nothing but signal.

Then came the sound: The low whir of machines. Millions of them. Devouring power, churning data, blinking their lifeless eyes. Servers scattered across deserts, mountains, and rainforests. Places whose destruction he had silently financed.

He stumbled through rubble with his mechanical legs, down into a place without technology. A root system. Fungal threads weaving through soil. Tiny filaments passing messages between trees. Language older than code. Connection without interface.

He gasped, lungs filling not with data, but with air. Dropping to his knees, his hands finally flesh and bone again, pressed into the earth. Tears came, but not from shame, instead from gratitude. A quiet knowing bloomed in his heart. The system could be rewritten.

A gentle pull from a cord brought him back to the circle. His heartbeat was the rhythm of all existence.

Monica chanted:

Sun's fire and moon's glow, woven as one. Mother Earth breathes in one shared breath.

Tree and man, forever entwined. Darkness transforms, life reborn in light. One moon, one sun, one song in space.

My life, your life, one life ablaze.

Monica danced by the firelight, singing the Icaros of the Shapibo people of the forest. She knew the weight of the men's fears, the ecstasy of their joy, and the tears of their pain. Like the mother vine herself, her consciousness was entangled with theirs. She wasn't only experiencing their emotions; she was experiencing their memories. She lived their lives, their triumphs and regrets, and knew their sorrows and love.

Smoke tendrils curled around her face as the Ayahuasca pulsed through her veins. A tremor ran through her, but it wasn't the usual signal of a purge; it was more like a cellular earthquake, each atom splitting, birthing universes within. Her consciousness slipped into Mykle's.

At first, she floated. His vision rose like a hymn—clean energy drove vehicles through cities woven with green rooftops and vertical gardens. There was pride in him. Hope too. And love. Real love for the planet. He wanted to save it. She felt it in her marrow.

But beneath it, something else.

The entire bright world began to collapse. They fell, down through headlines hailing him as the climate billionaire, the eco-visionary, the man who had found a way.

They landed hard.

A girl stood before them, thin, barefoot, and covered in mud. Behind her, cities flooded with rising water. Roads buckled. Smoke blocked the sun.

She stared at them, not with accusation, but with exhaustion. "You made it better. But only for those who could pay. You were the best of them, but you were still one of them."

Monica felt Mykle's heart break. He hadn't meant to withhold anything. But every solution had a price tag. Every advance rolled out first to the elite. His greed was the quiet kind. The kind that cloaked itself in purpose. The insistence that doing good could justify holding on to more than anyone should.

Monica bowed her head, Mykle's grief heavy in her chest, his breath rasping in her ear.

※

Thalia sat with her legs wide, Monica's back propped up against her chest. Monica's weary body swayed in unison with hers as Thalia sang to her in Shipibo:

Darkness and light, one love binds man and spirit as one. With love, we weave worlds as one. Mother Earth breathes one life.

Children of moonlight, hand in hand. With love, we bind earth and sky. One life, one breath.

Held in Thalia's strength, Monica made contact with Josh. She wasn't only his guide; she was his fellow traveler, dragged into a reckoning of his family history.

The air bit with a chill as they were yanked through time. Stone walls closed in, streaked with soot and stained with blood. A woman with frostbitten fingers cradled a dead infant against her chest. Men with hollow cheeks staggered through streets, hands raw from digging graves.

A voice, rough with ash, spoke. "We crossed oceans with nothing. We buried children. We suffered kings and plagues. And you? What did you do with our survival? You became the king. You sat atop the world, and still you wanted more. We didn't suffer so you could poison the future."

Monica and Josh descended through the earth, roots piercing their bodies. Josh screamed as the tree of life grew from his chest, fed by oil and blood.

The branches formed a face. His grandfather's. "You think empire is legacy? You call this progress? We did not endure for this. We did not carry your name through the fire for you to scorch the world."

Monica felt Josh's anguish rising like a tide. But then there was light. Small and flickering like a firefly. She followed him as he chased the spark through meadows of memory, over the mountains of what he had built and what he had broken, into a stillness that felt like forgiveness.

With each vision of his father, and Pam and his boys, the walls he had built around him fell, revealing the raw, messy beauty of his soul.

Through her eyes, Josh saw himself, not as the world judged him, but as he truly was; enough. Tears washed away the dust of self-deception, and together they bathed in the golden glow of self-acceptance. Emerging, radiant, and reborn, they returned to the circle.

The night began to fade. Monica had one last voyage to undertake. She reached out, not with physical hands, but with her awareness, weaving all five men's threads into a single tapestry. A single story about the planet.

They were no longer individuals, but facets of a single crystal reflecting the same luminous truth. Through William's eyes, she witnessed the pain of deforestation, the lungs of the planet choked by greed. Matt's anger, a smoldering ember in his gut, kindled by the plight of endangered creatures, also burned within her. She tasted Josh's grief, a bitter salt on her tongue, mourning the polluted rivers and silent oceans.

But it wasn't only burdens they shared. They swam in Joel's peace, a cool river washing away doubts, witnessing the interconnectedness of all life, from the tiniest insect to the vast expanse of the universe. They soared with Mykle's hope, a vibrant bird taking flight, envisioning a future where humans and nature thrived in harmony.

Their consciousnesses melded together in a kaleidoscope of shared being. They experienced the same emotions. They saw the same threads connecting all of humanity. Earth was a single, pulsating organism. It was a sentient being full of life and love. They knew the interdependence of all things, from the ants on the ground to each and every human to the infinite galaxies in the limitless universe.

In their shared journey, they saw the truth. Their lives were inseparable. What affected one affected them all. Creation and destruction played out before them, revealing the ebb and flow of life and death, the infinite cycle of becoming. Their interconnectedness was evident, not only as humans, but as stardust, as energy, as consciousness itself.

As the first rays of dawn peaked over the horizon, Monica's vision receded. She opened her eyes, meeting those of her fellow voyagers. They didn't need words. They had all been to the same place. They had seen the same truth; sharing the knowledge that all stories, all lives, were threads in the same grand tapestry. In that knowledge, they found peace and a profound sense of belonging. Belonging to something far greater than themselves.

CHAPTER FORTY-SEVEN

Josh stretched his legs toward the fire, the warmth relaxed his muscles, wrung out after the night's ordeal. His eyelids drooped, then fluttered open, battling the pull of sleep. The tang of bile still lingered in his mouth, a bitter reminder of the purge, but that felt distant now, overshadowed by the surreal clarity that followed.

When Shannon appeared, balancing trays of steaming mugs and snacks, Josh sat up straighter, his body reacting before his mind registered her presence. He wrapped his hands around the ginger tea, savoring its heat as much as its soothing aroma. Across from him, Matt seemed absorbed in a piece of fruit, as if rediscovering the simple act of eating.

For a while, no one spoke. The fire crackled and snapped, filling the space as the men avoided each other's eyes. Vulnerability hung between them like a fragile filament, too thin to bear the weight of words. Josh traced the flower pattern on his mug with his finger, searching for something to say but coming up empty.

Finally, Mykle cleared his throat. "That was…" His voice trailed off before finishing the sentence.

Josh looked up, meeting Mykle's eyes. He nodded, knowing words couldn't capture what they'd been through. The others followed suit, each nodding in unspoken agreement.

It was Joel who broke the dam. "I thought I was above it all," he said quietly. "I designed the world from a distance. But I wasn't part of anything. Not really. I forgot what it meant to touch something real."

Josh found himself leaning forward, pulled in by the rawness in Joel's voice. William's sob startled him. The normally impassive man rubbed a hand across his face as he described his journey through hell.

"It was awful. Truly awful. So much death and destruction. So many screams and fire. The darkness of my soul. But I came out, and it was...light."

The stories tumbled out then, one after another. Josh listened, his own memories surfacing. He hesitated to speak, still shaken, but the open, unguarded faces around him gave him courage. When his turn came, his words flowed without effort, the firelight catching the moisture in his eyes as he spoke of his ancestors.

The conversation shifted as they grew more comfortable. Mykle shared a fond memory of his daughter's wedding, his voice soft with nostalgia. William cracked a joke about his grandkids' insatiable appetites, drawing laughter from the group. Josh found himself smiling more than he had in weeks. The antagonism that had defined so many of their earlier interactions giving way.

By the time the first streaks of daylight lit the horizon, the talk had turned to the world beyond the facility: to climate change, to solutions, to possibilities. The energy was electric, their earlier exhaustion forgotten as ideas sparked like embers in the fire. Josh's heart raced with a mix of hope and urgency. For the first time, a glimmer of belief grew within him. They might actually achieve something. They might get to go home.

Matt stretched, his arms reaching skyward as he groaned. "Guys, how about we take a quick break to shower and change?

We should meet back in the boardroom before we forget any of this."

Josh nodded and grinned. "Great idea. I'm sure I reek, but you're all too nice to point it out."

"Yes, a shower sounds like a good idea." William wrinkled his nose playfully. "And you do not smell that bad, Josh."

"I'm sorry to interrupt you," Thalia's voice broke through their chatter. "I know you want to get to work, and that's fantastic, but I think you should get some sleep and have some time with me or Monica to help you integrate what you've learned. Go home, shower, and sleep. Monica and I'll be in touch later in the afternoon."

Laughter rippled through the group as they stood, their movements stiff but spirits light. As they filed toward their apartments, Josh caught Matt mimicking Mykle's booming laugh, earning a playful swat from the older man. The camaraderie was new, fragile, but it held authenticity. All of Thalia's hopes for the ceremony appeared to be fulfilled. The walls had come down.

Thalia stood by the edge of the pool, arms wrapped loosely around herself, staring out at the prairie. The world beyond the facility felt impossibly still, as if nature was holding its breath, waiting for the men to succeed. She could still feel the hum of last night. Of something bigger than herself, bigger than all of them.

Behind her, she heard the low tones of the conversation between Mykle, Joel, and Monica. It wasn't an argument, not cold, just deliberate. Thoughtful. She turned to face them.

"I'm not saying we're never going to tell them." Joel's hands rested in his lap. "We're talking about timing. About protecting what's been accomplished."

"Protecting it from what?" Monica asked, her voice soft but probing. She sat with her legs crossed at the ankles, her posture open, and her expression impassive. "You've seen what the truth can do. It can heal."

Joel scratched at his scalp. "Sure. But it can also destroy. You think Josh, Matt, or William would still trust us if they knew we orchestrated this whole thing? If they found out this wasn't as organic as it seemed?"

"They might surprise you," Monica said.

Thalia watched Mykle. He hadn't spoken much, but seemed to be absorbing every word so he could calculate his response.

Finally, he spoke. "It's not about whether they'd forgive us. It's about whether telling them helps or hinders the work they're doing now."

"Mykle's right." Thalia wasn't used to taking sides. She was always the peace-keeper. Her upbringing had demanded it. On the ranch, harmony was enforced. Disputes were seen as threats to the family's unity, and unity was everything.

She could still remember her mother's hand on her shoulder after an argument had erupted among the sister wives. "You're the steady one, Thalia. You need to smooth things over so we can all get through the day."

And she had. Over and over. She'd learned to bury her own opinions so deeply that sometimes she wasn't sure she could still find them. But not now. She'd stepped up after Mel's death, and it felt good. Her judgment was as sound as anyone else's.

The three of them turned to her, surprise in their expressions. She hadn't spoken much since the ceremony had ended.

"I don't see the upside to doing it right now." Thalia put her hands on the back of the chair she wasn't occupying, and remained standing. "There might come a day when they can hear it, but we shouldn't jeopardize everything now. Monica, we get it. Truth is important, and none of us finds all the lies easy, but not now."

"Hey Thalia?" Josh's voice interrupted the conversation. "Can I talk to you? Do you have time now?"

"Sure, I'll be right there." She looked at Monica. "We really should be with them."

"Who's going to talk with Matt?" asked Joel.

Cath hadn't opened her door when Thalia went to tell her about the ceremony. No one had seen her for days.

"I'll do it." It wasn't that Thalia didn't think Monica could handle it, but she knew her own approach was softer. Monica's ceremony showed another side of her, but without the Ayahuasca, she had some edges, and Matt was still fragile.

Josh cleared his throat, unsure of where to start. He and Thalia were walking through the VR bamboo forest together. Words, once his sharpest tools, now felt unwieldy, too blunt for what needed to be said.

"I owe you an apology."

Thalia's expression was neutral. She didn't say anything in response, which only made him feel more exposed.

"When I first got here... well, actually, the whole time I've been here, I didn't see you. Not really. I mean, I saw you, but not..." He stopped walking and faced her. "I thought of you as... another woman to conquer."

She raised an eyebrow, but still, she said nothing.

"I was wrong."

She looked him in the eye. "What changed?"

He clicked his teeth together, the question needing thought. "I did," he finally said so quietly he wondered if she heard him. "Or, I'm trying to. All my life, I've been chasing money, power, admiration, and sex. It's never been enough. I've taken more than my share of everything and convinced myself I deserved it." He looked down at his hands, as if they were holding everything he'd taken. "But now, I want to be someone different."

They continued down the boardwalk, sharing tears and stories of their pasts and their dreams for the future.

Monica and William sat on a blanket with the Timmendorfer Strand stretching out before them.

"It's just lovely here. Thank you for suggesting it. I've never been here before." Monica looked out at the placid sea.

"It was my family's vacation spot when I was a child. I have not been back in decades." William's voice was tinged with nostalgia. "This technology is astounding."

The breeze carried the scent of salt and seaweed. He turned to Monica, unsure how to start. The ceremony had stirred something in him, but voicing it felt daunting. He wasn't used to being vulnerable.

"I've been thinking a lot about death," he said. He expected her to react, perhaps with discomfort.

"It's not easy to think about."

"No. No, it is not." He was grateful for her understanding. "I used to be terrified of it. And I was afraid I would die here, well, not here, but in the facility, away from Maria. I thought I would be erased."

The waves lapped gently against the shore. The steady rhythm urged him on.

"But last night, I saw something. I felt it. Death is not the end… it is a return like water in a river flowing into the sea. It does not disappear. It becomes part of something bigger."

He drew in a breath and looked at the water again. "And Maria… she will join me there. We will be a part of it together. Not gone. Just… changed.

For so long, the fear had consumed him, shaped him. He'd needed to ensure he had a legacy, so he'd be remembered. Now, it didn't matter. And letting it go felt like shedding a skin that had grown too tight.

Monica touched his arm. "That's a beautiful way to see it. Thank you for sharing with me."

He nodded, his throat tightening, but not with sorrow. "I cannot believe I say this, but I am grateful. Grateful you choose me."

Matt let his legs dangle in the pool. It was Thalia's suggestion. He'd avoided this spot, but now, with Thalia sitting beside him, he felt lighter. Not free of the guilt yet, but not drowning in it either.

They sat in companionable silence for a while before he spoke. "You were all right. The ceremony, even the mushrooms... such profound learning. I thought I knew what mattered. Building something, achieving something, proving something. But it turns out, it isn't what you do, but who you are."

Thalia looked at him with all the kindness you'd expect from a saint. He was still sorting through the pieces. It felt too big to explain. "And all I want to be," his voice hitched, "is love."

He expected the confession to be embarrassing, but it wasn't. It was the truth.

Thalia smiled. Her gentle energy wrapped around him. "That's a beautiful thing to want."

"It sounds naïve, doesn't it?"

"No," she said simply. "It sounds real."

Matt drew in a breath. "I think I might go to Bhutan. Study with the monks. Crazy, right?"

"No. Not crazy. It sounds like a beginning."

CHAPTER FORTY-EIGHT

REFRESHED AND CLEAN AFTER THEIR INTEGRATION CONVERSATIONS, the men reconvened in the boardroom. Josh stood at the whiteboard, where Mykle's list remained: water, weather, fire, plastic, emissions, fossil fuels, recycling, melting ice caps, livestock, deforestation.

"We have a starting point." He pulled the cap of the marker off with his teeth. "But here's the problem I keep coming back to: There are already thousands of companies, non-profits, and governments tackling these issues. The problem is they're working in silos, often competing for the same funding. What if we created a mechanism to unify them? A network where they could collaborate instead of wasting time and money fighting each other."

Mykle's eyes lit up. "Exactly. We could build a structure where each group focuses on its specialty, but they also coordinate with others on crossover projects. No more redundancies, no more wasted effort."

"There'd need to be a hierarchy," Matt interjected. "Some kind of leadership structure to keep everything organized. Elections within the groups maybe. But what if we went one step further?

What if we broke the problem into five categories and each of us took charge of one?"

Josh nodded, his mind buzzing. "And we'll need funding—significant funding. The women mentioned we could bring others here to help, but we'll need to be strategic about who. This isn't something we can do alone."

Joel, who had been pacing, stopped and turned toward them. "You're talking about a world government."

Josh hesitated, then nodded. "Not publicly. We can't announce we're building a world government. But yes, that's what's needed. A framework that can coordinate global efforts, hold people accountable, and make decisions at a level no *one* country can handle alone. Something that exists to solve climate change, and then equality and war, too. The things the women wanted us to solve."

William's brow furrowed. "It would need to have no bureaucracy. Maybe a council of global representatives, one for each major region, elected, of course."

"And no veto power," Matt added. "This can't become another U.N. gridlock situation. Decisions should be based on consensus, but with timelines. Actionable steps."

"And it has to be inclusive," Joel said. "Not just politicians and billionaires. Scientists, activists, indigenous leaders—people who understand the problems firsthand."

Josh scribbled furiously. He paused, glancing back at them. "We'd also need enforcement mechanisms. Not military power. We know that isn't the answer. But something to ensure countries and corporations actually follow through on agreements. Maybe economic incentives or penalties. But whatever we do, we can't allow the people to suffer."

"Yes, more carrot, less stick." Joel looked pensive. "The moment you start penalizing, it creates resistance. What about an international fund? Something to reward progress instead of punishing failure?"

The ideas ricocheted around the room like fireflies trapped in a jar. The barriers between them completely disappeared as their shared purpose took hold. They weren't prisoners anymore. They were a team.

"What if we ran some sort of contest?" Joel's voice broke through. "A global search for the best minds to join us. A million-dollar prize for a list. A list of fifty people who could make the most impact. Not only the wealthy, but also religious, cultural, and government leaders. The contest would be open to anyone, but with strict criteria. Submissions would need detailed justifications for each nominee. Why this person? What do they bring to the table? So it's not only billionaires getting a say in how the future is shaped."

Josh jotted it down, adding arrows and connections between ideas. "And these people—the fifty—they'd be tasked with refining and implementing this framework."

The whiteboard overflowed with bullet points and diagrams. When he ran out of space, Josh moved to the windows, the marker squeaking as he turned the glass into a canvas of interconnected ideas.

Time evaporated. The sun dipped below the horizon, and Shannon appeared with trays of soup and fresh bread.

"You must be famished." Her words held concern. "After your ceremony, it's best to have something light. Tomorrow, you can have more substantial meals. But please, don't work too late. You need rest."

The men ignored her as they grabbed bowls and kept brainstorming between bites. Josh took a moment to meet her eyes and offered a genuine "thank you" before turning back to the windows.

As night deepened, the initial burst of ideas gave way to harder questions. Matt leaned back, rubbing his shoulder. "This is all great in theory, but how do we make people care enough to change their habits? How do we shift their mindsets?"

Josh hesitated, then quietly sucked in air. "That's where the psychedelics come in."

The room fell silent, but he pressed on. "We've all seen what these experiences can do. How can they crack people open, make them see the world differently? Imagine if we could bring that to leaders, policymakers, and CEOs. People with real influence. If they felt what we've felt... You know, how interconnected everything is...there's no way they could go back to business as usual."

"That is a risky proposition." Skepticism clouded William's face. "You're talking about introductions of something that is still stigmas... stigmatic... no, stigmatized to people with a lot to lose."

"But it works." Matt's voice was gaining strength. "I've spent my life building tech to bring people together, and I've never felt as connected as I did last night. If it can do that for us, it can do that for them."

"And if we can get the people at the top on board, then they'll surely see the potential in letting everyone have access. Controlled access, of course. But think of the problems it could solve. Things like homelessness, depression, anxiety, maybe even gun violence. The possibilities are endless." Joel's voice cracked with enthusiasm.

The discussion grew more animated, the men bouncing between excitement and doubt. They talked logistics—how to implement psychedelic-assisted therapy on a global scale, how to ensure it was done ethically and safely, and how to handle the inevitable backlash.

By the time dawn painted the sky in hues of pink and gold, the men were bleary-eyed but undeterred. Bowls of forgotten soup sat cold on the table, and the windows were covered in layers of scrawled notes.

Josh looked around the room, taking in the faces of his unlikely allies. "We've got something here. It's rough, but it's something."

CHAPTER FORTY-NINE

"Cath?" Thalia knocked on the door again. "Cath, we're going home. They have a plan and we're releasing it today. Please come and watch with us. It wouldn't have happened without you. We need you and love you."

For a moment, there was only silence. She pressed her palm flat against the door as if trying to reach through it, her forehead leaning against the cool surface. "Cath, this is what we've been dreaming of. All the pain, all the sacrifices. It's all been for this. For this moment. Mel would want you to be with us."

The door opened a few inches, revealing Cath's face. Her eyes were swollen and rimmed with red, her cheeks blotchy as if scrubbed raw by the back of her hand. She avoided looking directly through the crack, but it was enough for Thalia.

"I know it's been unbearable, Cath. None of us is the same without her. But she believed in this... in us. Please don't let her sacrifice keep you away now. Please, Cath, please come be with us."

Cath's lips parted before she pressed them shut again. Thalia reached out, resting a hand on her arm. "Don't let the team break apart now. Come, just sit with us."

Cath opened the door wider, but she still didn't look Thalia in the eyes. "Okay."

"Thank you." Relief washed over her as she looped an arm around Cath's shoulders.

The camera light blinked red, and Josh filled his lungs. This was it. The culmination of weeks in captivity and a lifetime of mistakes and realizations. His hands clasped together on the boardroom table as he looked into the lens. The other men sat beside him in quiet solidarity. Their presence emboldened him, each of them fueling his resolve without saying a word.

"Hello world." His voice was steady. "We know you have many questions, and I'm afraid there are some we can't answer. What we can tell you is why we left and why we're back."

Josh glanced at Matt, who gave him a small, encouraging nod.

"We've been working on a plan to solve humanity's most pressing issue: climate change," he continued. "It's a problem touching everything from our water to our air to our very survival. I used to believe we couldn't fix it, that the only option was to look beyond this planet for a new start. But I was wrong. I was wrong about a lot of things."

His voice faltered for a second as he thought of the moments that had brought him here: The mushroom trips forcing him to confront the damage he'd done, the difficult conversations with Thalia, and the camaraderie that had blossomed among the men during the Ayahuasca ceremony. Each step had chipped away at his old self, revealing someone he didn't recognize. Someone he hoped the world would learn to trust.

"While we were gone, we broke the problem into five categories. Each of us will speak on one and explain how our plan addresses it. But before we get to that, let me say this: None of this would have been possible without the guidance we received.

Psychedelic-assisted therapy changed our perspective. It forced us to see the connections between ourselves and the world around us. We hope to use that same therapy as part of this plan, to help others—leaders, policymakers, and citizens—open their eyes to the urgency of this crisis."

He paused, letting the words sink in. The memory of Thalia's quiet encouragement earlier that day bolstered him.

"I'll turn it over to my good friend Matt Aronowitz to start," he said, resting a hand on Matt's shoulder. "He'll talk about greenhouse gas emissions, which encompass industrial processes, transportation, and agriculture. Then Joel Berg, one of the most brilliant people I've had the pleasure of working with, will walk you through renewable energy and technology. This might be the most exciting thing you'll hear today, as we already have several new technologies to show you that will have a huge impact. After Joel, William Becker, one of the kindest, most compassionate people I've ever met, will tell you about land use and deforestation, followed by everyone's favorite billionaire, Mykle Drexel, who'll discuss the human aspect, social and economic equity. Finally, it'll come back to me to end with biodiversity and ecosystems, which will include the plastics problem."

As each man took a turn speaking, he sat back with pride. Matt, with his toothy grin and genuine caring, Joel, so articulate, William, whose passion shone through his words, and Mykle, who brought an unexpected tenderness to his topic.

His turn came last. He felt the weight of every decision he had ever made. Omnicia's ventures, once fueled by ambition and greed, now seemed like relics of a different life. He spoke of plastics choking oceans, species pushed to the brink of extinction, and the urgent need for coordinated action.

"This is our chance." His voice was thick with emotion. "Our chance to undo the damage we've caused, to give future generations a world worth inheriting. But we can't do it alone. We need your help. This isn't about profit or power anymore. It's about survival. It's about hope."

As the camera light went dark, Josh exhaled. They'd done it. Whether the world would listen was another matter entirely.

On screens across the globe, the video feed shifted back to news anchors.

Walt Meyers's face was a mask of earnest intensity as he turned to the camera. "Well, there you have it." His voice was imbued with awe. "A message from five of the world's most powerful men, addressing what might be the most critical issue of our time. Joining me now are three individuals who can help us unpack the groundbreaking announcement. We have climate activist Helga Stienbrunner, CEO of Voltex Electric, and Trevor Bakker. And back with us is agent Randy Stenner of the FBI."

The camera panned to the three guests. Helga, whose cheeks were glistening with unrestrained tears, leaned forward as if she couldn't wait to speak. Trevor, arms crossed, wore a skeptical smirk, while Randy sat stiffly, his expression unreadable.

"Helga. Your reaction?"

"I am trying not to cry, Walt," she admitted, her Scandinavian accent thick. "This is… it is unprecedented. Their plan—what we just heard—could change everything. This is the first time I have felt genuine hope for the planet's future in years. Their approach is bold, collaborative, and inclusive. If they can inspire the world to rally behind this…"

Trevor cut in with a sharp laugh. "Hope is great, but let's be realistic. There's no way governments or corporations will fall in line as easily as they seem to think. They haven't accounted for the political gridlock or the sheer greed entrenched in every system. The whole thing is a pipe dream."

Walt leaned forward. "There's no doubt we'll be talking about this for months, if not years, to come. Whether their plan works or not, it's already sparked a global conversation, and that's something. Stay tuned, folks. We'll be unpacking this story with more guests and experts throughout the day. Up next, we'll have FBI agent Randy Stenner discussing where he thinks these men have been."

As the broadcast continued, Thalia and the others cheered triumphantly.

"To Mel!" Monica raised her glass of champagne, and the women followed.

For now, the men's message was out, the first stone cast into the waters of change. The wave was coming, and they'd be ready. The only question left: who else would rise to meet it?

ABOUT THE AUTHOR

I grew up in Kamloops, Canada, but at 25, I experienced a sexual assault that shattered my sense of direction. I packed my life—and my cats—into my car and crossed the border to Seattle to start over.

In 2018, I wasn't thinking about writing. I was suicidal. What saved me was an underground psychedelic-assisted therapy session that didn't just heal me—it changed the trajectory of my life. Today, I'm a trained psychedelic facilitator, committed to exploring how altered states of consciousness can heal individual trauma and collective systems.

The idea for *They Could Be Saviors* came to me during meditation—a quiet whisper I couldn't ignore. Through speculative fiction, I explore the intersection of climate change, inequality, and the soul sickness of unchecked capitalism.

I believe billionaires are dragons—hoarding wealth while the world burns—and I write to ask: what if we forced them to change? My writing is a hopeful act of rebellion.

www.ingramcontent.com/pod-product-compliance
Lightning Source LLC
Chambersburg PA
CBHW050011120726
47903CB00006B/1730